# SCANDALOUS

# SCANDALOUS

# RECHELLA

*www.urbanbooks.net*

Urban Books
74 Andrews Avenue
Wheatley Heights, NY 11798

ISBN 1-893196-30-5

First Printing January 2006
Printed in the United States of America

10 9 8 7 6 5 4 3 2 1

*This is a work of fiction. Any references or similarities to
actual events, real people, living, or dead, or to real locals
are intended to give the novel a sense of reality. Any
similarity in other names, characters, places, and incidents
is entirely coincidental.*

Submit Wholesale Orders to:
Kensington Publishing Corp.
C/O Penguin Group (USA) Inc.
Attention: Order Processing
405 Murray Hill Parkway
East Rutherford, NJ  07073-2316
Phone: 1-800-526-0275
Fax: 1-800-227-960

# <u>Acknowledgements</u>

First and foremost, I thank God for life, love, and the ability to dream. Secondly, I thank Him for His mercy and grace. Thanks to my family for being supportive and understanding as I dedicated much of my time to sitting at the computer working on this novel. As I think back over time, there are many people to thank for their encouragement and kind words. I pray that each of you know who you are, for if I have failed to acknowledge you down through the years, I know God hasn't and never will. Many thanks to Urban Books for the opportunity. And to my agent, Carol, for always listening. The dream of writing my first novel, I dedicate to the memories of Ms. Marie Clark, Ms. Catherine Price, Ms. Lucille Graham, and Ms. Minnie Clemons. They were awesome moms during the first seventeen years of my existence. I will forever be grateful for the way they allowed God to use them in my life.

# Chapter One

I knew I was wrong, but I just couldn't help myself. Of all the places to be lusting, a funeral just wasn't one of them. I'm not going to lie, I wanted her so bad I could almost taste her. I had damn near watched her through the whole service. I imagined myself pulling her clothes off piece by piece. Watching her like that was extremely bold, even for me. I'm surprised somebody didn't see me and wonder just why in the hell I was gazing at her so hard. Despite my efforts, ol' girl still didn't stoop to my level and pay me any attention in return. Good thing she didn't, because our family definitely didn't need extra drama—on that day, anyway. She had on a pair of dark shades that prevented me and the crowd from seeing her entire face. I figured she probably wore the shades to hide her red, swollen eyes. I talked to her around 1:00 A.M. on the night before the funeral. She was still up crying while going over things and making sure that the final preparations to bury her husband were in order.

The old wooden country church was no bigger than a chicken coop, but it was packed with family, friends, and a lot of people who just wanted to be nosy. All who couldn't fit in the church stood out in the hot sun almost a mile down the narrow, rocky road waiting to walk through and catch one glimpse of the dead body lying in the coffin. There was nothing but trees and pasture as far as you could see. More people were on the outside of the church than inside. I never did understand why more people turned out for a funeral than a wedding. Maybe it's because people are envious of happiness and don't want to see it, but they aren't jealous of tragedy. Or, of course, maybe they just like looking at dead people.

Services began at noon. It should have been one of the saddest days in my life. I'd lost one of my brothers to a heart attack. But anyone who really knew me wouldn't have been able to tell if I was sad or not by the expression on my face. I drifted through the majority of the ceremonial hours fantasizing about how good it was going to be to get back between her legs after almost a year. That was how long it had been since the last time she'd given me some of her prized pussy. Before that, I'd never gone without fucking her for more than a few weeks at a time. My brother's funeral sure as hell wasn't the time nor the place for all of my suppressed desires to be unraveling, but in my opinion, wasn't too much more damage that could be done. I'd been fucking her when he was alive, despite having a wife of my own and plenty other outside women who kept me busy. I didn't know what it was about her, but she seemed to be the only woman who could truly satisfy my hunger for passionate sex. Maybe because she was the so-called forbidden fruit, or maybe it was just the challenge of it all. I swear, I drooled at the mouth just hearing her name.

As I sat on the front pew, lost in thought about her, I felt my dick begin to grow. In only seconds, it had gotten so hard I thought it was going to bust through my pants. I briskly shook my head to come out of the daydreaming state that I was in, and turned my attention to the service. The part of the program that called for three minute expressions from any relative or friend who wished to speak was underway. Two of my younger brothers had already taken turns saying a few words, but being the oldest, I was usually the one who did most of the public speaking. The family expected me to take the floor. I cleared my throat and stood up to do what I'd always done so well, which was tell people what they wanted to hear whether it was true or not.

"First off, I wanna give honor to God, who is the head of my life," I stated in a somewhat subtle manner, clearing my throat yet again. "To the pastor, to all of you that came out to make up this great audience today, and last but certainly not least to my brother's wife, Sister Katie Jennings. We've gathered here for the home-goin' celebration of Brother Gregg. And it ain't gon' be no cryin' and hollin' up in here.

# ReChella

We gon' praise the Lord just like Gregg would've wanted us to. I think I speak for my mother, my brothers, and the entire Jennings family when I say this ain't no sad occasion. Shucks, my brother was saved, sanctified, and filled wit' the Holy Spirit. Can I get a amen, church?"

By the time I uttered the last sentence, I had heightened my voice to a much more spirited tone. I was about to get that crowd seriously hyped up. I never considered being a preacher or anything like that—shit, being a deacon in my church for well over twenty-five years was demanding enough. I mean, damn, how much playing holy can one man do? One thing I could say about my inspirational speaking was that people paid attention to me whenever and wherever I opened my mouth to talk. No matter how much bullshit I thought of on the spot, the ones listening always received it. Hell, sometimes I even managed to convince myself to believe the stuff I was saying. Maybe that was the reason it was so easy to make other people believe.

Despite all of my wicked ways, there were some genuine instances when I believed I'd been truly blessed with a real gift of ministering. Of course, if that were the case, then according to the Bible, the gift had sure enough been corrupted as a result of my disobedience and unruly behavior. If I found myself getting too caught up in feeling guilty about misusing God's word or the favor that I believe He'd placed on my life, I'd just chalk it up as "nobody's perfect." I wasn't the first man to do what I was doing, and damn sure wasn't going to be the last. Plenty of preachers and deacons all over the country, who spoke to greater multitudes than I, were doing the exact same thing if not worse. Hell, Jim Baker's a name that nobody will ever forget. Even my man, Jessie Jackson, managed to get himself tangled up in some baby momma drama shit. And why? 'Cause he was creeping for some coochie just like the rest of us and got caught.

The funeral crowd yelled in response to me right on cue. "Amen! Amen!" Their faces said they wanted me to bring it on.

"All right, then, that's what I'm talkin' 'bout!" I reached a hand up and adjusted my tie as I proceeded. "Talk to me like you wanna hear what I'm sayin' . . . and let's have some church today!"

As hot as it was in the church, I needed to make my words short and sweet, but that would have been too much like right. I took a white handkerchief from inside my suit coat pocket and wiped the sweat from my forehead. The small window unit in the front of the church wasn't putting out much air. On a regular Sunday service it did fine for the handful of members that belonged to the church, but the funeral crowd was too large to even know the air conditioner was running. Everybody fanned with hand fans to help keep them cool. Folks was crammed up in that little place like sardines in a can. There wasn't a bit of air stirring. I thought about taking my jacket off, but I wasn't about to take a chance of putting it down and giving some careless Negro the opportunity to sit on it and wrinkle it. A black, double-breasted suit and long-sleeved white shirt covered my milk chocolate skin tone, with a black and white striped tie that fitted snugly around my neck. Folded inside the upper left jacket pocket was a matching handkerchief. I wore some black Stacy Adams tie-ups that carried a spit-shine so deep they let off a glare.

Born and raised in Senatobia, Mississippi, in the heart of the country, but that didn't mean shit. I thought I was just as good or better than any of them would-be fancy folks up north. My deep southern accent revealed itself the minute I opened my mouth and mumbled a word. Some folks labeled me as arrogant, but to set the record straight, pure skill's the deal. No matter where I went or what I was doing, I dressed the part and always kept my low-trimmed, texturized hair in shape. At forty-eight years old, I exercised faithfully and kept my finely honed abs and firmed-up muscles in shape. At the risk of replicating my many female conquests' words, I didn't look a day over thirty-five. The wide range of homegirls who always showed me love did a

4

# ReChella

very good job of convincing me of my youthful appearance, too.

Even at the funeral as I stood before the people, I noticed a lot of women in the audience winking and eyeballing the hell out of me. To keep from getting too distracted, I glanced over at Gregg's flowers and coffin a few times to remind myself of why I was up. Gregg really had a nice put-away. He was laying up in that brand new, shiny gray casket, looking just like himself. If I hadn't known better, I could've sworn that he nodded his head once in agreement with the crowd as they praised my words.

"I'ma say it again, 'cause I don't think ya heard me, people! I said, do anybody wanna have church this evening?" I bellowed even more vigorously. I suddenly grabbed the microphone that was clamped onto the podium where I stood. "Gregg Jennings is on his way to Heaven, y'all, where we need to be preparin' ourselves to go. 'Cause the Lord is sho' nuff' on his way back, amen!"

"Amen! Amen!" The crowd became more and more hyped as I continued.

That was my exact intention. I wasn't going to sit my black ass down 'til somebody shouted. By now, I had began gesturing and sweating like a Hebrew slave. I had developed the preacher man's gruffness in my throat; the one that preacher's get when they've really gotten deep into the message that they're delivering and nobody can hardly understand what they're saying.

"Whoopin' and actin' like y'all ain't saved. I'm saved! So I ain't worried this evenin'. If God called me home right now, I'm ready! I got a question for all my sistahs and brothers! Are ya ready?" I held the mic so close to my lips I accidentally smacked a kiss right into it.

Sometimes I wondered if I even knew what the word "saved" meant. I should have known, because I'd been in church all of my life. I guess going every Sunday had become routine like anything else can be. My mother raised me, Gregg, and our other five brothers in the church. One thing for sure, I never wanted to disappoint Momma because she'd worked so hard as a single parent to bring us up the right way. From my young child years on through my teen years into my adulthood, I could hear Momma's keen voice repeating the same words. "Now, Charles, you the eldest of all your brothers, so you gots to be the one to set a good Christian example for them. I know you ain't gon' let me down, 'cause you a good chile and you know the Lawd is watchin' ya."

She always expected way more from me than she did from my other brothers, even after they had grown all up. During my teenage years, when my homeboys were partying out in the open and clubbing every weekend, plus fucking every girl who'd let them and bragging about it, I was training to be a deacon and going to church every week. But in my spare time, I managed to get my sneak going and catch up on some of the stuff I'd missed out on not being with my friends. For Momma's sake, I faked being the perfect son, and that led to me creating Mr. Public Figure. Having two faces tired my ass out big time, but at least it kept a smile on Momma's face. It also kept her from being publicly embarrassed over things that I could have otherwise been doing openly in our little community. Every now and again she heard a few nasty rumors floating around about me. A town that small, if gossip got out, it was hard to miss, but she never believed a word she heard. In her eyes, I could do no wrong. She always told me about the hearsay, but before I could even get a word in to answer for the charges, she'd end the conversation with one of her many pep speeches. "You see, Charles, folks a lie on ya just to try and brang ya down when ya livin' right. But don't you worry 'bout none of that mess, son. 'Cause they lied on Jesus Christ . . . and ain't no servant greater than his master. Boy, you just hold on and keep doin' what ya doin'. God got yo' back."

Living with expectations like that, I knew I had to keep up a good front, so people would believe that I was on the right path, but in reality, I never lied to myself. I knew I had been on the wrong path for a long time. When I was thirteen, I persuaded one of our church members' daughters to have sex with me behind the church. That little sexy thing was crazy about me and I knew it, so I told her if she didn't give me some I was going to find me another girlfriend. She gave it up right there on the spot. Ruth Jamison was her name. She was the prettiest thirteen-year-old I'd ever seen. A high-yellow gal with long, coal black hair. After I was done robbing her virginity and losing mine to her, I felt kind of bad about the way I had manipulated the situation. But it was all good, because she became my wife once we were of age.

At nineteen years old, she and I were joined in holy matrimony. We stayed together through the births of three daughters and twenty-nine years of marriage. Ruth died of kidney failure six weeks after our twenty-ninth wedding anniversary. She was one woman I could genuinely say I loved dearly. Yet, despite how much I cared for her during the many years that we were together, I still hung onto my mistresses and creeped throughout our entire marriage. If she wasn't able to keep me from doing my thing with the ladies, I knew damned well that no other female who came behind her was going to tame me.

Two months after Ruth's funeral, I married the woman who I figured was the next best candidate. I had been seeing Bettie Jackson while Ruth was still living. Bettie was special to me in her own way and I cared quite a bit for her, but there was no way for me to love her, or any other woman, for that matter, as much as I'd loved Ruth. Hell, Ruth was my first, and she bore my children. Plus, she had put up with my whoring for all those years without giving me too much lip, and still loved me as much as she did the day I married her. All in all, Ruth was as close to sainthood as any person I'd ever known. I damn sure couldn't be honest with Bettie and tell her I didn't love her as much as I'd loved Ruth, because she was always telling me how much she loved me, then turning right around and asking me to tell her the same. So, I carried on with the norm and convinced her that I loved her just as much as she said she loved me.

A little naïve maybe, but my new wife worshipped the ground I walked on. And man, did she come with added bonuses. Not only could she fuck her ass off, but she could cook just as well. Even though Bettie and I had been sneaking around for just about the entire last year of Ruth's illness, she didn't seem to think bad of me for cheating on a sick spouse. If she did, she never said a word about it to me in the beginning. There were times when she even met up with me in the parking lot at the hospital while Ruth was getting dialysis treatments. True enough, that was a lowdown and disrespectful thing to do, but it was real convenient at times. After we were married, Bettie always seemed like she was so happy to be in the Jennings family. She sat right next to my mother at the funeral.

I humped my back over and strutted back and forth in front of Gregg's casket, ministering like a true man of God. My sound had to be echoing in every ear, because I was shouting to the top of my voice and sweating like a hog on Thanksgiving morning.

"I said I'm wrapped up? Tied up! And tangled up all in Jesus this evening, ya'll! Are you saved?"

"Yes! Yes! Amen!" The crowd was on the verge of a high-spirited outbreak.

"I said are you saved! Are you ready to go through the pearly gates where my brother Gregg gone?"

"Amen! Amen," they continued bellowing.

Then it happened. The first female jumped up and started hollering "Go 'head, son," just as loud as I hollered. In only seconds, she fell out on the floor, jerking in a Holy Ghost fit. That started a chain reaction, and by the time I was done talking, nearly everybody in the church was up clapping, screaming, and shouting all over each other. Hats and pocketbooks were flying through the air like Frisbees on a windy day. There wasn't much need for our preacher to say anything. Just the same, 'cause he was too busy rootin' and hootin' right along with the other folks, draped in his long, burgundy pastoral robe with the words *Mt.*

*Pleasant* in mustard-gold color sewn down the left side.

He was a single, twenty-nine-year-old, eligible bachelor. I'd heard many women refer to him as a fine-ass preacher, but let me tell it, he was a fucked-up ass preacher. He and I didn't set horses too well. Everybody called him Pastor Deeberry, but I refused to call him by anything more than his last name. That was 'til Momma had me promise not to disrespect him publicly, then I only said Deeberry behind his back. Most of the members of the church respected him and hung onto his every whim, but I could see straight through all of his sheisty shit and mess. He was as crooked as they came. Being a master of deception myself, there wasn't a chance in hell for him to trick me with that fake-ass concern for the goodwill of all mankind hogwash. He charmed many of the women that belonged to the church with his boyish facial features and Boy Scout demeanor. I didn't know what was the excuse for some of the male members.

I finally went ahead and sat down in my seat after the crowd took over the show with all that rumbling and going on. I must have felt something sincere when I was up there gabbing, because before I realized it, I was dabbing tears from the corners of my dark brown eyes. Maybe the saying's true, that if a person pretends long enough, they might get saved for real. If so, it would have been right up my alley.

Deeberry's eulogy was brief, then the funeral directors opened the casket and directed the people down the aisle to view the body. Folks who were already standing around the walls and outside walked through first in a single line. They peeped into the coffin and examined as much of the body as they could see, then kept on out the side door.

Gregg's wife had managed to stay strong through it all, until she went up to view the remains of her beloved husband. She broke down hollering in a bad way. "Ooohh, Lord! Ooohh, Lord . . . Gregg, baby, why'd you leave me? I wanna go with you, baby! Please, baby, I love you sooo much. Gregg! Gregg! You're the only one that understand, baby." She snatched the shades from her eyes and dropped them. The way she sobbed and carried on, there wasn't a dry eye in the church. The bottom of her black, tea-length dress scoured the front of the casket as she tousled to embrace Gregg's stiff body. In all of the shuffling, one of the black leather shoes that she wore somehow maneuvered off her foot and onto the floor. She was too hysterical to notice. "You can't be gone! Lord, have mercy! Wake up. Wake up!" She tugged at his black suit coat, trying to pull him out of the coffin.

Her sons weren't able to keep their composure either. They screamed and cried for their father. "Daddy. Daddy. Don't go. We love you!"

The funeral directors tried to get Katie and the boys away from the coffin, but before they could do it, Momma and some of my nieces flocked around, crying and hollering even louder. So much weight was on the casket it began to tip over. The directors could not control the situation. I quickly jumped up and beckoned for a few other male members of the church to come help get Momma and the rest of the relatives away from the coffin.

Even after we'd seated everybody else, it was difficult to drag Katie away. She wasn't a big woman, no more than 160 pounds, but at that moment, she was stronger than an ox. Her perfectly made-up face dripped away with the tears that streamed down her cheeks. The bouncy ring curls in her dark brown, shoulder length hair drooped in the humid atmosphere. As refined and classy as she always kept herself, her mental control vanished. I tried to comfort her as I pried her hands, finger by finger, from the casket rim.

"Come on, Katie, have a seat. It's all right. He know how much you loved him. He's in a better place now. Gregg wouldn't want you to carry on this way. You gon' make ya'self sick," I pleaded. The other men and I wrestled to get her to the pew. After a few minutes, she calmed down. Some of what Katie felt had to be guilt. After fifteen years of being married to Gregg, I knew how much she loved him. Hell, I loved him too; he was my brother. But what could I do? I also loved fucking Katie.

# ReChella

The crowd settled down as the casket was being closed. Lo and behold, before the top was all the way down, a loud scream bellowed out. "Wait! Don't shut that casket!" A fretful voice came from the back entrance as the church doors flew open. I immediately looked up in the direction of the yell to see what was going on.

"Aw, hell, what now?" I mumbled, taking in a deep breath. "It's too hot for this shit. Folks gon' start fallin' out if we don't hurr' up and get out of this matchbox."

The female who burst in the church and yelled to the top of her lungs was none other than Gregg's ex-wife, Debra. Her two teenage kids were right along with her. Talking 'bout one crazy bitch, Debra was certifiably insane—not to mention she had probably been drinking too. She hollered again, even louder than she did when she first rushed in and captured everybody's attention. "Please! Wait! We need to see him too! The children need to see Gregg! These his kids, and they wanna see their daddy for the last time. My car broke down on the way here. Please let us see him!" Debra and the two teens rushed up the aisle and stood in front of the casket.

Folks stared in astonishment. Whispers and low chatter sounded throughout the church. The look on Katie's face was furious. For a second or two, I thought she was going to jump out of her seat and grab Debra, but she didn't say anything. I guess she kept her cool to avoid any additional scenes. God knows it was bad enough already. Debra was probably lying about her car breaking down, anyway. There was no doubt in my mind that she had pre-planned the whole dramatized entrance just to get attention and remind folks that she was once married to Gregg. That was just the kind of crazy-ass shit she was capable of. The directors went ahead and allowed Debra and the children to pay their respects before they closed the casket and signaled to the pallbearers.

Henry Wilkins, Joe Reynolds, William Pratch, Preston Boone, and Stan Washington were the active pallbearers on the program. They marched the casket down the aisle as

11

the ceremony ended. The five men were also close friends of mine and Gregg's. We sang together in a men's gospel group, The Mighty Spirituals. Most of the members of the group were from our hometown, Senatobia. William and I started the group when we were in our early twenties and then recruited the other four fellas. All of us possessed many of the same qualities and standards. The only thing we loved more than women was a bigger variety of women. As the old folks used to say, we could sang up a storm. Our voices sounded just that good.

Gregg didn't join the group until about six years later, and none of our other brothers had ever wanted to join. In our family, Gregg was next to me, but in the group, he was the youngest. He was a little bit more stand-offish and quiet than me and the other group members, but he was just as big a womanizer as the rest of us. Katie had even caught him with one of his many admirers once. That slowed him down for a few weeks, but it damn sure didn't stop him.

Being a part of our group had plenty of benefits. We knew as long as we looked holy, kept our personal appearance intact, and sung up a shout when we went on stage, we would always have a wide selection of pussy waiting for us after each program. The women were obsessed with that kind of styling and profiling, so we delivered. We weren't the only ones by far. Plenty of other gospel groups in our parts lived by the same code of ethics. If I say so myself, we just did it so much better than the rest of them. One of our hottest songs was "Amazing Grace," which happened to have been Gregg's favorite song. That's the tune that William and the boys softly hummed as they strolled the casket on out of the church.

# Chapter Two

Across the dusty gravel road at the cemetery, our family and a few close friends met one last time to bid a final farewell to Gregg. As we stood around waiting for Deeberry to conclude the burial, I glanced over at Debra and her children. The boy and girl looked fine, but Debra was standing only a short distance from Katie. That didn't rest too easy with me. Although Debra had calmed her ass down quite a bit and didn't look like she was contemplating causing anymore disruptions, the relaxed look on her face didn't mean a thing. When she was married to Gregg, he used to say she had four or five people living on the inside of her. So help me, he told us that he believed she was demonically possessed. That was one of the many reasons he divorced her. She could be easy-going one minute, and all of a sudden seem like something would come over her, and she would snap, crackle, and pop on anybody's ass that was nearby.

Those kids of hers probably caught more hell than a little bit. They weren't too talkative; they were more like Gregg in that area. Every so often, Gregg would pick them up and bring them to a family gathering or something that we were having so they wouldn't lose touch with our side of the family. I was glad that the children weren't as crazy as their mother.

They stood one on each side of her at the gravesite. Every piece of common sense I owned told me to ease over and put some more thickness between Debra and Katie, but I decided just to try to keep myself alert as our full of shit pastor took his damn time with the ritual. He really didn't know how bad I wanted to bitch-slap him and make him hurry the hell up with his annoying, sissy-like voice.

"Gregg Jennings was a soldier in God's army. He fought the good fight and ran the good race. God said it was time to take off his armor and go rest a while. Now, we gon' miss

13

him 'cause we love him, but God loves him best." Deeberry paused for a second and held a shiny cross up in one hand and sprinkled dirt on top of the casket with the other one. "Ashes to ashes, dust to dust. Dear Lord, our loved one we entrust."

We listened quietly as he carried on with the last rites. Every now and then, a cool breeze blew in and whisked away the hot rays that beamed down on us from the sun.

"Father God, take this soul . . ."

"Oh no! Stop, y'all! Don't put him in there!" I suddenly yelled out, interrupting Deeberry in the middle of his sentence. "He ain't dead! He ain't dead! Look at him! Get him out of there!"

The pallbearers were lowering the casket into the grave during my hysteria. I didn't understand why they were continuing to put the casket into the ground and Gregg was clearly not dead. He had somehow managed to push the top off the casket and was sitting up in it, staring directly at me. All I could think about was how big an error we'd all made in presuming him to be dead. My God, we were getting ready to bury a man alive. How could we have made a mistake like that? How could the funeral home have made a mistake like that? Things began to get very blurry around me. I was confused. By now, all I could see was Gregg getting up and standing in the coffin.

The peaceful look that rested on his face during the funeral service transformed right before me to the worst look of anger I'd ever seen. He began uttering a bunch of words in such a deafening tone that I could barely listen. I covered my ears with both hands, shut my eyes as tight as they'd fasten, and vigorously shook my head from side to side. It was obvious that he was upset, and given the way he was peering at me, I seemed to be the reason. I reopened my eyes in time to see him stretch one arm out and point at me. The overwhelming feeling that had come over me rendered me scared as hell. I was still covering my ears, but at the same time, I was desperately trying to make out what he was saying. Then all at once, his loud mumbo-jumbo dropped a notch or two and I was able to understand him. That made things even worse. What he said to me completely blew my mind. Not only did his words leave me speechless, I almost pissed in my pants standing right there. I was in a state of shock. The next thing I felt was someone tugging at my arm and softly chanting my name.

"Charles. Charles, what's wrong? It's all right." Bettie grabbed hold of me and hugged me. "Calm down, baby. We know you gon' miss him. We all are," she whispered, rubbing my back to soothe me.

William wasn't standing too far from Bettie and me. He hurriedly came to the rescue. He threw his hand on my shoulder and made an attempt to assist her in walking me away from the gravesite. Before we strolled off, I peeked over in the big grave hole and noticed that the casket was still intact. It didn't look at all like it had been opened, and there wasn't a sign of Gregg standing up anywhere. I skimmed over the crowd and saw how some of the family had broken into tears and others were staring at me like they felt deeply sorry for me. Now, I was as confused as ever. Question after question ran through my mind.

*What's going on? Did everybody else not see and hear Gregg like I did? If so, why ain't they sayin' somethin'? Where did he go so fast? I can't be losing my mind; I'm too strong for some shit like that.* Then, in the midst of my silent inquiry to myself, it registered with me that Bettie was holding onto one of my arms and William the other. They were leading me like I was some kind of deranged invalid. Ask me how fast I collected myself and pulled my arms away from both of them.

I turned to Bettie to try to ease her mind. "Hey, I'm all right. I just need to stir 'round. I'ma walk a li'l piece off. Go on back. I love you," I said, trying to sound calm. I kissed her on the cheek.

"I love you too," she spoke with softness and care, then reluctantly turned and rejoined the others.

I turned toward William and signaled with a nod to go forward. "Hey, man. Let me holla at you a minute."

# Scandalous

"A'ight. You sure you don't wanna go to your car, though? We can crank up the air conditioner and it won't be as hot, man," William proposed, cradling a concerned look.

"Nah, I'm cool." I inhaled a deep breath and began walking. I wasn't accustomed to losing my cool. I just needed to get a hold on things. William and I walked about fifty feet away and stopped near a tree. From all indications, nobody else had seen or heard what I had. At least nobody else was acting like it. I know my people, and there's no way in hell a crowd of black folks would have hung around if a dead man had gotten up out of a casket and started talking to them. Somebody would have tore some shit up getting the hell out of dodge. That being the logical case, I wasn't going to take a chance on nobody but William hearing what I was getting ready to say. Whether the other folks standing around had witnessed it or not, I simply could not dismiss my experience. The chances were very slim, but just in case my mind had done a little flipping out, I knew I could trust William.

All of the fellas in the group were like brothers to me. The six of us were close and knew more shit than a little on each other, but William and I were the oldest of the other guys. Our friendship went further back than even before the group. He and I were just closer. I knew he would be honest with me no matter what. I glanced around to make sure nobody was near us before I said anything.

"Did you see him? Did you see him? He sat up in the coffin and talked to me. Didn't you see him?"

"Who?" William frowned, looking just as confused as I was. "Did I see who?"

"Gregg," I whispered aggressively, looking dead serious. "I'm talkin' 'bout Gregg. You didn't see him get up in the coffin and talk to me?"

William stared at me like I was melting. He was clearly shocked at my question. That told me he hadn't seen anything out of the ordinary, except maybe the way I'd shot off in a panic.

# ReChella

"Charles, look, man. It's been a long day . . . you under a lot of stress . . . and it's hot out here. I understa—"

"Will, come on now. Don't be talkin' to me like I'm some li'l chile." I jumped in before he went any further. "I'm tellin' you I seen Gregg get up out of that casket. It ain't got nothin' to do wit' stress or how hot it is. He talked to me."

Will slumped his head over and slowly boggled it from side to side. "Gregg, ya say?" Will questioned without looking back up. "Let me get this straight. You tellin' me yo' dead brother got up in his coffin and said somethin' to you?"

"Hell yeah, he did. You don't believe me?" I guess I shouldn't have been upset that he didn't believe me. After all, the story was so far-fetched, who would?

"Come off it, Charles. You was seein' thangs, fella. Or better yet, you was in some sort of a daze. Look, before you went off and started yellin', I had already noticed the spaced-out look on yo' face, man. You looked like somebody had you hypnotized or somethin'. I thought you was gon' hit the ground any second; that's just how feeble you looked. I swear . . . just befo' I eased a few steps closer to ya so I could nudge you in the side and snap you out of it, you started screamin' and carryin' on. You grabbed yo' ears. Look like you was scared to death. But hey . . . everybody else started to get misty-eyed when the grave-diggers began to lower the casket down in the ground too. I figured reality was settin' in and you was panickin' at the thought of not seein' Gregg anymore. But, now you tellin' me you done talked to a dead man?" Will threw me out an incredulous look as he awaited my answer.

I peered right back at him as sure as sure could be. "That's what I'm tellin' you. I know it's hard to believe, but I damn sho' ain't makin it up, and I ain't crazy either. I can even tell you what he said to me."

"Look, man, I ain't sayin' you crazy. I'm just sayin' you was probably daydreamin' or somethin'. It's natural in a situation like this. I just told you . . . several mo' folks had started to break down when the casket was bein' put in the ground. You wasn't the only one. "

Of all the things Will and I had talked about over the years, seeing dead people wasn't on the list. I didn't enjoy pressing the issue, but I needed to make him understand how serious the experience was.

"Dammit, Will, listen to me, would ya?" I firmed my tone to accommodate my serious gaze. "I wasn't daydreamin', man."

"Well, how come I didn't see him? How come nobody else saw him?"

"Shit, I don't know," I exclaimed, becoming somewhat irritated. "But Gregg's words were somethin' like, 'How could you do it? You were my brother, my blood. We came out of the same womb. We had the same daddy. How could you do it? I swear, everything you do, I'ma be watchin' you, every move you make. I won't rest 'til I ruin you, you backstabbin' son of a bitch.' "

"Hold up. Wha—"

"No, let me finish." I wouldn't allow him to interrupt me at all. "Gregg spoke in a deep, creepy voice. 'Katie was my wife, not yours. I'm gon' reach out of this grave and tear your black, rusty dick off and put it in yo' mouth. I'ma let Momma and the rest of the family know what kind of sick bastard you really are. I swear, I'll get you, you, you.' I ain't lyin' to ya, Will. That's what he said."

Will had been gazing at me intensely the whole time I was telling him what Gregg said. A shit load of question marks were drawn all over Will's face. I braced myself to answer them. He raised one hand in front of him.

"Hold up, hold up. Let's back up a few steps . . . and, and say Gregg did come back from the dead to talk to you." Will sighed deeply, shaking his head. "Damn, I can't even say that wit' a straight face. But . . . let's just s'ppose he did, okay? Why in the hell would he say somethin' like that to you? I mean . . . his wife? What could you have possibly done to Katie that would make him wanna cut yo'dick off and cram it in yo' mouth? She yo' sistah-in-law . . . It ain't like you been coatin' ya own—" Will stopped in the middle of his sentence, wearing the same questionable expression, only this time, it was more of a mind-blowing look. I knew he was waiting on me to say something. All I could do was drop my head and park my eyes on the ground. I guess my silence spoke for me.

"Awwww, awww, man." Will sighed deeper as if a lightbulb clicked on in his head. "I don't believe it. Charles, tell me you ain't been fuckin' Katie."

I slowly raised my head and glared at him with guilty eyes. "For years."

"Get the fuck outta here," he exclaimed, taking a step back. I knew he was surprised, because as tight as we were, I hadn't even told him about my dealings with Katie. As far as that matter was concerned, only she and I knew the deal. We'd always said that we would never tell a soul or even be careless enough for so much as a whimper to leak out. And we'd done just that. We had managed to keep it on the down-low for all those years, so I don't know how in the hell Gregg could have known. He certainly never said anything over the years. Maybe it was some sort of a dead thing—whatever the hell that meant. I'd always heard old folks say the dead know what the living doing, but as far as I was concerned, that was one of many myths.

"Look, man . . ."

Look, man, my ass." Will took over my words. "How come you ain't told me 'bout this, and how long has it been goin' on?" He appeared to be a bit on the wounded side now.

"How 'bout I answer yo' last question first?"

"I don't give a damn which one you answer first. Just start talkin', nigga."

"Me and her been hookin' up 'bout twelve, thirteen years . . . give or take a few." I somewhat hesitated.

"That's bullshit, Charles. Ain't no way y'all been screwin' that long and you ain't told me 'bout it."

Will, come on, now. That ain't the kinda shit you just casually talk about."

He gave me an offended look. "What the hell you mean,

casually talk? I'm yo' best friend. It ain't nothin' we ain't talked about in all o' these years. Or, at least I thought it wasn't nothin'. I guess I was wrong."

"Come on, man. That's the only thing outta all this time I ain't told you 'bout. I just couldn't spill that one. I mean, like you said befo', she my sistah-in-law, for goodness sakes."

"That's yo' reason for not tellin' me?" He shrugged, widening his eyes. "If it is, that's a poor-ass reason, my brotha. All the shit I done confided in you 'bout."

"Nothin' like that, though. You ain't never told me nothin' 'bout you and yo' brother's wife messin' off." I pulled my same white handkerchief out of my pocket and dabbed the sweat beads off my face.

"Naw, ain't nothin' ever went on with me and my brotha's wife, but you must don't remember 'bout four or five years ago when I was foolin' 'round wit' Francine's hot-ass niece. Not only was she my wife's niece, but she was only seventeen. You talkin' 'bout some good, hot pussy . . . damn." By now, Will was staring into space with a smile on his face. He seemed to be re-living his encounter with his niece-in-law.

"Aww, yeah, I remember that." I snapped my finger and pointed at him. "'Cause you stopped screwin' her when she told you she thought she was pregnant."

Will cut his smile short and pasted his eyes back on me when I reminded him about the girl's so-called pregnancy. "Doggone right I did. It woulda killed Francine if that gal had'a gave birth to a baby lookin' like me. I was so damn glad to hear her say it was a false alarm. She swore she wasn't messin' 'round wit' nobody but me at the time. She was lyin', though. Mo' young boys was sniffin' behind her than she could keep up wit'."

Will was exactly right about him giving me the 411 on those little rendezvous with his niece-in-law. And from what I recalled, he never mentioned it to any of the other guys in the group either.

"You right, man. I shoulda' holla'd at you 'bout me and

Katie, but I guess I knew it was some cold-ass shit to do to my own brotha. So honestly, I felt bad about it, but I just couldn't stop seein' her, man." I boggled my head, expressing my helplessness when it came to Katie.

Will leaned forward and locked eyes with me. He wore a devilish smirk on his face. "The pussy that good, huh?" He chuckled and slightly punched me on my left shoulder.

His teasing action told me that he had accepted my reason for not sharing the issue with him and was no longer teed-off about it. The sound in his voice was just as familiar. He'd now switched to our *pussy is pussy and we gon' get all we can* group mode. He was ready for some wild details. Too bad there wasn't enough time to fill him in on the pleasurable side of the story. I would have to do that later, once everything got back to normal. Right then, I needed to get back to the real issue at hand.

"Yeah, man, she a'ight," I said modestly. "But I need to—"

"A'ight?" She gotta be better than just a'ight. Hell, you been hittin' it for twelve or thirteen years." Will cut me off before I could get back to the subject of seeing Gregg.

"Okay, okay, it's some of the best pussy I ever had . . . but look, Will, I need for you to undastand what I just told you 'bout me seein' Gregg."

Will chuckled as if he had it all figured out. "What's to undastand? The answer plain as daylight, but I still got one question for ya." He primped his mouth and eased his hands down in his pants pockets.

"What?" I eagerly anticipated, thinking his question was maybe going to be one step closer to he and I understanding more about what had happened to me.

"Does this mean you ain't fuckin' Katie no mo'?" A hasty, cunning laugh blurted through his lips.

I couldn't do nothing but look at him for a few seconds. "Aw, man, cut the shit. That ain't funny." I wanted to laugh too, but I restrained myself and turned away from him as he chuckled . Under any other circumstances, I would have been shucking and jiving along with him, but I needed some answers.

"I'm sorry, man. I just had to throw that in. But seriously, you think this incident may just be stemmin' from a guilty conscience? That's my undastandin' now that you done told me what was up." He ended his laugh. "I know as good a time as I had when I was fuckin' that li'l fast niece of Francine's, there were times when I felt guilty 'bout it. I ain't gon' front, I did."

I took in what Will said and made no reply, then looked out across the graveyard, lost in thought. *Maybe Will's right. After all, since Gregg' s death I've felt a li'l bit more guilt about wronging him all that time, and now that he's gone, I'll never be able to apologize for bein' such a lousy brother. Plus, nobody else saw or heard anything that disturbed them. Yep, I had to be daydreaming or something. Damn, I need to check myself if my conscience done started producing guilt this severe. No way I'm givin' in to no guilty shit. I do what I want, when I—*

"Charles. Charles." Will interrupted my thoughts.

I shook it off and turned my attention back to him. "Yeah, yeah . . . I was just thinkin' 'bout all this shit, man. And you right." I agreed with him because he had to be right, and there was no way that I was going to allow an overly active conscience to interrupt my lifestyle. My pride resurfaced and I squashed that guilty, seeing dead folks shit with the quickness. "So what? The deed already been done now. I can't change nothin' that happened, regardless if I feel bad about it or not. All I can do is move on. Ya feel me, man?" I stated very enthusiastically, gesturing my hand to do five with Will. We did the brotherly handshake and smiled at each other. He looked thrilled to see that I was now sounding like the Charles he knew. I felt that same confidence.

"That's what I'm talkin' 'bout, my brotha," Will said, nodding his head. "It's gon' be a'ight. "I guess if we didn't feel a li'l emotion sometime we wouldn't be human, huh?"

"Sho' ya right!" I reached up and adjusted my tie in case it had shifted during all the drama. I straightened my jacket and slid my thumb across each eyebrow. "Come on, man. Let's get on back up here wit' the rest of the folks so we can exit this graveyard. Hell, we could stay out here all night and ain't none of these dead folks gon' get up and walk or talk." I chuckled, glancing over the many headstones.

Will laughed along with me as we headed back toward Gregg's gravesite. Damn, I was good. I gathered my wits and transformed my personality to cool just that quick. The rest of the folks were dispersing to leave. Will went on to his car and I caught up with Bettie. She had Katie by the arm, escorting her to the funeral car. Katie patted tears that were dripping from her eyes with napkins.

"Katie, you a'ight?" I asked delicately.

"Yeah, I'm okay, Charles." She stopped and looked up at me. We had made our way to the black limousine that the funeral home provided for her and the boys. "I need to be asking you that question."

I knew she was referring to my scene during the last ritual. I had already prepared myself for any questions concerning that little unfortunate episode. "I'm fine. I . . . I." I slumped my head over and began boggling my head as if I were trying to fight back tears. "It didn't really sink in that he was gone . . . I mean really gone, until they was puttin' the casket down in the ground. I guess I didn't realize how bad I was gon' miss my brotha. I'm sorry if I upset y'all any more than you already was." I lifted my head up and glanced from Katie to Bettie. I needed my ass tore all to pieces for faking like that, but I sure as hell couldn't tell them the truth. Will had given me the perfect explanation for my uproar when he told me that in the beginning he thought the reason I'd shot off was that the reality of Gregg being gone forever was sinking in. I knew I was going to use that same reason for everybody who approached me about the incident.

Katie didn't comment after my reply. She turned around almost immediately to get into the limousine. One of the funeral directors had already cranked up, and the other director helped her in. Bettie and I backed away and strolled toward our vehicle. Bettie dropped a few tears and clutched my hand.

"I knew you was tryin' to be strong and it was gon' hit you sooner or later. You sure you all right?"

"Yeah, I'm fine, baby." I held open the passenger door to the pearl-white Cadillac SUV for Bettie to get in. I answered Bettie's question, but my mind wasn't on what she was talking about at all. The fact that Katie didn't say anything after I explained the reason for my outburst was bugging me. Bettie had obviously bought my act.

*What was Katie's problem?* I wondered. *Why didn't she say somethin' reassurin' like Bettie did after seein' how hurt I was? Who in the hell do I think I'm foolin'? I should've known Katie wasn't gon' believe that act. She probably only asked me was I all right just to see what I was gon' say. If anybody see through my charade, it's her.* I hopped in on the driver's side and cranked up.

# Chapter Three

When we made it to Katie's house, carloads of people were pulling in the driveway, dropping off home-cooked food for the family. Some stayed to eat and offer fellowship; some left right back out. Katie's house was as packed as the church had been. Bettie and Momma kept busy in the kitchen entertaining some of the company, while the rest of the family was scattered all over the place. Folks settled in and started to eat up a storm. Most of the children were on the outside, eating at the two picnic tables under the big shade tree in the backyard.

All of the feasting and yakking at the repast reminded me of the many family get-togethers we'd had at Gregg and Katie's house before he got sick with heart problems. I reminded myself how much fun we used to have down there playing games and eating 'til our stomachs poked out too full. As I strolled around, jumping in and out of brief conversation with different people, I couldn't help but notice that even though Gregg wasn't there, the fact that everything was going on the same way it had always gone on sure did make it seem like he would stroll through the house slightly grinning at any minute. On the real, I was going to miss him, but everybody's got to die sooner or later.

I chatted with Will, Preston, Henry, Joe, and Stan after each of them had grabbed a plate of food and was on his way out. They wanted to get on home to their families. I was glad to see that Debra didn't bring her ass down there. Not that she perhaps didn't want to.

I hadn't seen Katie since we first made it to the house. I'd been keeping an eye out for her, but I didn't want to ask anyone if they knew where she was because I was planning on catching her alone to have a word with her about her non-response in the church parking area. I wandered around until I ended up in the back of the house near the boys' bedrooms. She had to be somewhere 'round, and that was the only area of the house I hadn't checked. I noticed the basement door cracked a little, so I pushed it open further and stuck my head inside.

"Anybody down here?" I waited a sec to see if anyone would answer. "Hey, anybody—"

"Yeah, I'm down here." A soft female voice sounding like Katie interrupted me before I could ask the question again.

"That you, Katie?" I asked as I pushed the door all the way open and stepped in the dimly-lit room and stood at the top of the stairs. I closed the door behind me.

"Who does it sound like, Charles?" she answered in an annoyed tone.

Yep, it was definitely Katie talking to me in that manner. I shuffled down the stairs and walked over to the small, dark green sofa she was sitting on. She was still wearing her funeral dress, but her shoes were lying across the floor as if she'd kicked them off in a hurry. Her head rested on the back of the sofa and she appeared to be just as annoyed as her tone of voice sounded. But at least she wasn't crying.

"You a'ight?" I sat down on the sofa beside her.

"I'll be a lot better when some of them folks upstairs start disappearing." She didn't bother to open her eyes when she answered me.

"I know what you mean. A lotta traffic up there. It's gon' thin out pretty soon, though. A few folks already done left including that weak link, Deeberry. Say he had some kinda night service he'd been invited to at another church." I looked down at my watch. "How long you been down here, anyway?" A moment of silence passed and she didn't say anything. I went on to my next question. "Anybody else down here wit' ya?"

She raised her head and gave me that same annoyed look. "What kind of crazy question is that? You see anybody else in here? And stop askin' me so many questions. I ain't takin' no damn test."

"You ain't got to get smart 'bout it. I wanna know why

26

you turned away without sayin' anything after I told you and Bettie what happened to me at the gravesite."

"Nigga, please. You can waste that lie on somebody who don't know you. You wasn't carryin' on like that 'bout missin' Gregg." She rolled her eyes and rested her head on the back of the sofa again.

"In spite of what you may think, Katie, he was my brotha."

She sighed deeply. "Look, I don't even wanna talk about that mess. You know you can't fool me . . . and I know you can't fool me. I don't know what caused you to shoot off like that, but it wasn't the reason that you done told everybody. So drop it, and go on back up stairs wit' everybody else. I'll be up in a few." She closed her eyes as if she was meditating.

I knew she was right. Everybody else seemed to have bought my explanation for the scene, but there was no chance in me convincing her of the same, so I didn't linger on the subject. Damn, she looked like a cold glass of ice water on a hot summer day lying back on that sofa. Not to mention how good she smelled. Her perfume had always enticed me. She had her very own distinct scent.

My thoughts drifted back to when I was daydreaming about her during the funeral service. *It's been a long time since I had some of that,* I told myself silently while searching her body over. I felt a sudden twang in my pants. I knew my dick was getting ready to stand up and salute. *How bad would it be for me to fuck her right here, right now?* I asked myself in my mind. Before I knew it, I had reached my hand over and stroked the top of her thigh. She quickly raised her head up and looked at me like she was going to knock the hell out of me.

"What are you doing?" she snapped.

"I'm sorry . . . I couldn't help myself." I eyed her longingly. "Katie, you look so damn good, baby."

"You know what? This is too low even for you." She locked eyes with me and shook her head from side to side. "How can you even let a thought like what you're thinking

27

cross your mind at a time like this?" She got up and walked across the room and stood near the wall. "Get yo' black ass outta here before I throw you out."

I stood up. "Look, I didn't mean to upset ya. You know how I feel about ya, Katie. And I'm sorry to say, but my feelings don't have no certain day of the week attached to 'em. Believe me, I know this a bad time, but—"

"A bad time? Really? Is that what it is to you, a bad time?" She crossed her arms and threw me a disgusted look. "Damn, are you even human? A bad time is when your car done broke down and you stranded five miles from a gas station, or, or, when you've just had a tooth pulled and somebody calls you on the telephone wanting to talk. I told you the crap you was sayin' back on the church ground wasn't nothin' but bullshit." Her appalled look intensified. "Get out." She pointed to the stairs.

I disregarded her command and walked over and stood in front of her. "Calm down. I know you're upset, but we can work this out, Katie. Just listen to what I have to say. You know you feel the same way I do." I grabbed both of her arms.

"Let go of me, Charles." She tried to pull away. "And keep your voice down."

"I ain't talkin' that loud. Besides, you know can't nobody hear us way down here." I began to rub all over her. I couldn't contain myself, especially now that I had touched her warm, soft body. Even though she was fighting me at that moment, I hoped that if I didn't back down, I would turn her on like I was. The notion wasn't totally out of the question. There had been many times in the past when she'd told me no but really meant yes.

"You are too talkin' loud . . . and folks can hear down here. I ain't takin' no chance like this. Let me out of here before somebody come lookin' for me." She pushed against my solid chest with both hands, trying to move me out of her way. I ignored the minor blows, pulled her close, and hugged tightly while reaching down to take both hands full of her ass cheeks.

# ReChella

"It's been a year since we made love. I need some of you, Katie." I quickly moved my hands to her breasts then massaged and squeezed uncontrollably.

"No," she aggressively whispered. "I told you we were through doin' this. We never made love anyway. We fucked. I can't handle the guilt, Charles." She fought to keep me off.

"You don't have to be guilty no mo'. He dead. I stayed away just like you wanted when he first started having heart problems. I stepped back and gave you plenty of time to take care of him. But now he gone and I need you back." A longing stare penetrated from my eyes to hers as I rubbed her breasts and pressed my rock-solid erection against the inside of her thighs.

Our rendezvous were always intense. I knew Katie better than she gave me credit for. She wanted to fuck just as much as I did, but she wouldn't have admitted it. She needed someone to blame her guilt on after we finished doing it. If she had really wanted me to leave her alone, I wouldn't have gotten the chance to lay a finger on her, and damn sure wouldn't have gotten close enough to squeeze her breasts and grab her ass. When a woman really means *no,* a man's going to know.

Hell, when I first started flirting with her, I knew by the way she responded that it was only a matter of time before I bedded her. My desiring her was nothing personal against Gregg; she just had it going on. In fact, I had him to thank for driving her to finally give me some. It was about a year after they were married. She found out he was cheating, and I guess for her, fucking me was the ultimate way to get revenge. I didn't give a damn why she did it, I was just glad she chose to do it with me. She told me that it was only going to be that one time, but after I got a taste of her, I couldn't stand the thought of giving it up. Shit, I hounded her like a dog in heat from then on.

A few years into our arrangement, I trusted her wholeheartedly. I even discussed my other women with her. In my opinion, she was the only woman who really knew me—the real me. She always told me that she didn't mind my naughtiness, and she'd never breathe a word about it 'cause she had no intentions of leaving Gregg, despite what he'd done. Besides, she had as much to lose as I did, and she didn't want me blabbing either. We knew realistically that what we had would never amount to nothing but hot, sizzling sex. For all those years, we milked it for everything it was worth.

When I decided to marry Bettie, Katie was the first to know. I even asked her opinion. She flat out told me that she thought Bettie was just as fake as I was, so we would probably get along fine. After Bettie and I were married, whenever I'd ask Katie about getting together with me, she'd always bring Bettie's name into the conversation, claiming I needed to be spending that time with her since we hadn't been married that long. Personally, I thought she was a little on the jealous side, but that's another thing she would never have admitted. I knew it wasn't going to be long before she brought Bettie up as we were tousling down in the basement.

"Charles, you don't need me. You just want some pussy. You got a nice-lookin' wife. What about her?" Katie continued to push me away.

"What about her?" I asked in a belittling manner. "I know I got a pretty, brown-skin woman wit' long, shiny hair; big round titties; and a plump ass that shake like Jell-O when she on top ridin' me. And I ain't gon' even mention how deep her throat is." All while I was rambling on about Bettie's body parts, I got more and more aggressive with Katie. "But guess what, baby?" I halted to look in Katie's face. "She still can't do for me what you do."

"I don't see why not." Katie curled her lips and raised her eyebrows with an attitude. "'Cause bro' man, I ain't suckin' no dick. If she ain't everything you need then go get one of your other women. After all, you got plenty of 'em. Let's not forget about Lora Powers. She been rollin wit' ya a long time. What's it been sixteen, seventeen years for y'all?"

"You know I don't mess off wit' her no mo'. Me and her ain't hooked up in a long time." I wasn't thinking about nothing Katie was saying, 'cause my dick was about to jump out of my pants.

"Well, I'm sure if you give her a call, she'll be more than willing."

"Forget that," I said with a look of hunger in my eyes. "Nobody do for me what you do. You know that. This nut I been carryin' 'round all this time, you got to bust it."

Katie sighed and squinted her eyes at me. "How can you live wit' yourself, Charles? You done hemmed me up down here in the basement trying to fuck me on the day of your brother's funeral, while your whole family upstairs grieving. Do you have any integrity at all?" She turned her nose up and shook her head in disgust.

I paused and stared back at her, raising my eyebrows with certainty. "I know you ain't all of a sudden tryin' to grow no morals. For all these years, you fucked me just as hard and long as I fucked you."

"You right, I did. At first it was out of revenge, I confess. Then it got completely out of hand, but it's over now, and has been for almost a year. So, why can't you just forget about it?" She dropped her arms and stopped fighting, I guess thinking I would develop a conscience and leave her alone. She should have know me better than that, though.

"Okay, I tell you what. You want me to leave you alone, right?" I sounded as if I was getting ready to give up.

"Yes, I do," she quickly asserted.

"If you give me one last quickie for the road, I won't bother you no mo'. Now, that's as reasonable as I can be." I was just saying that shit for the moment, so I could go on and get me some. The minute I got through fucking her, I was probably going to be thinking up what to say the next time to get some more. I began to unfasten my belt buckle as if I knew she was going to agree.

"You sick bastard. You so full of shit it's pitiful." She sighed. "We can't do this down here, now."

"Sure we can. You wastin' time." I wiped my tongue across my top teeth and unzipped my fly.

"You ain't gon' give up, are ya?" She frowned, sounding

defeated.

"Nope," I quickly uttered.

"Damn, just get it over with." She leaned her back against the wall, folded her arms and looked away as I dropped my pants and underwear down to my ankles.

My long, chocolate dick sprang out about nine inches. With no help from her, I reached down and pulled her dress up to her waist and held it there with one hand. Then I viciously tore the crotch of her panties out and rubbed my fingers through her moistened pussy.

"For somebody who don't wanna fuck me, you sho' is soakin' wet." I pushed my middle finger inside her and slid it in and out. I kissed over her face and licked around her mouth. She slowly began to open her legs and ease her tongue out.

"No, no. Please, I can't. I hate feelin' like this," she uttered weakly. Her sound told me she wanted it, but she hated that she wanted it. She closed her eyes and turned her head from side to side with this vulnerable but yearning look on her face. She was fighting hard not to like what I was doing. At the same, time she had to know from our past experience that I could lead her down the road to a fulfilling orgasm that would help relieve some of the stress she was feeling from the funeral and everything.

I kept at it with the strong foreplay. Tiny teardrops ran down her face on the same trail as the ones she'd dispersed at the funeral. "I loved him . . . I did. I didn't want it to be like this. Oh God, why?" She was weak, she confessed through loud whispers. I felt a little sorry for her, but I swear, her tears and cries turned me on all the more.

"Undo these buttons for me. My mouth waterin' for some titty," I urged seductively. I knew that if I touched her breast with my warm, wet tongue one time, she would melt like butter. She loved for her titties to be sucked.

She opened the buttons as I requested. I caught a mouthful of one breast and sucked away. Her grunts told me she liked it. It was like old times. From that point on, it was smooth sailing. She grabbed my dick and caressed it with vigor. My finger was still drenching around up in her. She bundled and tucked the bulk of her dress underneath the stretchy waist section.

"Ohh, ohh, fuck me. Fuck me right now." She turned her face to the wall and bent over, waiting for me to fill her up with my thick dick. In a split second, I worked it in and began thrusting in and out. The harder I worked at it, the more she begged. "Come on, give it to me. Give it to me hard. Oooh, yeah." Her heavy breathing joined with mine.

"Umm, umm, whew," I moaned and maintained a steady, forceful motion. My balls slapped against her ass repeatedly. I'd been inside her no more than one or two minutes, but I was about to erupt like a volcano. "I'm fixin' to cum. Ohh, ohh, Katie. I'm fixin' to cum, baby." I gripped the sides of her thick, curvy hips with both hands.

She pressed against me and rocked back and forth. I heard the pitter-patter of footsteps upstairs, but I never broke a stroke. Like Clarence Carter sang in his song, I was *strokin'*.

I slid one of my hands around her hip to her sweltering pussy. It was dripping wet with pre-cum. I caressed her hard clit with three fingers. It sprang up through each finger split. She opened her legs wider. She was really fucking me now. Her ass was rolling like a whore in a room full of millionaires. Like me, she probably could have fucked off and on the rest of the night.

"It's good. It's so good. Make me cum," she begged.

"Oooh, it's cummin' down. It's cummin' down." I felt my stuff getting ready to gush out. I all but foamed at the mouth. The steam from her pussy was smoldering my dick. I groaned like a madman. A hundred frowns of pleasure embarked on my forehead.

"Make me cum. Make me cum too." She drooled and slobbered like a mare in heat. The way she was carrying on, she had to have missed my humungous cock knocking against her fervent walls during the time we hadn't been together.

"You wanna cum, sistah-in-law? Huh, huh, you wanna

33

cum?" I panted and raved, still stroking and fingering her clit. It turned me on even more to call her sistah-in-law. "Say it. I wanna hear you say it. Say my name, sistah-in-law." I rammed in and out of her wet pussy, demanding her to say my name.

"Charles, oooh, oooh, Charles," she wailed out my name just like I wanted. She arched against me and rolled her ass frantically. I think we both got some kind of kinky thrill from knowing that we were supposed to have been off limits to each other.

"Say it again if you wanna cum. Say it again." I stroked harder. I slid the hand from her hip and the saturated hand from her pussy up her stomach, dragging a trail of slick sexual juices, and palmed both of her breasts. She turned her head to the side and looked up at me from the corner of her left eye. Her mouth watered. She dangled her wet tongue across her top lip, enticing me to bend down and kiss her. Still humping, I leaned even more, pressed into her back and licked my tongue against hers. My sweaty, slimed-up palms fondling her hard nipples and the tongue-teasing play sent our bodies into red-hot ecstasy. She arched. I hard-pressed. We gyrated simultaneously.

"Oooh, oooh, oooh, Charles," she uttered sensually. We huffed and gasped out of breath as we climaxed in unison. I kissed her back several times. She went along with the flow for a minute or two, then I guess she snapped out of it and the true circumstances of everything came rushing back to her mind.

"Let me go. I need to get myself together." She motioned to pull away.

I slowly pulled my creamed dick out of her and reached down to pull up my shorts and pants.

"Ohh, damn." I heaved a sigh. "Woman, you good. As much pussy as I get, ain't none like yours. I swear I can't begin to count the wet dreams I have 'bout you." I felt nothing but pure relief and gratification.

She, on the other hand, sounded somewhat edgy again. "You know what, Charles? The only thing you got goin' for

# ReChella

yourself is that big dick. If it wasn't for that, you wouldn't be worth shit." She pulled her dress down and straightened it. Her panties were torn up, so my cum, mixed with hers, had to be dripping down the inside of her thighs.

"How long we been down here anyway?" She looked at her watch.

"Twelve minutes, baby. I ain't been out of pocket but twelve minutes. It don't take all day to do nothin'." I sniggered while tucking in my shirt and dusting my pants off.

She rolled her eyes and took in a long breath. "Get the hell outta here, crook." She walked into the small basement bath to tidy up.

# Chapter Four

After I neatened up, I resurfaced among the others without raising any suspicion whatsoever. I went straight to Bettie to cover my tracks, just in case somebody saw me leave the basement, then saw Katie leave right behind me. Luckily, Bettie didn't seem like she had been looking for me. She was still in the kitchen with Momma and several more family members, chatting and keeping everything in order. Enough noise was going on that only Bettie could hear what I was saying once I got close to her.

"Hey, baby." I walked up, grasped Bettie from behind in her two-piece black jacket and skirt, and kissed her on the cheek while she situated some of the food on the kitchen counter. "You and Momma got everything under control."

Bettie turned her head upward and pecked my jaw with a return kiss. "Yeah, baby. You ready to eat somethin' yet?"

"That sounds good, hun. But before you fix me a plate, I need you to do somethin' else." I lowered my voice to a serious tone.

Bettie then turned around to face me as she wiped her hands with a paper towel. "Sure, what is it?"

I displayed a concerned look. She gave me her undivided attention despite all the noise that we were in the midst of. "I been down in the basement tryin' to talk to Katie, and I don't know if I helped her or made her worse."

"What's wrong with Katie?" Bettie asked in a disturbed voice.

"Baby, she losin' it. She still cryin' and tryin' to avoid everybody. You think you can talk to her?" I poured it on thick with no shame. It may have been a lie, but it was damn sure justification.

"Of course." She agreed willingly. "Where you say she at?"

"In the basement."

"Okay, I'll be back." Bettie headed toward the kitchen

door. "Momma, I'm comin' right back."

"All right, Bettie," Momma answered.

I strolled on back into the living room with my chest sticking out, proud of the superb job I'd done in getting what I wanted and tying up any loose ends. There didn't seem to be as many people around as before I'd gone down in the basement, but folks were still scattered about laughing, talking, eating, and occupying themselves. Several people questioned me about Katie's whereabouts and told me that they wanted to see her before they left for the evening. I simply told them that Bettie went to check on her and she'd probably join us soon. I dropped down on the sofa with my brother, Kenny, and his wife, Linda, to talk for a while.

The three-bedroom, tan brick house wasn't all that fancy, but an eye-catcher. Katie had it decorated from wall to wall with pretty black art paintings and silk flower arrangements in big vases sitting in various corners. Flowered border ran around the top rim of the walls in each room. Color coordination in ivory, burgundy, and hunter green was blended throughout, except the boys' bedrooms. Navy blue and brown pleased that hyperactive trio.

Both Katie and Gregg always seemed to have taken pride in owning such a nice and tidy little home with a finished basement. The house sat on two-and-a-half acres of land and was located only seven or eight minutes on the outskirts of west Senatobia. Nobody else who lived in their small community was quite so lucky to have the comforting reassurance of an extra room off from the rest of their house, equipped with everything needed to survive for several weeks in the event of a natural disaster. According to what Gregg told me shortly after purchasing the house, the previous owner was a paranoid Army veteran who believed in being well resourced for storms and tornados. Never mind the fact that our fair southern town rarely got severe weather, mostly weather warnings and occasional damage off rubble and debris from high winds. The basement was at the very end of the long hallway around a corner. Soft mauve carpet ran throughout the living room into the hall. The hall bathroom sat on the left and the master bath and bedroom were on the opposite end of the house. Nice and cozy best described it.

### Katie

*I can't believe I just finished screwin' Charles on the same day I buried Gregg,* I thought as I took my time climbing the basement stairs. *Have I really become that pathetic? Who am I foolin'? I did that the first time I let him touch me. And on top of everything, I've been dodgin' these folks since I got home. I might as well go on and face the music, 'cause some of 'em ain't gon' leave 'til they get a chance to look in my face. I don't know why. I sure don't wanna look in theirs.*

The reason I'd gone down in the basement in the beginning was to be alone for a while because I was having a hard time keeping myself together in front of everybody. But how was I going to face them now? Things were even worse than when I first went down there.

*Damn, how'd I let that slick bastard hem me up?* I repeated in my head. As bad as I hated to admit it, and I would have never admitted it to Charles, those few minutes that he was doing me were the first time I'd felt any pleasure in a while. Gregg had been sick for so long, with no signs of getting better. The doctors had given up and told me to prepare myself for the inevitable. Even so, it still hit me pretty hard the day they pronounced him dead. Gregg was no saint, but I loved him dearly, and out of all the stuff he'd done, I still didn't believe that he was as bad as Charles when it came to morality.

As ruthless as Charles was when it came to women, he sure never lacked for any. Females lined up for his ass. He didn't even look all that good, either. Maybe for a lot of the women it was the way he worked that nice-sized penis of his. I know that was one of the main reasons I kept messing with him for as long as I did. He could make me do and say things that I wouldn't dare bring up around Gregg. Gregg was a very good lover, but Charles had certain devious qualities that extracted all of my hidden naughtiness. Still, that was no call for him to be so deceptive. But who was I to judge, considering what I had been doing with him all that time?

Over the years, I'd told myself many times that I was going to put an end to the disgraceful mess that we were caught up in, but every time he came calling, I'd put up just enough fight to get heated up and then before I could blink my eyes, we'd be all over each other. I always tried to blame him for being slick and dragging me into bed. That wasn't the whole truth and I knew it. Charles couldn't do any more than I wanted him to. When I really meant for him to stay away from me during the last year of Gregg's illness, I sure as hell didn't have a problem getting my message across. That told me if I wanted him out of my life, I could have made it happen. Boy, that sure was a reality check.

*What would Gregg say if he could see me now?* I shook off my last thought as I finally reached the top of the stairs. I turned the doorknob and pulled the door open.

"Whoa!" I jerked, slightly startled.

"Ooh, Katie." Bettie yanked her hand back and thrust it to her chest, seemingly just as startled as I. Evidently, both of us were turning the knob to open the door at the same time. "I was just coming down there to check on you." She slightly exhaled.

"Oh, ahh . . . well, here I am." I hesitated awfully. Thoughts of me and her husband going at it not even fifteen minutes from that very moment flickered in my mind. Her face was the last face that I expected to see *first* among the crowd.

*Calm down, Katie. Don't look so nervous. You gon' tell on yourself,* I repeated in my head.

"What's up?" I blurted out, trying not to sound so jittery.

Now she looked as if she was lost in thought about something while gazing at me. Could she have sensed the guilt in my hesitation when I answered her? Was the shit written all over my face, or what? She briskly shook her head, batting her eyes.

"Yeah . . . ah, you okay? Charles, ah, told me you were down here." Her words were somewhat hesitant too. And the way her eyelids were fluttering, I thought something was in her damn eye. Being a female myself, I knew she was letting off signs that something didn't feel right to her. I needed to get my shit on the track, pronto.

"Yeah, I wasn't feeling that great, so I came down here to get myself together. You know, away from the crowd." I made strong eye to eye contact with her. And now I didn't sound as surprised and nervous as I was in the beginning. But, why in the hell Charles had sent her, of all people, after me was one I needed an answer to.

"Believe me, I understand. There was a lot of traffic, but it's slowin' down a little." She seemed more comfortable and direct too.

"I hope so." I exhaled, sounding tired on purpose.

"Charles was worried. He told me he'd been down in the basement trying to comfort you. You know men, though. He figured he didn't help any." She reached out and took my hand. "You sure you're better?"

"Yeah, I'm sure." I smiled mildly and closed the basement door with my other hand. Knowing how cunning Charles was, I guessed he had probably fed Bettie the *comforting me* lie to justify him being in the basement, in case anything came off as suspicious. "Lyin' bastard," I turned my head in the direction to go up the hall and whispered under my breath.

"Pardon?" Bettie turned my hand loose and we started up the hall.

"Oh, nothin'. I was just thinkin' out loud about how I appreciate everybody's help."

"Don't be silly. That's what family's for," Bettie said confidently. "How 'bout something to eat? I know you gotta be hungry by now."

"Not right now. Thank you, though. Have the boys

40

eaten anything yet?" I tried to make conversation, seeing that she was trying hard to be helpful. But I was still thinking about the damn lie that Charles had the nerve to tell her. Actually, I was quite pissed, but I knew I needed to get that out of my head and prepare myself mentally to chat with all of those people. So, that's what I did.

"No, the boys haven't eaten either. They're outside playing basketball, I think. But the rest of the children have already eaten. I asked the boys if they wanted to go 'head and eat with the other children, and they told me they weren't hungry."

"That's my boys. They'd rather play first and eat last. Lord, but when they do get ready to eat, they try to eat up the refrigerator." I exhaled. "Ain't it too hot out there for basketball?"

"To us, maybe, but not to them." Bettie smiled, slightly nodding her head to me. Just before we reached the end of the hall, she paused. "You know, you would probably be a lot more comfortable if you changed your clothes. After all, you're at home. Everybody would understand that."

I glanced down at my clothes. "You're probably right, but since I didn't change when I first got here, I'm not gon' worry about it now. I'ma go 'head and talk wit' some of these people. Go on back and finish what you were doin'. I'm fine now."

"Okay."

Bettie wasn't such a bad person, and it wasn't that I disliked her. Actually, I liked her quite a bit. When Charles first brought her around to meet the family right before announcing their plans for marriage, she came off as some kind of uppity, goody two-shoes with fake credentials. Now, that rubbed me the wrong way a tad, and I think it did the same to everyone else. But, maybe that was just her, defense mechanism when meeting new people, because after we all got to know her she seemed to fall right in with the rest of us. I thought she was a bit overzealous about being in the family and having the Jennings name, but hey, it wasn't my business.

# Scandalous

She gave me a quick hug, and I inhaled a deep breath as we entered the living room. Bettie walked on through to the kitchen.

"Hey, Katie," a deep, scratchy voice called out from across the room. "Come on over here, sistah-in-law."

I strolled over, smiling, to where Kenny and Linda were standing. "Hey, Kenny. Linda."

He opened his arms to hug me. Linda smiled and flashed a wave at me while Kenny and I embraced.

"You hangin' in there?" Kenny asked gently as we retracted from the hug.

"Yeah, I'm . . . I'm hangin' in there." I took a once-over look at him and widened my smile. "You lookin' mighty handsome, fella."

"Sho' ya right!" He expanded his smile to match mine, then suddenly twirled around and posed masculine-style. "You liiike?" We both laughed out loud. Linda crossed her arms and continued to grin.

"Yes, I do. Gregg would be shocked . . . and proud to see you in a suit," I stated excitedly.

Kenny narrowed his smile and gave me a caring look. "I know. He never stopped tryin' to convince me to wear suits; especially to church." We exchanged caring gazes from that warm memory of Gregg.

Now, Kenny was a real brother to Gregg. In spite of my explicit behavior with Charles, the only thing Gregg's other brothers and I ever felt for each other was wholesome brotherly and sisterly love.

"Well, Kenny, he's watchin' from heaven, so he's smilin'," I said with assurance.

"I believe that, too. Look, sistah-in-law, if you and the boys need anything, you got me and Linda's number. All you got to do is call us." Kenny's sincerity glowed like a neon light. He loved Gregg a great deal, and they often went fishing together to get in that brotherly time, as they called it. Gregg and each of his brothers had their own individual relationship, but he and Kenny were closest. Every Sunday after worship service was over, Gregg never failed to approach Kenny about wearing a suit and tie instead of just a shirt and tie. Kenny always laughed and told him that his shirt and tie was as close as he was going to get to wearing a suit.

As different as each of them were, I had to give it to the Jennings family, even black-ass, crooked Charles. They always managed to hang in there as a pretty tight family no matter what kind of ups and downs came their way. I sometimes felt closer to Gregg's family than I did my own; excluding the thing with Charles, of course. I certainly spent more time with the Jennings family.

Their mother brought them up doing just about everything together, and it stayed with them over the years. She was big on family eat-outs and gatherings. Truth be told, only one of my sisters and I got along well. I hadn't seen or talked to the other two in a very long time. But, the way things always sped downhill with us, it was in our best interest not to be in each other's company anyway.

Oftentimes, I thought how bad it was that our mother hadn't raised us to be as close as Gregg's mother had raised them to be. Yep, Ms. Mildred Jennings deserved her props for that. Another thing she wouldn't hear of was one of her daughters-in-law calling her Ms. Jennings or Ms. Mildred. She always treated her sons' wives like her own daughters, and insisted we call her Momma. So, Momma it was. That is, unless she thought her sons were being mistreated or hurt in some way by their wives. Then she was like a bear protecting her cubs. The one thing I didn't care for about her was she didn't think her boys could do no wrong— especially Charles. He had the wool over her eyes so thick it was ridiculous. But, I guess like any other family, they had their own way of doing things.

Gregg and I were alike in many ways; being talkative wasn't one of them. He rarely spoke up unless he was spoken to first. Now, Kenny and Linda were opposite in that area. While Kenny kept the conversation going, Linda hardly said anything at all. Plenty of times at family dinners, I'd almost forget she was in the room she was so quiet. A professional-looking, brown-skinned lady with a neck-length bobbed hairdo, medium height, medium weight, she was very conservative in her choice of clothing, and her demeanor could only be taken as serious. Even as Kenny and I stood in the living room and joked about him finally wearing a suit, Linda was tickled pink, but she still looked just as serious as always. The earnestness in her encouraging words to me were very moving.

"Be strong, Katie. Dying is a part of living, and we all must travel that same road at some time or another." She wrapped her arms around me affectionately. "I know your faith is boundless. You'll be fine, just fine."

Of my three sisters-in-law, Linda was the most likable to me. Then Sharon; then Bettie.

"I know I will. God gon' see to that." We withdrew from the hug. "Thank you, Linda." She and I shared the same warm look as Kenny and I. "Have y'all had anything to eat yet?" I felt a few tears trying to surface, so I quickly changed the subject.

"Well, I had a li'l somethin' earlier, but we were tryin' to let some of the company get finished befo' we really let loose," Kenny answered rather jolly while patting his stomach. "You know how Momma is 'bout bein' courteous to comp—"

"Excuse me, y'all." Mr. Dixon eased up with his wife and interrupted Kenny's words. "We just wanted to holla at Katie before we get on outta here."

"Hello."

"Hi."

"Hey." Kenny, Linda, and I spoke simultaneously as I reached out to shake the Dixons' hands.

"Well, how y'all comin' 'long?" Mr. Dixon asked in his old, shaky voice.

"Doin' well, Mr. Dixon, very well," Kenny answered, then smacked his hands together one time. "Listen, me and Linda gon' go on, grab a bite and let y'all talk." Kenny excused himself, and he and Linda headed for the kitchen.

"Brother and Sister Dixon, everything's fine. I guess

about as well as can be expected." I took in a long breath.

"Well, chile, just hold on to God's unchangin' hands, ya hear," Sister Dixon uttered distortedly, sounding like her throat was filled with phlegm.

"I am. I am." I nodded yes.

The Dixons were also members of Mt. Pleasant Church, along with the rest of us. In fact, they'd been members probably longer than anyone in the church. The old couple was in their mid-seventies, but they got around as well as any twenty-year-old. I talked with them a while, then my mother and I stole a few minutes alone to go over a few concerns of hers. I was the one in need of support, but as usual, she was the one who wanted something. She wasn't a great mother when we were young, then when my father died, she really went down. The only thing certain about her after his death was the way she drank and wallowed in self-pity. That was one of the many reasons we'd drifted apart over the years. Can't say I wasn't glad to see her moseying on out the door with her man friend to go home.

Afterward, other guests made their way around to chat with me. I didn't realize how exhausted I was from talking so much until the last person left. The front room was now quiet. As I closed the door and locked it, the only noise in the house was coming from the kitchen, where just family remained.

### Charles

When I finally finished filling up on some of the funeral grub, I turned my chair over to Wayne so he could sit down for a bite, or at least another bite. He swore he hadn't done anything but taste a little something to tide him over when I'd seen him chewing earlier. I told him if what he'd had on his plate was tasting, I didn't want to see him eat a full meal. I was used to his healthy appetite, though. He and I laughed it off.

The ones who hadn't eaten fixed a plate and pulled a chair up to the kitchen table, and the rest of us stood around and talked. My brothers could eat their asses off. I'd always had a healthy appetite, but they could put away much more food than me, especially my youngest brother, Bo, and my middle brother, Wayne.

"Wayne, you think you got enough on yo' plate?" Momma laughed, staring at Wayne's food like she was getting full just watching.

Wayne's mouth was too full to respond. He kept right on chewing. So much food was on his plate, every time he forked up a mouthful of something, bits of something else spilled from the edges. His wife, Sharon, always joked about how hard it was to feed him, their little boy and little girl.

Kenny was probably right behind Wayne in eating the most. But in age, Kenny was next to Gregg at thirty-seven, then Wayne at thirty-four, Richard thirty, AJ twenty-eight, and Bo twenty-five. None of my brothers were what you called fat. They were strong, healthy-sized men with much more muscle than me. Any stranger could look at us and tell that we were brothers. Our family resemblance was undeniable.

Wayne finally swallowed his food and restrained from refilling his mouth long enough to reply to Momma. "Ain't that much on my plate, Momma. Look at Jon Jon and Li'l Gregg. For them to be so skinny, they ain't short-stoppin'." Wayne then forked up a mouth of greens and began chewing again.

Jon Jon and Li'l Gregg were thirteen and fifteen. They were Gregg and Katie's sons. Then there was little Jeremy, who was eight. He could devour as much grub as his two older brothers.

"But, Uncle Wayne, that's yo' third plate," Jon Jon said rather comically.

Everyone in the kitchen burst into laughter. And that was just what we all needed after such a tense day—a good laugh.

"Hold up, hold up. Forget about who eatin' what, y'all." Richard cut into our laughter, putting his corn on the cob back down on his plate. "Can somebody please tell me what in the hell Debra came bustin' in the church like that for? Excuse my language, Momma."

"I know that's right. I bet folks still talkin' 'bout that," AJ remarked right before he bit into a crispy chicken leg.

Momma raised her voice. "Still talkin'? They ain't never quit. You know how Senatobia is. That shit everywhere by now."

Another thing about Momma, she was a fiesty old lady. I guess raising seven boys, she had to be. She always spoke her mind, and didn't take no crap off nobody. Yet, at the same time she was sweet as anyone allowed her to be. Richard, AJ, and Bo still lived with her. None of them had gotten married and moved out on their own, but you better believe she was on them every day like flies on stank about getting their own places.

"Well, I'm glad Katie didn't say nothin', but I sho' wanted to," Kenny blurted out, breaking a corn muffin in half.

"Glad Katie didn't say nothin' 'bout what?" Katie asked as she strolled through the kitchen door. I guess she'd finally seen the last of the company out.

"About that crazy Debra," Kenny told her.

"Oh, well, even if I had said somethin', it would've only made it worse. She wanted to give people somethin' to talk about, anyway." Katie sounded rather irritated.

"I think you handled it perfectly," Sharon stated. "'Cause if it had been me, I woulda threw her out on her a–"

"Sharon, that ain't called for. She did right by not sayin' nothin'," Wayne interrupted his wife before she finished her sentence.

We all laughed again. Sharon was by no means quiet like my other sister-in-law, Linda. Sharon was in her mid-thirties, short tapered hair, butter pecan complexion and slim figure. She could raise more hell than the law allowed. The day Wayne brought her to one of Momma's Sunday dinners and introduced her, I knew off the top not to ever get out of place with her. One of two things would have probably happened: She would have either cursed me out on the spot or told everybody in town, including Wayne. Maybe both. I also kept my cool with Kenny's wife, Linda. She was so damn quiet and serious, I couldn't size her up too well. Hell, the only person she ever looked like she was concentrating on was Kenny. Not that I sat around wondering if my brothers' wives would go to bed with me if I approached them. It wasn't like that. When a beautiful woman was in my presence, my antennas just automatically popped up. I had to keep abreast on who to fuck with and who not to. Besides, Katie was the only one of 'em that I'd felt that certain something for from day one.

"Katie, get yo' plate out o' the microwave. I fixed it for ya earlier," Momma said with concern as she observed Katie.

Momma was always looking out for the family. She made sure Katie, Li'l Gregg, Jon Jon, and Little Jeremy had a plate put to the side. She probably felt that Katie wasn't going to feel up to doing it herself after spending so much time talking with so many people. And from the looks of Katie, she was right.

"Thank you, Momma." Katie took the plate from the microwave and peeked under the foil. "Dang, you musta thought you was fixin' this plate for Wayne."

"Hey, watch ya'self," Wayne grumbled, squinting his eyes and still stuffing his face.

"It's the truth, Wayne." Katie giggled, putting her plate back in the microwave.

"You ain't gon' eat now, Katie?" Momma asked, deepening her concerned look.

"Nah, I might try to eat a little bit later. I just don't feel up to it right now."

Katie walked over to the sink, leaned and rested her elbows on the counter. I couldn't resist snatching a glance at her ass as she bent over, remembering our nice quickie in the basement. I played off my naughty peek by making conversation. "Sistah-in-law, you look exhausted. You probably need to turn in early tonight," I told her.

*That good fuck I gave ya had to wear yo' ass out. I*

smiled on the inside, reflecting.

"Maybe so," she answered nonchalantly.

"He's right, Katie. And soon as everybody finish eatin', we gon' put everything up, so you won't have to be in here tryin' to do it," Bettie added. "That way you can go straight to bed."

"I know that's right. You gotta be tired, 'cause I can hardly wait for my head to hit the pillow," Sharon uttered strongly.

Linda made no comment, but shook her head in agreement with Sharon and Bettie.

"I sure do appreciate y'all," Katie mumbled.

"Charles, y'all got a program next weekend?" Momma asked, changing the subject. She loved to follow the gospel singing. She and a couple of her lady friends came to just about every program that our group was booked on, and many that we weren't.

"Yeah, Momma, we gon' be at the Civic Center on that big gospel explosion program next Saturday," I answered.

"Ain't the Melody Angels and Harmonettes on that same program?" She raised her eyebrows with interest.

"I believe so. You gon' make it?" I asked her.

"Man, what you mean is she gon' make it? Her and Ms. Hattie already there," Bo said, smiling, then took a big gulp of Coca-Cola.

"And don't forget about the third stooge, Mrs. Sadie Mae. She gon' be right up in there too," AJ added, slightly grinning.

"Aw, hush," Momma uttered. "I need to hog-tie the three of y'all and drag ya on up there wit' us. Maybe you'll find some nice church girls and get married like ya brothers."

"But I didn't say nothin', Momma," Richard uttered innocently.

"So." Momma didn't take no mercy on Richard. "That don't mean you don't need me to drag you on up there too. I don't see no wife'a yo's standin' 'round in this kitchen, do you?"

# Scandalous

Richard laughed and the rest of us joined in with him. I figured Momma was quite possibly getting ready to deliver her usual sermon about Richard, AJ, and Bo getting married. They knew she didn't want them playing the field with a whole lot of different women. But I still didn't think she was as hard on them as she'd been on me when I was their ages. She often used Gregg's, Kenny's, Wayne's, and my marriage as examples of good family-based marriages, saying that she wanted her younger sons to find their soul mates and be just as happy as we were—or seemed to be.

Gregg and I had the same father, Percy Jennings. He died when Gregg was just a year old. He was the only man that Momma had ever been married to, and the only one she spoke of fondly. The rest of my brothers shared the same father, Joe Louis Arnold. According to Momma, Joe was much different than Gregg's and my dad. Momma claimed he wasn't the marrying type. The one thing she continually repeated about him was, 'The only happiness that damn Joe Louis Arnold ever gave me was my five sons. Other than that, he wasn't worth two farts in hell. God rest my dear old momma's soul, she always warned me to never trust a man wit' three first names.' I guess that told us that even though Mildred Jennings in the flesh was saved, she hadn't always made the best of choices either. Still, I didn't know a soul in town who didn't like or respect my momma.

Two things that little short, brown lady was well known for were cooking and feeding anybody who wanted to eat. Sundays at her house were like being at Piccadilly Restaurant in Memphis. Then on top of that, she cooked every day for Richard, AJ, and Bo. Who could blame 'em for not wanting to leave home? She had 'em spoiled as ever. Being the baby boy, Bo got away with a lot of stuff that we hadn't even tried when we were growing up. He knew Momma was full of spunk, so sometimes he pretended to raise his voice and talk back to her just to get a rise out of her.

"Momma, how many times have I told you? We ain't got to always be at church to meet a nice woman. Sometimes the folks at church worse than the folks at the club." Bo stood up from the table and pointed his finger at Momma as if he were chastising her. "Now, get on up and let's go to the house, woman, befo' I leave you down here." He could hardly keep a straight face. He burst into laughter, right before the rest of us did the same.

Momma didn't say a word. In fact, her expression said that she wasn't even paying him any attention. Bo wasn't crazy enough to disrespect her like that for real, nor were the rest of us. She would have gotten a stick and beat the hell out of him on sight. At sixty-five, her high-pitched voice was as strong as ever. She was determined to stay young and vibrant. She loved pretty dresses, matching shoes, and big hats. At Christmas time, we couldn't go wrong buying her stuff like that.

"What's ya hurry, Bo?" I asked, standing behind Bettie, massaging her shoulders.

"I got a hot date. I ain't on lock-down like the rest o' y'all ole married boys." Bo reached down and shook Kenny's shoulder with one hand while laughing. "Ain't that right, Kenny boy?"

Kenny didn't comment right away. He just smiled and shook his head from side to side as if Bo should have been ashamed of himself. "Charles, you gon' whup this boy or what?" Kenny finally said.

"Naw, I'ma let Momma get him," I said lively.

A muffled ringing sound came from underneath one of the cabinets.

"Hush. Listen, y'all." Richard halted his hand in front of him, signaling us to stop talking. "I hear somebody's cell phone rangin'."

"Me too. Sound like it's—" Bo started to say.

"That's my phone," Bettie stated quickly as she bent down and opened the cabinet where the stifled ring came from.

She opened her black leather purse in a hurry. "Hello, hello." Bettie paused while holding the phone to her ear and pasted her eyes directly on me.

# Scandalous

Her volume had to be up to the maximum, because I heard the music loud and clear through the phone. "I don't see nothin' wrong, wit' a little bump-n-grind . . . I don't see..."

"You know who this is, don't you?" Bettie whispered to me while covering the mouth of the phone with her hand. I smiled as she and I listened to her hot-headed twenty-four-year-old sister singing along with the R. Kelly song that was playing in the background. A couple of seconds passed, and Bettie seemed as if she was becoming annoyed.

"Hello, Keshundra. Keshu!" Bettie exclaimed.

"Damn, why you hollin' up in the phone like that, gull?" Keshundra's country alto voice finally screeched out to Bettie through the phone waves. I heard her loud and clear right before Bettie pushed the button to turn the volume down.

If everybody else hadn't already started back on their own conversation, they probably would have heard her too. I turned my attention back to the others and noticed Momma glancing around the kitchen as if she was looking for something.

"You tryin' to find somethin', Momma?" I asked.

"Yeah, I'm looking for my pocketbook," she replied, still eyeing from place to place. "Anybody seen it?"

"Ain't this it under ya chair, Momma?" Sharon asked, bending over to pick up a brown purse.

"Yeah, that's it. Thank ya, baby," Momma said with gratitude as she reached for the purse. "Look, I reckon we gon' get on outta here, y'all, befo' I have to whup Bo's ass," Momma stated, backing her chair away from the table, then stood up and looked over at Katie. "'Less you need me to stay on longer, Katie."

"No, I'm fine, Momma. You go on home and get some rest yourself," Katie said.

Momma walked over and hugged Katie. Everybody was done eating, so they started making preparations to leave too. Linda and Sharon had already started clearing away food and doing dishes. No sooner than Bettie hung up the

52

phone, she told me that Keshundra had locked herself out of the house and needed to get in as soon as possible 'cause the mosquitoes were wearing her out. Bettie joined in and helped with the kitchen, and as soon as they were done, we headed home. We lived on the outskirts of east Senatobia, about as far away from town as Katie's house. Both areas were considered to be the wooded country. So, I knew if anybody was out that time of the evening without any mosquito spray, they were getting the hell bitten out of 'em.

# Chapter Five

Now, Keshundra was hotter'n a firecracker in a pile of dry hay. From the first day I met her, all she bragged about was fucking and how good she could give head to her men. The last place she needed to be was under my roof, but how could Bettie refuse her own sister when she asked to stay with us a few months until she got an apartment in town? And for what reason would Bettie have refused her anyway? As far as I knew, the two of them had a great sisterly relationship. Their parents were older, settled folks. Bettie told me how they always complained about Keshundra's lifestyle. I guess they'd put up with it as long as they could, because they finally told her if she didn't settle on one man, she was going to have to get her own place. That, of course, landed her at our doorstep for the time being. I never got the very first chance to throw a few lines her way to see if she would bite. Hell, when Bettie wasn't around, she'd beat me to it.

Some of the shit Keshundra talked about concerning sex left me speechless. It was a sight, too. Me, speechless? Keshundra hadn't been staying with us no more than a month. She always had her hand out asking Bettie for something. Wasn't long before she started asking me for a loan or two here and there. She never paid me back, though. But it was cool. I knew my generosity was going to come in handy one day.

She always tried to get me to tell her how well off I was financially. Swore that one day she was going to have a man to take care of her just like I was taking care of Bettie. Keshundra believed as fine as she looked, she shouldn't have to lift a finger. She wanted to be some man's trophy wife. I never gave her any specific information about my finances, but I did tell her enough to whet her appetite. The fact that I had driven my own truck for years probably told her I made top pay. No, Bettie didn't have to work if she didn't want to, but after we got married, she chose to stay on part-time instead of full-time at Crye-leike Realtors, which was a good thing, 'cause she was just my second wife, not the heiress to my fortune.

When we pulled into the driveway, Keshundra was sitting on the garage steps listening to the radio. We parked the truck right next to the champagne-gold Lexus in the garage. I gathered the stuff from the back seat to take in, and Bettie walked toward the garage door where Keshundra sat, rolling her eyes like she was mad at the world. Her bark was worse than her bite, though. We were used to her little tantrums.

"It sho' did take long enough. These damn mosquitoes gon' have knots all over my sexy body," Keshundra complained. "Y'all better be glad I found some Off spray in the storage room."

Bettie didn't reply right away. She held the keys out to Keshundra in a way that said she wasn't paying her no mind. "Girl, we had to straighten up for Katie and make sure her and the boys were settled in for the night."

Keshundra threw out a puzzled look with attitude, then snatched the keys from Bettie's hand. "Make sure she was settled in? She lost her husband, not her mind."

Bettie maintained her *you ain't talkin' 'bout nothin'* look at Keshundra and changed the subject. "No wonder you gon' have knots all over. You ain't got no clothes coverin' ya." Bettie started up the steps.

Keshundra stood up and slowly rolled her eyes and neck as she reached for the knob to unlock the door. "I got clothes on. I ain't no old maid. I'm not gon' be walkin' 'round dressed like somebody's grandma."

Keshundra should have been in Nelly's Ms. Apple-bottom search. She had an ass out the frame. Not too big, not too small. She barely had any waistline. Move on up her rack a little further, maybe a 36B bra size. She had shoulder length hair the same as Bettie, but she always wore it pulled back off her face; said she didn't want nothing hiding her big, brown eyes. She wore a black sports bra and some red short pants that were so tiny, the bottom of her cheeks peeped out every time she slightly bent over.

Keshundra fumbled with the lock before she turned the key and opened the door to my five-bedroom, three-and-a-half bath, two-story brick house that was paid for in full. For many years, good ole Ruth graciously occupied the territory that Bettie had now taken over.

Together, Ruth and I had raised our three daughters in that beautiful, spacious home, and never let them lack for anything. My two older daughters, Amy and Karen, were married with their own families and living in New Jersey. My youngest daughter, Tina, was on her third year at Delta State University. She had her own apartment in Cleveland, not far from the college.

Neither of the girls approved of me replacing their mother so soon after her death. After a while, they came right out and told me that they'd lost a lot of respect for me. And they damn sure didn't make no secret of how they felt about Bettie. They didn't care for her at all. I couldn't keep up with the number of times they'd asked me what kind of woman could move into another woman's house and sleep in the same bed that she'd taken her last breath in, two months after she'd died. A few of them times, I had to keep them from confronting Bettie with the same question. Bettie knew how they felt about her, so she made it her business to keep quiet on that issue in order to keep the peace.

My girls also told me more times than a few that they knew Bettie was already in the picture before their momma passed on, but they just couldn't prove it. Of course I denied it, since I knew they were only guessing. That left nothing more for them to do, although it hurt like hell when they told me that as long as Bettie was in their mother's house, they were going to steer clear. At first I thought it was just their hurt talking, but after many weeks turned into many months, and then the months turned into a year or so and counting, I realized they weren't bullshitting at all. I wasn't used to my girls not coming home to visit for holidays and various occasions, but what could I do? I couldn't divorce Bettie and throw her out on the street. I had to acknowledge her as the new-fangled woman of the house. But I certainly did make it crystal clear to her from the git-go that my property would always stay in the Jennings family.

I flat-foot told Bettie that Ruth and I had worked hard for what we had acquired over the years, and if she ever decided to leave me for any reason, she would just have to leave without any of the property that I already had when we got married. I didn't say it to her in a ugly way, of course, but she needed to know where I stood on that, especially, since I'd had it all stipulated in a pre-nup agreement that she had to sign before we were married. Whether she had a problem with it or not, she sure didn't hesitate to sign her John Hancock on the signature line.

When Bettie moved in, she really didn't have anything to do to the house, because it was already beautifully decorated. But, I guess she really needed to feel like the woman in charge, so she moved a few things around and about, and mixed and matched a little bit here and there to add her own taste.

The kitchen hallway was the way of entering through the garage. Bettie and Keshundra stood in the kitchen as I brought a couple of plates in the house that Bettie had fixed to go before we left Katie's. I set them on the table then glanced over at Keshundra.

"Bettie," I called out. "Which one of these plates belong to fang face?" I turned back to look at Keshundra with my face screwed into a cross-eyed, mocking expression as a joke.

Keshundra gave me the same eye-roll she'd given Bettie. "Ha, ha, ha, that's so funny." She abruptly slapped me on the shoulder. "I know you ain't callin' me fang face, wit' yo' rat face."

"Rat face?" I gasped.

"That's right, rat face. Look like you 'bout to break out a hunk o' cheese and start gnawing any minute," Keshundra snarled then burst into laughter.

Bettie jumped right in giggling with her. I smiled in silence as I watched them get a kick out of her little so-called clever remark. Keshundra and I had been playing the dozens since the very beginning. It was our way of chilling out with each other; it was also a habit. I guess it sort of gave us that sister-and-brother-going-at-it type edge. Except for the times when Bettie wasn't around, of course. During those times, we maintained our joking around, but the subject just took a raw turn to shit that we knew we shouldn't have been discussing with each other.

I was somewhat disappointed in myself that Keshundra had been in the house with us for that long and I hadn't tapped that ass yet. With all of the *let's fuck* signs she was ramming in my face, and then proclaiming to be so close to her sister, a brother had to wonder was she for real or was she just trying to set a trap to see if I'd bite. And if I did bite, Bettie would quite possibly jump from behind a piece of furniture or something and yell, "Got yo' ass." That little thought is what kept me in check for a minute. I damn sure talked much shit with Keshundra, but I still carefully calculated my moves to be on the safe side.

"All right, I'ma let you have that one this time." I chuckled, then went on down the hall to my bedroom, visualizing the eyeful of Keshundra's tits and ass I'd just helped myself to.

### Keshundra

I removed the foil from the plate that BJ brought for me and sat down at the table to eat. I was hungrier than a mug, plus them mosquitoes had tore my ass up out in that damn garage. It was well worth it, though. That drunk, horny-ass nigga down the street gave me a hundred dollars just to sit out there on the steps and talk with him while he searched my sexy body over. That was all he was going to get, too—a look. Limp-dick bastard. Hell, even if I had wanted to fuck, he probably wouldn't have been able to get it up as much liquor as he was drinking.

# ReChella

*The things a girl gotta put up wit' just to keep the cash flowin',* I thought as I sniffed the aroma of the hearty meal before me.

"BJ, hand me a fork?" I watched my sister slow-poke around the kitchen like she was an old woman who'd been out in the cotton field all day.

I'd been calling her BJ since I could remember. Our two older brothers never found it fitting to call her anything but Bettie Jean, though. But then again, they were too stiff necks anyway. For BJ to have been so much older than me, she was kinda cool. She acted more like a hip mother than a sister. Me and her had always been thick as thieves, and we pretty much talked about whatever was on our minds. Of course, I had a few hush-hushes that I wouldn't have told her about, and I'm sure she had a few secrets that she hadn't shared, but it was all good, 'cause it didn't affect our relationship. Besides, there's certain kinds of personal shit that need to stay on the DL anyway.

"Girl, I been on my feet all day. I'm tired," BJ grunted, handing me the fork. "Put all this stuff up for me when you finish. I'm gon' take a long, hot bath and turn in."

"This early? It ain't but 7:30," I said. "I forgot. Y'all some old-ass folks." I twirled spaghetti around the fork and slid it in my mouth.

BJ threw me a look that said I had lost my mind. "Shit, you got wax in yo' ears? I just told you I was tired, didn't I?" She raised her voice.

One thing about the country, everybody had a few choice cuss words. Even prissy, goody two-shoes like BJ. Yes, even though I loved my sister dearly, she tried her best to make other people think she hadn't sinned a day in her life. She put on this holy-roller act like she was the little blameless princess in the palace, but I knew the truth. In fact, she was the one who first showed me the ropes in the relationship game. Then I excelled past her, of course. Yep, she was just as devious and gold-digging as people labeled me. The only thing was, she didn't have anymore use for her "giving up the pussy for pay" skills now that she'd found one man to provide her with the entire package. She buried her gifts of deceitfulness after she met her beloved husband, Charles. I had to admit, she acted like she really loved him. Over the years, her sharp cunning senses seemed to be getting a bit rusty, since she didn't use them anymore. But I'm sure the tricky traits were still there. I'd seen time when she wouldn't have been thinking about going to no bed at 7:30 at night. Hell, she would've just been preparing to get her prowl on at that hour. I was curious to know why she was so tired, though, because to my knowledge, all she'd done was attend a funeral.

"You that tired?" I widened my eyes but never stopped eating. "That's why I ain't never gettin' married. Married folks don't get none. Me and my friend get some every day. I ain't messin' that up." Shiiit, I was blunt. Whatever came up, came out. Anybody who knew me, knew that.

"Believe me, we get plenty, baby girl." BJ plopped her hands on her hips, staring at me. "And you ain't gettin' no younger, ya know. Twenty-four, knockin' the hell outta twenty-five."

"Haah." I looked at her with a leer. "I might be, but my man only twenty. He a young stud, baby. And the rest of 'em that want me ain't much older than him. That's how I like 'em, young and trainable."

"So, you sayin' if the right man came along and there was only one year difference in your ages, you wouldn't be interested because he was older?" BJ maintained her stare with her hands on her hips as she awaited my reply.

The food was good, but I had eaten all that I was going to eat except for the chocolate cake. I picked off of the thick slice with my fingertips. "I ain't crazy now, gull," I answered. "If he can handle the work, I'll give him the job." I licked the icing from my red, air-brushed nails. "Otherwise, the ones standin' in line already know the routine," I gloated.

"I thought you really liked Derrick, Keesh?" BJ asked. Keesh was BJ's nickname for me, another for-short name our brothers wouldn't have used.

# ReChella

"I do like Derrick. But you think I'ma say no when other guys wanna take me out and treat me to nice gifts and stuff? It ain't that serious. I gotta get mine." I got up from the table and rinsed my hands off at the sink.

BJ shook her head at me like she was disgusted. "All right, just don't ever get caught, ya hear. When men think you using 'em, that kinda shit can backfire on you. Some things you need to quit while you're ahead." She turned to go down the hall toward her room.

One thing I detested with a passion was folks who'd done the exact same shit as I was doing, but 'cause they claimed they didn't desire to do it anymore, they tried to act all high and fuckin' mighty. BJ had to know she was going to piss me off by making that uncalled-for statement. Like I was so lost that she needed to save me. Hell, her and that harlot, Jezabel, was the ones who invented fucking for money and goods. I knew I should have kept my mouth closed, but I couldn't resist. I had to give her ass a reality check to make sure she hadn't outgrown her damn roots—in other words, forgot where she'd come from.

"I guess you ought to know, seein' that you experienced it first hand," I sniggered as I cleared the table and put the remaining plates in the fridge. I glimpsed BJ out the corner of my eye when she spun back around after hearing my remark.

"Girl, shut yo' damn mouth," she whispered aggressively. "That crap in the past . . . way in the past." People learn from their mistakes. And you know for yourself I've learned from my past."

"I know that's what you say, so why you soundin' all uppity 'cause I ain't there yet?" I nodded my head at her while still sniggering. "I was just makin' sure you hadn't got all holy on me and forgot about it. You know, got too big for ya britches as Momma used to say. After all, I learned how to shuffle them niggas from the best . . . my big sistah." I tried to sound proud of her teachings on purpose. I knew it would get under her skin, 'cause she never wanted to talk about or remember any of it.

61

# Scandalous

As I walked past her I saw the aggravated expression on her face. I ignored it and leaned over to give her a little kiss on the cheek and whispered sarcastically. "Thanks for the lessons, sis. Niiighty-night." I went upstairs to the room that I was using while I stayed with her and Charles.

I really didn't have time to be thinking about BJ and her small-time issues anyway. She had her security blanket already in the mix. I needed to be working on getting me some new dicks lined up. My mean-green stash was getting a little low because I had over-spent on a new wardrobe I'd been itching for. Even though my usual male connections was still putttin' out some bread, a couple of 'em had started to slack a little by coming up short. I definitely knew how to remedy that, though. If they wanted to play games, I knew a shit load of games. Short on pay, short on pussy; simple as that. Negros wasn't smart. Thought they were going to be getting some freebies. Not. Hell, I didn't have a 9-to-5 job, but I had plenty of bills that needed paying. My Macy's card, Dillard's card, and Mastercards and Visas weren't going to get paid with good intentions. And my damn Nissan Altima car note sure as hell wasn't going to get paid by hoping. I laid across the bed, reflecting over the evening's activities.

*Damn, I could've got a couple'a more hundred outta that nigga down the street if he hadn't o' been drinkin' so much. I woulda put this pussy on him and that woulda been it. Oh well, so much for that. No need in cryin' over spilled milked. Maybe I'll catch up wit' his ass tomorrow. I might as well go on take a bath and wash this mosquito spray off,* I told myself silently.

As I raised up from the bed to gather my things for the bath, a thought hit me. *Charles! That's it! Ole Charlesee pooh. Nah, I can't do that. Can I?* I walked over to the dresser mirror.

"Are you gon' have a moral dilemma 'cause that's your sistah's man, or are you gon' go 'head and get paid, girlfriend? How's she gon' ever find out anyway?" After staring into the mirror and asking myself those questions, I knew I was seriously getting ready to fuck my sister's husband.

Sure, I had considered it many times before, but the cash stash wasn't as low as it was now. Maybe that was one of the things that had kept me under control with him as long as I'd been. All of the flirting and playing around that he and I had been doing had finally ended up in the only place that it could have. That was definitely among the hush-hush stuff that I hadn't talked about with BJ. Besides, back in the day when she was teaching me the ropes and things, she'd hammered it in my head that as long as I stayed two steps ahead of the game, there weren't any specific rules when it came to getting what you want. According to what I'd learned from her, she would have done the same thing if the occasion had called for it. So, that gave me my answer, or at least it justified what I was about to do. Charles Jennings wasn't just my brother-in-law. Hell, he was a man with plenty of benefits and even more money. And damn, I needed both of those goods real bad right about now.

The ethics question mark on my face that I'd been staring at in the mirror had transformed into a motivational smile. I vamped from the mirror 'cause I didn't have no more time to dwell on that "what if" shit. I had to make preparations for the ultimate seduction. Even though I felt like ole Charles would be just like a dog with a bone if he was given the right incentives, I still had to hype him up with plenty of old-fashioned temptation, then leave his mouth watering for some Keshundra.

One thing I knew from being in the house with BJ and Charles for the month that I'd been there was they had a few routines that they stuck to like clockwork. When she got in that Jacuzzi, she would be there for a minute or two. And during the time she was aroma-therapying herself, or whatever the hell she called it, he always came upstairs and sat in his office on the other end of the hall from my bedroom. He'd be fumbling around with some papers and things at his desk with his office door wide open. I never bothered to ask what he was doing, but I knew that he could probably see everything that went on in the hallway and much of what went on in my room if I left the door open and stood at the end of the bed.

Now the plan was coming together. I knew exactly what I was going to do. I quickly jumped in the shower before Charles made his nightly visit to his office, and sure enough, by the time I was finished, he was sitting at his desk, wearing his silk burgundy pajama set, looking at some papers and writing with the door wide open as usual.

I conveniently forgot to take a dry-off towel in the bathroom with me. I walked out into the hallway butt-naked and dripping wet; didn't even look all the way in the direction of the office, but I'd quickly glanced him out the corner of my eye. Hell, I acted like I didn't even know he was there. The linen closet was directly across the hall from the bathroom. I took my time getting a towel, giving him a full view of everything I had to offer. I tucked the big, folded towel underneath my arm and slowly walked to the end of the hall, water dripping all over the soft Dupont carpet, and went into my room. I left the door open for him to look straight ahead from where he was seated and watch me. I kept my back to him.

Before I started drying off, I grabbed a small CD headset off the bed and put it on. As I dabbed my body with the folded towel, I began to roll and twist my ass provocatively along with the slow jam that was playing in my ears. Shiiit, I damn near felt his eyes crawling over my whole body, even in the distance. My thick, round apple cheeks wavered. Seducing a man always took me to the ultimate high, and as much as I hated to admit it, at that very moment, not even the threat of BJ catching me was going to deprive me of that intense feeling. Hell, I was about to get off just rolling my ass for him. Besides, I counted on BJ being safely tucked away for at least an hour in the long, hot bath she'd told me she was going to take.

I rolled and grinded continuously. I knew if I made him masturbate while watching, he'd want to do me for sure.

# ReChella

The more I rolled my ass, the hotter I got. Then it happened. Even though my back was still to the door, I saw him out the corner of my eye ease up and stand in the side of the doorway. That nigga was definitely trying to get a closer look. He just didn't know I was fixing to put on a show for him that he wouldn't ever forget. I never stopped rolling and pretending to dry myself.

After a while, I laid the towel on the bed and closed my eyes to make it seem like I was all into the music, then gradually danced around to face him. I rubbed myself all over while I danced, caressing my melon-sized breasts with both hands as they bounced up and down. All the while, my eyes remained closed. I was dying to see the look on his face, but I maintained. Couldn't let the jig be up too soon. I smoothly moved one hand down to my thighs to massage them over as I continued using the other one to work both breasts. I busted a move and started doing one of my favorite dances called the booty dance. That damn dance should've been X-rated, 'cause in order to do it, I had to stretch my legs out far apart and surge my bare pussy all the way to the floor over and over again. Each time I went down, I knew he was glancing at my wide open pussy. Just a little bit more, I kept telling myself. It was almost time to open my eyes and catch him sneaking and peeking. I wondered if I should pretend to be startled or just act natural. Hell no. Being startled by a man looking at me wasn't my style. If anything, I would've been scared as hell if I'd been putting on a show like that and the man wasn't watching. A little more dancing and pussy-popping, I felt I had him just where I wanted him. I raised my lids and made eye contact with him.

To let him know I wasn't startled, I pasted a devilish smirk on my face. I halted my dancing and took off the earphones, then laid them on the bed. I leaned my head to one side to look at him. That nigga was drooling like a mad dog. He was even clutching his dick real tight through his silk pants. Look like he was about five seconds from jumping on me and sticking it in. Damn, I had to give it to myself. I was good at my job. The look on his face told me so. I verbalized my tease.

"What you doin' in here, peepin' Tom?"

He was flushed. He stared me down. His bottom lip almost hung to his chin. I never attempted to pick up the towel and cover myself. Finally, he opened his mouth to speak.

"Gal, you one fine-ass, sexy thang. You sho' got me all 'roused up. Name it and you got it." He was direct as hell.

I started inching toward him. "What you mean, nigga?"

He couldn't take his eyes off my big, round titties. "You know what I mean. Gimme a li'l bit and I'll get you anything you want," he stated with no hesitation.

I stopped close enough in front of him to brush a tiny hint of my firm nipples against his chest through his shirt. "You want some pussy?" I frowned, trying to look as if I was puzzled. "Is that what you sayin'?"

"Yeah, it is." He nodded like a donkey.

"Why on earth would I do somethin' like that to my sistah? Give me one good reason." I tried to look blameless. Ah, yeah, standing there naked as a jaybird, then had the nerve to be trying to look innocent.

"Ain't no good reason. But she won't ever know, and you can get whatever you want," he stated plainly.

That was all I needed to hear. My plan was coming together right on time. Dollar signs began dancing in my eyes. "Don't be bullshittin' me. You tellin' me I can get anything I want?" I raised my eyebrows with enthusiasm.

"An-y-thing you want." The words glided from his lips as his head turned from side to side. His eyes traveled from one of my breasts to the other, and I knew without a doubt I had him just where I wanted him. I intensified the situation even more by referencing his dick.

"Damn, look like you got a nice piece of hardware." I opened my hand and used my palm to caress the tip of his dick as it pushed through his silk pajama pants. He squeezed and stroked one of my breasts.

"You got some big, pretty, plump . . ." he began to

mumble.

"Shut up." I cut his words short, continuing to press my palm against his dick-tip with more force. "Every fuckin' thing about me pretty and plump. Got it?" I gave an order as if I was a goddess, and he was the peasant boy. Damn, ask me did I take advantage of his weakened state.

"Got it." He agreed to that shit, too. He was clearly still captivated by my seductive power. He was at my mercy, but he sure as hell didn't seem to give a hoot. I removed my hand from his dick and positioned both hands underneath my breasts, boosting them up and down while gradually moving toward his mouth. He lowered his head to meet the big, brown half-dollar ends pasted on my tits. He opened his mouth wide and filled it with my soft, succulent titty and gristle-hard nipple. He sucked so hard and licked so forcefully that saliva ran down the corners of his mouth onto my titties. That proved I was damn right 'bout him watering at the mouth while watching me dance. As he stooped over sucking my breast, I peered over his shoulder, on the lookout for BJ. There was no sign of her. I suddenly pushed his mouth away.

"What's wrong?" he asked, swiftly peeking behind him. I assumed it was to check for BJ, as I'd already done.

"Shhhh." I glued my index finger to my lips, gesturing him to be quiet. Neither one of us attempted to move all the way into the room away from the door.

*I'm 'bout to fuck yo' mind all the way up, Mr. Charlesee pooh,* I said in my head right before I squatted to his knees with my legs wide open, and pulled his dick out of his pajamas. The elastic waist pants snapped and landed under his sizeable balls. He wore no underwear. That made it easier for me to hold on to his dick, slip it in my mouth, and move back and forth on it, pleasuring him. Every now and then I licked around the tip and glazed my lips with the sappy liquids he let off. "Ummm." I looked up into his eyes to let him know that I was a bold bitch who knew how to get the job done right. He stood steadfast and stiff, gripping the back of my head with both hands as I sucked away. I tilted my head and took his balls in my mouth while using one of my hands to invigorate movement on his dick—treat his meat, ya feel me? I knew we were playing with fire, BJ being right downstairs and nobody else in the house except the three of us. But hell, he was the one married to her and he didn't seem to care, so who was I to complain?

"Ummmm. Umm." I hoped my low moans expressed to him how much I was enjoying the taste of his man-sized cock. Out of all the bragging I'd done to him about how good I could do a nigga up on deep-throating, he had to know now that I hadn't been playing one bit about that shit.

"Ahhhh," he moaned back. He was acting like he wasn't too far from his sweet peak of ecstasy. I easily rotated my sucking and massaging by taking his balls in my mouth and letting my hand take over swift massaging of his dick. I kept the fast-paced caressing of his dick in motion as I juggled his sac around in my mouth. After a little while more, I re-inserted only the head of his dick into my mouth and clamped down on it with my tongue and jaws, trying to make it feel like he was halfway inside the walls of my tight, twenty-four-year-old pussy. He began to roll his ass slowly and work it in my mouth little by little, or should I say inch by inch. I quickly changed my squatting position to knees and took it all in the throat. He rolled a little harder and faster. While rubbing my hands over his tight abs, I took that fast rolling from him also. He once again gripped the back of my head with both his masculine hands and increased the stroking rhythm. I still took it all.

"Oooh oooh." He let out soft moans, but he probably wanted to roar like a lion.

I loosened my jaws and slowly pulled his dick out of my mouth and stood up, while at the same time deliciously wiping my tongue around the outside of my lips. I did that to keep his mind focused on me. He seemed a bit puzzled, but still looked mesmerized. I could tell he wanted to know what in the hell was up; why'd I stop? But he remained silent while watching my tongue dangle and play over my lips as I moved backwards toward the foot of the bed. I never broke eye contact with him.

I sat down on the flowered comforter at the very end of the bed, spread my legs and stirred around in my wet pussy with my middle finger while waiting for him to make his move. Slick bastard. I saw him take another fleeting look behind him right before he sprinted over to join me. Then the unthinkable happened. Yep, he messed around and fucked up the whole mood. I guess since I had worked his shit so good orally, he was real close to cumming. Evidently, he figured he would just go on, stick it in and get his quick nut off and call it a night. He stood between my legs and rested his knees on the foot of the bed, gripping his dick, then crouched down and tried to plunk it in the pussy in a hurry. I blocked that shit real quick and threw him a frown that looked like somebody had injected me with lemon juice.

"Hold up. What you doin?" I demanded.

He stopped and looked at me in surprise. "What you mean? Ain't we fuckin'?"

I spurted a tiny laugh then rocked my head back and forth with attitude. "You ain't earned the right to fuck me yet. You better taste this sweet pussy first, then I'll tell you if I'm gon' let you fuck me or not."

His surprised look intensified, and for a moment he looked to be at a loss for words. I guess my bold statement wasn't expected. Still the same, I maintained my authoritative gawk as I awaited his reply.

I knew Charles was much older than me and probably had plenty old-school ways, like a lot of men from back in his day, so I didn't expect for him to be no expert on new-generation sex technique. But damn, he was acting like he'd never even seen a pussy looking good as mine that close up before. His expression damn near said that he didn't know what to do with the kitty-kat. I was getting impatient as hell laying up there with my shit gapped wide open and he hadn't started eating it yet.

"What you waitin' on, a fuckin' invitation? You act like

you ain't never ate no pussy befo'." I motioned as if to get up, but he took hold of my thighs and held them in place to keep me where I was.

"Now, just hold on a minute, babygirl. I"m 'bout to be yo' candy licka. I lost my thoughts for a minute wondering if we really had enough time. I was just tryin' to hurr-up fo' we get interrupted. That would be a disaster, now, wouldn't it?" He smiled, gazing into my eyes. I stared back at his ass suspiciously, but I didn't remark.

He kneeled and held even firmer to my thighs and began to kiss the inside of them, while at the same time looking like he was relying on nature to take its course. I simmered on down and went with the flow, but he wasn't fooling me one bit. I could tell he wasn't used to going downtown. That's what the hold-up was. That meant BJ wasn't getting no tongue action in the coochie.

*Damn, she must really love him to put up with some shit like that. Hell, she need to be thanking me for breaking his ass in for her,* I thought, smiling as he gradually made his way up to the edge of my neatly shaved vagina. He began kissing all around it. Every now and then he pinched and enclosed my fat, pussy lips between his lips, then slowly ran the tip of his tongue over the top of my split without going too deep. He teased at it.

It must have tasted real good to him, because at the bat of an eye, his tongue ejected and swiped a deep lick all the way from the bottom to the top; then another, then another. Yeah, he was liking that sweet stuff.

He went farther inside of me and thrust his tongue in and out, using two fingers to part me open more and expose my stout clit. He dangled my clit and sucked it. Now, I began to moan for it.

"Ummm, ummm." My moans must have told him that he'd found a good spot to work on, because he sucked it with more intensity. I moaned deeper and clutched the back of his head with both hands. I mowed my fingers through his short, black hair, while at the same time pressing his head closer into my pussy and rolling.

"Shit. Oooh, shit. That's it, keep it up." I lifted my head and looked down to watch him eat. "I'm fixin' to cum in yo' mouth," I muttered. He was damn sure a fast learner, 'cause that shit was getting good.

*Beep, beep, beep, beep!*

A keen beeping noise all of a sudden sounded. I quickly pushed him away and jumped to my feet, startled as hell. I just knew we were caught. I grabbed the towel off the bed and began wrapping my nude body in it. He on the other hand, looked a wee bit more calm than I was.

"Shit." He sounded irritated, while reaching in his pajama shirt pocket for something.

"What's that noise?" I asked fretfully.

"Damn, it's my beeper. I had it set to go off around the time yo' sistah would get out of the Jacuzzi," he replied, turning the beeper off.

"How'd you know how long she was gon' be in there?" A curious look stretched over my face.

"She always stay in for a certain amount of time every night."

"You mean you came up here knowin' you was gon' try to do somethin' wit' me while BJ was downstairs bathing?" I know I looked offended, 'cause I had an attitude now.

"Well, I didn't know how far I would get, but I was gon' try. You a li'l hard to resist, ya know." He chuckled. "My boy here need to calm on down now, though." He looked down and talked at his penis as he grasped it and pushed it inside his pants, but it was still hard and sticking out. He began taking short breaths in and out, I guess to concentrate on making it settle.

"Hold up. Wait." I halted my hand in his face. "You planned this?" I squinted my eyes at him. He stared me back, but made no response. "You no-good low life. This shit messed up."

I guess I shouldn't have been mad since I'd done the exact same thing, but I think one of the reasons I was so upset was realizing that I wasn't the only master-minding schemer. Obviously, he'd been making his own plans to do me all that time. I hated when a man out-thought me, or even thought on my level.

"What's yo' problem? You wasn't doin' all that rollin' and grindin' for the walls. You knew I was watchin' you. That's why you made it so easy, ain't it?" He spoke with a bit of an attitude now.

*Damn, he tryin' to call me on my plot. I can't have that,* I said in my head.

"I don't know what you talkin' 'bout." "I hurried over to the door and pointed out into the hall. "Get the hell outta my room befo' BJ come up here and catch you."

"I'm goin', I'm goin'." He winked at me.

On his way out, he made it quite clear that we would finish where we left off the first opportunity that presented itself. I didn't say shit when I closed the door behind him. I sprinted back over to the bed and lay down to go over everything that had just taken place.

# Chapter Six

I dashed my ass on back across the hall to my office and sat down at the desk. True enough, I was saved by the beeper, but talk about bad timing. Keshundra's stuff was getting better and better, too. I never thought I would actually enjoy eating pussy like that. After getting a sample of that hot tenderoni's stuff, I knew my old-school rule of not going down on a woman was all the way out the window. If all pussy was as soft and good as hers, I was in for life. All that time Bettie had been doing it to me just like I wanted, but I'd never returned the favor. If only she'd known that she needed to thank her little sister for putting me in a position of having to do it or else.

If by chance Bettie had dropped in on me while I was sitting at my desk pondering, I was going to be looking just like a spellbound fool, 'cause my mind drifted back to the way Keshundra was sucking my dick even before I'd helped myself to her treats. Damn, was she some kind of expert or something? Out of all the bragging she'd done about how good she could give head, I realized that she hadn't exaggerated one bit. The way I'd shoved my dick in and out of her mouth, I almost couldn't tell that I wasn't thrusting in her tight pussy. Hell, I thought Bettie could deep throat like no other, but after getting it Keshundra style, Bettie hurriedly moved to second place.

*I can't believe how much of my dick Keshundra swallowed. She sucked it like a oversized pacifier, and was groaning the entire time. She was enjoying every damn second of it, too. Damn, that girl done whipped me and I ain't even fucked her yet*, I said in my head. Yeah, she had messed my mind up for real. All I could think about was trying to find a way to get back in there and finish what she and I had started.

The telephone interrupted my thoughts. "Hello."

"Hello, Uncle Charles. My momma told me to call you

and tell you that Debra out in the yard tryin' to start somethin' wit' her. She bammin' real hard on the door, too, Uncle Char—"

"Who is this?" I asked with concern.

The caller was so panicked and talking so loud, I couldn't make out the voice, nor much of what was said.

"This Jon Jon, Uncle Charles," the caller replied.

"Jon Jon?" I confirmed.

"Yes, sir!"

"Jon Jon, slow down. Now, who you say over there, and what's goin' on?"

"Debra. Debra," Jon Jon exclaimed.

"What she want?" I was trying to take it step by step and make sense of what Jon Jon was saying.

"She tryin' to start a fight wit' my momma," Jon Jon cried.

"What? Jon Jon, put yo' momma on the phone," I urged.

A few seconds went by and Katie answered the phone. "Hello," she yelled into the phone.

"Katie, what's goin' on down there?" I asked again. By now I was becoming a bit uneasy about whatever the commotion was, especially since I'd heard Debra's name mentioned.

"Debra done brought her drunk ass down here tryin' to fight. She—" Katie cut her explanation off. "Get away from that door, Jeremy." Katie was so upset, she was at the top of her voice.

"Y'all done called the police yet?" I asked, knowing that if Debra was anywhere on the scene trying to fight, that's exactly what was going to have to happen. No wonder she hadn't tried to come down to Katie's with everybody else after the funeral. She had made plans to slip down there after all the company was gone.

"I was tryin' to keep from doin' that," Katie snapped. "She got her kids wit' her. They cryin' and tryin' to get her in the car to leave, but she won't go. I hate for 'em to see her go to jail. And I'll tell ya somethin' else. If I open this door and go out there, I'ma hurt her ass real bad."

In spite of Debra's irrational behavior, the fact that Katie hadn't phoned the police indicated that she was trying to be as reasonable as possible.

"All right. I'll be there in a few minutes. Just don't open the door 'til I get there." I hung up and ran downstairs to my room to throw on some clothes. Bettie had gotten out of the Jacuzzi and was already dressed for bed. She wanted to know what was going on and why I was in such a hurry. I explained the telephone call and everything as I dressed. Bettie quickly dressed and insisted on going with me.

We jumped in the truck and drove off. Bettie called back to the house to tell Keshundra why we'd rush away. A short eighteen-minute drive landed us in Katie's driveway about 9:05 P.M.

"Will you look? That crazy woman disturbing everybody in the neighborhood," Bettie said with concern. I turned off the motor.

"What is she tryin' to do?" I jumped out of the truck and rushed toward the house.

Bettie followed and stopped near the children. They stood at the end of the porch, pleading with their mother to get into the car, but she refused and remained at the door, shouting and daring Katie to come out.

"Come on, bitch! You ain't got the guts to come out and face me, 'cause you know you guilty. Yeah, you, you guilty. I know it, and you know it," Debra blasted.

The headlights and sound of the vehicle hadn't budged Debra one bit. She'd obviously been drinking, because she blundered over her words and staggered when she attempted to move around. It had been dark a little better than an hour. I guess most of Katie's neighbors were already inside for the night, but the ones who weren't watched the loud scene from their porches. Thanks to the bright post-light, they had a fairly decent view. Bettie persuaded the children to get in their car, and she stood watching from out in the yard as I approached Debra.

"Hey, hey, hey. Debra, what's goin' on, girl?" I walked

up behind her, speaking at a moderate tone in an attempt not to set her off any more than she already was. "What you doin' out here, sistah-in-law?" I addressed her as sistah-in-law so she wouldn't feel isolated from the Jennings family. Even though she was crazy as a June-bug in the summertime, I knew she still cared for Gregg even after all those years, so she probably had a little vulnerability mixed in with that ignorance of hers.

"Sistah-in-law. You damn right, sistah-in-law." Debra agreed with my choice of words. "What's up, Charles?" She tottered her skinny, lanky body around to look at me as she spoke back. The bangs of her medium-length, auburn streaked hair partially hid her dark forehead. "See, that's what I'm talkin' 'bout. You know the truth. You know I'm yo' real sistah-in-law, and she ain't nothin' but a fake-ass wanna-be. I was Gregg's first wife . . . and . . . and the first wife is the only one that count, ain't it? Don't the Bible say that, Charles? What you doin' down here, Charles?" She took a staggering step toward me to hug me and almost fell.

I caught her and held around her waist. "Whoa. You a little off balance today, ain't ya?"

"Ain't we all? But, but least some of us got guts 'nough to admit it." She primped her mouth and drew a big frown as tears began to flood her face. I felt a tinge of sorry for her. I pulled her close and held her to my chest, then stroked her back to calm her as she muttered her squabbling words. "She didn't love Gregg like I did, and Gregg knew she was screwin' somebody else too. He just didn't know who. He told me so." She sniffled and snotted all over the black Nike T-shirt that I was wearing. Tears constantly flowed. "Don't you see? That bitch, Katie, broke his heart and helped kill him." Debra softly pounded against my chest and cried like there was no tomorrow. "Oohhhhhhhhh, oohhh, I can't let her get away wit' dat."

In that tiny brain of hers, she actually believed the nonsense she was saying. The whole time that I was trying to calm Debra and get her off of the porch, I noticed Katie watching from the window through a crack in the curtain.

"Now, now, come on." I soothed her with gentle words. "You got to get yo'self together, Debra. Yo' children out here, and you scarin' them. This just ain't the place for you to be. Not on this woman's property. What if she call the police and they come take you to jai? What's gon' happen to the kids then? Think about them, huh?"

I lifted her chin up to look at me. The smell of her alcohol breath reeked in my face, but I managed to persuade her to a slow yes as I nodded. Richard and AJ drove up just as she and I began to walk off the porch. I guess Katie had called Momma 'nem and told them what was going on after she called me.

I almost had Debra to her car, and Katie had to get brave and bring her ass out on the damn porch. As soon as Debra saw her, she went crazy. She broke away from me and ran, or better yet, wobbled real fast back up on the porch and threw a blow at Katie before I could catch her. Katie swung back, and they entangled in a cat fight. Now, why in the hell Katie didn't just stay in the house 'til the coast was clear was unbeknownst to me. As unbalanced and project as Debra was, by the time the brawl was over, Katie was probably going to be wishing she had. Maybe that was why she hadn't come out 'til somebody else got there to restrain Debra, 'cause she was somewhat on the scared side. Debra was screaming to the top of her voice and swinging like a wild woman.

"You killed him, you evil bitch!" She was way out of control.

"Drunk slut. Get the hell away from me befo' I kill you," Katie yelled back as she rendered several licks onto Debra. She was a lot bigger than Debra, and she seemed to have the ups on her, but Debra still hung in there. She sank her fingernails into the side of Katie's neck and left a long, three-track scratch. Katie really got mad then.

"I'm gon' have you locked up. Maybe you'll come to yo' senses," Katie shrieked, taking another swing. By now I had grabbed hold of Debra, and Richard grabbed Katie. AJ helped us pulled them apart. Debra continued to yell and scuffle to get loose as AJ and I dragged her back to the car.

"You didn't mean nothin' to Gregg . . . that's right, you didn't! Me and him was still sleepin' togetha, and we was gon' get back togetha, too," Debra yelled.

Boy, did Debra trigger a nerve in Katie when she said that.

"Po' ho! Gregg didn't want you. That's why he left yo' triflin' ass. Keep talkin', I'ma come out there and knock them two gold teeth out yo' damn mouth. What kind of woman wash her ass and cook outta the same pot, anyway?" Katie was undoubtedly hell-bent on hitting Debra with the worst insults she could think of, 'cause that was some cold-ass shit to say out loud, even if it was true. And believe me, Gregg had complained about how nasty Debra was more times than a few when they were married. She was one female that I could honestly say I'd never desired to make a pass at.

Finally, Debra got in the car with the kids, and AJ and Bettie worked on keeping her calm. I walked back up on the porch just in time to hear Richard talking to Katie about her behavior.

"Katie. Katie," Richard uttered, standing in front of her, gently shaking her with both his hands locked around her arms. "Look at these folks out here instigatin'. All they want is somethin' on a saved, church-goin' woman like ya'self to talk about. Don't give it to em' by arguin' back wit' Debra. She drunk. You didn't fall for her mess at the funeral, so don't fall for it now." Richard looked like he was trying to stay in front of Katie and block her view of Debra. "They ain't gon' talk about her like a dog, 'cause she ain't 'bout nothin' anyway. They gon' be talkin' 'bout you," he continued.

A few of Katie's tears hit the porch as she inhaled. Her expression read that she was taking everything Richard said to heart. Jon Jon and Jeremy were still in the house watching from the window. Li'l Gregg had made an attempt to run out on the porch and jump in the fight when his momma and Debra was going at it, but AJ grabbed him and made him go back in the house. I knew we needed to go on and get Debra's ass out of Katie's driveway, so they both could calm the fuck down.

"Listen, Katie. Go on in the house and try to calm ya'self down like Richard tellin' ya." I opened the door and held it until she went in, then I whispered to Richard. "Hey, Richard. Try to keep her calm as you can, man. I'ma drive Debra 'nem on to her house in her car and let AJ follow me in his truck and bring me back. It's a miracle her and them kids made it down here in one piece, drunk as she is, anyway."

"I know that's right. A'ight, man," Richard agreed.

In addition to Richard staying with Katie, Bettie wanted to stay and make sure she was okay too. On the way to Debra's place, I didn't know what the funky-ass odor was coming from the back seat, but it smelled like stinky feet mixed with eight-day-old shit. I swear I was about to be sick. So much stuff was piled up and thrown around in her car, there was no telling what carried the smell. Rolling the window down barely helped. I didn't know how in the hell them children sat back there without getting sick. Hell, if we had gone just one more mile, I probably would've gotten sick myself. I was too glad when we pulled up in front of Debra's apartment at the Senatobia Projects in New Town. I jumped my ass out of that car in a hurry and said my goodbyes, then hopped in AJ's red F-150 truck.

On our way back to Katie's, AJ stopped at the Texaco gas station on the corner of Main Street and Scott Street to fill up.

"You want somethin' out of the store, Charles?" AJ asked as he got out.

"Naw, I'm cool."

I sat on the passenger side and rested my head on back of the seat, replaying all the drama and realizing I was a little pissed because it interfered with me fantasizing about how good Keshundra had made me feel.

*Damn, I hate I didn't get a chance to finish wit' her. If all this mess hadn't come up, maybe I coulda slipped back upstairs after Bettie went to sleep. Shit, I could be at home . . . that's it, I could be at home now,* I repeated in my head. Maybe the drama hadn't messed up my night after all. Maybe the drama had in fact helped my night, 'cause now that Bettie was out of the house, all I needed to do was come up with a reason to have AJ drop me off at home instead of back down to Katie's. The perfect opportunity was in my lap. Keshundra was home alone, and Bettie was probably going to stay with Katie awhile. I unclamped my cell phone from my belt and began dialing Bettie's cell.

"Hello," Bettie answered.

"Hey, baby," I said. "How's Katie?"

"She still cryin' a little, but she all right," Bettie answered.

"Listen, I got a terrible headache. Will you be okay driving home if I get AJ to take me on to the house so I can rest my head?" I grumbled, trying to sound as if I was feeling like crap.

"Of course. That's a good idea. You need some rest anyway. You got to be up early in the mornin'," she agreed.

"Thanks, babe. Tell Katie I'll talk to her tomorrow," I added.

"I will. I love you."

"Love you too." Just as I hung up, AJ was hopping back in the truck to leave.

"AJ, run me on to my house, man. My head throbbin'. I got to get some sleep." I frowned, demonstrating how bad I felt from the pain of my headache. "Okay," AJ agreed. "After I drop you off, I'ma scoop Richard up fast as I can, then I'm going home and get straight in the bed myself. I'm tired as hell too, man."

About ten minutes later, I unlocked the door and went into my almost dark, quiet house. You better know I headed straight upstairs for Keshundra. My mouth was watering. I could hardly wait to get back with her.

I knocked softly at her door. No answer. She may have been sleeping. I waited a few seconds and knocked again. Still no answer.

# ReChella

"Keshundra, this Charles. I came up to tell you that I'm back and Bettie comin' on later." There was no response from inside Keshundra's room. "Hey, you in there?" I asked louder. Still no answer. "I'm comin' in." I slowly opened the door and walked into the dark room. "Keshundra," I called again as I flipped on the light. She was nowhere in sight.

I poked around in the room a few minutes. Flashbacks of how Keshundra had rocked my world in that very room less than two hours from that moment popped in and out of my mind. I closed the door and checked the bedroom to the right of hers. The light was off, and there was no sign that anyone had been in that room at all. I walked down the hall to the bathroom. The light was off in there also, but the door was halfway open. "Keshundra." I stuck my head inside and called to her. No answer. The same in my office and the third bedroom to the left of my office.

Hustling back downstairs, I quickly walked through the wide-open dining room and living room before I dropped down on the ivory leather sofa in the large den. As usual, all of the lights in the house were turned off except for a soft, dim-lit halogen lamp in the corner of the den.

*Where could she be? Her car parked on the side of the house like always. Maybe she took a spur-of-the-moment run down the street,* I thought. However, I didn't intend to miss her on her way back in. I fluffed one of the lavender sofa pillows under my head and grabbed the remote control off the center table to thumb through some channels as I awaited her return. Before I knew it, I'd dozed off thinking about the hot time Keshundra and I could've been having before Bettie returned home.

A few minutes into my nap, I woke to a dark figure standing over me, looking down. I couldn't quite make out who it was because the person's back was to the television. I blinked my eyes rapidly, trying to focus in on the dark shadow. "Keshundra?" I called out, attempting to sit up on the sofa, but I couldn't rise.

Some kind of strong force, seemingly, was holding me down and preventing me from getting up, but the strange

81

thing was that the figure standing over me wasn't touching me. "Bettie?" I spoke out again, trying to find out who was standing there.

"Guess again, Charlie boy," a male voice replied. "Bet you didn't think I was comin' back to visit this soon, did ya?"

"Who are ya? Turn toward the light so I can see ya." I became fretful after hearing a man. It couldn't have been Will, 'cause he wouldn't have come up in my house like that without calling me first or something. I tried with all my might to rise and get a plain view of the person before me, but I couldn't.

"Shut up! Stupid nigga! You know exactly who I am. You 'bout to get yo'self in a world of trouble messin wit' Bettie's sistah, and you don't even know it. If you had any sense, you'd walk away and forget about her, but I know you can't do that. Can ya? Can ya? Can ya?" The deep voice became stronger and more intense as it kept repeating the same question to me.

By now I knew the incident was connected to the one at the gravesite earlier that day, and since I'd dismissed the first one as my imagination, the logical thing was to dismiss that one as the same. A sourball of knots launched in the pit of my stomach, telling me that I was frightened again. I didn't like it one damn bit. Although I still couldn't rise from the sofa, I somehow managed to move my arms around. I began fighting at the naked air to be loosed from whatever powerful force was keeping me down. I screamed out. "Stop! Stop!" The more I fought, the tighter the hold. I turned my head away from the figure for only a second or two. Then a hand reached down and tapped me on my shoulder. As soon as the hand touched me, I was able to move my entire body. I jumped up, still swinging with pillows falling.

"Stop, stop, stop!" I cried out.

"Wake yo' ass up, nigga. What's the matter wit' you?" Keshundra screeched. "You betta not hit me, fool." She backed away from me to avoid catching a lick that was obviously meant for someone else. A few seconds and things became clearer to me.

"Ohh, uhh, uhh. What happened?" I asked, almost out of breath and rubbing my hands over my face to snap out of it.

"I guess you was dreamin' or havin' a nightmare or somethin'," Keshundra replied.

"I was wide awake. I couldn't make out who you was, but I saw you standin' there. I couldn't have been dreamin'," I said, still gasping for air. Even though I couldn't get up when I was lying on the sofa, I felt conscious, because I'd questioned the person standing over me. "Didn't you hear me askin' who you was?" I asked Keshundra.

She sighed, thrusting one hand on her hip. "Pay attention, 'cause I ain't sayin' this but once. When I walked through the kitchen door, all I heard was you mumblin' out loud. I didn't understand what you was sayin' 'cause it sounded like some Chinese shit. I walked over here and looked at you, and yo' eyes was not open. Got it? Not open, they was closed. They didn't open 'til I reached down and tried to wake you up. Then you jumped up hollin' and hittin' and shit. Any part of that you don't understand?" she asked unsympathetically.

"All right, whatever." I decided to let it go. I didn't want her to think I was losing it. Besides, it was obviously just a dream.

"Damn right, whatever. Stay off that pork, yo' ass might not dream so much," Keshundra stated, turning to walk away.

"Where you been, anyway?" I glanced at the clock on the walnut-oak, full-wall, entertainment center. "I got here 'bout thirty minutes ago. I been lookin' for you."

"Oh, really. Where BJ at?" Keshundra asked as she crossed her arms and cocked her eyes to one side. "Evidently, you done misplaced yo' wife and got me mixed up, asking me all my damn business."

"Bettie stayed wit' Katie. She probably gon' be down

there a while." I picked up the pillows off the floor and threw them back on the sofa. "Can we finish what we started?" I composed a humble look.

"We can if you ready to put yo' money where yo' mouth at."

*What the hell she mean by that? Not money, I hope,* I said to myself silently. "You know, I really like you. Not just—" I started to say, trying to avoid her statement.

"Cut the crap." She abruptly jumped in. "We both know this little rendezvous 'bout two thangs . . . and two thangs only. Sex and Money. So, don't patronize me by talkin' shit, 'cause ain't none of yo' tired old lines gon' work wit' me. I done heard it all befo' I'm immune to it. Sex and money ain't nothin' but a power trip. If you can hang on, you can go for the ride o' yo' life. If you can't, then sit yo' ass down. And last but not least, by all means, don't waste my time wit' empty conversation."

Damn, I knew she had an over-sized ego, but I was obviously not prepared for her invigorating gust of confidence. I'd had a lot of female conquests in my time, but that little feisty mama was quite a refreshing breath of challenge. I was much more accustomed to women treating me like it was their honor to be with me. That shit she threw caught me off guard, especially after she'd been so willing and free when she'd sucked my dick upstairs earlier.

"So, it's all about the Benjamins wit' you, huh," I stated.

"You damn straight. I ain't givin' up nothin' free."

"What was that upstairs earlier?" I held my hands out in front of me as if I was clueless.

"Do you have a habit of makin' investments in somethin' you ain't never tasted—I mean tested?" She smirked.

"Oh, you just knew if I tasted a little bit, I'd want some more. Is that what you sayin'?"

"I guess it is, if that's what you hearin'. Don't look so surprised. Men been takin' advantage of women since the beginnin' of time. Gettin' all the pussy they can get and

84

tellin' mo' lies than humanely sane. The way I see it, if we can't beat ya, join ya. And while we at it, get all we can. Tell me somethin', though." She raked her eyes all the way from my feet to my eyes.

"What?" I was now a bit distrustful after hearing what she thought was a logical way of thinking. Don't get me wrong, I wasn't hatin' on her or mad that she was trying to get paid for her services, 'cause she was damn sure worth a few bucks, but she didn't have to be that cold to a brother.

"How do it feel to have the tables turned? Ha, haaa!" Her insensitive laugh sealed her moral position.

I couldn't do nothing but shake my head from side to side at her. As bad as I hated to admit it, no matter what she stood there and said, I still had to have me some of that good pussy of hers.

"A'ight then, I guess I better start callin' you Heidi Fleiss." I smiled, indicating that I'd jumped on the bandwagon with her.

"Heidi Fleiss was a ho. I'm a mo'," Keshundra stated bluntly.

"A what?" I looked baffled.

"A mo'," she repeated, then told me the meaning. "The mo' you get, the mo' you want."

She winked at me and walked to the stairs, probably knowing all the time that I was weak on her. I guess she could just about smell my yearning to get her ass into bed. Maybe that's why she blew me away with her next, even more blunt statement. "One thousand dollars cash in ten minutes upstairs, non-negotiable, take it or leave it." She started up the stairs. I stood and watched as she strode away.

"Damn, a thousand dollars." I shook my head and mumbled. "She must think she Heidi Fleiss fo' real."

I went in my room and closed the door behind me. The clock was ticking and Bettie was probably going to be heading home soon. If I was going to do the damn thing, I needed to be going on and doing it. I went into my closet safe where I kept extra money in case of emergencies, and got the thousand dollars. Then I headed upstairs and knocked on Keshundra's door.

"Come in." She answered in a sexy voice.

I didn't know if she thought I was actually going to give her the thousand-dollars or what, but the way she told me to come in, she sure sounded confident of it. I walked into the candle-lit, perfumed room and closed the door behind me.

*Damn, it sho' didn't smell like this when I was up here while ago,* I said to myself. She was lying across the foot of the bed in a sensual side-pose, wearing a short, white, see-through negligee. Her hair hugged the sides of her face as she'd combed it into its original bouncy wrap-style. I got an instant hard-on as I walked over to the bed and dropped the ten neatly stacked one-hundred-dollar bills down bedside her. I could have sworn she looked like she was trying to suppress a surprised expression as she scooped up the money and threw it in the nightstand drawer next to the bed. Neither of us spoke a word. Now her ego had probably tripled in size by me coming through with the substantial cash.

I stood at the foot of the bed over her. She moved herself in front of me. While sitting on her folded legs, she took off her negligee. Then slowly unzipped my pants and pulled them all the way down to my feet. I stepped out of them and removed my black Nike T-shirt and dropped it on the floor near my pants. We presented ourselves butt-naked before each other. She began kissing on my dick and licked it, grabbing around to my ass with both hands and squeezing my cheeks over and over as she began to suck.

I craved to taste her just the way she tasted me. As she devoured my chocolate pleasure pole, I bent over her back, enclosing her head in my crotch, and began smacking my tongue on the back of her jiggly ass. I gradually moved to position myself in the bed underneath her, spreading her legs on opposite sides of my face to finish sampling where I'd left off earlier. We lay straight up and down with her on top of me and our heads at opposite ends of each other. I saturated my mouth through her slick pussy while it hovered over my face. She continued slushing on my dick. We took full advantage of our new position, number sixty-nine.

"Ummmm." Our moans laced the air in harmony.

"Ohh, ohhh." A high-pitched keen cry screeched through me during which I spurted and creamed her entire mouth.

It had been suppressed from the first time we were interrupted, and I couldn't hold it back any longer. It felt so good. I breathed a sigh of relief and didn't move from my spot. That first one was out of the way. Now I could prepare to fuck her extensively. I guess she'd already anticipated that I would come as I did, because she grabbed a large towel from the head of the bed and wiped her mouth, then immediately straddled me face-to-face. Still no words. We began a passionate kiss, filling each other's mouths with wet tongues, smacking and breathing as if it was our first time around. I savored the essence of her pussy on my lips and tongue, and she had to still taste the residue of my cum around her mouth. Gapped over me and lapping up my every gesture, she was performing as if she was determined to give me a night to remember. At that moment, the things she was doing to me, I would've given her another thousand dollars if she had asked for it. That's just how good she was putting it on me. Luckily, there were plenty more thousands where that one came from, though.

"I want yo' cock in me," she whispered as she wrapped my ear in her soggy tongue and stood to her feet, just high enough to mimic froggy position.

Reaching one hand down, she placed the tip of my dick barely inside the edge of her entrance, then rolled and gyrated a tease on me like no other. I held my head afloat and peered at the rotation of her relentless ass-twist. Her pussy gapped wide for my viewing pleasure. After a generous amount of rolling and teasing, she dropped down and rammed my erection inside her all at once.

"Damn," I bawled.

She repeated it again and again right before she clasped down on me and stroked long and hard. I joined in the motion by clutching the sides of her hips and meeting each of her strong down-strokes with a hard up-stroke. I moved one hand to the front and fondled her clit with my thumb during our stroking. When I did that, her clit swelled to a rigid bud and sent her into orgasm paradise.

"Ohhhh, ohhh, ohhh," she squealed as she let loose a flood.

I felt the cum dripping down my dick and amidst my hairs, but get this; she never stopped stroking. Her stroking escalated into humping and surging. It reminded me of when she did the booty dance in the doorway. The way she was going at it told me that she desired multiple orgasms, and that's just what she got, 'cause I fucked her long and hard. My dick struck her insides repeatedly as I experienced her riding me like a thoroughbred race horse.

"Come on, baby. That's it. Keep it comin'." I encouraged her as I felt myself approaching yet another heightened finish.

She continued clinging her tightly folded legs to the sides of my humid thighs and swayed over me as her energetic plunging seemed uncontrollable. Her breasts bopped against my masculine torso. I groped them with one hand and squeezed her fluffy ass-quarters with the other. Staring each other eye into eye, our lips smashed together like magnets into another intense mesh-play until our bodies cruised into elated bliss.

"Ohhh . . . yeah," she uttered rather gratifyingly.

"Whooaaa," I hollered as she rolled off me onto her back. We lay looking up at the ceiling, satisfied and fulfilled.

"You ain't half bad for a old man." She laughed, puffing for air.

"Old man?" I took a momentary look at her profile. "I bet you a hundred dollars ain't none of them so-called young studs you foolin' wit' big enough to play in my league."

She chuckled with no response. That told me she knew I was right on the money, she just didn't want to admit it.

"You a'ight," she said jokingly.

"I guess you ain't half bad for a young tender wit' not even half my experience," I taunted her back.

"Whatever, Charles. On that note, I'ma pee." She slid out of the bed and opened the door to go to the bathroom. "Be ready for round two when I get back."

"I ain't goin' nowhere, baby." I pulled myself up and turned the covers back, then crawled underneath to await her return.

# Chapter Seven

While I rested my head on the pillow, I noticed Keshundra's cell phone lighting up over on the nightstand. It was silently ringing when I picked it up to look at the caller ID. *P. DEEBERRY---662-555-0990* was the name and number displayed. I sat straight up in the bed.

"What the hell," I mumbled, noticing the time of the call. "Why is this Negro callin' her phone this late? It sho' ain't for no spiritual counselin'." I heard the bathroom door open, so I quickly put the phone back down and pretended to be napping. Keshundra walked in the room and took immediate notice of me sleeping.

"Just like a lazy nigga to fall asleep right after," she said as she sat down on the side of the bed opposite me.

"I ain't 'sleep. In fact, I think you better return the call you just got," I suggested smugly.

She grabbed her cell and clicked its light on. "Damn. Missed him, and he didn't leave no message either." She punched a few keys rather anxiously.

"What a shame. Maybe he'll call back. Anybody I know?" I asked, imposing a blameless stare.

Keshundra stopped fidgeting with the keys and lay the phone back down. "Stop being ignorant. What I tell you earlier 'bout useless conversation. Hell, I already know you saw the name on that call. A scoundrel like you wouldn't miss no opportunity like that to get info," she asserted.

I couldn't do nothing but grin. "Birds of a feather, huh?" I rubbed my hand gently across her hand as it lay flat on the bed. "So, what's the deal wit' good ole Deeberry, anyway? Y'all a couple now?"

"That man ain't married. He more a couple wit' me than you are," she exclaimed.

"But, the pastor, though?" I frowned. "Let him tell it, he too into the Word to entertain women company. At least that's the lie he tell every Sunday."

"I know you ain't judgin' him. You a married deacon, and look where you at right now." She raised her brows with attitude. "Let the truth be told, ain't neither one of y'all so-called men of God worth nothin'. He be preachin', hoopin' and shoutin' all over the church, then right after he get through, he be chasin' any skirt-tail that look good to him."

"Come to think of it, how you know Deeberry anyway? I can't recall you ever goin' to church wit' me and yo' sistah," I asked baffled.

"Don't worry 'bout howww I met him," she emphasized. "Point is, he asked me for my number almost immediately after our introduction. I sniffed out what he was about right then. And don't be tryin' to keep the subject just on him. I said you and him both ain't worth nothin'.'"

"What you mean?" I gave her my most innocent gaze.

"I mean you and yo' singin' buddies, and all the rest of them gospel groups be singin' and runnin' all over the place actin' like ya shoutin' at them gospel programs. And befo' it's even over, y'all be scoping out your next victim in the crowd." She spoke frank and with no shame.

I don't know why I expected anything more than straight candor from her, no matter what the subject.

"Do yo' sistah know you think that way about gospel groups?"

"Hell, my sistah was one of 'em."

I now raised my eyebrows with much curiosity. "What you talkin' 'bout?"

Keshundra gave me her famous devious smirk. "Surely you didn't think men was the only ones gettin' down like that. Some of these women groups do the same crap. Way back in her much younger days, BJ was a quartet-head just like some of these other desperate females that be runnin' behind y'all like y'all some real R&B stars. But after she got fucked enough times, she changed positions and started doin' the fuckin'—and might I add, gettin' a lot o' duckies to go wit' it." Keshundra boasted a proud expression while bragging about her sister's authoritative manner.

I know I still looked baffled as hell to her, but I didn't comment. Many questionable thoughts of Bettie darted through my mind at that moment. Keshundra must have picked up on them by my facial manifestation. Her abrupt words interrupted my thoughts. "Don't even play! You know what a damn quartet-head is?"

"Maybe I don't, but since you know so much, why don't you tell me?" I propositioned her, not because I didn't already know what she was talking about, but because I wanted her to keep gabbing so I could hear as much as possible about her comments concerning Bettie.

"A'ight, definition time. Quartet-heads are females who dress up every weekend and follow the singin' all over the place, standing in line waitin' to fuck one of y'all self-styled superstars of gospel. And the worst part about it is most of 'em don't get shit out of it . . . except the fuck, of course. But then, that's okay too, 'cause that's all they be wanting. See, if them bitches was smart, they'd be getting paid. Couldn't be me." She spoke as if she was above it all, but then, I guess she was seeing that she'd just gotten a thousand dollars out of me.

"You sayin' every woman that go to the singin' do that?" I asked.

"Naw, I ain't sayin' all women that go to singin' do that. A handful of 'em on the real. But for the ones who put on that phony holy-roller act, they need to stop coverin' up and just be who they are. I may not be much, but at least I ain't no hypocrite." Keshundra's imaginative answer didn't surprise me at all.

"Oh, you ain't?" I asked sarcastically.

"Naw, I ain't." She rolled her eyes. "I ain't afraid to admit who I am. I love sex and I love money. And I ain't dressin' up in no two-piece suits and pumps jumpin' round in church tellin' folks that I'm perfect and they need to be like me 'cause I walked on the water wit' Jesus."

I knew she was right on target in what she was saying, but I still couldn't eliminate my questions about Bettie's part in all of that.

"Anyway, what you mean bout' yo' sista' changin' positions and doin' the fuckin'?" I tried to sound as nonchalant as I could, so she wouldn't pick up on how bad I wanted the information.

"I mean she could sing a little, so she became a singer instead of followin' 'em around. That gave her first choice to get who she wanted instead of waiting in line for sloppy seconds. Smart, huh?" Keshundra held fast to a sly grin. My dumb-founded look surfaced again. "Aww, poor baby. You thought you picked BJ all by yo'self, didn't you? Would it make you feel any better if you thought y'all picked each other?" Her words were aggravating the hell out of me, but I managed to suppress my annoyance in order to get as much information as I could.

"Who were some of the ones she hooked up wit' befo' my time?" I continued my inquiry.

Keshundra quickly flipped her switch on the defense. "Don't insult my intelligence by tryin' to fish info out of me about my sistah. If you wanna get a interview, you need to ask her. I ain't tellin' the business. The only reason I told you as much as I did is 'cause I chose to," she stated firmly.

She obviously had her own motive for sharing the little piece of information about Bettie with me, and it certainly didn't seem to be for my benefit.

"Look, I ain't tryin' to pick you. I just asked. If you don't wanna answer, that's fine. I'm through wit' it." I tried to sound insulted by her jumping on the defense.

Before she could answer me, we captured sudden eye contact with each other to the sound of the house alarm beeping.

"Aw man, it's BJ," Keshundra exclaimed edgily.

"What she doin' here this quick? I thought she woulda stayed a li'l longer than this," I said, leaping out of the bed and hustling to put my clothes on while Keshundra blew out the candles and threw on another less revealing gown from her dresser drawer. I knew the second Bettie walked into our bedroom and didn't find me, she was coming straight upstairs to my office, and from there to ask Keshundra if she'd seen me.

Keshundra probably knew that too. That's why she was rushing me. "Get the hell outta here and go on in yo' office, nigga." She looked out in the hall to make sure Bettie wasn't in sight.

When I saw the coast was clear, I sprinted across the hall to my office, turned the light on and shut the door behind me. I sat at the desk and pulled out some paperwork and started writing. A few minutes drifted, and just as I figured, Bettie knocked at the door twice before she entered.

"Hey, baby, you still up? I thought you would've been in the bed 'sleep by the time I made it here," she said.

"Yeah, that was my plan, but no sooner than I walked through the door I thought about some work that I needed to finish, so here I am," I said calmly.

"How much longer you gon' be?"

"Ummm, 'bout ten minutes and I should be windin' it up."

"Okay, uhhh . . . okay, I'll be downstairs." She hesitated a bit. She seemed somewhat troubled.

"Is something wrong, baby?" I asked, wondering about her visibly uncertain state.

"Well, I'm not sure. I was gon' wait to talk to you tomorrow, but since you still up, it just ran back across my mind," she said.

I inhaled. "Well, give me a few more minutes on this and I'll be down and we can talk." I tried to go that extra mile to convince her that I was really doing paperwork.

"Okay." She agreed and closed the door behind her when she left.

A bit later, I made my way to our bathroom and freshened up right before I stuffed myself between the sheets next to Bettie. I had to make sure that no traces of Keshundra were left lingering on me.

"Baby, I'm all yours. Now, what's troubling ya?" I asked.

Bettie looked like she was lost in thought. She sat up in

94

the bed and fluffed a pillow behind her. "It's Katie," Bettie said.

"Katie. What about her?" I asked.

"I feel so sorry for her," Bettie stated sympathetically.

"Yeah, I know. Debra really had her goin' for—"

"No. That's not what I'm talkin' 'bout," Bettie interrupted me. "Charles, she told me she saw Gregg and talked to him." There was an enormous amount of concern lagging in Bettie's eyes as she spoke.

"Saw him and talked to him? When?" I frowned, and at the same time a disturbed feeling crept upon me as I recalled my weird dream right before Keshundra woke me up.

"She told me that shortly after we cleaned up the kitchen and left, the boys went to their room, and she dozed off on top of the covers in her bed. That's when it supposedly happened. She said she woke up to him softly callin' her name. He was sittin' in that big La-Z-boy chair across from the head of her bed. And baby, she said he was cryin'."

"Cryin'?" I repeated. "Gregg was cryin'?"

"Yep, she said tears was drippin' down his cheeks and he kept askin' her why, why, why," Bettie continued. "She also said he told her that he know he wasn't a perfect husband and he'd made plenty of mistakes, but he always loved her more than anything in the world. He said he understood why she did what she did, but he didn't understand why she did it wit' the person she did it wit'. Because that person was nothing but a cold-hearted leech who didn't have no fear of God in him at all."

I was getting nervous as hell now. Some strange-ass shit was definitely in the mix, but I simply was not going to accept it as anything other than imagination or dreaming. "Baby, you sure she wasn't dreamin' or somethin'?" I asked, sounding very certain.

"That was the first question I asked her, and she said she was sure she wasn't dreamin'," Bettie replied.

My nervousness was now making me somewhat

annoyed. "Well, even if she wasn't dreamin', which I doubt very seriously, what do it all mean?" I awaited Bettie's answer, since she seemed to have one for everything.

She repositioned herself on the pillow, turning more toward me with extra serious eyes now. "Charles, Katie confided in me. She had an affair on Gregg. And in the dream or vision or whatever it was, she said Greg told her that he'd suspected it when he was livin', but he didn't know who the man was that she was messin' wit'." Bettie paused and took a momentary look down at the covers then back at me. "I guess that sayin' is true; the dead know what the livin' doin', because Katie said that when Gregg came to her, he told her that he'd finally found out who the man was, and if he had known who he was when he was alive, he would've killed him."

I almost pissed in the bed. I was thunderstruck. I knew then that all of that shit couldn't have just been coincidence. But who was going to really believe any of it? Even hearing Katie's story and my story together, a normal person would've just written us both off as two extremely guilty consciences. After all, we were the ones who'd done the damn dirt. As my eyes traveled back and forth over the bedroom from the dresser and full-length mirror to the chest and wall art, a tormenting thought hit me. Just how much did Katie confess to Bettie? One reassuring thought held me together. It was obvious that Katie hadn't divulged who the mystery man was that she'd had the affair with, because Bettie was still in the bed beside me and didn't look like she was making preparations to go anywhere. All the same, I still needed to hear straight from the horse's mouth that my name would never be revealed.

"Wow, that's quite a story. She must really be goin' through somethin' if she told you all that." I moved around and began fluffing my pillow to keep from appearing so restless.

"Yeah, she is. I mean, there's a lot of guilt that she's inflicting on herself," Bettie said.

"Did she tell you who the man was? I mean, the man

she was, you know . . . seein'?" I asked, trying to come off as cool as possible.

"No. She didn't say who he was, but I asked her why she did it." Bettie paused, neglecting to deliver Katie's answer to the question. I waited a while, but she still held out. Looked like she was lost in thought.

"And?" I wanted to know.

"Oh." She took a sudden brisk headshake. "I'm sorry, I was just kinda remembering how sad Katie was. Anyway, she told me about the time she caught Gregg cheatin' on her and how she'd lost a lot of trust in him, then eventually it led to her havin' an affair. It's funny, though. I never pegged her as being the cheatin' type. The first day I met her and Gregg, they looked like the perfect couple." Bettie was plainly feeling the anguish that Katie was going through.

"Baby, they were a good couple. They just had some problems like all couples have," I said with care. My words were lined with relief after hearing that Katie hadn't squealed every detail of the business away.

"Like all couples have?" Bettie leaned her head back. "Well, I know couples have problems, but infidelity is one I hope we don't ever have. When I said *I do,* I meant for it to last forever."

"So did I. I was married to Ruth for twenty-nine years and we had a good life. So, guess what?" I tapped the end of Bettie's nose playfully with my fingertip.

"What?" She peered into my eyes.

"I plan to be married twenty-nine or thirty-nine to you and have the same kinda good life." I boasted to boost her confidence, then we melted into a tight embrace and kissed.

"Hey. You better not start nothin' you too tired to finish." She joked about me arousing her, then reached over to turn off the lamp on her nightstand. I fell back on my fluffy pillow to finally get some sleep.

"Baby, I'm so tired, I don't think I could get it up if I tried," I muttered, gradually nodding off.

"Oh, believe me, I could get it up if it needed to be up,

baby. But I feel ya on that tired thing," she said, then pulled the covers up and said goodnight.

The next day, I started my deliveries on schedule at 7:00 A.M. I could hardly wait to confront Katie about her sudden urge to tell Bettie all of her business, and quite possibly tell mine next. I also wanted to hear about her so-called visit from Gregg. I started calling her around 8:00 A.M. There was no answer. I called her all the way up to 3:00 and still didn't get an answer.

On my way back to Senatobia from Memphis after making the last delivery, I got off Interstate 55 onto Main Street and stopped at Jo Jo's Mart for gas and a soda. Main Street's the second busiest street in town, and after about a mile west, it runs smack-dab into Highway 51, which is the first busiest street with all the Wal-mart Super Center and new outlet stores traffic. As I filled my truck, I scanned over a few of the stores, restaurants, and businesses on both sides of Main. Next door to Jo Jo's, our fair town had been industrious enough to home Wendy's, Kentucky Fried Chicken, Motel 6 with a built-on Waffle House, Texaco gas, and on the other side, a BP Supermart gas station, Popeye's Chicken, and Pizza Hut. Further on down the business area of Main Street included the post office, city hall, the court house, public utilities offices, the police department, and other professional buildings, many of which were being remodeled and expanded due to the city's growing population.

I hung up the gas nozzle, still puzzled about my inability to reach Katie all day, so I decided to make a quick trip to her house before I went home for the evening, only to get there and find the house deserted. Katie and the kids were nowhere in sight. Confused even more and having no clue as to where they were, I left and arrived home just in time to catch a call from Momma.

"Hello." I picked up the phone as I walked into my bedroom.

"Hey, Charles," she said.

"Hey, Momma."

"How you doin'?" she asked.

"I'm fine. Y'all doin' all right up there?" I threw the mail down on the dresser.

"Yeah, everybody all right," she said. "I was callin' to tell y'all that Katie and the boys went to her sistah's house in Memphis. She called me 'bout five this mornin' to let me know, and told me to tell the rest of the family so nobody would be worried."

My damn heart flopped at the news, but I made no indication to Momma.

*So, that's where she been all day,* I thought.

"Aww, I'm glad to know that, 'cause I been callin' down there all day tryin' to check on 'em. I even went by right befo' I came on home," I told Momma.

"Ya did? Well, I called you on yo' mobile phone a couple'a times around mid-mornin', but I kept gettin' a *not available* message. So, I just decided to wait 'til I thought you or Bettie was at home," Momma explained.

"So, is she goin' up there just for today or what?" I asked.

"Naw, she said she probably gon' stay a while. Say she just can't bear to stay in the house right now. And since her sistah don't work, she say she'll have some company every day, all day," Momma told me.

Hearing Momma tell me that Katie had left indefinitely sent an ailing pain through me. *How in the hell am I gonna get to her to find out what's goin' on and she way up there? And then on top of it, wit' her sistah every damn day,* I thought as I dropped down on the bed. I was desperate to talk to her, and I didn't like the idea of waiting to conciliate my suspicions one bit.

"A'ight, Momma, I'll let Bettie know. Is that it? I mean, Katie didn't say nothin' else?" I asked, trying to indirectly find out if Katie had had the same stroke of conscience and told Momma any of what she'd told Bettie.

"Naw, that's 'bout it, but I could tell she was real bad off after what that crazy-ass Debra did last night. I asked her if she wanted to wait and let AJ or Bo see her up there when they got off work this evenin', but she said she wanted to go 'head and leave early in the mornin',"  Momma explained.

"Well, you keep us posted and let us know how she doin'," I said.

"I will. Bye-bye." Momma hung up.

As bad as I hated it, I had no choice but to accept the hand that Katie had dealt. "Damn, when I do catch up wit' her, it ain't gon' be pretty," I told myself softly as I ran the Jacuzzi full of water to soak and relax in for a while.

### Bettie

I could hardly wait to get home and unwind. I'd made plans to spend a nice, pleasant evening with Charles, and when I walked into the bedroom and saw him lying across the bed fast asleep wearing only his underwear, I knew that he'd probably already been in the Jacuzzi relaxing so he could do the same with me. The week leading up to the funeral had been so depressing and not to mention time consuming, with all of the family having to help Katie make the final preparations and all. Thank goodness it was finally over and things could start to get back to normal. Katie and her troubles had been on my mind off and on all day, but now that I was home with my husband, I didn't want to think about any of it. I hadn't had any of Charles in two days. My body was craving that big, delicious dick of his, and I knew he was probably craving some of me too. Yeah, this was our time for some good ole enjoyment, Charles and Bettie style.

I walked carefully around in the bedroom, gathering my things for a quick shower. I'd spent about an hour and a half in the Jacuzzi the night before, thinking that when I got out, Charles and I would get a little bit right before we fell off to sleep, but instead, we were derailed into preventing a catastrophe at Katie's. It was all good though, 'cause now he and I were each other's for the taking. The second I stepped out of the shower and dried off, I began lotioning and body-spraying myself up.

*Oh man, I sure do wish I had some of that spray or perfume or whatever it was that I smelled coming from Keshundra's room last night. That aroma was almost magical. I've never smelled anything like it. I can't imagine what it could be. Then again, if I was able to smell it on the outside of her room with the door closed, maybe it's too strong,* I thought.

Keshundra had probably been in the hallway from a visit to the bathroom or something right before I made my way up to see Charles. So, the fragrance may not have been too strong after all. I made a mental note to ask her the name of it so I could pick some up the next time I was at the mall. I just knew Charles would love that scent the minute I smelled it.

The more I thought about it, the more I realized that that crazy sister of mine was in her room alone preparing for bed, yet she was still spraying herself down like she was getting ready to have male company. What a waste. She sure as hell stayed true to the game in all aspects. No way I would've been using an alluring and seductive perfume like that all by myself. I would've had to be getting ready to spin my web and lay it on my man real thick, just like I was fixing to do when I slid in the bed right bedside Charles after I finished rubbing myself down. He looked so peaceful lying on his stomach asleep.

"Baaaaaaby. Baaaaaaby," I whispered in his ear while leaning my upper body on his back and caressing his shoulders. "Baaaaaaby," I continued softly as he began to awake.

"Yeah?" he answered, very groggy.

"I got somethin' for ya," I teased.

"What?"

"Somethin' you like." I began to kiss up and down his back, swiping a tongue-slash every now and then.

"Ummm, this feels nice to wake up to," he garbled.

"You think this is nice, just wait a sec." I slightly rose up off him. "Turn over and lay on your back, baby."

# Scandalous

He toddled over on his back. I pulled his shorts down and unveiled him semi-hard, then stuffed my mouth full at the blink of an eye. Within seconds, he swelled to his full potential inside my jaws. There was no shame in my game. I'd always been a take-charge tyrannosaurus in the bedroom. I didn't have time to be waiting on no man to roll over and make love to me when he felt like it. That old mess was reserved for them ancient sisters from back in the day. The way I saw it, if I wanted to have some sex, then I was going to get off my behind and have some sex. I boldly told Charles at the beginning of our relationship that his penis was my own personal lollipop, and that's just how I treated it. Man oh man, did I love the taste of his golfball duo and the sniff of his soapy-scented hairs. As I continued pumping my mouth up and down, I throated him almost to a choke, thinking I was going to leave him breathless with a high-powered ejaculation, then afterward straddle him to be hardcore fucked like usual.

But he had his own new ideas; ideas I certainly wasn't expecting that left me darn near speechless. He suddenly lifted my face out of his crotch and flipped me down on the bed and swapped places with me. Before I could get a word out to ask him what was wrong, I watched his face descend between my legs. I was considerably puzzled. Then I felt his warm tongue rambling inside of me. I screamed out in both sensation and surprise. I hadn't had a tongue down there in so long, I'd almost forgotten how it felt. He scoured through my pussy doggedly, making me absorb every whim and thrash. I just couldn't believe what I was experiencing with him. He didn't mumble a word, just kept going at it like he was in hog heaven.

As good as it felt to me, I simply could not concentrate solely on the fact that he'd finally gone downtown on me after all those years. Charles made it abundantly clear when we first started seeing each other that he'd never gone down on a woman and wasn't into doing it. Well, that was certainly no problem with me. You don't get rid of a new Cadillac just 'cause it has a small dent in it, nor do you dispose of a good man just 'cause he has a few old-fashioned reservations. I accepted Charles' rule with no complaints. But now, out of nowhere, he was eating my pussy like he'd been doing it all his life. I couldn't help but wonder what in the hell was going on. Question after question flickered in my mind.

*Where'd he learn how to do this, and who's he been practicing on? Oooh, it's so good. Damn, it's good. But he's never done it to me before. He told me he'd never done it to any woman before. So, why is he doin' it so damn good? Ahhhhh, yeah, yeah, yeah. Keep it up. Yeah, yeah,* I repeated in my head. For a while, the sensation of it all overpowered my suspicious mind, and when I knew anything, I was rolling my pussy over his face, almost near cumming stage.

Every time I raised my ass up off the bed, gyrating, damn if he wasn't clinging his mouth to my clit and holding on for dear life, while following the pussy in every direction. He was loving every minute of it. Just as I was about to turn into a complete wild woman, another reality hit me.

*Maybe he was just shy about it. Yeah, that's it. He was shy about it. But shy people don't eat no pussy the way he eatin' it. He got to be done did it to somebody else recently and found out he like it. But who? Naw, that's crazy. Charles wouldn't do that to me. I know he wouldn't. He loves me too much,* I rationalized silently. Eventually, I somehow managed to rid myself of all the negative thoughts and concentrated on enjoying my first oral performance from my husband. 'Cause it was good to the very last lick.

After he'd led me all the way to a fulfilling orgasm, he climbed on top of me and penetrated his manhood inside, thrusting deep and hard. That even lasted astonishingly much longer. Our earth-shattering finale landed about nine on a Richter scale from one to ten. We lay wrapped in each others arms and fell asleep.

Don't get me wrong, Charles' dick was gigantic and he'd always pleased the hell out of me during sex, but that particular performance was off the damn chain, as

# Scandalous

Keshundra would've said. I was so proud that my boo had done away with his long-running but very old-time rule, just for me. Now, that was love. I felt so blessed and happy to be married to a man as attentive and caring as Charles. His kind of selfless love was the exact thing that I'd been trying my darndest to get my hard-headed sister to understand and prepare herself for, but all she could relate to was the old me. The me that had been in love more times than I could count and dogged out by every one of the no-good bastards. Of course, that was during my late teens and early twenties. By the time I made it to my mid-twenties, the only thing I felt I had left to do was become a victimizer instead of a victim. But right before my change-over, that last boyfriend of mine used me up and threw me away like Alabama trash. The very next day, Bettie, the black widow was born. That's right, I adapted the malicious spirit of the female black widow spider: screw 'em then devour 'em.

I swore that no man would ever hurt me again. So, for many years, I was out in the streets servicing my every need and want by taking all I could get my hands on from any decent-looking working man that was in a position to pamper and pay me. And to be honest, I was proud of my lavish life. All I had to do was lay on my back or climb on top and please whoever the man for the moment was. I never even considered my prospering from having a good time anything other than just that, prospering from having a good time. The way I saw it, the men was getting it for free and still being dogs with every woman who'd let 'em, so why not make them pay? That way, everybody would get to go home satisfied. Needless to say, one of my worst mistakes was turning Keshundra on to the game when she turned eighteen. She'd been seeing a guy that was a couple of years older than her, and had fallen head over heels for him. As I expected, he hung around long enough to take her virginity and move on to the next girl. It hurt her pretty bad, so I didn't hesitate in showing her how the real game worked. What I didn't realize was that I'd created a monster. She took it all to an entirely different level and became way out of control.

See, I'd always kept my business on the down-low, especially since our father was a preacher and he and my mother were well respected in our church. But, Keshundra was another story. She just plain didn't give a damn who knew what she was doing or who she was doing it with. After a while, she started calling me old-timed and telling me how bad I'd begun to slip because I constantly urged her to slow things down a bit. She even told me that I was turning into a goody two-shoes. Truth is, I had been playing for so long that I'd just gotten tired of the game. And I certainly wasn't getting any younger. Somewhere down that long and meaningless road, I'd started to believe again that there had to be a true love somewhere out there for me, but if I kept on spinning my web of lies and deceit, I'd never find him.

Then I met Charles, a dedicated father and husband of twenty-five years plus, who'd been dealt a sad hand with a terminally ill wife. Even though he and I saw each other during his wife's illness, he still remained by her side and took care of her 'til the day she died. That told me that he was the kind of man I wanted to be with for the rest of my life. I was ready and willing then to give up the old life and mend my ways. I actually spent time in church doing something other than trying to meet men. In Keshundra's eyes, I'd really become a holy-rolling loser now. She swore the only reason I was giving up the game and marrying him was because he was so well off. The fact that he was financially secure was definitely a plus, but I just couldn't make her believe that it wasn't the sole reason I wanted to be with him. If only she'd known that I'd agreed to sign a pre-nup before he and I got married.

I wouldn't have told her that, though, because she never would've let me live it down. Still the same, I felt responsible that she was now on that same lonely, meaningless road that I'd traveled for years. I promised myself I wouldn't stop 'til I made her realize that it was nothing but false hopes and empty wishes to think that material things would always make her happy.

I didn't hesitate in signing the pre-nup for Charles because I'd already had every material thing that money could buy, and I now wanted something non-materialistic. Charles had given me the intangible for four wonderful years, and it made me happier than I'd ever been in my life. That was another reason I was disappointed in myself for thinking the worst when he came out of the blue and pleasured me the same way that I had been pleasuring him for so long. Just another demonstration of his love for me. I'd re-taught myself how to trust when I fell in love with him and not to jump to conclusions before hearing the facts.

Boy, did I give myself the third degree while in the kitchen cooking, and I couldn't wait to chat with my boo about his newly discovered talent. He was still sleeping. I'd already awoke, slipped out of bed and prepared him a quick but delectable late evening meal. Instead of waking him myself, I decide to let the aroma from the food do it for me. Sure enough, by the time I was putting the finishing touches on everything, he strolled through the kitchen door wearing his gray jogging pants and a gray T-shirt.

The scrumptious aroma led him right to the kitchen table as I'd expected. He sat down and looked up at me as I stood near the stove, buttering the biscuits.

"Baby, this twice in a row you done gave me a pleasant awakenin'. You sho' know how to make a man happy." He gave me a caring smile.

I gave him the same caring smile. "I'm glad you approve, my love." I quickly dashed over and gave him a big kiss on the lips. "I love you so much," I whispered as I hugged him tightly. Gosh, I could hardly wait to fix our plates and sit down, so we could chat about the way he'd just romanced me down.

"I love you too," he said. "Why didn't you wake me when you got up to start cookin'?"

"Oh, you looked so peaceful I couldn't bear to," I said playfully. "Besides, I knew the aroma would eventually drag you on in here."

"You sho' know how to make me smile, baby." He looked down at his plate after I sat it on the table in front of him.

"Do I? Well, I'm glad to know you're satisfied." I smiled as I equally portioned my plate with a slice of boned country ham, fried potatoes, squash, and homemade biscuits.

"Satisfied? That's a understatement." He took a big bite of ham.

"You certainly did a little satisfying earlier, didn't ya?" I made an attempt to ease into the oral sex conversation, because I didn't want to embarrass him, especially if he was shy about it.

"Huh?" He bit into a biscuit, drawing a frown as if he was confused. I smiled at him and raised my eyebrows teasingly. "Oh, oh . . . yeah, that." He softened his frown when he realized what I was talking about. "Well, I had been thinkin' 'bout it for a long time and I came to the conclusion that you deserve to feel as good as I do. So, I went for it," he stated most urgently—so urgently that it almost sounded like he was nervous and making up an excuse. That certainly turned the playful little smile on my face upside down.

"Oh really. So, it took all this time to come around, huh?" I questioned.

"Better late than never," he spurted out rather tackily, not even looking up from forking his food.

In the beginning, I wasn't sure how the conversation would go, but I certainly didn't think it would be that awkward. I was almost reluctant to say anything else, but I did anyway.

"That's true. It's always better late than never." I flinched my eyebrows up at him. "So, I guess I better be glad it was no later than it was, huh?"

"Why you say that?" He chewed hungrily, still seeming as if he was trying not to look nervous. I didn't know what was up, but the way he was acting was really bugging me.

"'Cause, if you had waited any longer, I wouldn't've had none left. You meant business. How'd you catch on so quick—dreaming?" I now spoke frank and with sarcasm.

"I didn't hear you complainin' when I was doin' it. And as far as catchin' on, it don't take no rocket scientist to figure out how to lick a—"

*Ring. Ring.* Saved by the bell. The telephone interrupted Charles before he finished another tacky answer in my opinion.

"I'll get it." He certainly didn't hesitate to get up. "Hello," he answered. "Hey, Will."

*Umph, what in the hell just happened here? Why did he seem nervous? And why did he seem so defensive annnnd illusive? So what, it was his first time. It shouldn't have been that damn big o' deal for him to talk about it. I've never had a problem talkin' openly about giving him head. Is it just me or is he hiding somethin'? Oh shit, this is ridiculous. Here I go again with the same mess. Of course he was nervous, because he was probably embarrassed. Lighten the hell up, Bettie,* I told myself while Charles was on the phone with Will. Once again, I'd managed to let my misplaced paranoia get the best of me. I again convinced myself that nothing was there, and to stop fishing so hard. And even if it was, did I really want to know? If I kept up with the crazy skepticism, I knew I was probably going to deeply offend Charles, and I definitely didn't want to do that. He'd never given me a reason to distrust him, and I didn't need to be inventing one. I decided to drop the conversation and change the subject.

Charles hung up the phone and sat back down at the table. "That was Will, baby. He was callin' to remind me that we got rehearsal tomorrow night instead of Thursday night, 'cause of that program at the Civic Center on Saturday."

"Oh, yeah. Y'all do have that program this weekend, don't ya?" I spoke more lively in an attempt to lift the atmosphere. "Who else gon' be there, baby?"

Charles looked at me with a brand new sentimental

smile now and spoke very gently. "Hey, you don't have to change the subject, ya know. I wanna finish where we left off. I know I probably sounded a li'l on the insensitive side a while ago." He reached across the table for my hand. "But I have to admit I was a teeny-tiny bit on the embarrassed side. I'm sorry if I hurt yo' feelings." He squeezed my hand caringly.

I could have kicked my own ass. I was so moved by his sweet and honest gesture. *I knew it was nothin' but a little shyness,* I said in my head. I sure as heck wasn't going to let him know what ridiculous thinking I'd been doing. "No. Don't be silly. I'm fine. I figured you were a tad on the shy side about it." I exhaled with relief, hopping out of my chair and dropping down in his lap to embrace him. "Oh, for the record, you got it goin' on." I squeezed him tighter as I complimented him to let him know how I enjoyed it.

"I'm glad to know that, 'cause you deserved it long before now." He kissed my cheek.

I was now back in the zone and as happy as ever.

# Chapter Eight

*Charles*

After rehearsal, I bid the rest of the fellas goodnight, but I asked Will to hang around a little while longer so I could talk to him. I didn't know which one of us was smiling the most when I was telling him all about my hot time with Keshundra, and how he'd saved my ass from a disaster with the phone call the night before. Talk about a close call. I was asking to be found out, diving into Bettie's pussy like that and eating it like there was no tomorrow, and hadn't ever done it to her before. I guess I just got too excited about my newly found fetish. Shit, I was like a kid in a candy shop; I wanted it all, whereas I should have gradually eased into it and acted as if I was willing to try it just for her. That way when she inquired, I wouldn't have been so uneasy about answering. My edgy actions probably increased her suspicions. Damn, Keshundra's shit must've really jumbled up my thoughts, because it wasn't until the very moment Bettie brought the subject up that the dead giveaway thing hit me. It worked out fine, though, 'cause after Will's phone call bought me some time to get my shit together, I put on a prize-winning performance that answered any doubts she had and won her right over into my lap.

He swore I owed him big-time for that one. "Yeah, man, you gots to pay up," he said, laughing. "I don't know, I might let ya slide since you didn't hold out on me 'bout this here sistah-in-law." He opened his car door to get in. We'd just locked up the community center where we always held our rehearsals.

"Well, I sho' do appreciate that. You all heart, my brotha." I laughed back at him. "Oh, I almost forgot. You did say we goin' on stage before the last group Saturday, right?"

"Yeah." Will shot me a suspicious look. "Don't do

nothin' I wouldn't do befo' the show. And ya betta be on time, too, nigga." He got in his car. I smiled and got in mine.

The Gospel Explosion Program at the Civic Center was the talk of the town for those few days leading up to it. People from all over showed up. The second I walked into the building, I recognized faces from Coldwater, Independence, Como, Sardis, Hernando, Memphis, and yes, Senatobia represented in big numbers. Nine groups went on that night. We were in the number eight spot. The minute we stepped on the stage in our sharp, gray suits and coordinated navy accessories, the women went crazy. I swear, look like we'd been melted and poured into those suits. That's just how tailor-made-to-fit they were. It wasn't an accident that me and my boys pretty much fit a similar description. In fact, it was a requirement to look, dress, and perform a certain way before even being considered to become a member. Being the founders, that's how Will and I set the standards for the group in the beginning. And by all means, we positively kept our whoring shit on the utmost down low. Every group performed well that night, but if I had to say so myself, The Mighty Spirituals shook that 1200 seat theater big time. The sold out crowd screamed for more.

As soon as we sang the last song and exited the stage, a small fan club of females were waiting for us in the lobby, just like after every program. The five of us stood and chatted with the women while the last group performed. Before long, the lobby was filled with dressed-up men and women standing around conversing. I happened to look down to the other end of the lobby, and to my surprise, spotted the very person that I'd been itching to see. Although I hoped she would make it to that program, I was very doubtful of it. Katie stood talking with the Melody Angels, dressed up and looking as good as ever. But then, the Melody Angels weren't looking too bad themselves. In fact, the female quartet group members sauntered around in their cream, two-piece, double-breasted skirt suits and cream-sequined shoes, as lively as they always were. A couple of ladies in the group, Cynthia and Sheila, lived in Senatobia. Katie had been friends with them for years. The remaining three, Pamela, Reesa, and Jen were bonafide Memphians. I stared down the lobby at them. It seemed that whatever they were talking about managed to make Katie laugh. That was certainly a step in the right direction, considering the last time I saw her she was upset and crying. I didn't want to interrupt their conversation, but I couldn't take a chance on letting Katie get away without me talking to her first.

## Katie

I figured just about everybody I knew and their mommas, too, were going to be at the big gospel program, so I started not to go. I just didn't feel up to pasting on no fake smile and answering a bunch of unnecessary questions about my dead husband and how I was taking it all. How the hell did they think? Besides, I'd done enough of that to last a lifetime after the funeral. The boys and I had been lounging around at my sister's house all week, and frankly, I was somewhat on the bored side. Plus, I knew some good old-fashioned gospel singing was probably just what I needed to help uplift me. That was the reason I got on up and went anyway.

Just as I expected, when the high-spirited singing was over, I was glad that I'd gone. Not to mention, I had a chance to chat with some girlfriends of mine who were booked to sing on the program. I was really happy to see them, 'cause I knew they weren't going to be yakking on about nothing and rehashing old memories about Gregg just to see me cry. They kept it real, just like I knew they would.

"Katie, I knew you was a fighter, girlfriend. Gimme love, gimme love," Cynthia said merrily, embracing me. "I told the girls at rehearsal Wednesday night that you was gon' make it to this program fo' sho'."

"She sho' said it. But I knew you was gon' be here too, my boo," Sheila added playfully, taking her turn to hug me.

"Well, God is able, ain't he?" I said, smiling while receiving a hug from Pamela, then Jen, then Reesa.

"Yes, He is. He the only one I know who's able," Pamela agreed.

"Y'all threw down tonight, didn't ya?" I said, giving my girls a soft handclap.

"And you know this, man." Sheila widened her grin and took a quick bow. She was the really silly one in the group, always ready to amuse no matter what the occasion.

"Come to think of it, Katie, I called you Thursday," Cynthia said. "Why didn't you answer yo' phone, gal? You knew that was me."

I didn't even get a chance to answer right away. Pamela jumped in rather comical and answered for me. "Now, how you figure she knew it was you, Cyn? Could she see you through the phone? Why you always assumin' everybody got caller ID? Some folks don't want all o' that junk on they phones. I done told you 'bout that mess, girl."

The rest of us burst into laughter, including Cynthia. Pamela was even tickled at herself. Cynthia raised her hand in front of Pamela. "Talk to the hand, 'cause ain't nobody else listenin'."

"Me and the boys been at my sistah Dee Dee's house in Memphis all week." I told them. "I just had to get out of my house for a little while."

"I can understand that." Cynthia patted my shoulder caringly.

"How you liking Memphis?" Sheila asked.

"It's all right for a visit, but I wouldn't wanna live there permanently," I quickly stated.

"The Golden Hummers and Mighty Spirituals tore the floor up tonight, didn't they?" Reesa noted, changing the subject.

"I know that's right, girl." Pamela stuck her hand out to give Reesa five. They shot mischievous winks at each other, then clapped their hands together.

It was no secret that Pamela and Reesa had it bad for a couple of the members of those two groups. Word had it in the singing community that they'd been hooking up with the men for quite some time. Only problem with that was the men were already married, and so were Pamela and Reesa.

"Come on, y'all, let's get on back to Memphis. I got to be at church at eight o'clock in the mornin'," Jen said, slightly yawning.

"Jen, you act like it's two in the mornin'. It ain't but 11:30, girl. This early compared to our regular let-out times," Pamela responded.

"And that's why I'm gon' take advantage of the chance to get some extra sleep. See ya." Jen waved her hand at Pamela and began walking toward the front lobby door.

The rest of us followed. People were gathered all over, laughing and talking. A tall, trendy-dressed woman approached us as we made our way on the outside. She stopped on the sidewalk in front of us.

"Excuse me. How are you all?" the nicely spoken, eager female blurted.

Everybody except Reesa smiled and spoke back.

Reesa held an unsure look and spoke rather slowly. "Good . . . evening."

I assumed that the stoutly built, professional-looking woman probably wanted contact information about booking their group. She parked her bright eyes directly into Reesa's uncertain gaze and spoke in a disturbed manner. "Since you refused to talk to me Tuesday morning, you mind if I have a word with you now?"

The rest of us glanced around at each other in silence, obviously puzzled after hearing the woman's somewhat bitter request of Reesa.

Reesa didn't make it any better. She responded to the woman with just as much hostility. "I'm gettin' ready to leave. I don't have time to stand out here talkin' to you, Mrs . . . Mrs. whatever yo' name is," Reesa snapped.

I frowned, seizing eye contact with Cynthia, who was

frowning and looking even more puzzled than her other group members. The woman quickly snapped back at Reesa. "Oh, so, he didn't even tell you my name? Humph. Verlinda Walker. That's my name." She raised one hand to her hip.

Reesa seemed to be getting more impatient. She was the quick-tempered one in the group, the only quick-tempered one. I'd witnessed her over-react in the simplest situations, so I didn't even want to imagine where this was going to lead. She shifted all 230 pounds of her weight onto one leg, and threw a vicious glare at Verlinda.

"Listen, honey, why don't you go home and talk to yo' husband. I don't have nothin' to say to you," Reesa stated bitterly.

Verlinda didn't break a sweat. Her light-toned voice was cool and relaxed. "You don't hear well at all, do you? I said my name is Verlinda, not honey. And for your information, I kicked Mr. Walker out, so he's all yours now."

"I don't want him," Reesa quickly asserted.

"Really. Well, it certainly didn't look that way at the China Palace restaurant on Elvis Presley, Tuesday morning." Verlinda smirked.

My eyes widened, along with the other four girls as we listened. Reesa, on the other hand, looked like the cat that had swallowed the canary.

"The best thing for you to do is get out of my face before you regret it." Reesa's threat didn't seem to move Verlinda one bit.

If anything, Verlinda was now sarcastic. She pointed at Reesa's stomach area and chuckled. "Your skirt is twisted, darling. Hmmmm . . . perhaps if you had gotten a size larger than that twenty. I wear a sixteen in suits, and you're much larger than me."

Reesa definitely didn't take kindly to Verlinda making fun of her. I could tell by the squint in Reesa's eyes that it was on now.

"You, stupid bitch—" Ressa exclaimed.

"Reesa." Jen abruptly jumped in. "Come on, now. Don't

be cussin' like that. These folks out here gonna hear you. We just got out of service."

"Yeah, Reesa, did you forget that you just got through shouting all over the stage?" Verlinda taunted.

"Ahhh, Verlinda," Pamela said softly. "That's your name, right?"

Verlinda turned her attention to Pamela and nodded. "Yes, it is."

"Why don't y'all talk about this another time?" Pamela asked with reason. "I mean, we all just got out of a high-spirited service, and, well, this just ain't the time nor the place."

Verlinda seemed to be sensible. She didn't resist Pamela's rational suggestion at all.

"I agree with you. All I wanted to do was let your friend Reesa know that Pastor Walker got the clap. I caught him with a nasty four hundred pound woman who belongs to the church that he pastors in Collierville. About a week after that, he had to go to the doctor because of penis-burning, and that's when he found out he had the clap. I figured he wasn't going to be honest and tell her, so that's why I took it upon myself to try and help her. When I saw him and her in the restaurant, I spoke to her because I knew she was one of the Melody Angels' lead singers."

Pamela gasped as her eyes widened. "Well, ahh . . . now she know."

I was outdone. I glanced around at the other girls and noticed their looks of disbelief at Verlinda's unemotional bluntness. If Reesa's look could have killed, Verlinda would've been dead on the spot. I decided to throw in my two cents to try and persuade Verlinda to leave before things really got out of hand.

"Excuse me, Verlinda. You look like an intelligent, professional woman. So, I know you know that Pamela is right about this not being the time or the place for nothing like this." I gave her a pleading look.

In return, she sprouted me a big grin. "Yeah, I'm gone. My good deed here is done." She flung both her hands up and laughed as she strolled away. "My good deed here is done."

Damn, what a show she'd put on. Her jolly laugh and self-gratifying strut clearly said that she'd cleverly done what she'd set out to do, to publicly humiliate Reesa. As bad as I hoped the incident was over now that Verlinda had walked away, I knew Reesa went for bad, and so did the rest of the girls. I couldn't see her letting Verlinda have the last word, then stroll away laughing about it.

Just as I figured, Verlinda hadn't gotten a good twenty feet away when Reesa retorted. "I think it's mighty sick of you to go around lying on your husband while he counseling other women . . . just 'cause you jealous! After all, with him being a pastor, that's part of his job description, so you shouldn't worry about it!" Reesa's loud outburst captured the attention of other folks now.

*Oh my God. Please, Lord, don't let this happen here now,* I said in my head. Too late, though. Verlinda stopped in her tracks and turned back around, still smiling and looking as calm as ever.

"Oh, I agree with you. That's why I don't worry about him since I put him out of my house. But when I was worrying, it wasn't the counseling women that bothered me, it was the fucking them that did." Verlinda never lost touch with her smug grin.

I could hear muffled sniggling and "whoo"-ing among the crowd. The disgracing statement even seemed to bowl Reesa over, because she didn't respond immediately. However, Verlinda wasn't done just yet. "Listen, darling. If you desperate enough to keep on screwing a self-made, tired-ass, thirty-nine-year-old whorish preacher with the clap, that's your prerogative." And with that, Verlinda turned and began walking away again.

Folks really laughed out now. I knew that Reesa had taken all she was going to take, especially now that more heard what Verlinda had accused her of. At the blink of an eye, Reesa took off behind Verlinda. Jen grabbed at her arm and Cynthia jumped in her path, but she brushed them off like lightweight feathers.

Verlinda must have heard the clapping sound of Reesa's heels against the pavement, 'cause she spun around just in time to catch a lick in the face from Reesa. The lick didn't seem to faze Verlinda, though. In retaliation, Verlinda quickly landed a solid fist right back in Reesa's face. As they fought, landing blow after blow, me and the other girls struggled to break them apart. But they were like angry bears. Verlinda grabbed a handful of Reesa's long, black hair as they tousled. The way she was yanking it, I just knew she was going to pull a damn patch right from the roots. Reesa's weakening position gave Verlinda the power to really work her ass over; scratches, punches, you name it. It was almost as if we weren't even trying to break them apart. Reesa scraped and yanked at Verlinda's hand to loose the stronghold on her hair, but she was unsuccessful until Charles and some other man came out of nowhere and grabbed hold of Verlinda. Then another man took hold of Reesa and helped us try to restrain her. Although Verlinda tried to get loose, Charles and the other man held on to her. "Hey, hey, come on, now. Calm down," I heard Charles saying as they made their way down the sidewalk.

I knew it was way past time for me to go, after all that drama, and right after a good singing program too. Just proved that church folks can act a fool anywhere, anytime, and make worldly folks look like they're the ones with the sense. All the scrapping and scraping reminded me of my brawl with crazy-ass Debra earlier that week. The nosy folks at home could get off me and her incident now, 'cause after that, they'd have something fresh to gossip about. I already knew the headlines: Reesa, of the Melody Angels, somebody named Verlinda, and her preacher husband with the clap. Come sun up the next day, that was going to be the talk of the town. I went ahead and said my goodbyes to the girls and headed to my car. Right before I reached my car I heard a familiar voice calling my name.

I didn't even look up, 'cause I was dreading who it

sounded like. Instead, I ignored him and picked up the pace. He was first in line of the people that I didn't want to talk to at the program. I had done well avoiding him up to that point.

"Katie," he called out again. This time I went ahead and looked up. "Hey sistah-in-law. Why you in such a hurry?"

"It's late, Charles. I don't want the kids or my sistah worryin'. I need to get on back to Memphis." My reply was direct. Any fool could have seen that I didn't want to be bothered. But not Charles. He always had to have his way, no matter what.

"Is something wrong? You seem uptight."

"Well, excuse me for not being in better cheer, but I was just caught in the middle of two grown women fighting right after church." As I spoke, I purposely avoided eye contact with him.

"Yeah, that was unfortunate. Is the lady that sing wit' the group all right?" he asked.

"They finally calmed her down. I'm sure she'll be fine."

"That's good. The other lady done cooled off too," he said, stretching his neck as if he was looking for someone. "That's funny. I just left her standing over there. I guess she done rolled out too. That was mighty quick."

"Well, I'm sure you can catch her if you hurry," I said, unconcerned as I unlocked my car door to get in. Charles' doggedness never ceased to amaze me. He'd probably hit on Verlinda once he got her by herself.

"Wait a minute, now. I need to talk to you, Katie." He sounded annoyed by my eagerness to leave, but I didn't care.

I paused before getting into the car. "Will you go on and say what you wanna say? I told you my sistah and the kids waitin' on me."

"How long you gon' stay in Memphis?" he asked.

"That really ain't ya business, but if it'll speed you on yo' way, I'm stayin' as long as I want to. The kids out of school for the summer, so we ain't got to rush back. They needed to get out of Senatobia for a while anyway," I responded rapidly.

"They needed to or you needed to? Bettie told me 'bout yo' li'l dream concernin' Gregg." He now spoke firmer.

I knew the issue of Gregg's visit was somewhere on his narrowed-minded list to be mentioned, and the second he said it as if it was some kind of a joke, it offended the hell out of me.

"Little dream? If Bettie told you about a dream I had, she lied," I snapped. "When my husband came to me, I was wide awake. That was no dream, and that's what I told her."

"You don't have to get upset about it."

"I ain't gettin' upset. I just don't want nobody changin' my words around. What's it to you, anyway?" I was fuming.

"What's it to me? I tell you what it is to me. You told Bettie all that stuff 'bout you cheatin' on Gregg, and how he know who the man is now that he dead." Charles looked to be as upset as I was now.

"That was my business I shared with her. I didn't mention yo' name."

"Not that time, but how long befo' you do?" he insisted.

"Is that all you worried about, that somebody's gon' tell on you? The experience I had is bigger than me or you. I don't care whether you believe me or not, but one thing fo' sho', Gregg was right about yo' black ass," I snarled rather low.

"What's that s'pose to mean?" he asked disgustedly.

As the conversation continued, both of us became more and more wound up.

"He warned me to stay away from you and yo' treachery, 'cause it won't be long befo' you crash and burn, and anybody involved with you goin' down too. So, you stay the hell away from me." I jumped in my car and slammed the door behind me.

"So, that's it?" He leaned down to fix his dead-ass eyes on me, but I only gave him my side profile as I let my window down. I still refused to hold eye contact with him. I focused straight ahead and didn't even answer him. "You hear me talkin' to ya. You just gon' go 'round thinkin' you done talked to a dead man and tellin' all about it, huh? That's crazy and you know it. Once a person dead, they dead. You know that for yo'self. I tell ya what, though. Keep that shit up and folks gon' say you crazy fo' sho'."

Since he just wouldn't shut up, I went ahead and gave him one last piece of my mind. "Listen, Charles, I don't give a damn about what folks say, and I definitely can't change the past. The only thing I can do is try to make a better future by not making the same mistakes that I've already made over the years. When Gregg came to me, he told me that he'd forgiven me and he wanted me to put this whole mess behind me and go on with my life. That's all that matters to me." When I first let the window down and began talking, my intentions were to set Charles straight for trying to mock my experience with Gregg, but somewhere in the midst of my words, something different happened.

I began to feel uplifted as I told Charles of my newly found hope. My eyes filled with tears. I felt an amazing sense of confidence and faith. What was happening to me? I wasn't sure, but whatever it was, it was beautiful. I even turned to look at Charles, and when I did, I saw him in a completely different light than ever before. I was actually relieved that I'd told him the truth face to face about what was going on with me. Because now, I didn't have to dodge him anymore. He had to have seen the sincerity in my eyes, and maybe even felt the compelling vibes of honesty coming from me; I just knew he did. Then something else unexpected happened as I was gazing into his eyes. The way he stared back at me. I'd never seen such a powerless stare upon him. Even though he didn't admit anything to me verbally, as I held eye contact with him, everything was confirmed for me on the spot. Charles' vulnerable expression told me he knew that I wasn't bogus like all of those times before when I'd made an attempt to end our disgraceful relationship. I didn't have to say another word. He began slowly backing away from the car without uttering so much as one word of opposition. I drove off, knowing deep in my heart that I was finally free of him.

# Chapter Nine

*Charles*

Up until the two ladies got to scrapping, it had been a pretty good night. From that point on, things took a turn for the worse. No doubt about it, Katie was damn sure convinced that she'd talked to Gregg, and not in a dream. Even though I'd tried my best to make her realize how mixed up she was, her certainty did remind me of the gravesite incident when I was so sure that I'd spoken to him too. Then Will set me straight, right before I set my own ass straight. I just couldn't help thinking that if I had so much as breathed a word about my little "Gregg episode," Katie would've straight-up clicked, believing then that she had indisputable proof of seeing him. She may have even fell into a full confession about every damn thing. That would've been a fucking disaster, 'cause all of my business would have been in the streets then.

All in all, I still didn't know exactly what to make of the conversation I'd had with her. What I did know is it left me feeling empty as hell, and I hated that feeling. I just couldn't get the sincere look that was in her eyes out of my mind. I had seen her cry and put on the *I'm through with you* act many times over the years, but it was different this time. Something became gradually overwhelming about her persona right before me. It was almost spooky. As I'd leaned over at her car window listening to her talk, it was like a voice whispered in my ear and said, *You'll never touch her again.*

My natural instincts were to try to change her mind, manipulate the situation a little bit like I'd always done, but for some weird-ass reason, I felt like it would be a waste of energy. In fact, my heart was so heavy and I felt so powerless, I couldn't say a damn word, so I just backed away from the car and let her drive off.

As I strolled back to the front of the building to catch

up with Will and the fellas before they left, a thought hit me. *Damn, have I really lost Katie this time? I got to do somethin'. But what?*

"Hey, Charles," Stan called out, interrupting my thoughts as I approached them. "Did you get that woman to her car without gettin' any bruises on ya?" He swayed over in laughter, and the rest of the guys laughed with him.

I frowned, somewhat puzzled for a few seconds, then I realized he was talking about the woman in the fight, Verlinda, and not Katie. Whew, that Katie shit was really screwing with my mind.

"Man, you had a serious load on yo' hands, didn't ya?" Joe asked, still laughing.

"Yeah, Charles. By the time we made it outside, I looked down the sidewalk and couldn't see nothin' but her slangin' you and that other fella from side to side. The two of y'all could hardly handle that big woman," Henry sniggered. "For a minute I thought she was fightin' y'all."

"You ain't got whiplash, do ya?" Stan was really keeping the laugh alive with his joning.

I glanced around at them while shaking my head, then cracked a laugh too. "Y'all seen me and dude strugglin'. Why didn't one of ya help us out? Man, forget y'all. Where my wife at, anyway?" I scoped over the thinned-out remaining people, trying to spot Bettie.

"Her and yo' momma, and y'all's pastor was headed that way a few minutes ago." Joe pointed to the other side of the parking lot.

"Who, Deeberry?" My smile turned into a frown.

"That's y'all's pastor, ain't he?" Joe asked, grinning on the sly, 'cause he knew I couldn't stand Deeberry.

I didn't reply. I waved Joe off and began walking in the direction of my car. By now, the other guys were walking to their vehicles to leave too.

"Hey, Charles, what time we meetin' at yo' house for the cook-out tomorrow?" Preston hollered.

"Five-thirty," I answered. "I'll see y'all later."

On the other side of the parking lot, Momma and her

two friends, Ms. Hattie and Mrs. Sadie Mae, and Bettie and Sharon were all gathered around, deciding where they wanted to go eat. That was a traditional thing, for groups and singing-goers to stop at a twenty-four hour restaurant or truck stop in the area where the program was held to grab a late meal.

As I stood in the midst of everybody, I couldn't believe my eyes. I witnessed another shocker for the night. While Bettie and everybody else discussed the eating arrangements, Deeberry and Keshundra were quite cozy, standing a little piece off to themselves, chatting. They must have been so caught up in their conversation that they didn't even notice me joining the crowd. Neither one of 'em so much as flinched a brow to speak. That shit annoyed the hell out of me.

*No wonder he up here. He sniffing behind Keshundra like a damn prairie hound,* I thought.

"Charles, who was that woman that got to fightin' wit' the Melody Angel gal?" Momma asked, interrupting my thoughts.

"Some preacher's wife from Memphis," I replied. "I think her name was Verlinda."

"What happened?" Bettie asked, changing her facial expression to a frown. "I mean, why were they fighting?"

"I don't really know. But according to what the woman said, the girl that sang lead for the group was messin' round wit' her husband, and she caught 'em," I answered.

"Did she catch em' here at the program tonight?" Sharon asked.

"I don't think so. I think she said she caught em' earlier this week at some restaurant in Memphis," I replied, then waited for whatever unsolicited opinion Sharon was getting ready to throw out.

"Well, excuse me for sayin' so, but if she caught 'em at a restaurant, then that's where she should've acted the fool at, rather than comin' out here after a gospel program clownin'. I swear, black folks know they can clown somethin' awful when they want to," Sharon declared in her usual outspoken tone.

"Fo' real. I agree. Some of us do all the wrong things in all the wrong places at all the wrong times." Bettie looked appalled. "I'm glad a bigger percentage of us know better than to act that way, though."

I decided to tease Sharon a little, just to get another one of her snappy responses. "Sistah-in-law, my brotha let you out tonight?"

Even before she answered, her eye-roll gave me attitude. "Let me out? I know you didn't say *let me out*. In his dreams." She flung her famous neck-roll at me.

The six of us laughed, but Deeberry and Keshundra remained in their own little world.

"Why didn't he come with y'all, Sharon?" I grinned.

"Pa'leeeease. You know Wayne wasn't 'bout to get up off that couch and put no clothes on after he got off work this evenin'," Sharon replied.

"Charles, did you see Katie?" Momma asked.

"Yeah, I talked to her briefly." I nodded. "Did any of y'all get a chance to talk to her?"

"Me and Bettie talked to her when we first got here, but she didn't seem well at all. I asked her why didn't her sistah or somebody come wit' her," Momma said.

"What she say?" Sharon asked.

"She didn't really say too much of nothin'. She just seemed so distant," Bettie hesitated in reply.

"Yeah, I picked that up too," I added. "But she gon' be all right. We just got to keep on prayin' for her."

"Ain't that the truth," Momma agreed.

"Baby, we decided to go to IHOP to eat." Bettie changed the subject. "Is that okay with you, or do you wanna go somewhere else?"

I didn't answer right away. Shit, I could hardly pay attention to my own conversation with them for trying to sneak a peek in on Deeberry and Keshundra every now and then. "Ahh . . ."

"Hey, if y'all done made ya minds up, I'm ready," Deeberry called out, cutting my words off. "Aw, Brother

Charles, I didn't see you come up." He excused himself from Keshundra and strolled over to greet me. "You all right tonight?" We shook hands.

"Yeah, Pastor, I'm good. How you doin'?" I pasted on a fake smile.

"Aww man, blessed and highly favored enough to be in the company of these beautiful black sistahs tonight," he replied, sporting his black, single-breasted suit and shiny black shoes.

"I heard that." I momentarily envisioned myself throwing him down on the pavement and whupping that okey-dokey, charm-the-beautiful-black-sistahs bit out of him on the spot.

A couple of my boys in the group once joned me, saying I was hatin' on Deeberry 'cause he was much younger than me and had more game. But I begged to differ. That nigga's game was way too weak for me to be hatin' on. He probably practiced them tired old lines at home in the mirror. I didn't have to practice anything, 'cause my shit came natural.

"Yeah, these sistahs represented in a big way tonight, Brotha Charles," he exclaimed very animatedly. Hell, the way he was more keyed up than usual and couldn't be still, I could've sworn he'd been sipping in somebody's yack-bottle.

"So, Dee . . . umm, Pastor, you enjoy the program tonight?" I held to my fake smile and reluctantly kept the conversation going. Almost fucked up and said Deeberry, though. Momma's chastising eyes fell right on me.

"Man, did I? Y'all boys know y'all can work it out! I guarantee ya, the angels was up in heaven doin' the Electric Slide on the streets of gold, 'bout to waste their milk and honey. Haah, ha!" He suddenly jerked his body like he had a twitch going on or something, or like he was getting ready to shout right there.

See, that was the kind of crap that I was talking about. All of them dramatics wasn't called for. Why couldn't he have just complimented the group and shut the fuck up? I held onto my same smile for a moment, pretending to be gratified by his phony praise. "All right then. Look, I'ma let y'all go on grab a bite befo' it get too late." I hoped that no one could see how annoyed I was.

"You ain't goin' wit' us, man?" Deeberry asked, trying to look displeased.

*Hell naw, I ain't goin'*, I said to myself. I had no intentions of sitting down to a meal for a whole hour or two listening to his bullshit. I made my quick excuse. "Naw, I got to get on to the house. I'm a li'l tired, but I'll see y'all first thing in the mornin' at Sunday school."

I noticed Bettie threw me a surprised look, but she didn't interrupt Deeberry.

"A'ight, Charles. Well, if you'll excuse me, I'ma get back over here to my lovely company. Ms. Keshundra gon' be headin' down the highway to home in a minute too. Make sure you see her on in for me now, ya hear?" He halted his hand in front of him. "Oh, and ahh, Brother Charles, I told yo' wife that she and her sistah got the same kinda meek spirit. It just don't get no better than that. When sistah Bettie introduced her in church several weeks ago, I immediately saw the resemblance in them. You know the Lord sho' will bless ya wit' nice company to keep." He grinned as he strolled on back over to Keshundra.

*Nigga, please. You don't wanna be blessed wit' no good company. You just want some of that pussy. And the first time you saw her you didn't even notice her face. You probably didn't see nothin' but them big titties and ass. You ain't foolin' nobody*, I said in my head.

I'd noticed that Keshundra's attire was completely different than usual. She was actually dressed respectably, a fitted dress just above her knees and no cleavage or crack showing. I made my greeting to her. "Li'l sistah, you enjoy the program?" I interrupted her and Sharon as they shared in low-volume chatter.

"I surely did, big brotha." Keshundra nodded.

Sharon jumped in and offered her unsolicited experience, yet again. "I did too, but that lead singer for the Clanton Spirits know he need to chill out. He start cryin' and jumpin' around befo' he even sang the first word. From that point on, you can't understand nothin' he sayin'. What's up wit' that?" "Sho' do," Mrs. Sadie Mae agreed. "I thought I was the only one who couldn't undastand him. If I didn't hear his songs on the radio, I wouldn't know what he was sangin' 'bout."

"Look, now, y'all can talk about all o' that when we get to the IHOP. I'm hungry. Come on here, befo' I take a bite outta some o' ya," Ms. Hattie stated rather comically, opening the truck door to get in.

Momma, Sharon, and Mrs. Sadie Mae followed. Evidently, all of them rode to the program with Bettie.

"Goodnight, people," I said, walking toward my car with Bettie alongside me.

"Baby, why aren't you goin' with us to eat?" Bettie asked sadly.

"Ain't no particular reason. I'm just feelin' my bed a li'l bit mo' than I'm feelin' my empty stomach." I tried to play it off. "Now, I got a question for you," I said playfully.

"Okay."

"How did Deeberry end up wit' y'all, and what is he sniffin' behind yo' sistah for?"

"That's two questions." Bettie smiled.

"You gon' answer 'em, or do I have to guess?" I sounded teasingly.

"Maybe I will if I can get a big, sloppy kiss," she said.

"How 'bout a small, neat kiss now and a big, sloppy kiss later?" I grabbed her around the waist from the back to make it seem like I was more interested in her than in her answering my questions.

"Got ya'self a deal." She readily told me what I wanted to know. "After Bible study Wednesday night, Pastor told me that he was gon' invite Keesh to the program tonight, and he asked if it was okay with me. I told him I thought it was a fantastic idea, and that I thought Keesh would like it."

"So that's how he met her, the Sunday that me and the group went outta town to sang? She went to church wit'

# ReChella

you?" I recalled what Deeberry had said about being introduced to Keshundra several weeks ago at church.

"Yeah, that's the same weekend," Bettie answered.

"You didn't tell me she went to church wit' you, baby."

"It probably slipped my mind. At the time, it didn't seem like a big issue. You already know she go to service at Momma and Daddy's church sometimes, anyway."

I delayed my next question momentarily while squeezing Bettie tighter. "So, what you think?" I asked carefully.

"What I think about what?" she asked, sounding puzzled.

"You know he ain't her type, now, don't ya?" I came on out with my rather rash and selfish opinion.

"Yeah, I know. But what's the big deal?" Bettie humped up her shoulders. "Who knows? Maybe this'll be a nice, positive change of pace for her. She need somethin' to slow her down anyway, and maybe he's just the one to do that." Bettie seemed a little more serious now.

Though I was somewhat hesitant, I still went ahead and said the rest of what was on my mind. "But is she ready? I mean, you can't expect somebody like Keshundra to turn into a respected pastor's wife and Sunday school teacher overnight. That's stretchin' it, even for her great mind of pretending. Don't get me wrong, now. I'll be the first to admit that Deeberry is a li'l shady, but he still standin' in the shoes of a pastor. The relationship between him and Keshundra's just too mix-match." There, I'd said it all.

Bettie slowly removed my hands from around her waist and turned to face me. Even before she said a word, I could tell by the expression on her face that she was not pleased with my views on the matter.

"What's it to you, Charles?" She plopped her hands on her hips with attitude. "Don't get me wrong, I respect the fact that you think of her as a sistah, and you're concerned, but I know the real Keshundra inside and out. I'm her blood." Bettie tapped her chest with her fingertips. She looked like she was getting ready to put me in my place,

129

then a voice called out to her.

"Hey, BJ! I'm gone," Keshundra yelled from her car as she was pulling off.

"Okay, drive safely," Bettie exclaimed, watching her leave. No sooner than Keshundra drove off, Bettie turned her attention back to me. "I wanna know exactly what you meant when you said, 'can't expect somebody like Keshundra to turn into a respected—'"

"You takin' it all wrong, baby," I cut in, halting my hand up to silence her. "All I meant was—"

"I know what you meant," Bettie snapped, cutting my words off now. I must have really struck a nerve, because she rarely disagreed with me. And she sure as hell didn't raise her voice very much. She continued. "Who are you to judge my sistah? I mean, who am I or anyone to judge her, as a matter of fact? We've all done some things that I'm sure we don't care to remember."

"Now, hold on just a minute." I jumped back in with a very easing tone and attempted to fix up what I'd said for the sake of peace. But damn, she snapped me up again. I swear, I'd never seen her like that before. But then, I'd never trashed her sister to her face, either.

"No, you hold on. I listened to you, now you gon' listen to me," she insisted in a firm tone. "Deep down, Keshundra's a good person. She's a little misguided, 'cause she thinks she's got her whole plan for life figured out at twenty-four, but she'll learn as time go on. Keesh deserves somebody in her life to be patient with her and help her to be all she can be. Regardless of what you think, Charles, she ain't just another gold-diggin' ho that look good. She's got a heart too."

*Tell that to the fuckin' thousand dollars I gave her last week,* I said in my head.

"Look, baby, I'm sorry if I offended you, or if you thought I was down-talkin' yo' sistah. You right . . . I shouldn't have said all of that. I didn't mean to be insensitive, though." I stuttered my way to an apology. "You know as well as I do, Keshundra ain't 'shame of who she is or how she is. She don't mind admittin' it one bit. I was only sayin' what she done already said." I gave Bettie a deliberate, remorseful look. She bought it, hook, line, and sinker.

Her face softened and her words were much gentler. "Yeah, I know that, but I hope to change her way of thinkin'. And I also know some of the reason you trippin' out is 'cause you ain't all that crazy 'bout Pastor, either. You think he try to be a player on the sly, don't you?"

"Yeah, but, he done met his match now. The playa might get played this time." I chuckled, referring to Keshundra. "Go on and laugh. You know you want to."

Bettie narrowed her eyes and tightened her lips, trying not to laugh at my comment, but she spurted her giggle out anyway.

"Get outta here and go eat, so you can hurry on home," I told her playfully. "And by the way, why ain't li'l sistah goin' wit' her new boyfriend to eat?"

"She told me she needed to meet Derrick after the program. Said he'd been blowin' her cell up all night. Good thing she had it on vibrate, huh?" Bettie said, sounding much more merry now.

"Deeberry wasn't disappointed?" I widened my eyes.

"I'm sure he was, but you know Keesh probably made up somethin' convincin' to tell him," Bettie said, looking down at her watch. "I'll see you at home, baby. I don't wanna keep 'em waitin' no longer.

I reached out to hug her. "I love you," I whispered in her ear as we embraced.

"I love you too. And don't think I don't know the real reason you ain't goin' to eat with us. It's 'cause Pastor goin'. You can't fool me." She smiled as she began walking in the direction of the truck.

# Chapter Ten

To my surprise when I made it home, Keshundra's car was already parked in the driveway. I could hardly wait to fall up in the door and question her about dickless Deeberry. I almost broke my damn neck trying to get in the house. I didn't even take time to pull my jacket off. I trotted straight up the stairs.

The door to Keshundra's room was open, but the light was off. I stuck my head in and flipped on the switch. There was no one. I looked down the hall and noticed my office door open. The lights were off, but it seemed that a candle was burning on my desk. The second I stepped in the door, Keshundra and I captured eye contact from her seat on the sofa near the right wall. Though the room was quiet, I got a nice loud whiff of her same magical perfume from our last rendezvous.

"It's about time you got here," she said in a low, sexy tone. "I thought truck drivers knew how to handle the road."

"How long you been here?" I asked rather dryly.

"Long enough." Her sensual body pose caught my eyes.

"So, what's up?" I propped my arm against the door.

"Don't we have some unfinished business?" She searched me once over.

"Do we?" I threw a sharp, sour look back at her. She must have detected the friction.

"What's wrong wit' you?" Her forehead wrinkled.

"Ain't nothin' wrong wit' me. I just thought maybe you was gon' stay out wit' yo' new man tonight." I couldn't seem to shake my dry tone. Hell, who was I kidding? I didn't want to. I was still irritated about her seeing Deeberry the dog. Not that I had any grounds, but who gives a shit about being relationship correct?

"Who, Pastor?" She looked puzzled. "First of all, he ain't my man. And secondly, if he was, I know you ain't trippin'

132

'bout it. Why you so jealous of him anyway?"

"Who said I was jealous?" I snapped.

"It's plain as daylight. But let me ease yo' mind a little." She stood up and gradually moved toward me. "Pay attention, 'cause I ain't gon' say this but once. You know how I feel about idle talk. I coulda stayed out wit' him tonight . . . and fucked him if I had wanted to. But instead, I chose to lie to my sistah, ditch all of 'em, and make it back here in time enough to finish where you and me left off last week. Me and Pastor's business ain't got nothin' to do wit' me and yo' business. Besides, he may be handsome and all, but he talk a weak-ass game." She stopped directly in front of me. "I been fantasizin' 'bout gettin' some of this big, hard rod all week." She reached down and grasped my crotch, now speaking in a more sexy tone. "Now let me tell you how I want it, daddy."

Although I remained silent, I responded by embracing her and sliding my hands down her back to her beefy cheeks, grabbing handfuls of them. She whispered in my ear.

"I didn't think it could happen, but it's so big, I think I'm hooked. Damn, I guess I'ma have to pay you now, huh?" She began kissing at random under my neck and around my jaws, while continuing to rub over my crotch. She worked her way around and flipped her tongue in my mouth. We shared a passionate kiss. I had to admit, I did feel somewhat relieved after hearing Keshundra say that Pastor was no competition against me, and that she'd ditched that jack-legged bastard just to come home and fuck me. I tell ya, a brother's ego was about ten times its original size now. And to top it off, hearing her say that my shit was so good she might've had to start paying me, that meant I didn't have to keep giving her so much money. She wanted my heavy hardware just as much as I wanted her young tightness. Shiiiit, somebody should've told the young, call-himself-handsome Deeberry that experience, age, and big dicks rule over all else. Damn if Keshundra hadn't lifted things up for me after they'd been heading downhill for a minute. And thennn, I was about to get some of that good pussy.

"Ummm," I moaned, sucking on her tongue.

"Fuck me on the desk," she whispered as she licked around to my ear.

We began inching toward the desk, while kissing and feeling each other's bodies through our clothes. I lifted her up onto the desk, hoisted up her dress, and spread her thighs while standing between them. She quickly helped me unzip my pants, so I could let loose the hard dick that she'd so craved. She tightly wrapped her legs around my thighs and locked me in between. I stretched her across the desk and took hold of my solid erection with one hand, then rubbed the head of it over her vagina. Her panties remained intact, but as I pressed and rubbed over the crotch, they became wet from our butter-like secretions.

She palmed my ass with both hands, then pulled me up close to her repeatedly, urging to get me inside.

"Ummm." I couldn't wait to penetrate her tight pussy.

"Come on, I want it in." She moved one hand down and held the crotch of her panties to one side, exposing her big pussy lips. I then stuffed her and began thrusting back and forth. We eyed each other with faces of steaming madness. My bottom lip wagged, leaving my mouth cracked open just a tad as I increased the stroking. If I hadn't known better, I would've sworn that her pussy was even hotter than the first time we did it. She may have been laying up on that hard-ass desk, but she was gracefully taking every rugged inch of me pumping in her.

"Oooh, yeah, that's it. It's so big . . . I been waitin' on this," she uttered as her eyes dazzled in luscious lust.

I may not have been talking as much as her, but that shit was so good I soon drifted off into my own little world. I was giving it to her just like she'd asked for it. The more we went at it, the more I felt myself losing control. I thrust and rolled almost into a violent rage. But the weird-ass part is what came next. I was peering into the tiny candle flame that sat on the desk to the left of us when all of these conflicting thoughts started flickering in my head. I felt so confused and mixed up, I could hardly remember who I was fucking. My body began trembling as I felt an orgasm creeping on.

"Ahhh, ahhh," I suddenly exclaimed. "Come on, sistah-in-law. Let me hear you say it," I demanded, gripping tight to the sides of Keshundra's hips and continually pumping.

"It's good. Keep it comin'," Keshundra shrieked, keeping up with the flow.

"Umph, ummm. Say it, baby. Please, say it like you always say it," I begged her. I peered into her eyes and continuously ordered her to say it, say it. She stared back at me, looking real confused, like she was wondering what in the hell I kept begging her to say. Even though she wasn't saying what I wanted to hear, I still didn't let up. "Please, sistah-in-law, say it. It's comin', it's comin'."

"I'm cummin' too," she panted and rolled with force.

Just as we arrived at our extreme finish, I really lost it momentarily. "Ohhh, ohhh, Katie. Say it, Katie. Say—"

"What you say?" Keshundra demanded, cutting my words off, then rendered a sudden push to my chest. "Katie? I know fuckin' well you didn't call me no Katie!" Keshundra exploded and hurried off the desk, pulling her dress down.

It wasn't until that very moment I snapped out of my confused state and realized what I'd done. I was too stunned to say anything right away, but Keshundra was angrier than a pit bull that somebody had fed hot sauce.

"You lowdown, black, no-good, cheatin' son-of-a-bitch. You been fuckin' yo' dead brotha's wife?" Keshundra looked appalled. "I knew I shouldn't have got mixed up wit' yo' low-life ass."

I finally opened my mouth to speak after I'd pulled up my pants and fastened them. "Keshundra, listen . . ."

"Keshundra, nothin'. Don't be callin' my damn name," she barked. "You know that shit fucked up. Yo' brotha' just died. How long you been screwin' his wife, anyway?" Keshundra slapped her hands on her hips, waiting for my answer. "Forget it. You probably been doin' it since the day after their wedding. I don't believe this shit." She was furious. She glared at me while shaking her head from side to side.

"Kehundra, you so full of shit it's hard to believe," I exclaimed.

"Me?" She slapped one hand on her chest.

"That's right, you," I stated unapologetically. "You the one person I thought would always keep it real."

"What's that supposed to mean?" She somewhat lowered her tone now.

"Say if I was messin' wit' Katie . . . I'm not, but say if I was." I pointed my finger around. "Well, what's the difference in me foolin' around wit' my brother's wife and you foolin' around wit' yo' sistah's husband?" I asked with no sensitivity whatsoever.

Keshundra cocked her eyes up in anger, refusing to answer. She had to know that was a legitimate-ass question.

"Forget you, Charles." She rolled her eyes and crossed her arms.

"Nawwww, now. Let's just be real. What's the difference?" I asked again. She puffed out a big sigh, but made no comment. I continued. "A'ight, I'll answer for ya. Ain't no difference. Gregg was my blood, and Bettie yours."

"Whatever. I'm through wit' yo' black ass." Keshundra motioned to walk out.

"Yeah, whatever." I mimicked her. "How you gon' have two sets of rules? You ain't trippin' off me betrayin' my brother no way. Like you told me 'bout Deeberry and me bein' jealous . . . you jealous too, 'cause you think Katie been wit' me."

"That's a damn lie," Keshundra snapped, turning back around. "I ain't jealous of no female. Katie and nobody else can't mess up the flow on my rockin' chair, nigga. I just see the bigger picture. If you been screwin' Katie, now I'm added to the list, and ain't no tellin' how many mo' females you got stashed away. Whewww, you messin' over my sistah big time. And what's even sadder is she bein' faithful to you." Keshundra dropped her head, shaking it from side to side.

I didn't believe my eyes, but I could have sworn she was getting ready to cry.

"So, I'm a sick person. Is that what you gon' tell me? You do this kinda'shit for a livin', Keshundra," I reminded her before she started some sniveling shit.

"Nooo, I ain't gon' tell ya shit, 'cause whatever it is, evidently you think you already know," she snarled.

I tried to hurry up and change the subject, 'cause I swear I just didn't feel like listening to another female dwelling on some more sorrowful guilt trip shit. Two in one night? Hell no. I was already fuming mad at myself for losing control long enough to let Katie's name slip out of my mouth.

"Keshundra, we can talk all night, but you still didn't answer my question. What's the difference in what I did and what you did?" I asked bluntly.

She shot her middle finger up at me and stormed out of the room without saying another word. I beat my head against the wall for quite some time, trying to figure out how in the hell I could've made a mistake like that. I remembered one time joking with a friend of mine about it happening to him, but in all my days, I'd never fucked up and forgot who I was fucking. As bad as I hated to admit it, Katie had left me distraught. Only thing left to do was hit the sack and hope for a better tomorrow.


### Bettie

Running late for church was never my thing, and that was exactly what Charles and I ended up doing the Sunday morning after the gospel program. I didn't know if the alarm clock failed to go off, or if I'd just forgotten to set it when I made it home from IHOP. How-be-it-ever, he and I rushed through our room getting dressed, leaving stuff all over the place. We still managed to arrive at Sunday school only five minutes after starting time. Immediately after Sunday school was over, Sunday service began at 11:00 A.M. and was over by 1:00 P.M.

Still hurrying, he and I went straight home after worship to began preparations for the cook-out that we'd been planning for the group for quite some time. We changed into jeans and T-shirts. Charles went ahead and fired up the grill in the backyard and loaded the first pan of ribs on. I stayed in the kitchen making baked beans, spaghetti, coleslaw, tossed salad, and wrapping corn on the cob in foil sheets for the grill.

Keshundra had gone to Sunday service at our parents' church and hadn't made it home yet. I couldn't wait to talk to her and hear her version of the evening with Pastor. He'd already told me at IHOP how much he enjoyed her company and was really disappointed that she wasn't able to join us there to eat. It would've been nice if he'd been able to make it to the cook-out.

After I finally got all of the food to cooking, I went ahead and started straightening up my bedroom. What a mess it was. Clothes from the previous night, mixed with the church clothes that we'd recently changed out of, were just as we'd left them. I began separating everything into two piles; one pile for the cleaners, and one pile for the household laundry. As I fumbled through the clothes, a strangely familiar scent caught my attention. The more I shuffled, the stronger the fumes became, but I couldn't seem to remember where I'd smelled the distinct vapors before. I picked up piece after piece, but couldn't find the primary piece holding the fumes. Then I sniffed Charles' shirt from the night before and it seemed to be the piece that I was searching for. I sniffed it again just to make sure. *What is that? I know that smell,* I said to myself. I put it down then picked up his pants that he'd worn with the shirt and sniffed them. They held the same fumes.

"What in the world?" I murmured low. Even though the scent wasn't like anything I'd ever owned, I really felt like I had somehow been in contact with it before, so I rummaged my brain, trying to recall where I'd already been familiarized with it. No doubt, whoever the female was that the sweet-smelling fragrance belonged to had to have been hugging him mighty tight for it to still reek in his clothes the next day. In fact, she just about had to have been all over him. No quick, friendly hug would've left a trail like that behind.

*Maybe somebody wasted somethin' on him . . . That's it, a spill,* I told myself. I entertained several notions before I finally gave up. One thing I refused to do again was jump to a lot of crazy, paranoid conclusions and get all wound up only to find out later how off-base I was. After I re-piled the two stacks of clothes, I went ahead and straightened the bathroom up. The clumsy in me must have been on duty, because I accidentally broke a bottle of my favorite body spray from Ralph Lauren. Knocked it right off the rim of the Jacuzzi as I gathered some towels to go in the hamper. "Crap," I uttered in complaint. "A half a bottle, too."

The moment I finished cleaning up the spill, a thought hit me, and I stopped cold in my tracks. *Perfume, perfume,* I repeated in my head. "That's it. I knew I'd smelled it . . ."

Suddenly, a very sickening feeling came over me. By now, I was already ruffling back through the clothes that were piled for the cleaners. After inhaling several sniffs of Charles' same shirt and slacks from before, I was stricken motionless for a few seconds. I then composed myself and darted upstairs to Keshundra's room, and sniffed from each one of her perfume bottles that sat on the dresser. Nothing on the dresser was similar to the distinct scent.

*Damn, I could've sworn I smelled that same scent comin' outta here a few nights ago,* I told myself. I went through several of her drawers and still didn't find anything. When I came to the drawer that contained her lingerie, I noticed a cute little bottle of perfume called Slave. The second I removed the top and smelled it, I knew.

"This is it," I mumbled. My heart sank to the pit of my stomach and my eyes filled with tears, but I wasn't sure why. "Why would Keesh's perfume be trapped in Charles' clothes? I didn't see them make any physical contact last night. It doesn't make any sense," I whispered as my heart pounded with uneasiness.

So many unanswered questions and thoughts sped through my mind. I couldn't help but imagine the worst, because everything that I remembered connected Charles and Keshundra. Just when I thought things were bad enough, I remembered Charles' sudden interest in oral sex. And to put the icing on the cake, I recalled Keshundra's so-called no-eat-no-fuck policy. For several years, Keshundra had bragged to me about how oral sex was her initiation for a man, and if for some reason the man wasn't into it, then she wouldn't let him have sex with her. I knew she meant every word of it, so that one factor alone told me where Charles had learned his new trick. No, I didn't have any ironclad proof, but just thinking of the possibility that my beloved husband had at some point put his tongue between my sister's legs was bad enough. I swear, I was about to be sick right there.

*That's why he didn't want to discuss it with me afterward. And that's why he was so critical about Pastor and Keshundra gettin' together,* I reminded myself silently. All of the telltale signs were staring me in the face, and sadly, I didn't miss any of them.

"BJ, you up here?" Keshundra called out, interrupting my thoughts.

I quickly put the perfume back in the drawer and shut it, then dabbed the tears from my eyes. Damn, I was busted. I had to think fast and act natural.

"I'm in here, Keesh," I hollered back to her. "I'm in your room."

She strolled into the room and threw her purse on the bed. "What you doin' in here nosyin' around?" she snapped, eyeing me with attitude as I stood in front of the dresser, pretending to look through her perfumes.

I kept my cool and acted as if being in there wasn't a big deal. "Hey, girl, I guess I don't have to steal it now." I looked at her and smiled, which was not easy considering the circumstances.

"Steal what?" She dropped down on the bed as if she was tired.

"Some of your perfume," I said playfully. "Girrrrrl, I was about to snatch me a bottle for tonight. I dropped mine on the marble floor in my bathroom and it shattered everywhere. But, now I guess I can get permission since you caught me."

"Where you goin' tonight? She frowned, looking puzzled.

"Nowhere. After the cookout, me and Charles got a little business to take care of, if ya know what I mean." I shot a bubbly wink at her.

"Yeah, right. Y'all old folks need to sit down somewhere." She smirked. I could tell she was buying my reason for being in her room.

"So, which one can I take?" I pretended to smell each of them.

"I don't care, BJ. Take whichever one you want. And while you up here tryin' to steal somethin', you better go check on them pots. I thought I smelled somethin' burnin'," she said nonchalantly, laying back on the bed. I grabbed a bottle and took off downstairs to check on the food.

The hours rapidly rolled by, and before long, people were piling in for a pleasant evening of eating, drinking, and fun. The group members were right on time. Most of Charles' family, and a few members from my side showed up. Also, a few close friends and associates stopped by. Everything was laid out beautifully, and everybody seemed to be enjoying themselves. Some played volleyball in the big backyard, while others tried their hand at Spade. I deliberately kept myself busy trying to laugh and talk with everybody, so my mind wouldn't keep drifting back to the disturbing information that I'd stumbled onto. My happy face was painted on the outside, but I was in shambles on the inside.

# Chapter Eleven

*Charles*

Who says a man can't forget about his problems when he's having a good time? My disastrous Saturday night was the last thing on my mind during the cook-out. I was kicking it down-south style with the fellas and my brothers. I wasn't about to let an evening of fun be spoiled over no crazy females and their issues. So, I pushed that shit on the back burner for the time being. I could always work on a solution later. The boys and I had a card game going that was all the way live. We'd set the table and chairs under the shade tree where the breeze was plentiful.

"Who winnin', y'all?" I asked, returning from a short bathroom break in the house.

"It sho' ain't our dreary opponents." Bo laughed out loud, giving AJ a high five over the table. Bo and AJ were partners, partners who rarely got beat in Spades, if ever. "Hey man, you and Stan stick to singin', ya hear," Bo said, still laughing and teasing their opponents, Henry and Stan.

"Look, it's time for somebody to get y'all up outta them seats," I stated to Bo.

"Yeaaah, man, I wanna get up, 'cause I want somethin' else to eat. But, ahhh, who good enough to beat us and make us get up?" Bo bellowed out another laugh. I knew he was right, and so did everybody else, so all we could do was laugh along with him.

"Me and Preston next, so y'all might as well get ready to give up the seats," I declared, trying to sound confident.

"Big brotha, if my memory serves me correctly, me and AJ done already put you and William away, annnd you and Joe got slaughtered right before that. Maaaan, when you and Preston bite the dust, y'all won't have no mo' group members left to beat." Bo chuckled.

"A'ight, keep makin' fun. You gon' be cryin' when we end ya lucky streak. You gon' have to swallow all o' this hot air you been lettin' out, " I replied, smiling.

Preston laughed and threw me a five in agreement. Even though AJ and Bo had always been the card champions in our family, me and my other brothers longed to beat them just to wipe that silly smirk off of Bo's face if only for one time. AJ didn't brag as much as Bo. He just subtly cheered him on while throwing out a word or two here and there.

Unfortunately, after our turn, Preston and I got up from our seats not nearly as happy as when we'd first sat down. We failed miserably, leaving Bo and AJ still the reigning champions. Up next were Wayne and Kenny.

"Somebody call in the Army, National Guard, and Air force!" Bo yelled, standing up, shaking his fists in the air, champion style.

"Sit down, shut up, and take yo' beatin like a man, li'l brotha," Wayne said, interrupting Bo's triumphant speech. Now, Wayne may have lost just as much as the rest of us, but he never ran low on bragging. "It takes a Jennings to beat a Jennings. Come on, Kenny, let's lay these boys to rest nicely." Wayne rubbed his hands together as he took a seat at the table.

I shot Wayne a disagreeing look. "What I s'pose to be, a stepchild?" I asked.

"Naw, my brotha," Wayne said, looking up at me, smiling deviously. "You a Jennings, no doubt. But you didn't have the whole package when you was playin'. See, you and the group need to stick to what y'all good at. In fact, sing me and Kenny a song or somethin' while we winnin'." Wayne howled.

Nearly everybody in the yard heard his comment and fell into laughter. I noticed Momma laughing and shaking her head too.

"Man, forget you," Stan said, still laughing and rubbing one hand across his low haircut.

At first dark, I turned the outside lights on and we kept the game going into the night. It wasn't until 8:30 or 9:00 when everybody started leaving. I had sparingly mentioned my unfortunate slip-up with Keshundra to Will before he left, and he was somewhat concerned. We got together and talked about it in my office after everybody else was gone.

"So, man, you think she gon' run her mouth?" Will asked, sitting on the opposite end of the sofa from me.

"Why would she? Hell, she got just as much to lose as I do. Bettie her sistah," I replied.

Will looked to be in thought for a minute. "Yeah, you right. She got to be smarter than that." He sighed. "All I know is this is one of them situations that need to get unfucked real quick."

I'd taken the time to tell Will all about the incident with Keshundra, but I conveniently left out most of the details concerning what happened with Katie and me. There was no need in going down the same dead end road twice. His views on the, seeing-dead-folks issue was probably still the same anyway.

"Ain't that the truth. Who'd think a—"

*Knock. Knock.*

"Excuse me, man," I told him. "Come in."

Bettie opened the door and stuck her head in. "Sorry for interruptin' y'all, but Charles, I just got a call from Marilyn on my cell. Somethin's goin' on wit' her, and she didn't wanna talk about it on the phone, so I told her I'd drive over there and sit wit' her a while," Bettie said. Marilyn was one of Bettie's good friends.

"Okay, baby, that's fine. Drive safely," I uttered.

"All right. See ya, Will." Bettie said as she closed the door.

"Goodnight," William responded, then turned back to me. "Look, man, all I got to say is when you can't handle that hot, sexy Keshundra no mo', please let a brotha know." He stood up smiling. "I gots to roll on out. I'm tired as hell."

I stood up with him. "Aw, now, you know I can handle it. I just got to get her straightened out." Will and I did the brotherly handshake, then Will opened the door to leave.

After I saw him out, I scurried back upstairs and knocked at Keshundra's door.

"Come in," she hollered.

I opened the door and closed it behind me. "Hey." I stood still, gazing at her.

"Can I help you?" she asked with attitude, peering up at me while she lay across the bed with her cell phone to her ear.

"Is it all right if I talk to you for a minute?" I asked humbly. She gave me a slight eye-roll as she sat up.

"Let me call you back," she said to whoever she was talking to on the phone. "What you want?" She laid the phone down on the nightstand.

"You still mad? Look like you been avoiding me all day." I chose my words very cautiously.

She sighed, sounding annoyed. "I wasn't mad to start wit'. A li'l disappointed, but not mad. Anyway, I ain't trippin' off that crap no mo'. You ain't my husband. I ain't got to deal wit' ya."

I eased out a short breath of relief. "So, do that mean our li'l arrangement over and done wit'?" I asked humbly.

"Humph." She hastily eyed me from head to toe. "You got some money, you can get some pussy," she said bluntly.

I shook my head in disappointment. "So, it's like that, huh? I got to pay now?"

"Damn right, you do," she snapped. "You the one who fucked up. I ain't gon' lie . . . yo' dick the shit. That joint had my legs tightening together and cravin' for it all last week. So, yeah, I was probably gon' break my rule once or twice and do a few fucks for fun, but that shit is over now. No freebies."

Naturally, I was a little disappointed about the money, but it wasn't the end of the world. Hearing her say what she said gave me the green light to go at her once again. I didn't say another word. I simply walked over to the side of the bed, dropped to my knees in front of her and took hold of her thighs. She didn't resist at all. I then pulled her to the edge of the bed. She wore a short blue skirt and a blue flowered blouse. I pulled her skirt up to her waist and laid her back on the bed, then pulled her red thong on one side of her pussy lips and began licking inside her. She rubbed over my head with both hands as I ate her sweet pussy.

"Ohhhh, that's it. I taught you well," she bragged softly as she started to roll for it. Just as we began to get into it, the door swung open.

"Noooooooooooo! What you doin'? Noooooooo!" Bettie charged into the room, screaming and yelling, with tears gushing from her eyes.

I instantly jumped up. "Baby!" I yelled in shock.

Keshundra sprang to her feet, scrambling to pull down her skirt. "BJ, I'm sorry! I'm so sorry!" Keshundra shrieked as she began to cry.

"Shut up, bitch! After everything I've done for you, how could you do this to me? I'ma kill you!" Bettie dashed toward Keshundra, grabbed her and started beating on her with her fists and kicking her.

Keshundra didn't try to fight back. She just threw her arms over her head and face to shield herself from Bettie's licks.

"Please, BJ!"

Bettie's eyes were blood-shot red from anger and crying. She was way out of control. "Bitch, I hate you! You stankin' slut. I'ma kill you," Bettie continued screaming, throwing lick after lick.

"BJ, stop! You hurtin' me. Stop! I'm sorry," Keshundra begged over and over again, tears steadily falling.

I grabbed a hold of Bettie from the back to get her off of Keshundra. As soon as Bettie felt my hands touch her, she freaked out even more.

"Get yo' hands off me, you sick bastard! Stop it! Stop it! Why you protecting her? I'm your wife!" she shrieked, fighting and clawing to get my hands off her. "I ain't protecting her. I'm tryin' to calm you down befo' you do somethin' you might regret," I stated, trying to control her.

"Why ain't you grabbin' on her? Get yo' fuckin' hands off me!" Bettie ceased fire on Keshundra and began hitting me like a wild woman. "How could you do this to me?" Bettie's cries sounded like she was in pure agony.

# ReChella

I struggled and scuffled to keep her restrained. It wasn't easy with her going crazy hitting me, but at least she was off of Keshundra now. For a minute, I thought she was really going to do something that we would've all regretted.

"I told you, baby, I'm sorry!" I barked. "What else you want me to do?"

"Die, you filthy pig! Both of y'all just die!" Bettie screamed, finally breaking loose from the firm hold of my grip. She slowly backed away from me and Keshundra until she reached the door. As she stood in the doorway, still pouring out tears, she quietly swept her eyes from me to Keshundra. If her look had been lethal, Keshundra and I would've died instantly. Keshundra had crammed herself between the nightstand and the head of the bed and was as quiet as her muffled crying allowed her to be. I felt real bad watching Bettie as she stood in the doorway, sobbing up a storm.

*How the fuck am I gon' get out of this?* I thought. "Baby, please," I said calmly.

She held both hands to her temples as if she had a terrible headache. "Don't baby me," she uttered in a much lower tone now. It wasn't what I wanted to hear, but at least she wasn't yelling anymore. "This ain't nothin' but a nightmare. How can you call me baby? Huh? How? I just walked in and caught you wit' yo' head between my sistah's legs." Bettie's frowns were so deep they almost looked to be permanent.

I didn't know what in the hell to say. What could I say? I was busted. But I had to try, so I just threw some shit out and hoped for the best.

"Let me explain, ba—I mean . . . let me explain. If you would stop talkin' a minute and hear what I got to say," I said peacefully, trying not to fuck up and set her off by saying baby again.

"What can you possibly say to explain this, huh, Charles?" She went from wriggling her hands together to folding her arms and rubbing up and down them like a crack-head craving crack. Her agitation was abundantly

147

clear. I didn't know what she was going to do next.

I took one step toward her and raised my hand in front of me as a sign of defeat. "Look, let's go downstairs to our bedroom and talk, just you and me. Believe me, I know how wrong this is, and I'm going to be honest with you," I suggested, looking as sorrowful as I could.

She stared at me like she couldn't believe what I'd just said. "Just you and me? Are you crazy? Nigga, you was fuckin' my sistah, and now you want just you and me to talk like she ain't got nothin' to do wit' it? Oh, I see, you wanna get me alone so you can try to feed me a bunch of damn lies. Well, you know what? It ain't gon' happen. 'Cause I want the truth, and ain't nobody leavin' this room 'til I get it," she insisted.

"Bettie, don't do this, please," I continued begging.

"Shut up, Charles. I wanna know how long this shit been goin' on," she snapped, but still didn't raise her voice nearly as high as in the beginning. She looked over at Keshundra still weeping on the low-low, stuffed in her spot between the nightstand and bed. "Bitch, you hear me. How long?" Bettie demanded.

Keshundra looked like she was in a horror movie and the monsters were closing in to eat her ass up. She was scared to death. "BJ, I swear this just the second time," Keshundra answered, her voice trembling. "I didn't mean to hurt you."

"Well, it's a little late for that now, isn't it?" Bettie gave her a sour look. "Boy, boy, if Momma and Daddy could see you now. I knew deep down in my heart that you wasn't nothin' but a ho, but I still tried to help you and give you the benefit of the doubt. At least I know now why my concerned husband was all worried about you and Pastor last night. He didn't want Pastor in the picture 'cause he was already fuckin' ya." Bettie humped up in her shoulders then threw me the same sour look. "Two sistahs under the same roof. What did you do, fuck one upstairs one night, and the other one downstairs the next night?"

"Why you doin' this?" I frowned.

"Why am I doin' this?" She mocked me. "Why am I doin' this? Well, I think you need to be askin' you and yo' little ho that question. In fact, I'ma give both of y'all about eight minutes to come clean and fill in the gaps." The firmness in Bettie's voice left no doubt in my mind that she wasn't bullshitting, but I still challenged her demand.

"What you wanna know, details? This is crazy. I mean, what good is it really gon' do?" I waved my hands in the air and motioned to leave the room. "If you wanna talk to me, I'll be downstairs."

She really got ugly then. "You sick son-of-a-bitch. I'll call yo' momma, yo' group members, and every last one of yo' brothers and relatives and tell them what kind of bastard you really are if you fuckin' push me." She squinted her eyes and slowly twisted her head as she threatened me. "I'll even make a public speech in the center of town and ruin your so-called upstanding reputation if I have to. Move one single muscle and you're over."

I backed my black ass up real quick, 'cause her eyes told me that she meant every damn word. Bottom line, she held all of the cards, and I didn't feel like being the next town scandal, so I had to play ball according to her rules.

"A'ight, you got the loaded gun. Fire away," I reluctantly uttered. Bad choice of words, though. Everything about her said she want to shoot a brother.

"I'll ask again. When did this shit first start? And I want the truth this time." She talked through tightened lips.

I held fast to my angry expression, but Keshundra looked like she just wanted to fall out and die. Neither of us answered right away.

Bettie waited quietly for only a few seconds. "Well?" she reasserted.

"BJ, it started last Sunday night. That was the first time," Keshundra stuttered slowly.

"Last Sunday night?" Bettie pondered a second or two. "That was the night I was at Katie's, sittin' wit' her." Bettie developed a flustered look.

"BJ, I'm sorry," Keshundra repeated for the damn

hundredth time.

"Shut up wit' the apologies and keep talkin'," Bettie urged.

"Last night when me and him got together, I realized how—"

"Wait, wait, hold up." Bettie halted one hand in the air and interrupted Keshundra. "Last night? Y'all got together last night? So you lied about meetin' Derrick, ditched Pastor—well, ditched all of us, and came back here to screw him? Is that what you sayin'?" Bettie asked, looking like she was getting sicker by the minute.

I honestly couldn't believe my ears. That crazy-ass Keshundra was sitting up there volunteering information that Bettie didn't know and didn't even have to know. Nobody could've made me believe that Keshundra was that damn ignorant. In the end, it's always the ones with the most mouth that don't have their shit together, though. Her in-control mentality was obviously just an act. I could've stapled her lips together, but she kept talking.

"But see . . . it was last night when I realized—"

"Realized what?" Bettie cut her ass off again. "Let me tell you somethin', little sistah. Whatever you think you realized last night, it didn't help you, because here you are, yet again. And this time you got caught. If you gon' try to shift the blame over on one person, you wastin' yo' time. I know that this was both of y'alls doin'." Bettie turned her nose up at Keshundra. "Let me guess what you keep tryin' to say, though. Last night you realized that he was just usin' you and that he'd use anybody to get what he want. That is what you were gon' say, right?" Bettie's bitter sarcasm smacked Keshundra right in the face.

Keshundra quietly turned her eyes down at the floor, looking like she knew she didn't have any choice but to accept that the situation was hopeless. Personally, I was glad she shut the fuck up before she did any more unnecessary damage, like bring up that I gave her ass a thousand dollars.

Bettie finally heaved a deep sigh. "Y'all wanna know

what I think? I think the hell wit' both of ya. I'm outta here." She turned to walk out of the door, then briefly paused. "But before I go, I just gotta tell ya how stupid both of you are. First of all, y'all left a trail a mile long. After I picked up the clues and pieced it all together this mornin', I figured the first chance y'all got at being alone, you'd try somethin'. Too bad I was right. Bitch, you got thirty minutes to pack yo' shit and get the fuck out of here. Not only are we no longer sisters, I never wanna see your ass again." Bettie sounded cold and heartless, and not to mention she was cussing up a damn storm. At that very moment, she made John Gotti look like John Candy.

Kehundra seemed really hurt by Bettie's harsh words and tried once more to reach out to her. "BJ, pleeease forgive me. Pleeease. I'm so sorry." Keshundra wailed and wallowed, pleaded and begged, but Bettie walked out of the room as if she didn't even hear her.

I was right on Bettie's heels when she hurried down the stairs and went into our bedroom.

"Baby, please, tell me you ain't leavin'," I begged.

"I ain't leavin'," she said very direct as she walked into our bathroom and began washing her face.

I was surprised at her answer. "You ain't?" I drew a perplexed look.

She never looked up from the sink as she rubbed handfuls of water over her face from the running faucet. "No. I'm not goin' anywhere," she stated real cool, "but it's gonna cost ya,"

"Cost me?" I frowned, still puzzled.

"You heard me. I don't stutter when I talk." Her voice firmed up as she turned to me while dabbing her face with a towel. "You fucked me over big-time when we first got married wit' that damn pre-nup. But you know what? It didn't matter to me that you wanted me to sign it, because I loved you just that much. I thought you were different from the rest of these no-good men. Oh, I knew you weren't perfect, but hey, who is? Now, the only difference I see in you and the trash on the streets is that you're a lot worse. I broke all of my rules for you, Charles. Every single one of 'em." She paused and peered at me hatefully. "If you want me to stay here and keep pretending to be the happy little wife and keep my mouth shut, then you got to pay."

"What you talkin' 'bout?" I asked nervously.

"Nigga, you ain't deaf. If you want my mouth to stay closed, you got to pull up some cold cash," she repeated.

"You gon' blackmail me?" I stared at her suspiciously.

"For starters, I want ten thousand dollars deposited into my own personal account, and I want that damn prenup done away with," she stated firmly, and from what I could tell, with no remorse.

"And if I don't?" I gave her an insulted look.

"Then you don't." Her nonchalant expression told me that she didn't give a damn about what happened to me, and she would definitely scream to the high heavens. I rested one hand behind my head, pondering and absorbing it all. Again, she was still holding all of the cards. My options were few.

"I'll call my attorney tomorrow," I stated at once.

"Good. Now, if you don't mind, please let the window all the way down behind you and lock it. I thought I closed it after I climbed in, but I guess I was too busy concentratin' on gettin' upstairs," she said with attitude.

"You crawled through the window?" I asked, turning to look at the partially open window.

"Humph, that ain't all, player," she said with superiority. "Not only did I unlock the window so I could climb back in; I never even left."

I didn't want to piss her off, but I could have sworn her car was gone from the driveway when I saw Will out, so I carefully mentioned it. "You never left the house?" I asked. "When Will left, the car wasn't in the driveway."

"No, it wasn't. I parked it down the street behind those trees at that dead end curve, then walked back to the house, damn fool." She smirked and walked out of the bathroom.

I saw her glance at the clock on the nightstand.

# ReChella

According to the thirty minutes that she'd given Keshundra to vacate the premises, there was only fifteen left. Bettie sat down on the side of the bed, rested her elbows in her lap and hid her face in the palms of her hands. I sat down opposite her.

"I didn't mean to hurt you," I softly muttered, but didn't dare touch her.

She raised her head, dabbing her teary eyes with a napkin. "So, how much did you give her the first time?"

"Baaaby, what?" I asked, trying to sound completely stumped.

"Please, Charles," she said softly, sounding to be at her rope's end. "Don't try to make up a lie. I know Keshundra wouldn't have slept with you the first time without gettin' somethin' in return . . . along with the oral sex, that is. So, for a change, just tell the truth. Otherwise, I'll just go ask her while she's in the guilty confession stage."

"A thousand dollars," I stated pitifully.

"It was that important for you to fuck her? She was worth that much?" A dull weariness seemed to be about Bettie as she questioned me.

"It wasn't important, it was . . . I was just stupid. I can't really explain it, but I need for you to forgive me so we can get past this. I love you." I know I sounded desperate and pathetic.

"Plenty of words are circling 'round in my head right now, but *forgive* ain't one of 'em," Bettie admitted.

The house alarm beeped, indicating that one of the doors was being opened. Bettie got up and walked into the kitchen. I followed only to the den in peeping distance, but if either of them had said anything, believe me, I was going to hear. Keshundra carried her suitcases out one by one and put them in her car. As she walked out with the last one, Bettie walked behind her, I assumed to lock the door.

"I hope you took everything, 'cause you'll never get back on the inside of this door again as long as I'm here," Bettie said, crossing her arms.

"I did," Keshundra replied pitifully. "BJ, can I speak to

153

you for just five minutes out in the garage?"

"I don't have anything else to say to you. I wish you'd just go."

"BJ, please? Five minutes is all I ask," Keshundra pleaded.

"Five minutes, that's it," Bettie said reluctantly. She closed the kitchen door behind them when they went out. I attempted a couple of times to plant my ear near the door and eavesdrop, but it would've looked real bad if I had gotten caught, so I let it go. I was curious as hell to know what Keshundra wanted to say outside that she couldn't have said standing right there. After about six or seven minutes, Bettie came into the bedroom and informed me that I wouldn't be sleeping in our room with her. So, I trotted on upstairs to the bedroom next to my office, and that's where I slept for the next two weeks.

# Chapter Twelve

*Bettie*

At least that lying, cheating, bastard husband of mine had come through with the ten thousand dollars that I'd extorted from him. Damn, had things really gotten that bad for me? Extortion? I'm afraid they had. The lowdown shit that Charles and Keshundra had done to me was almost unbearable. Even after the two weeks that had gone by since the night I'd caught them, the hurt was still just as strong. I hadn't really decided how I was going to deal with the two swindlers just yet, but I knew I was going to stop beating myself up over something they'd done. Yeah, I kicked myself time and time again for opening my heart back up and trusting another no-good nigga, then I kicked myself some more for ignoring my gut feeling and trusting a whore in the same house with my no-good husband. True enough, I'd done a lot of messed up stuff in my day, and with a lot of men. That I didn't deny. But never would I have fucked my sister's husband right in their house—not in any house, for that matter.

Anyhow, there was no need in crying over spilled milk. After much more contemplating, I just couldn't take it anymore. I realized that I couldn't stand the sight of Charles, nor could I stand being in that house anymore. Oh, sure, he'd been working his ass off trying to impress me and work his way back into my good graces by hanging on to my every whim, and so far, nobody other than Keshundra, he and I knew the gory details of what happened on that horrific night. That is, unless one of them had told. To the outside world, things appeared as they always had with him and me, but I was becoming more restless with the passing of each day. I had to make a move.

One Friday evening right at dark, Charles came home from work claiming to have a terrible headache. He said his head was pounding so bad, he couldn't even make it upstairs to the bed that he'd been sleeping in. He plopped down on the sofa in the den. Perfect timing for me, 'cause that just so happened to have been the day that I knew exactly what I was going to do about my sad situation. And it wasn't pretty.

"Oh, I almost forgot to tell you, Charles, Katie and the boys came back home today," I said, standing behind the sofa, looking down at him. "I visited with her for several hours, and boy, did she have a lot to talk about." I exaggerated on purpose.

Charles opened his eyes, but didn't move. "Aw, yeah? How they doin'?" he asked.

"They're all fine. The getaway seemed to do 'em good." I made general talk in a cool manner as if I didn't have a hidden agenda for bringing up the subject concerning Katie.

"That's nice," he said, closing his eyes again. I made it my business to observe his every reaction, and he seemed to be trying to act like me mentioning Katie didn't matter.

I raised the stakes a little more with my next statement. "Funny thing . . . she told me a lot of weird stuff too. And on top of it, gave me some very disturbing news while I was there. I been tryin' to understand how somethin' like what she said can happen, but I just can't seem to come to grips with it," I exaggerated more. "Oh, well."

Charles reopened his eyes and frowned, but didn't comment immediately. He seemed to be contemplating on what to say.

"Wha—"

"Oh yeah," I cut him off on purpose before he even got a whole word out. "I almost forgot to ask you, has your attorney finished with the contract yet?" I deliberately switched subjects to see how fast he would go back to what I'd implied about Katie. He just didn't know I was playing him like a new tune.

"Naw, I'll call and check on it tomorrow," he stated quickly. "What did Katie tell you that was so disturbin'?" He now sat up on the sofa and turned to look at me.

I couldn't do nothing but shake my head in disgust.

# ReChella

Just as I'd suspected, he redirected the conversation right back to the subject of Katie. I went ahead and obliged him for my own curious benefit. He was clearly worried about whatever he thought I knew concerning Katie.

"She told me that I should pack my things up and get as far away from you as I can," I stated firmly.

"What? Why would she tell you some shit like that?" He raised his voice.

"Because it's true," I replied with ease. "Charles, you have about as much integrity as a piss-ant. I musta been outta my damn mind to stay here another minute after catching you with my sister. And I'll tell you somethin' else. I know you haven't talked with your attorney about eliminating that pre-nup, either. That's right, I know because I did some checking behind you," I admitted with no shame.

"Listen . . ."

"No, you listen." I snapped. "You lie so much 'til I don't think you even know what the truth is. Your whole life is based on lie after lie after lie, and I fell right into it. For the last couple of weeks, I been goin' back over these wasted years with you, and I can see so plainly now. Just about everything you ever told me was a lie. I believed you not because I was stupid, but because I loved you just that much and wanted to believe in you. Hell, when I was out in the world dating, I helped invent most of these shitty relationship games. I know it's not an excuse, but at least I was single. I didn't have a husband at home that I was doin' all of this crap to. After I married you, I became faithful." I felt my regret and sorrow begin to surface. The last thing I wanted to do was cry in front of him again, so I momentarily drooped my head down.

With me being silent now, he must have felt it was a good chance for him to say what he wanted to say. "Look, Bettie, I don't know why you listenin'—"

"I'm not done yet, so please stop interrupting me," I said calmly, raising my head to look at him again. I didn't feel like hearing his nonsense, but I was determined to

157

speak every drop of what I wanted to say. I needed to do that for me.

"I guess all of this heartache is my re-payment for the terrible things that me and you did to your helpless, sick wife, Ruth, when she was on her death bed. I couldn't see it before, but reaping what a person sows brings about a change in 'em. Rest assured, whenever you reap yours, Charles, you better pray it don't kill you.

"All of those nights, sweet, innocent Ruth lay up in that hospital suffering with pain and aches probably runnin' all through her weak body, no doubt needing her husband there to comfort her, just maybe hold her hand if nothing else. And you and me, well, we were layin' up in the hotel right across the street from the hospital." As I continued, I felt remorseful as hell standing there confessing my horrible sins, but I had to get it all out.

"I should've known that if you could do that to her after almost thirty years of marriage and three children, you could do even worse to me. But the thing is, I lied to myself and sugar-coated the truth. When we were running around on her, I told myself that you just needed someone to comfort you and be there for you, because you were stressed so much from having to deal with her and couldn't really help her. Yep, I did that. I actually convinced myself that the only reason you cheated on her was because you knew she was going to die and you needed somebody who loved you and who you loved to be there for you. Pathetic, isn't it? Well, I've asked Ruth to forgive me, and I've asked God to forgive me too. I just hope one day I can forgive myself." I ended my words and motioned to walk away.

For a brief moment, he seemed to be absorbing what I'd said, then he messed up and opened his mouth. "Why are you bringin' up somethin' that can't neither one of us do nothin' about?" he asked softly. "All of that's in the past now. I ain't nowhere close to bein' perfect, but I was there for Ruth as much as I coulda been." He acted in his own defense.

"Whatever. Charles, I'm finished with it. My conscience

is clear on that, just like it's clear on the deal we made about the ten thousand dollars and the elimination of the pre-nup. You only completed half of our agreement, and you know it. But I kept my end of the bargain," I said with confidence. "Now, you can tell it to the judge."

"Okay, okay, you right. I ain't gon' lie 'bout it," Charles interjected. "But the only reason I been hesitating to eliminate the nup is 'cause I thought you was 'gon leave anyway," he admitted.

"That's fine, Charles. It doesn't even matter now. There's nothin' in this world you could say to me or give me to make me stay here with you another minute," I insisted.

A look of anger spread over his face. "I can't believe you makin' a decision like this based on a bunch of lies Katie done fed you," he exclaimed.

"Katie ain't fed me nothin, baby boy. In fact, I haven't even seen Katie," I confessed, standing tall and proud.

"Well, that's what you said a few minutes ago," he recalled.

"I only said that about Katie to see how you'd respond. Can't say I was surprised at how nervous you became all of a sudden. Guilt always go back to the scene." I smirked.

"What you talkin' 'bout, woman?" he boggled his head like he didn't understand.

I patted myself on the back for the way I'd used Katie's name just to see his reaction. In all truth, I wasn't even sure about the shit that Keshundra had told me about him and Katie the night I put her out. I figured it was one final attempt to try and shift all the blame on Charles manipulating her. I didn't even make any indications that I believed her when I slammed the garage door in her face and went back in the house. On the other hand, I did tell myself that one sure-fire way of getting to the truth was to drop a few crumbs and wait to see if Charles would pick at them.

"Are you sure you wanna know what I'm talkin' 'bout?" I glared at him hostilely. He just didn't know I was getting ready to drop the next bomb on him. "Out of curiosity, how long you been fuckin' her?" I asked bluntly.

"Fuckin' who?" His confused look was just as fake as he was.

"You know damn well who I'm talkin' 'bout. Katie, that's who," I snarled.

"Are you crazy? How can you ask me somethin' like that? I know Katie ain't told you that."

"I told you, I haven't seen Katie. So, no, she ain't told me nothin'.'."

"Well, why would you say that? Better yet, why don't you ask her the same thang?" he suggested with sarcasm.

"I don't have to ask anybody anything, because I already know. And I would've known sooner if I had paid attention to the thoughts that kept popping into my head," I told him.

"Thoughts? What kinda thoughts?"

"For one, the disgraceful thought that crept into my head at the repast when you came into the kitchen and sent me down to the basement to check on Katie. When I told her what you said about her being upset and wanted me to talk to her, she didn't have a clue as to what I was talkin' 'bout. Seem like she just went along with it. Then, me and her walked up the hall and I smelled the same scent on her that I'd smelled on you when you hugged me. I thought maybe it was because both of you had been down in the basement and some kind of fumes there had gotten into your clothes, but it was more of an intimate, sex-like smell. I was ashamed for my thoughts to even go there, so I rushed them away immediately." I was sure to tell him everything that I could possibly remember, even though it disgusted the hell out of me.

"You got to be outta yo' mind . . . and you shoulda been 'shame for thinkin' some shit like that. And at a time like that, too. That's wrong, Bettie," he said, trying to make me feel guilty about my own intuitional hunches.

"The jig is up, nigga. You can't dominate me no more," I exclaimed. "And as for Katie, well, her conscious eatin' her up like colon cancer after what y'all did behind Gregg's back. To be honest with you, it should. Gregg, or his memory, or somethin' should haunt you and her from now 'til doomsday." This time when I motioned to walk away, I kept going.

I returned a few minutes later carrying a large suitcase with one last piece of info to drop on him. "Just so you know, Keshundra's the one who clued me in on you and Katie. The night I put her out, she asked me to step out in the garage. When I did, she ran her mouth like a busted water pipe. See ya, son of a bitch.

"Hey, where you goin'?" Charles jumped up as I headed toward the door.

"I'm leavin'," I stated plainly.

"Leavin'."

"That's right, you heard me." I tugged the suitcase out to the garage, put it in the trunk of my car and went back in to get the rest of my already packed belongings. All the while, Charles was right on my heels.

"Baby, now, you know this ain't right. I been bustin' my ass for the past several weeks tryin' to prove to you how sincere I am. I been at your beck and call, now you throwin' it all back in my face." He sounded wounded.

"Call it what you want, but you and I both know that you ain't nothin' but a sick, twisted bastard, and soon everybody's gon' know." I placed the last of my things in the car. "I feel sorry for the next female who fall for you, thinkin' she got somethin'."

"Look, baby, I swear I'll call my attorney first thing in the mornin' and make the pre-nup arrangements that I promised," He actually sounded sincere that time, but I was no longer interested.

"No, thank you." I opened the car door to get in.

Man, was he quick. He jumped subjects real fast. "Bettie, if you leavin', I ain't got no choice but to accept it. But why don't you bury all this talk 'bout puttin' our business in the streets?" He gave me a pleading look to match his desperate plea.

"I guess you should've thought about that before you

fucked both of your sisters-in-law," I stated uncaringly and drove off, accepting that this chapter in my life had now come to an end.

### Charles

Out of all my days, I'd never experienced so much out of control shit with women. I tried my damndest to figure out how I'd allowed things to get so bad, so quick. What wrong turn had I taken? Well, I hadn't quite figured out the answer to that, but I did know that Bettie had definitely made good on her promise to sing like a damn canary about our business. The same night she left—as a matter of fact, only two or three hours after she left—my telephone started ringing off the hook. Thank goodness for caller ID. I didn't necessarily have to talk to nobody who I felt was calling, pretending to be concerned, but really being nosy. Nevertheless, there was one specific call that I was not looking forward to answering. I knew for a fact that if she didn't get me on the line sooner or later, she was going to be standing at my doorstep before long, so I decided to go on and face the music. The next time she called, I answered.

"Hello." I tried to sound as unruffled as I could.

"Charles, I been callin' down there for the past hour. How come you ain't answered the telephone?" Momma asked fretfully. "What's goin' on wit' you and Bettie, and why is she tellin' all o' these lies on you? You know she done called over yonder and told Sharon 'nem a whole bunch o' shit that don't even make no sense at all? What done happened wit' y'all to make her do somethin' like that?" Momma finally stopped for a breather.

"Momma, slow down, please," I said gently. "Calm ya'self, and I'll tell you what happened, okay?"

I heard her inhale a deep breath through the phone. "Okay, I'm calm. Now, what's goin' on?"

I already had my "roundabout lie" together. Not that I needed a real big one for Momma, 'cause she had already expressed how upset she was for Bettie lying on me, anyhow. Like always, Momma took the liberty of taking my side, so I don't know why I was so hesitant in answering the phone when she called in the first place. I told her what she needed to hear to be at ease.

"It was nothin' but a big, horrible misunderstandin', Momma. That's all. Bettie grabbed the cat by the tail and ran off without even tryin' to straighten things out. I tried everything to let her know that she was making a real big mistake, but she refused to listen to reason. Now, you go 'head and tell me what she told Sharon and the rest of 'em." I spoke with the utmost confidence to assure Momma that the situation wasn't as bad as it probably sounded. In addition, I needed to find out exactly how much Bettie had told, so I would know what I was facing with everybody else. When Momma was done telling me all that Bettie had blabbed, I was even more upset and my headache had increased threefold, but I didn't let on.

Apparently, Bettie had told the entire story without any mercy whatsoever. Seem like my fucking ten thousand dollars should have persuaded her to keep at least half the shit quiet. One thing I had to give her credit for, she sure as hell chose the right person to tell first. Sharon had the biggest motor mouth in the whole damn South. When she got wind of the news, that meant the whole Jennings family was going to know before the night was over. She wasn't too keen on telling outside folks, but she sure as hell was going to make sure all of the family folks knew. By the time Momma and I got off the phone, I didn't feel like doing nothing but taking a quick shower and hitting the sack.

That Saturday morning, I woke to the sound of the phone ringing, which was certainly no surprise since it was still ringing when I went to bed the night before.

"Hello," I garbled, knowing it was Will from the caller ID.

"Hey, man, how you holdin' up?" he asked kindly.

"Aw, I'm cool, man," I replied, sitting up on the bed and noticing through my sleep-filled eyes that the time was 9:15

A.M. "So, when you hear?"

"Preston called me first thang this mornin' and told me he tried to call you last night, but he didn't get no answer."

"What time he call?"

"He didn't say."

"Well, his call musta got mixed up wit' some o' them that I wasn't answering, or he may have called after I stopped lookin' at the damn ID and just went on to bed. I had a pretty big headache and that phone was worryin' the hell outta me." I sighed.

"Shit, I know you did. What the fuck happened, man?"

After I gave Will the real rundown on what happened, we actually ended the conversation with a slight bit of laughter. Hell, we both agreed there was no need in stressing all the way out. What was done, was done. And like everything else, it would eventually blow over.

The phone call from Will must have been my wake up call to get me on up into the day. Too bad I didn't follow it. Usually, on Saturday morning around that time I would already be rambling about, but since no one else was there with me, I dozed back off when Will and I hung up.

I hadn't been napping but a few minutes when I was startled by the sound of the same male voice belonging to the shadowy figure that stood over me in the den the night Keshundra walked in and rescued me. The only thing different this time was I saw no figure before me. I scanned the room all over and didn't set eyes on anything, but I damn sure heard loud and clear. He didn't sound as angry as the last time. In fact, he was tickled to death over my bad luck.

"Ha, ha, ha, ha, ha, ha. Ohhhh, ha, ha, ha, ha," he bellowed out. "How does it feel to finally get a dose of your own medicine, Charlie boy? Huh? Bet ya didn't see that one comin', did ya? I wish you'd seen the look on your own face when she walked in and caught you red-handed. Ha, ha, ha, ha, ha, ha, ha. I would've came to see you sooner, but I wanted to wait 'til she got fed up wit' ya and exposed you to everybody." He paused briefly.

# ReChella

"This is only the beginning. There's plenty more of the same, unless you make it right . . . make it all right. There's only one way to make it right, and deep down, you know what it is. But if I know you, you'll die before you even consider doing it. And that's just fine by me, because then I'll get to see you tormented. Ha, ha, ha, ha, ha, ha. See ya later, Charlie boy. And remember, make it right and you'll be free; don't, and you'll pay the ultimate price."

Talk about having the creeps when I finally got up and stirring shortly afterward. I replayed it in my head several times and kept reminding myself of Will's and my conclusion about all of it being nothing more than a little guilt trip that my conscience was taking. A guilt trip that was becoming one pain-in-the-ass ride. Oh, how I wanted it to hurry up and be over. When I took into consideration the unexpected bad turn that my personal life had taken, naturally, one of the first things I thought about was Gregg's threat to ruin me, but I still refused to believe that a dead man was sabotaging me from the grave. Bottom line, the circumstances surrounding everything was purely coincidental, so I went ahead and did what I was good at, moved on to the next order of business for the day.

# Chapter Thirteen

It had been two and a half months since my unfortunate episode, and finally, the aftermath was pretty close to dying down. I'd often heard it said that time is the best healer for anything. Well, I could definitely attest to that, because as the days and nights drifted along, me and my boys had joked about the incident so much that we actually named it The Night Charles Fell in Hell. So, it was all good again.

To add to my bettering situation, it was Friday night, seven o'clock, and I had a date at eight. I picked my new hottie up right on time. We had dinner reservations at Western Sizzling Steak House on Norfleet Drive in Senatobia. Reena was just what the doctor ordered; tall and slim, dark and delicious, with a nice plump ass.

On the real, I had been somewhat chilling out with the ladies, giving things time to settle back into the norm, whatever the norm was. So, I didn't per se have a main lady yet, but that sure as hell didn't mean I hadn't been getting no pussy. I'd been hittin' it here and there with some of the quartet-heads who bombarded us after programs in search of a good fuck from one of us, but I hadn't run across a real good gal who'd blown me away yet. If it was one thing me and my boys knew, there's a big difference between a good fuck and a good female. Every woman that can fuck ain't necessarily relationship material, but when the package is combined, it's delightful. Reena damn sure looked the part, but the evening had just begun. There was a lot to learn.

She and I sat at a cozy little table in the area of the restaurant called the blue room. It was supposed to be the most intimate room there. I liked Reena's down to earth demeanor and witty personality. We chatted while waiting to place our orders.

"Reena, what you gon' have?" I asked, smiling.

"I think I'll have the ribeye and loaded baked potato,"

she said smooth and easy.

"What about a salad wit' that?" I suggested.

"Yes, I believe I'll do a salad." She smiled back at me.

The waitress made her way around to take our order, then brought us sodas. The evening had gotten off to a pretty good start.

"That's a mighty pretty dress you wearin'," I complimented her.

"Thank you." She smiled. "You look very nice yourself."

"Soooo, everything been goin' all right wit' you?" I asked, making general conversation.

"Everything's wonderful with me," she said all perky-like. "Isn't that the question I need to be asking you?" She raised her brows, looking at me as if she knew the question was a no-no.

After hearing her question, I really didn't want to believe that she was steering the conversation in the direction that I suspected. So, I gave her the benefit of the doubt and didn't jump the gun with my reply. "Why would you need to be askin' me that question? I'm picture perfect, but thanks," I said peacefully.

She furrowed her brows, giving me a *you know exactly what I'm talking about look* this time. "Oh, come on, Charles. You know what I'm talking about, and I want the exclusive, too. That is, if somebody else hasn't already beat me to it."

I gave her a slightly offended look. "I may be wrong by assuming you're talkin' 'bout all the garbage that's been floatin' around about me in the past few months."

"Oh, so that's what it is, garbage?" She screwed her face into an accusing look.

"What else would you call a bunch of lies that ain't true?"

"If they weren't true, I guess I'd call them garbage too," she agreed. So, does that mean you're officially denying the rumors about you and both of your sisters-in-law?" she asked candidly.

I smart-mouthed her before I knew it. "What are you,

some kind of a reporter? First, you want an exclusive, second, am I officially denying . . . what's up? Not only am I officially denying 'em, I'm banning 'em from this conversation. That's just how crazy all of it is," I exclaimed sternly. I tried to fake a smile behind my little temper tantrum. She didn't seem to get too disheveled about my little sound-off, but she did defend her inquiry. "Hold your saddle, cowboy. I'm not a reporter. I'm not even one to spread or believe rumors, but you gotta admit, it's only natural for any female coming behind a messy display like that to have questions about it. Even if this is only a date." She widened a grin.

"I can understand that." I nodded in agreement. "But, you know that old sayin'; believe none of what you hear, and only half of what you see."

"You're not going to give me any of the inside details, are you?" She tilted her head to one side, holding her large grin.

"Listen, I don't know what you want me to say, but all of that mess is behind me now. I'm one who looks ahead, not back. My ex-wife and her sistah, and my other sistah-in-law, and all of them lies been packed up and locked away for good. Now, are we gon' talk about what's in the past all night or what could possibly be in the future?" I was now a bit more firm.

"Enough said," she uttered instantly, gesturing with one hand that the conversation was now closed. "I'm off the subject. Let's talk about—"

"Excuse me," a soft female voice interrupted Reena. Three women had eased up and stood in front of our table. "We just wanted to come over and say good evening on our way out. We were sitting on the other side and saw when you all came in," one of the women said eagerly while blushing all over the place.

"Good evening," I said, looking up at her, then the other two ladies.

"Hello," Reena said, glancing at each of the women.

"Well, ladies, did y'all have a nice dinner?" I asked

# ReChella

considerately.

"Oh, yes, it was very nice." The lady doing all of the talking answered, then took a slight pause as if she was dying to say something. "Charles, you do know who I am, don't you?" she asked. The two ladies standing alongside her were blushing and smiling just as much as she was, only in silence.

"Of course I do. Big supporters like y'all, how could I not know who you are? Myra, right?" I pointed at her. Luckily, just as she asked me the question, I'd already recalled who she was.

"That's right," she exclaimed, even more excited now because I'd remembered who she was without her telling me. "So, when's the next program, and where is it going to be? Not that it matters, because we're going to be there regardless. We don't mind driving to wherever y'all are to see you—I mean to see you and the group . . . your group and you." She stumbled over her words terribly as she tried to fix the slip-up.

"Well, thank you, Myra. I know my group members appreciate the support, just like I do," I stated politely in hopes of helping to smooth over her blunder. "Actually, our next program is not far off at all. It's at the B-I Center in Hernando next Saturday."

Myra widened her smile and clapped her hands together once, appearing to be overjoyed. "Oh, oh, next weekend, that's great," she exclaimed. She turned and looked at her girlfriends and the three of them seemed to lift off in total dynamism after learning of the program.

It wasn't hard for me to remember Myra, because she damn near lived on the second row at every program. And afterward, she'd always be among the big crowd of women waiting to see us off stage. I'd chatted with her and her friends on several occasions, but I hadn't gotten around to fucking her yet.

Reena sat and observed the women without saying a word, but the annoyed expression on her face spoke loud and clear. Myra didn't seem to be concerned with Reena's displeasure, because she didn't take her eyes off me long enough to notice anything else.

"Well, ahh, we're certainly glad to hear that . . . and we'll be there, front and center, as usual," Myra said, gazing at me like she was about to jump in my lap and kiss me. "Meantime, we'll let you all get back to your evening." Myra's eyes were still burning deep into mine. I tried not to look directly at her for Reena's sake, so I glanced from one to the other.

"All right, it was nice seein' y'all again," I said, bidding them farewell as they walked away.

Reena let out an irritated sigh. "My goodness, it might've been a lot easier if they'd just went ahead and dropped their drawers right there in the middle of the floor," she uttered displeasingly.

"What you mean?" I displayed a baffled look.

"Awww, come on, don't even go there. Them wenches got it bad and you know it." Reena looked insulted. "I can't believe they did that right in front of me."

"Did what?" I was determined to play dim-witted. "They were just fans who wanted to find out about our next program."

Reena tilted her head and broadened her eyes. "Fans? You have got to be kidding me. When did people start calling women like that fans? They ain't nothing but star-struck easies, better known as quartet-heads, and you know it, Charles."

"Come on now, Reena. They didn't mean nothin'." I reached over and stroked her hand as it lay on the table. "Besides, as beautiful as you are, them females the last thing on my mind," I said very convincingly.

Reena paused for a momentary blush after my comment. Her brown, layered hair bounced every time she made a slight move.

"Well, I guess their lusting display, no matter how pathetic it was, did help me see the truth about things," she said gently.

"The truth about what things?" I was a bit puzzled for

real now.

"You and the rest of your group members must get that kind of treatment from women all the time; therefore, you couldn't have been hard up for no woman, least of all your own sisters-in-law. So you see, good things can sometimes come out of the weirdest circumstances. Not that I didn't believe you before, but, but . . . well, you know what I mean," Reena uttered playfully, sounding as if a tiny weight had been lifted off her shoulders.

I drooped my head, pretending to be hurt. "Yeah, I do know what you mean, unfortunately. You didn't believe me, so you had to find your own logical explanation through some strangers. I'm so scarred."

"No, no, it's not like that . . ."

"I know. I was just messin' wit' you," I interrupted her, smiling.

We were getting somewhere now. I don't think Reena even realized it, but at that point, she was acting just as infatuated as Myra and her two friends, whose timing, by the way, couldn't have been more perfect if I had staged it myself.

Throughout dinner and the rest of the evening, Reena was much more uninhibited. We chatted our way through a pleasant dinner and left the restaurant shortly before 10:00 P.M.

"Hey, you mind riding up to Southaven to buy a nice, chilled bottle of wine?" I asked Reena, opening the truck door for her.

"That sounds great. Too bad Senatobia is still a dry county. We wouldn't have to go so far to buy a bottle if the city would reconsider alcohol license," Reena said.

"I tell you what, I ain't gon' hold my breath waitin' for that to happen." I closed her door then got in on the driver's side.

"You got a particular kind of wine in mind?" she asked.

"A nice Chardonnay if it's okay wit' you."

"Sure is." She fastened her seatbelt.

Twenty-five minutes later we were pulling in front of the

liquor store. Traffic was somewhat heavy for 10:30 on a Friday night, but we were on our way back to Senatobia in no time.

"Charles, is there somewhere I can maybe run in and use the ladies' room?" Reena asked.

"This is Goodman Road. There are plenty of restrooms. Just take ya pick," I told her.

"Whatever's convenient."

"How 'bout the Waffle House on Church Road? It's still in town, but it's on the way out of the traffic," I suggested.

"That's fine."

The parking lot at Waffle House was so packed, we couldn't even turn in, let alone park.

"I tell you what, if we get stuck in that crowd, we'll be forever gettin' out," I said, peering at the bumper-to-bumper on the lot.

"I know," she agreed, observing also. "Hey, turn into the parking lot at the Fairfield Inn and I walk straight across on the sidewalk to the Waffle House."

"You sure? I don't want nobody to snatch you away from me, now," I teased.

She laughed and blushed at the same time. I knew it was just a matter of time before I raked her on in, hook, line, and sinker.

"Don't be silly." She opened the door after I parked and hopped out of the truck. "I'll be right back."

"If you ain't back in five minutes, I'm comin' after you wit' back-up." I rolled my window down and continued joking as she walked away from the truck, smiling.

I had been waiting for Reena only a few minutes when I noticed a bright red car that closely resembled one of the fellas' cars, pulling in the parking spot right next to me. When the driver got out, sure enough, it was Preston. I hopped out of the truck.

"Hey, Preston. How you doin', man?" I said, smiling.

"Hey, Charles." He closed his car door. "What's up, man?"

"Nothin', fella. Waitin' on my lady friend." I walked

172

around to the rear of his car to meet him. We did our brotherly handshake. "Me and her drove up to buy a bottle of wine and she stopped to go to the ladies' room.

"I heard that," Preston said, continually looking back at the hotel entrance as if he was watching for somebody.

Just that quick, I'd already done the math on ole Pres and our "by chance" meet-up. It was a Friday night, he was parking at a hotel quite the ways from Senatobia, and his wife was nowhere in sight. It didn't take a brain surgeon to guess what my buddy was up to. I couldn't resist fucking with him since him and the other fellas had joned me so much about my little mishap.

"Man, I ain't holdin' you up or nothin', am I? You seem a little anxious. You up this way for the night?" I grinned, nodding at the hotel devilishly.

After my question, he seemed even more edgy. "Naw, man, I'm just hollerin' at a friend for a few minutes. I ain't doin' nothin'," he answered, almost sounding like he was making up an excuse, which was odd as hell, as much cheating and fucking-off the five of us often covered up for each other. If I hadn't known better, I would've thought he didn't want me to know that he was up there with somebody. The more he talked, the more his tenseness grew. He knew for a fact that I was the last person for him to be edgy around. I swear, seeing him like that was new for me. I was confused as a mug. I figured something else was going on with him, so I decided to go ahead and let him get back to his business. He'd tell us about it later.

"A'ight, Preston. I'ma—" I started to say, but stopped my own words as I caught sight of a more than familiar face coming out of the hotel entrance, walking in our direction.

It was obvious that she wasn't paying much attention to the few folks standing around in the parking lot, because as soon as she saw me, she stopped dead in her tracks. Too late, she'd already come half the way now. The expression on her face said she was absolutely shocked. Preston stared at me while I stared at her.

"Charles, look, man, this ain't what you think," he

uttered nervously.

"It's not?" I glanced at him then fixed my eyes back on her. "Well, what is it, my brotha? You and my ex-wife either on y'all's way in the Fairfield Hotel or on your way out. Now, that's what I think. You tellin' me any different?" My eyes traveled from him to her.

He slumped his head. "Naw, man. I wouldn't insult you by tryin' to make up no two-bit lie," he confessed.

Bettie was now slowing around, evidently prolonging the inevitable of facing me. I didn't make it any better by mouthing off. "What you waitin' for? Come on over so I can say good evenin'," I exclaimed, beckoning for her.

"Look, Charles, I don't want no trouble, man. Hell, she called me up," Preston said at a low tone before Bettie made it to us.

I looked at him, slightly disappointed. At least I now knew why he was so uneasy before. "No doubt. I can believe that. She definitely believe in gettin' what she want." I turned my eyes back to her as she approached us and stood near him. "How you doin' this evenin', Bettie?" I extended my hand to shake hers.

"You already said that, and I'm not shakin' your hand," she snapped, sounding just as bitter as the night she left my house for good. "I don't know what you tryin' to prove by bein' here, but what I do is none of your business anymore." She rolled her eyes all snobby-like.

"There's no need for animosity, Bettie," I said calmly. "We all grown folks, and we all know each other. And what's even more important is we know how to handle ourselves." I folded my arms.

By now, Preston possessed a seriously worried look. "Charles, I'm sorry, but I think we should all talk about this another time. Like I said, I ain't tryin' to start no trouble." He reasoned carefully.

Despite the tiny ounce of disloyalty I felt concerning Preston, for some reason I had the urge to let him know that I wasn't real upset and didn't fault him for going on being a man and doing his thing.

# ReChella

"Don't worry 'bout it, Preston. You and me cool. I ain't the one you need to worry 'bout puttin' yo' business in the streets, or maybe where yo' wife and kids can pick it up. Anyhow, you and I both know a man ain't gon' do no more than a woman let him do," I said boldly, glaring at Bettie. She glared me back loathingly.

"Just what in the hell is that supposed to mean?" Bettie demanded.

My smart-alecky mouth was laying for her. "It's self-explanatory, baby. You s'ppose to be so smart. Why you gotta ask for a explanation?" I shot off.

"Aww . . . come . . ." Preston began glumly.

"Okay, man," I jumped in, knowing he was trying to keep things from getting out of hand. "You right, Preston. This ain't the place for nothin' like this to go down. But before we leave I got one question, just one. And it's for the lady, if you please." I held my index finger up peacefully.

Bettie tried to come off as unconcerned by not remarking. My eyes burned in hers.

"You threw a pity party for ya'self the night you walked out," I stated calmly but firmly. "If my memory recalls correctly, you wailed about how remorseful you was for betrayin' my poor, helpless wife, Ruth. You even said how you was reapin' all of it. Said you'd asked my dead wife to forgive you." I paused, still watching her like a hawk and nodded at Preston. "What about his wife? Are you gon' ask his wife to forgive you too? I mean, she may not be sick or helpless, but she still a woman who can be hurt. I thought you said you'd changed. Oh, I get it. You went ahead and forgave ya'self so you could get back in the action befo' you missed out on somethin'?" My frown intensified as I ended my words.

She still didn't say shit, just rolled her eyes as if she wasn't paying me any attention. But I could tell I'd wounded her pride or something. Preston, on the other hand, was as nervous as a long-tailed cat in a room full of rocking chairs.

"Look, I still don't think it's a good idea for us to be

standin' out here like this. Bettie please, just get in the car," Preston politely asked, giving Bettie a pleading look.

Before any of us had a chance to disburse and get in our vehicles, Reena walked up and joined us.

"Good evening," Reena said, skimming from Bettie to Preston.

Neither of them said anything right away. For a moment, things were even more awkward than when I first discovered that Bettie and Preston were together.

"Good evenin'," Preston answered, forcing a smile.

"We're leaving," Bettie snapped, rolling her eyes and ignoring Reena's greeting.

I guess Reena was able to sense the thick atmosphere, especially with Bettie's unwarranted response. "Did I . . . interrupt something, Charles?" Reena asked hesitantly.

"As a matter of fact, no. You didn't interrupt anything at all," Bettie snapped, eyeballing Reena. "Sooo, you're the next victim, huh?" Bettie shot her a snobbish twice-over from head to toe.

Reena frowned, obviously puzzled. "I beg your pardon?" Reena asked peacefully.

"Oh, you heard what—" Bettie began to snap again.

"Excuse me," Reena cut in before Bettie could finish. "I think you need to change your tone." Reena was now doing the snapping. "I don't see any children out here, and the way you talking, it's got to be directed at some children."

"Look, honey, I was just tryin' to give you a word to the wise, but since you insist on being ignorant, so be it." Bettie stated, turning her nose up.

The provoking look in Reena's eyes had grown, and evidently, her estimation of the circumstances weren't far off either. She surprised me with her next statement, and by the looks on their faces, she surprised Bettie and Preston too.

"A word to the wise?" Reena repeated mockingly. "Tell you what. Why don't I give you a word to the wise? You've already been married to and divorced from one of The Mighty Spirituals. I don't think it's a good idea to fuck your way through the rest of them. Why, folks might get the wrong idea and think you're a slut or something." Reena sneered at Bettie and waited as if she were daring her to move. I was becoming more and more impressed with Reena by the minute. Hadn't nobody breathed a word to Reena about what was going on, yet she still hit the nail on the head about Bettie and Preston.

Bettie really looked upset now. "Listen, bitch," she snarled.

"Bitch?" Reena barked, cutting her off again. "You the bitch. I will sweep this parking lot up with your lying, phony ass." Reena took a step toward Bettie. Bettie looked surprised, and like she was about to break out and run.

"Please, y'all. Calm down," Preston urged as he glanced around to see if anybody else was watching.

"Let's go, sugar." I said, grasping Reena's hand.

"Yeah, we better leave before South Memphis come straight up out of me and land on her ass," Reena stated angrily, walking along with me to get in the truck. "I can't believe what I'm seeing, Charles. She laying up in a hotel with one of your group members then trying to act all dignified."

"Go ahead and get in, sweety," I said, opening the door. She abided peacefully.

When I made it back to the other side, Bettie had already gotten into Preston's car, but he was waiting behind the car with a deep look of regret upon him.

"Charles, you don't know how sorry I am about all of this. Man, we been too close of friends for too long for someth—"

"Look, Preston." I stopped him. "Ain't no secrets among us . . . on how we as men in the group do things. We know the way we conduct these willing females. As far as I'm concerned, Bettie is just another piece of ass like all the rest of them quartet-heads. I don't have no ill feelings for you, my brotha. Hell, if it had been me, I probably would've done the same thing. And anyway, didn't you say she called you up?" I asked.

Preston looked somewhat relieved after my exoneration speech to him.

"Yeah, she did," he said willingly. "I saw her in town in Senatobia about two weeks ago. We stopped and chatted about general stuff for a few minutes, then when we got ready to leave, she asked for my cell phone number. I ain't gon' lie . . . I wasn't gon' make no move on her, but I was kinda anxious for her to make one. She sho' acted like she was gon' call, too. I figured all the shit that went down wit' y'all, you wasn't ever gon' be wit' her no mo'," he explained.

"Well, you figured right." I nodded. "A word of advice, though. Be careful. She try to be smart and conniving, and she can be ruthless when she want to. Keep in mind the shit I told y'all she tried to get me to do before she left."

He seemed to be thinking hard about what I was telling him as he nodded his head. "A'ight, man. We'll talk later. . . in more detail," he said. We got in our vehicles and took off.

A moment of silence surrounded Reena and I as we rode down the interstate, but only a moment. She soon let her thoughts fly freely.

"I'm sorry, Charles, I just have to speak my mind," she uttered all of a sudden. "If he calls himself your friend, he's just as guilty as she is. It's both of their fault. What did he have to say, Charles?" She still sounded pissed, turning to look at me.

"He was telling me how Bettie was the one who called him up and initiated the whole thing. I told him his explanation wasn't necessary, 'cause I already know how she is. She did the same thang when me and her first started seein' each other, so I know he ain't lyin'," I said.

Reena shook her head as if disgusted. "That's pitiful. What's she going to do, screw all of your group members because you and her didn't work out? It's women like her who give decent women a bad name," Reena said unapologetically. "She ought to be ashamed of herself, getting caught at the hotel with one of your best friends. Umph, umph, umph. Even if she had been telling the truth about what happened with you and her sister back then, who'd believe her now . . . after seeing that? Of course, it's plain as day now. She had to make up lies on you just to cover her own tracks. Damn, you poor man. You know what?" she said softly, peering at me with sympathy.

I quickly transformed my expression to resemble that of a wounded puppy, since she was gazing at me that way.

"What?" I asked gently.

"I've found out something very interesting about you," she said.

"What's that?" Shit, I was almost whining like a sick puppy now.

"You haven't really said anything bad about your ex-wife yet." Reena spoke softly as she reached over and stroked my lower thigh and knee. "I mean, at the beginning of this evening when I confronted you, you simply told me that you'd been lied on. You maintained your innocence, but you never went into any detail trying to convince me or justify anything . . . and now look what's happened. All the proof you'll ever need for me to believe in you has happened right here, tonight," Reena said, piercing her stare deep into mine. I swear, her eyes said she wanted to stop and fuck right there on the highway.

I poured a sincere smile on her and reached one hand out to stroke her cheek. "Thank you for believing in me," I said, almost convincing myself that I was genuine.

# Chapter Fourteen

Reena held my hand to her face and ran her soft cheek against my palm. The titillating feeling was arousing. She began to kiss my palm. Damp kisses. She was mine for the taking. She painted me as a victim and she was going to rescue me. All I needed to do was pull over and get me some.

"Hey, you know you ain't gon' be able to keep much more of that up. I can't concentrate on the road," I whispered, not really wanting her to stop.

She began gliding her tongue between my fingers, and sliding one finger at a time in and out of her mouth.

"You've got to focus," she mumbled. "You concentrate on the road and let me concentrate on you." She dropped a few kisses up my arm and in a flash, her head disappeared down in my lap.

She rubbed and caressed my growing stiffness through my fastened pants. I felt myself swelling tighter and tighter. She began kissing and softly biting at it, then she gradually unfastened my belt and unzipped my pants, opening them enough to pull down my Hanes and free my erection. Next thing I knew she had a mouthful of my dick.

"Ummm, umm." she moaned.

"That's good, baby." I tenderly breathed in and out. "But ain't no way for me to drive like this." I stroked through her hair with my free hand as she continued. Luckily, I was coming up on the rest area exit in Hernando. I quickly got off the interstate without disturbing Reena's deed, and parked around back of the rest stop center near some trees, hoping to be at least reasonably hidden. Since it was an almost deserted rest stop, I didn't think too many passersby would be interrupting us that time of night. I pushed the button, letting the seat back as far as it could go, giving us plenty of leg room.

"Oooh, that's good," I grunted.

# ReChella

At that point, I was able to hold her head with both hands as she slowly slithered her tongue up to the tip of my head and plunged back down on my dick. I swear, I could feel the back of her throat. I hadn't had dick-job that good since Keshundra.

"Baby, it's so good." I still moaned.

She hummed in delight while moving up and down, jawing me. She suddenly lifted her head without saying anything, then grabbed her purse and began fumbling through it. The moonlight softly shone into the truck through the semi-dark tint. I caught sight of a tiny, reddish bottle that she took from her purse. She twisted off the top and poured all of whatever it was into her mouth, then quickly leaned her head back down and refilled her mouth with my hard cock. The second she began sucking me off again, I let out a scream so loud I just knew somebody somewhere heard it.

"Oooohhhhh." I quivered uncontrollably, cramming her head up and down on my dick repeatedly. I didn't want to choke her, but I couldn't help myself. At that moment, I needed to be as deep in her throat as I could go. I couldn't explain it.

"Ummmmm," she sounded in enjoyment.

She didn't pull away from my thrusts, nor did she seem to mind me ramming the way that I was. My mass couldn't be held back any longer. Whatever Reena poured into her mouth delivered a cool, tingly sensation on my dick, and it made me completely crazy. I hadn't had anything like it. I exploded everywhere, her face, mouth, hair, and body.

"Aaaahhhh." I continued holding tight to her head, even after cumming.

My ejaculation had always been an enormous amount, but it seemed to be double the load that time. Reena licked and rolled her face around in the thick, white, juicy substance that was mixed with her secret red potion, then she began swallowing it. She was the first female I'd witnessed to swallow, but hell, however she got her kicks was fine with me.

"Ummm, come on, give me some of this big, humongous dick," she whispered while rising up and pulling her dress up to her waist. Before she straddled me, I helped her out of her panties, then gripped her ass cheeks.

"Unzip my dress and taste my breasts," she begged, kissing me and smearing leftover cum from her jaws and face onto mine. Her lips tasted of raspberry cum, and she was not interested in cleaning it off.

I unzipped the back of her dress and she yanked her arms out of the sleeves, then dropped one of her breasts in my mouth. I suckled around the nipple and soon stuffed the entire tit into my mouth time and again. She was warm and wet as I pumped my middle finger in and out of her cunt-hole.

"You ready, Charles?" she asked as she licked over my face. "Here I come." She positioned my dick-tip under her and the second I pulled my finger out, she dropped down on me. "Oooohhh." She thrust up and down viciously, stopping every few seconds to press down tighter and roll her pussy over my cock.

Then she reached around to her cheeks for one of my hands and affixed my fingers directly on her clit as she pursued her hard rolls. I rubbed and patted her clit as she'd directed, and used one finger from the other hand to stroll up and down her back. She liked it. Her peculiar high-pitched, squeal said so. "Mmm. Mmm. Mmm. Mmm," she jerked and screeched. She had multiple orgasms right before our big, colossal orgasm together.

Having the two orgasms back to back was awesome and equally as gratifying for me, but both of them did what was expected. They drained me. I'd been involved in a lot of weird shit in my days, but I wasn't prepared for what happened next.

Reena had this fiendish look of hunger in her eyes.

"I don't think I'm going to be needing this anymore tonight," she stated in a deep, forceful voice. This voice was much different than the high-pitched, squealing voice I'd just heard from her. "How about I get rid of it?" she asked, pulling at her dress.

She remained straddling me and peered deep into my eyes as she began ripping her dress off. She tore that bastard off like it was made of toilet paper and threw it down on the floor of the truck. She then grabbed her purse again and turned it upside down, pouring its contents on the seat. She began rambling through her shit like a dog digging for a bone. I was too astonished to respond. I sat right there speechless as I watched her lose her wits. *This is one freaky fucker,* I thought.

"My pussy still throbbing," she snarled. "It needs more of your big cock in it." She abruptly rose up and pulled my slumming chunk out of her, then lay flat on her back on the seat with her pussy facing me.

Unfortunately, I'd already gone limp after the second orgasm, but I looked closely as she rolled and wiggled, touching herself from place to place in hopes that I'd soon be aroused again.

"Hey, you," she called out in that same deep voice, only a little more sexy now. "Once it get turned on, I can't turn it off until it's fully satisfied. You're going to have to fuck me all night," she said, her eyes dancing.

I fixed my eyes on her and took in a deep breath, knowing that it was virtually impossible for me to get back on it right then, but I felt very optimistic that another round wouldn't be too far off.

"Keep doin' what you doin', and I'll be cranked back up in no time." I watched attentively as she worked her fingers in and out and around her cunt, non-stop. After several minutes had gone by, she used one hand and felt down alongside the seat and picked up a tiny bottle resembling the first raspberry one that she'd emptied into her mouth earlier. She drained the entire bottle over her pussy and began massaging it inside her.

"Oooouuuuhhhhh," she cried out in enjoyment.

I remembered the electrifying sensation that I'd felt when she first deposited a mouthful of the tasty, gelled substance onto me and caressed it over my penis. I understood exactly why she was yelling out. Before I realized it, I was up on my knees with my head buried between her legs, slurping and smacking like a kitten drinking warm milk.

"That's it, eat it all up, Charlesee poo," she said, palming my head with one hand and navigating my moves as she held her full, somewhat hairy lips open and fed herself to me. "Ooooohhh, right there. Don't move," she squealed, yet again, in that same peculiar sound.

I increased my sucking in the spot she specified and within seconds, I was tasting her sweet, raspberry-filled cum all over my mouth. Her delivery was immense. I was pleased to aid her in such a pleasure-filled ending. At that moment, I realized that I was re-energized and hard as ever. In fact, my hard-on was jumping and thumping for somewhere to land. She inhaled a deep breath, her eyes still dancing bright.

"Wowww, you're amaaazing," she murmured.

By the time she was done complimenting me, I had pulled my pants and shorts off and plunked my dick on top of her exposed pussy. I slid it in and began humping away. She welcomed me with clawing fingers on my thick, muscular cheeks, scraping handfuls of my ass as she pleaded for more of it. I plummeted. She gripped and received. I rolled, she rolled back.

The more hard strikes I slapped her with, the more wild and violent she became. She began whacking and pounding the back of my ass vigorously with her fists, then let off an unyielding scream like a dog in heat. Shortly following that, she began flapping her body like a fish out of water. She smacked against the leather seats as I rammed in her. Her head hammered the inside of the passenger door. I couldn't see her pupils at all, only the white of her eyes. Each time I attempted to call her name, just to make sure she was all right, she grunted louder, became more violent, and thrust back at me all the more hard. I was a tiny bit concerned, but not enough to stop the action. The pussy was getting better and better. I maintained the rush and hoped that she

184

didn't hurt herself or knock herself unconscious 'til I got my nut off. The way she expressed her satisfaction was different, but at the same time it was fascinating. We banged and knocked straight to the finish line, yet another time.

"Mmm. Mmm. Mmm. Mmm," she squealed the same noise that I still hadn't gotten used to hearing. "Ohhhh, that was so good, Charles. Thank you. I haven't had it like that in a long time. Thank you. You're the man." She finally opened her eyes and began talking to me.

"I agree. It was more than good." I panted, trying to catch my breath from the intense work-out as I raised up off her and backed away to get my clothes and put them on.

"I guess I'll have to stay the night at your house since I don't have any clothes to wear home," she said, looking at me after she'd picked her torn-up dress off the floor and examined it.

I nodded to her dress. "I guess you will."

She grinned deviously. "I lose control during sex, especially good sex with a good partner," she said, I guess trying to explain some of that weird shit I'd just witnessed her do.

"Losing control's a understatement. You get damn right crazy, baby. But I dig that shit," I said, winking at her. "The place for you is in my bed." I cranked the truck up. "You ready? I think we've worn our welcome out at this rest stop."

"Yeah, I'm ready." She laid the ragged dress on her lap and slid herself as close to me as she could get and rested her head on my shoulders. We took off. I could only imagine what it would have been like if some freak car accident or car trouble had happened on our way home. Her being butt naked could never have been made any sense of to a third party.

Luckily, we arrived at my house safely about 12:00 A.M. To our knowledge, nobody saw her go into the house without any clothes on. Both of us went straight for the showers. I allowed her my bathroom facilities, while I took the upstairs shower. I accommodated her with one of my T-shirts and some jogging pants to wear around the house. She declined the jogging pants. I encouraged her to make herself at home. She took a grand tour of the house, then we relaxed on the bed in my bedroom.

"I'm really impressed with your home, Charles," she said, lying beside me, stroking my bare stomach.

I lay on my back at the head of the bed with my arms folded behind my neck. *What an incredible night,* I thought. Everything that happened worked in my favor. I couldn't complain at all. I'd started the night off thinking Reena was a good candidate to be the next Mrs. Charles Jennings, and by now I was all the more sure of it.

"Do you ever get lonely in this big ole house all by yourself?" she asked playfully.

"Well, I've only been alone in it for a few months now. Before that, I'd never spent too much time by myself," I answered, my attention wavering.

She began kissing around my naval area.

"You better cut that out befo' you get somethin' else started," I said.

"I hope so." She kept at it. "I could use another round, you know. That is if you got anything left," she teased.

"I got plenty. Can you handle some more?" I asked, turning over to kiss her.

We went another short round. After that, it was lights out and sleep on. The next morning, I arose to find Reena not laying beside me, but a delectable aroma filled the air. I hopped out of bed and stuffed myself into my pajama pants. The aroma led me straight to the kitchen. There, Reena stood over the stove putting the finishing touches on a good-looking breakfast.

"It's only eight-thirty. You got to be done been up awhile to do all of this," I said, strolling over to the stove, then kissed her on the cheek.

She gave me a broad smile. "Good morning," she sang happily. "I figured since I invaded your home last night without notice, the least I could do was get up and make you some breakfast. Oh, yeah, I found a unopened toothbrush in your bathroom cabinet. I hope you don't mind I used it."

"No, that's fine. I see you found your way around the kitchen pretty good."

"It wasn't hard. You keep an extremely organized place to be a bachelor. Plenty of food in the fridge and no dishes in the sink. My kinda man," she bragged, moving from place to place as cheery as a songbird in the spring.

"Are you always this jolly first thing in the mornin'?" I asked, yawning.

"Only when I wake up in a big, beautiful house with a handsome man who rocked my world . . . and made my spine tingle non-stop the night before." She was actually glowing as she talked.

"Is that a fact? Well how 'bout we make that happen every night?" I asked, smiling broad like her now.

"What do you mean?" She put on some oven mitts, then pulled freshly-baked homemade biscuits out of the oven.

"I mean let's get married. Think it over and get back to me," I blurted out without any hesitation whatsoever. *Damn, did I just say that out loud?* I asked myself silently. I was sure enough thinking it, and all of a sudden it just popped out of my mouth. I wondered for a second or two did it surprise Reena as much as hearing it aloud surprised me. I guess so, since she'd stopped in her tracks with her mouth hanging open, looking stunned. The aroma from the food was making my mouth water.

"My goodness, those biscuits smell so good," I said, walking back toward the kitchen door. "Baby, I'm gon' wash my face and brush my teeth. I don't want this food gettin' cold on me."

I left her still standing in the same spot, looking stunned, holding the pan of biscuits. When I returned, she was sitting at the table as quiet as a mouse.

"Hey, everythang ready?" I clapped my hands together and sat in a chair next to her.

She still didn't say anything, just sat looking at me.

"Baby, is something wrong?" I asked, reaching for her hand and gripping it tightly.

"Of course something's wrong," she uttered, looking very serious. "Charles, you just asked me to marry you. Unless you were only kidding around."

I purposely came off as relaxed. "First of all, no, I wasn't kidding around. And second, why does me asking you to marry me make something wrong? Oh, I get it now." I gasped, making it seem like I'd figured out what the problem was. "I guess I was just thinkin' out loud. I'm sorry. I shouldn't have blurted it out like that, huh?" I carried on as if the conversation was no big deal at all. "I should have made it more romantic, right?"

She was really looking confused now. "Are you serious? You don't even really know me. And you certainly don't love me," she stated.

"I'm getting to know you, and so far, everythang I know, I like." I took a big swallow of orange juice from the glass that she'd poured for me. "And love, well, what's not to love about you? You funny, you smart, you beautiful, you verrrry sexy, and you can turn me on in a hot minute." I paused. "Oh, and last but certainly not least, you can cook." I waved my hand over the table of food, acknowledging her grand breakfast.

"Is that it?" she asked.

"No, that's not it. But I've told you some of what you are to me. I guess I was hoping to hear some of what I might be to you."

She still seemed uncertain and a bit confused. "Well, Charles, you're a lot to me. You're adventurous, handsome, successful, and a grrreat lover, but it's been barely twenty-four hours that we've shared together." As she continued talking, she picked up an empty plate and began fixing it with bacon, hash browns, eggs, rice, and biscuits, then she set it down in front of me. "I mean, is that really enough to base a decision like marriage on? You want jelly or syrup?" She stopped and looked at me.

I'd watched her as she chattered and fixed the plate all

at the same time, therefore, I couldn't help but to make a mindful observation.

"All while you were talkin', you were fixin' my plate. Don't you see? You just automatically did it. You have the instincts of a wife . . . and a caring wife, I might add. But don't get me wrong, now." I hurriedly defended my point of view. "I didn't ask you to marry me just to do stuff for me," I stated, making sure she didn't get the wrong idea.

"Well, I'm glad you cleared that up. I would've hated to continue this conversation thinking all you want from me is a female to serve you," she said, smiling, but I somehow got the feeling that she really wasn't joking about that.

She began fixing her plate.

"So, tell me. Why did you ask me to marry you, Charles?" Her question was filled with skepticism.

"Honestly?" I maintained my cool.

"Honestly." She paused, gazing at me.

"I think we would be good together. Plus, I can't stand the thought of somebody else gettin' a piece of that action you gave me last night," I said humorously, then winked at her. She didn't say a word. That told me I needed to be more serious. "Aww, come on, Reena. What can I say? It just feels right. We're so comfortable, even sittin' here together. I realize last night was our first night out, but you don't think it was unusually comfortable for a first time?"

She gently nodded, agreeing with me. "I admit . . . it was really relaxed after we crossed a few hurdles," she said softly. "But there's so much that you don't know about me. Are you really willing to take a big chance like this?" she asked as she finally began to eat.

"I'm not the only one takin' a chance. You're takin' a big one on me too."

"What about your family? What will they think? What will they say?" she asked, sounding worried.

"I don't live my family's lives and they don't live mine. They don't have a say in what I do . . . or who I do it with. Besides, they'll love you. Like I said earlier, what's not to love about you?"

# Scandalous

A few minutes of silence went by as we finished eating.

"Whewww." I pushed my chair away from the table and leaned back, patting my full stomach.

"Let's do it," she exclaimed, standing up, then plopping down on my lap. "Let's go for it!"

"All right," I exclaimed, embracing her tightly. "I knew you was up for it."

Reena and I spent the rest of that Saturday chilling out, getting to know a little more about each other. She even drove my truck to her place and brought some of her things back. For over two months, I'd been alone in that big-ass house. Her being there made me realize just how bad I missed having somebody to share my bed with on a permanent basis. That was the main reason I popped the question on her so fast. I'd had a wife since I was nineteen years old. It was one of those things in life that I considered necessary for a completely great canvas. Besides, old habits die hard, and if it was one thing I knew for a fact, I was a man of habit. I tell ya another thing, too. Reena hit the nail on the head when she made note of me wanting a female to serve me. Damn straight I did. A man of my stature need shit like that, and I wasn't up for waiting another year to find it. I'd been keeping my eye out for the right gal, and I felt like Reena was that gal, so I went for it. That ain't no damn crime.

I willingly opened my home and life to Reena. Of course, not before she understood that she was going to have to sign on the pre-nup line. She was a little nervous about meeting my family, but both of us agreed that she would meet everybody that Sunday afternoon following church services. Truth is, I hadn't been attending regular services much since all of that shit happened, but I'd been promising Momma that I was going to get back on track soon.

# Chapter Fifteen

When Reena and I made it to Mt. Pleasant, 11 o'clock service had just begun. We quietly made our way up the center aisle and took two seats on the far end of the second pew, which was just about where I usually sat every Sunday. I could feel the many eyes peering at me and her from across the church as we joined in with the choir during a short devotional hymn. After the hymn ended, Brother Simmie Powell rose for the morning scripture reading. Reena and I opened our Bibles and read along. After that, Deacon Dixon kneeled at the altar for the prayer. As he cleared his throat, we all awaited his old, shaky but powerful voice to crank up. The choir softly hummed in the background.

"Let us bow our heads, please?" Deacon Dixon requested. The members bowed. "This mornin', our Father, we kneel befo' You as humble as we know how." Deacon Dixon prayed his usual spirit-filled prayer, and by the time he was done, his wife, Sister Dixon, had gotten happy like always.

She was like an alarm clock; she knew just when to sound off. "Uuhhh, thank ya, Lawd! Uuhhh, thank ya nigh, nigh, Lawd," she shouted out.

We settled down following the prayer. Then the announcements and upcoming church business, followed by acknowledgements to any guests, were read aloud by sister Bertha Rowland, the church announcer, a fair-skinned, low-key, homely woman, no more than thirty. Sister Rowland stood behind the podium with the same stern expression she'd always worn.

"This invitation is from Saint Matthew's Senior Choir. It reads, 'We the members of Saint Matthews' Senior Choir would like to cordially invite the Senior Choir of Mount Pleasant Baptist church to our annual choir day, which will be held on the third Sunday in November, the nineteenth, at three o'clock in the evening. Please contact our choir president, Sister Villa Mae Huntley, to be placed on the program.'" Sister Rowland folded that invitation and moved to the next one. "We have a thank you card addressed to the members of Mount Pleasant from Sister Katie Jennings. It reads, 'To the Mount Pleasant Congregation, I would like to take this time to thank each and every one of you for your support and prayers through me and my sons' time of sorrow and grief. During the fifteen years that I have been a member at Mount. Pleasant, each of you never failed to show me and my family kindness and generosity. That's why I have found it to be an extremely difficult task to write this letter. Although my heart and thoughts will always be with the Mount Pleasant church family, I am requesting that my name and my sons' names be permanently removed from the church membership role. I will be reviving membership at my home church, New Genesis Baptist Church in Panola County. This is where we have been attending for the past several months. In the meantime, continue to pray for us and we will continue to pray for you all. Sincerely, Sister Katie Jennings, Gregg Jennings Junior, Jon Jon Jennings, and Jeremy Jennings.'" Sister Rowland closed the card.

As Sister Rowland was preparing for whatever was next on her list, I noticed how the members were looking around in dismay after hearing the contents of Katie's card.

"At this time, I'd like to ask all guests to please stand," Sister Rowland uttered, looking over the church.

Reena stood, and two other women on the right side of the church stood as well. Sister Rowland addressed the new visitors in our church's customary way. "To the visitors that are standing, Mount Pleasant Baptist Church members would like to take this time to welcome you all to our home. We would like to say that you're not strangers here, you're our sisters in Christ. We would also like to invite you back to come worship with us each Sunday morning at eleven A.M., and Sunday school at 10:00 A.M. Would any of you like to have a word?" Sister Rowland swept her eyes over each lady. They all declined. "Then you may be seated." Sister Rowland then took her seat.

Every Sunday morning, Sister Rowland stood to make the announcements and after that, nobody heard anything else from her throughout the rest of service. She always kept to herself. I glanced over at Reena to make sure she was hanging in there after standing up in front of everybody.

"You all right?" I whispered.

"Yeah. I'm fine. Thanks for asking," she whispered back.

Deeberry's sermon wasn't too long for a change, but he just couldn't seem to stop gazing at me and Reena every chance he got. From the time he rose to preach, his eyes boggled back and forth on us throughout the entire service. That nigga didn't have a bit of business up in that pulpit. Maybe I was being a hypocrite, but that was just how I felt.

"In conclusion, church, I want to say that we all must one day answer for the choices that we make in life, may they be good ones or bad ones. Can I get a amen?" Deeberry shouted, gesturing from behind the pulpit.

"Amen! Amen!" the church members yelled in response.

"Come on, boy. Say that. Say that." One of the old mothers on the mother board boosted him on.

"GOD! Will hold us accountable on that grrrreat gettin' up day! So we better be careful, folk, when we tempted to do wrong," Deeberry stated, then wiped across his mouth with a white handkerchief. "Runnin' round sleepin' wit' anything and anybody that look halfway decent and know it's wrong . . . I tell ya, God is not pleased!" He dropped his eyes directly on me and Reena after that statement.

That was another thing I hated about him. He wouldn't preach from the Bible. He always preached about folks' private lives. He always talked about things he'd heard or things he suspected, not knowing if any of it was lies or not. I was glad to see him end his pitiful, misguided sermon.

"Let us stand and lift our hands toward Heaven as we dismiss the service, please," he instructed. The congregation stood and we lifted our hands. "May the Lord watch between me and thee while we are absent one from another. Amen. You are dismissed in Jesus' name," he concluded.

Everybody began to scatter about, mingling and hugging one another in fellowship. Reena remained at my side.

"What did you think about the service?" I asked her as we attempted to move through the crowd to get to Momma.

"If you've been in one small town service, you've been in 'em all," she said softly, clutching my hand.

As Reena and I maneuvered through the people, I noticed that Momma was standing by herself in the mother board area. I knew her being alone wouldn't last but a few minutes, so I tried to get to her as quickly as possible.

"Hey, Momma," I said, kissing her cheek when I approached her.

"Hey, Charles," she said. "Glad you made it out this mornin'. You musta got the message I left on yo' machine last night. I left one and Bo left one too."

"Naw, I didn't even check my messages last night. Was it anything urgent?"

"I was just remindin' you to make sho' you made it to church this mornin', 'cause we all goin' out to the cemetery and lay flowers on the family plot, then everybody meetin' up at my house for dinner," Momma explained, glancing at Reena while talking.

"Well, in that case, I'm glad I didn't miss today." I smiled at her.

Momma narrowed her eyes at me. "You ain't got no business missin' anyhow," she stated.

"Momma, I'd like for you to meet Reena," I said, widening my smile.

Momma sprouted a big grin while reaching for Reena's hand to shake it. "You got a last name, baby? I don't know what's wrong wit' my son today," Momma said pleasantly.

Reena grasped her hand and returned the same big smile. "Yes, ma'am, I do. My last name is Hickman. Reena

Hickman," she said.

Momma paused, still clutching Reena's hand. "Hickman, Hickman," Momma said, pondering. "You any kin to Joe Lee and Francis Hickman?"

"I sure am. That's my mother and father," Reena said proudly.

"Hush now, gull," Momma said enthusiastically as she finally turned Reena's hand loose. "I know yo' folks, baby. Been knowin' 'em for years. They still live out in Marshall County?"

"Yes, ma'am, they sure do," Reena said, grinning.

"Tell me, how is they doin'?" Momma asked.

"Oh, they're just fine. Both of them still up and about and in good health," Reena answered.

"That's good to hear, 'cause I ain't seen 'em in years," Momma said cheerfully. "They was always friendly people. Matter of fact, they two of the finest folks I ever knowed. And you know what they say, the apple don't fall far from the tree. You seem to be a fine gull ya'self."

"Thank you, ma'am. I really appreciate hearing that," Reena said warmly as she gazed into Momma's eyes.

"Aww, stop callin' me ma'am. Everybody call me Ms. Mildred, so you do the same," Momma insisted.

"All right, I will, Ms. Mildred." Reena glanced at me, really smiling now. I winked at her and smiled back.

She definitely wasn't as nervous and uneasy as before she met Momma. But then, that was one of Momma's many gifts. She was able to charm a person into feeling the utmost comfort in any kind of situation.

"Well, Reena. You did say Reena, right?" Momma asked.

"Yes, ma'am . . . I mean, yes, ma'am, Ms. Mildred," Reena blundered over her words trying to get it right.

"I'm reckonin' my son gon' be bringin' you on over to eat some dinner wit' us, ain't he?" Momma asked politely.

"Ahh, well . . . ahh." Reena hesitated, looking at me for an answer.

"Yeah, Momma. She comin' wit' me," I cut in.

Wayne walked up and joined us, followed by Richard and Bo. I was so caught up in the conversation with Momma and Reena I didn't even see them approaching.

"Hey, Momma, Charles, and how you, miss?" Wayne spoke to each of us.

"How y'all doin'?" Richard said, then Bo greeted right after that.

"All right, how y'all doin'?" I said.

"Hey," Momma said.

"Hi there," Reena replied, glancing at each of them.

"Momma, you 'bout ready?" Bo asked eagerly. "Ain't no need o' standin' 'round here talkin' all day, now.

I know my brothers, and I could tell by the looks on their faces they were wondering who Reena was.

Momma rolled her eyes and shook her head at Bo. "Good Lord. The food gon' be at the house when you get there, Bo," Momma said sternly.

Bo grinned without commenting. All of us laughed.

"Charles, you gon' introduce us to the lady? Where yo' manners at, man?" Wayne asked, grinning, not able to hold in his curiosity anymore.

"I sho' am," I answered. "Boys, this is Reena Hickman." I held my hand in front of her. "And Reena, these are my brothers, Wayne, Richard, and Bo." I pointed at each of them.

"How are y'all doin?" Reena extended her hand to each of them.

The moment they finished shaking hands, a few more members slipped up and joined our little circle.

"Hey, there, Sister Mildred," Sister Dixon said as she and Sister Kirkwood stood next to Momma.

"Hey, y'all," Momma spoke back.

"Mildred, these folks keep on talkin' 'bout this big dinner you havin' later on. If I hear one mo' word 'bout it, I'ma have to come by and get me a plate or somethin'," Sister Kirkwood said lightheartedly.

"Well, you do just that. You know you welcome," Momma replied. "I guess we need to be gettin' on outta

here, so I can get home and get everythang warmed up."
Momma made that statement just in time.

Deeberry had finished talking with most of the other
members and was on his way to our little group. The
second he walked up, the atmosphere just shifted into
downhill mode. At least for me it did.

"Well, how's all of y'all doin'?" he said, eyeballing each
of us. "Charles, glad to see you made it this mornin'."

"I'm glad to be here, Pastor," I spoke sharply. "You
preached a good sermon." I could barely get that lie out of
my mouth, but if I was going to say anything to him, those
words were my best choice.

"Thank ya, thank ya very much," he said then turned to
Momma with a more serious look. "Sis' Mildred, I hate to
hear Sis' Katie and the boys gon' be leavin' the church."

"Well, we do too, but if that's what she feels is right for
her, and if God is pointin' her in that direction, then that's
what she got to do," Momma said sternly.

"You sho' right, sistah," he replied. Well, when you see
her, give her my love, and tell her that her and the boys
always welcome to come back home and visit wit' us
anytime." He pasted that phony beam on his face that I so
despised.

Wayne and I seized eye contact instantly. Wayne's sly
look told me that he knew what I was thinking about
Deeberry. So did Richard and Bo. They gave me the exact
same look as Wayne, and at the same time, they were
barely holding back their laughs.

"Well, we gon' head on out, y'all," I said, attempting to
expedite my visit with Deeberry. "Bo, where'd AJ go?" I
scanned over the church, pretending to look for AJ just to
keep Deeberry from interrupting me as Reena and I walked
away.

"The last I seen of him, he was headin' out toward the
cemetery," Bo answered, still trying to keep from laughing
at me.

"A'ight, man," I said to Bo then turned to Reena and
whispered, "Let's go." I saw how Deeberry was watching

197

Reena's and my every move, It was no surprise to me when he quickly plugged a spot to be nosy.

"Miss? You come back to see us, now, ya hear?" Deeberry uttered, staring at Reena as we motioned to walk off.

"I will. Thank y—"

"I don't believe I caught your name, though." Deeberry cut her off before she could even finish her "thank you."

I jumped in to her rescue. "That's 'cause she didn't throw it at ya, and fur—"

"Charles! Wayne!" Momma quickly called out, stopping me from telling Deeberry off. "Y'all go on out to the cemetery wit' Kenny and AJ and get them flowers laid out, please. We got to hurr-up. Time movin' on."

Wayne, Richard, and Bo was trying their best to keep from laughing out. Reena looked really confused.

"Come on, y'all, let's roll out. We don't wanna get the old lady riled up," Bo teased.

The five of us left Momma, Deeberry, Sister Dixon, and Sister Kirkwood standing in the middle of the floor. Out at the cemetery, Kenny and AJ had already started placing flowers on the family plot. It wasn't long before we were finished with the whole plot. Shortly after, we all gathered around the dining room table at Momma's house. The ones who didn't get a chance to meet Reena at church were introduced to her at the house. Reena seemed to be enjoying herself, listening to my crazy brothers clown around. Sharon, Ms. Hattie, and Momma were busy warming up the food and putting it on the dining room table. Momma's house was filled with laughter and excitement like usual during her Sunday dinners. I felt somewhat warmhearted as I observed how everybody seemed to be in the greatest of moods. I hastily decided it was as good a time as any to lay the news on 'em.

"Excuse me, everybody. I have an announcement to make," I said aloud, raising one hand in the air. The noise ceased and all eyes turned to me. Reena looked at me in wonder like everybody else.

# ReChella

"Is everybody in here? Everybody listening?" I asked, scrolling my eyes over the room.

"Yeah, man, everybody in here," Wayne answered, sounding impatient. "Now come on wit' the come on. I don't need nothin' to be distractin' me from dinner, so hurry up."

"Aw, hush, Wayne. Even if it is somethin' distractin', I doubt very seriously if it's gon' keep you from eatin'," Kenny said, laughing.

"I know that's right," Sharon agreed as she and Momma walked in with the last of the food and put it down on the table.

"Well, me and Reena would like for all of you to be the first to hear our good news," I said pleasantly. Reena's eyes widened with alarm. She was obviously not expecting what she figured was coming next. She probably didn't think I was going to tell everybody so soon. Too late to turn back now, so I carried on. "I asked Reena to marry me and she accepted."

Silence combed over the room as I waited for somebody to say something. Nobody mumbled a word. Not even Reena. She remained confined to a very nervous smile. Some of my family stared at me in astonishment, while the rest of them glanced around at each other.

"This is not the response I thought we'd get. Is anybody gon' say anything?" I said, looking around.

Momma looked like she was going to faint, but she managed to stumble through a few words. "Yeah . . . sho' we are. Congratulations, ahhh, to . . . to y'all. Right? Everybody? Open ya mouths," she demanded.

Even after Momma demanded that the others speak, still nobody said anything. Damn, I expected them to be surprised, but completely speechless? Reena looked like she was about to hyperventilate. Therefore, I had to take up everybody else's slack.

"I know it may seem a little sudden, but the fact is, me and Reena love each other and we just wanna make it right," I stated, still scanning around at everybody.

I knew I was stretching it with that "we love each other"

bit. Hell, like Reena said in the beginning, we hadn't really known each other long enough for love to be the reason. But if we were going to be convincing to my family and to others, we would have to play the entire role. Momma slowly looked around at everybody again, then re-parked her eyes on me.

"Well, ya see, we all think it's wonderful . . . and well, I guess maybe," Momma began to say, then paused. She slumped her head over, shaking it from side to side, then quickly raised it again. "What I'm tryin' to say is . . ."

"What she tryin' to say, Charles, is that we all happy for you and Reena, but we just didn't see it comin', 'cause this is our first time meetin' her and all," Kenny jumped in and finished Momma's explanation, then addressed Reena. "And, well, Reena our silence and surprise don't mean no disrespect to you, and we hope you don't take it in any way offensive." Kenny did a great job of smoothing everything over for Reena's sake. Shit, I was happy as hell to hear how he fixed things up.

"That's right, sugar. We don't mean no harm to you," Momma said softly, looking to have a better hold on things now.

Not a face in the dining room wore anything less than seriousness.

Reena looked at Momma with the same gentleness that she'd given her.

"Thank you, Ms. Mildred, and thank you too, Kenny, for being honest. And no, I'm not offended at all," Reena said, smiling from Momma to Kenny.

I appreciated my family's concern, and even though things seemed to be smoothing over, I had become somewhat on the annoyed side at how everybody was making such an issue of it.

"Is all of this really necessary? I mean, it's really not that big of a deal, y'all," I stated firmly.

Momma turned to me. "Charles, let's go talk about this in private," she said peacefully.

"Naw, Momma," Kenny interrupted, protesting before I

could answer. "If you don't mind me sayin', I don't think that's a good idea. I mean, everybody in here done already heard the announcement, and I'm sure everybody already thinkin' whatever they wanna think. We may as well say what we gon' say out loud instead of makin' it seem like we talkin' behind somebody's back or in secret." Kenny made all the sense in the world. I nodded for his suggestion.

"That's right. I agree wit' Kenny," I said. "Besides, I don't want Reena to feel uncomfortable."

"Too late," Ms. Hattie exclaimed, pointing at Reena. "Look at her. Y'all done terrified the po' woman." Ms. Hattie was serious as suicide, but her way of expression always came off as some kind of joking. It was hard to keep from laughing at the way Ms. Hattie made her statement about Reena being frightened.

"No. No. I'm fine," Reena said with assurance. "In fact, I admire you all's honesty. I can see that you all love Charles very much, and just want what's best for him. Well, so do I."

"Charles, I just think you may be rushin' thangs a li'l," Momma said, looking concerned. "Boy, you just went through a messy divorce wit' a woman who ran all over town spreadin' lies on ya." Momma raised her voice three octaves. That told me she was not for any playing around.

"Aw, now, Momma, come on," Wayne interrupted, dragging his words as if he were tired. "Ain't no need'a bringin' all o' that up. This woman ain't got nothin' to do wit' what Bettie did."

"That's true, Mildred. I know Charles yo' son and you love him, but he a grown man, sugar. He know what he doin'," Ms. Hattie stated bluntly, agreeing with Wayne, and sounding to still be speaking from jokes-ville.

"Wayne, I didn't ask you or Hattie a darn thang. Now, please, speak when y'all spoken to," Momma said honestly then turned back to me. "Charles, you don't think you rushin' this? I mean, y'all got plenty time to get to know each other. As a matter of fact, how long you been seein' each other, anyhow?"

# Scandalous

"Momma, that don't matter. All that matters is how we feel about each other," I urged. I dared not tell them that Reena and I had only known each other for two days. I would've probably had to rush everybody to the emergency room for going into cardiac-arrest.

"Momma, I'm wit' Charles. He a grown man. He old enough to know what he doin'," Bo said, grabbing a roll off the table, trying to be as serious as he could be. "Let's look at the facts here. Charles been married longer than some of us been livin'. If he don't know what to expect by now, I'm afraid ain't no hope at all for me, Richard, and AJ." Bo looked around rather nonchalantly, noticing how everybody was quietly peering at him like we wanted to smack him one up side his head. His silly way of trying to get his message across reminded me of Ms. Hattie.

"What?" he exclaimed. "It's the truth."

"Boy. If you say one mo' word, I'm gon' sock you one, so help me. Then I'm sendin' ya out wit' no dinner," Momma declared.

Everybody began to laugh. Thank goodness that comment broke the serious mood just a little.

"May I say somethin', please?" Reena softly uttered.

"Sho', you can say whatever you feel. You in this too," Momma replied smoothly. We quietly turned our attention to Reena.

"Thank you, Ms. Mildred." Reena gestured with one hand. "I didn't mean to cause any family problems or anything. Obviously, you all are close enough to discuss everything as a family. That alone tells me I wouldn't want to be in this family without being welcomed by each one of you. I know that Charles and I are adults and we can make our own decisions, but honestly, I don't even want us to be married unless we have your blessings. In fact, now that I'm sitting here listening to everybody, I realize I have a question that I'd like Charles to answer. I didn't feel that it was relevant to us, but maybe it is." Reena turned her teary eyes to me, looking as innocent as a newborn baby's eyes.

Her voice was delicate, shaking even. She definitely

captured everybody's undivided attention, then she came out with it. "Honey, please believe. I don't mean any harm, but I have to know the answer to this question. It's been popping in and out of my head since you asked me to marry you, but I kept driving it out. Is it all right for me to ask you this in front of everybody?" Reena asked humbly.

I had no idea where all of those dramatics were coming from, so now I was nervous and skeptical as hell, but I went ahead and reluctantly agreed.

"Baby, if you feel comfortable askin' me, then by all means, ask me right here," I stated warily.

I quickly recalled all the talk that she and I had done Saturday morning. I couldn't figure out what her question was going to be. I uneasily waited, hoping that I wasn't showing any signs of my skepticism.

"Thank you." Reena's eyes burned deep into mine. "Did your asking me to marry you have anything to do with how much Bettie hurt you when she told all those lies on you after you suspected she was cheating with one of your group members . . . then you caught her red-handed with your best friend, Preston?" Reena maintained her innocent look, but I almost pissed in my pants. I didn't see that one coming, nor did I understand what it had to do with anything.

"What?"

"I know you lyin!"

"You caught 'em, Charles?"

"When?"

"Where?"

"I know it wasn't Preston!"

"Now, that's some shit."

"She was foolin' wit' Preston?"

So many questions and comments were flying about in the air, I couldn't tell who was saying what. Reena watched the fireworks go off amongst the family. I couldn't deny to them that the incident with Bettie had taken place, but because of my oath to the group, I was not going to confirm even for my family that the man with Bettie was Preston.

But at the same time, I had no control over what Reena told. After all, she did see them with her own eyes.

"Hold up. Hold up. Wait a minute, y'all! I don't understand a word nobody sayin'," I exclaimed, waving both hands in the air. Everybody calmed down.

"Charles, is that true?" Momma asked, infuriated. "Did you catch Bettie?"

"Yeah, Momma, I did," I answered pitifully.

"And how long was that goin' on?" Momma continued.

"To tell you the truth, I really don't know. The only thing I'm fo' sho' of is when I caught her," I said.

"And when was that?" Richard asked.

"Reena and I drove to Southaven to get a bottle of wine," I replied to Richard. "On the way back home, we stopped for her to use the ladies' room at Waffle House on Church Road. The parking lot was so crowded, I pulled in right next door at the Fairfield Inn and waited for her there. That's when I saw Bettie and the man she was wit' at the hotel. Then me and Bettie got into a confrontation."

Momma bore a face of fury. She looked like she wanted to kill somebody.

"I knew that heifer wasn't no good for you," Momma stated frantically. "All them lies she told, she wasn't doin' nothin' but tryin' to throw the bloodhounds off her own damn trail." Momma pulled out a seat and sat down at the table.

"Was it really Preston wit' her?" AJ asked.

I knew I wasn't going to answer that one. "It really don't make no difference who was wit' her, y'all. The fact of the matter is she got caught in her own web of lies," I said, avoiding answering AJ's question.

Just when I thought I'd successfully evaded it, big mouth Sharon finally exploded into the interrogation.

"That's a lie! It make plenty of difference who she was wit'. 'Cause if she was wit' somebody you call a friend, then obviously that friend wasn't a friend from the git-go," Sharon exclaimed, widening her eyes.

I was puzzled anyhow as to what had taken her so long

to add her two cents. Sharon staying quiet for as long as she had was a new record. Why couldn't she just sit her loud ass down and stay quiet for a change, like Linda? Linda sat in her chair and listened without so much as breathing too loud. Finally, everybody who wasn't already sitting pulled up a chair and sat down at the table and began fixing their plates.

The conversation for the rest of the evening was about lying, cheating, low-down Bettie. And naturally, they all tried to sway me into confirming who the man was with Bettie. I didn't. As I listened to the family yak on and on, I realized I never got a chance to answer Reena's question. It, of course, was what brought on the yakking. The more I thought about it, the more I kept arriving at the conclusion that Reena's question wasn't one that she really wanted an answer to. I figured out that she'd used the question as a diversion to get my family off the subject of me and her getting married and onto something else. Slick heifer, but it worked.

# Chapter Sixteen

A few weeks had gone by and Reena and I soon found ourselves standing at the altar of Mount Pleasant Baptist Church, draped in our lovely wedding attire. She wore a beautiful cream-colored satiny wedding dress, trimmed in lace and pearls, and a nice clamp-on head-piece to match. There was no outrageously long wedding dress train or unusually decorated veil. We kept it simple but elegant. Two bridesmaids, Linda and Sharon, and two groomsmen, Wayne and Kenny. Reena didn't have any sisters, but her best friend, Eileen Chambers, was her maid of honor. Richard, AJ, and Bo pulled straws for my best man role, since none of them were gung-ho about renting or wearing the "uncomfortable tuxedo," as they put it. When AJ won the best man title by pulling the shortest straw, the family teased him all the way up 'til the big day. I stood in my cream-colored tailed tuxedo and watched as my eight-year-old niece, Jasmine, the little flower girl, delighted herself in scattering flower petals all over the aisle, while smiling every chance she got at her mommy and daddy, Wayne and Sharon. As soon as Jasmine reached the front of the church, she stopped and took in a deep breath, smiling.

"I made it up here, Mommy and Daddy," she exclaimed in her soft, little voice. The wedding party along with the entire audience laughed softly at her cute little scene.

"That's nice, baby," Sharon whispered. "Now, hurry and take your place over here."

Then came the ringing of the traditional wedding song, and along with that my stunning bride. I had to admit, over time I'd grown very fond of Reena. In fact, I could honestly say that I cared about her. Reena's father escorted her up the aisle. She was as beautiful as a story-book bride, and she didn't seem nervous at all as she sauntered up the aisle wearing a faint smile on her face. I watched her and prepared to take her hand.

# ReChella

"Who gives this bride?" the minister asked promptly.

"I do," Reena's father answered, then she took her place beside me.

Reena's pastor, Pastor Milam, did the honors of marrying us. Deeberry was never even considered for the job. I'd already explained to Reena my problems with him. Reena and I stood at the altar side by side. Pastor Milam engrossed a stern but gracious expression as he nodded to us then began the sacred vows proceedings. "Dearly beloved, we are gathered here today to join in Holy Matrimony, Charles and Reena."

The ceremony was short and sweet, and the small, intimate reception was even shorter and sweeter. We all had a great time, though. Later that night, Reena and I checked into the big, beautiful Marquis Hotel in Memphis as Mr. and Mrs. Charles Jennings. We celebrated all weekend. Damn, I honestly didn't think there were so many different ways of fucking, but Reena showed me some thangs. We did everything short of hang out on the tenth floor window ledge. That first time she and I had sex in my truck at the rest stop, and everything we'd done leading up to the wedding night wasn't nothing compared to some of the shit we did in that damn hotel. The second we closed our room door, she shut herself up in the bathroom for about fifteen minutes, and when she was ready to come out, she insisted I close my eyes and don't peek. She eased up behind me and covered my eyes with both her hands, then whispered in my ear.

"I've got a surprise for you, baby."

I could hear the enthusiasm in her voice, so I became enthusiastic too. "Well, uncover my eyes already so I can see it," I said.

When she moved her hands away and I turned around, I almost jumped out of my skin. "What the fuck?" I yelled before I knew it.

She had on a skin-tight leopard suit with a long-ass tail sticking out the back and two big holes for her breasts to hang out. As if that wasn't weird enough, she had on a matching leopard mask with whiskers dangling on each side of the nose.

"Damn, baby. You scared me for a minute." I searched her twice-over, trying to figure out just what the fuck she was.

"You like it? she asked, purring like a cat. "I bought it just for you."

Hell, it sounded like Eartha Kitt was up in there with all that purring going on.

"It's interesting," I said, still stunned.

She suddenly leaped on the bed just like a real leopard and flipped onto her back, spreading her legs wide open.

"If you think the suit's interesting, check this out," she purred, pointing downward.

*Well, I'll be damned,* I said in my head. The crotch area of the suit had a big, round hole in it for her pussy to be exposed just like her breasts were. She didn't even have to take the damn thing off for me to fuck her. The more I stared at her and thought about it, the more she resembled the hell out of a leaping leopard. *Where in the hell did she come up with some sick shit like this?* I thought.

"What are you waiting for, tiger? Come and get it." She purred again.

I didn't want to put a damper on the moment, but that purring shit was gon' have to go. It was weird enough that it looked like I was getting ready to fuck somebody from *Wild Kingdom*, but to sound like it too, I couldn't handle that. Luckily, by the time I stripped off my clothes and dived on her, she was talking normal again. I rubbed my dick over her exposed pussy then rammed it inside her, thrusting in and out. After we worked that way for a while, she backed that ass up to me and we did it doggy-style up in the bed. She used her hands to support her as she spread her legs and ass open, rolling over my dick non-stop. While she rolled, I slapped that ass repeatedly, watching it jiggle like jelly through the suit.

Her titties were hanging through the titty-holes of the suit and swinging back and forth. I took my hands from her ass cheeks and reached down under her, grabbing both big, soft titties. I squeezed them tight and caressed them as she continued working her pussy on my dick. Sometime later that night, after we'd done plenty more kinky shit, we finally simmered down and fell asleep. I remember thinking before I fell off, it was official; Reena was a bona fide sex fiend. I never thought I'd hear myself say it, but I could hardly wait to get home so I could get some rest.

# Chapter Seventeen

Will jabbed me with his elbow as we made our way out of the church and stood in the lobby. "Charles, do I have a surprise for you, my brotha," he said, grinning wider than all outside. We'd just finished singing on a program at the Pilgrim Zion church in Memphis.

"What's up, man?" I asked. He looked like he could hardly hold whatever the surprise was.

"I got a blast from the past for ya."

"A blast from the past?" I gave him a curious look, wanting him to go ahead and tell me about the surprise.

"One of yo' old flames stepped in the building tonight. One you haven't seen for a good minute."

"Well, don't keep me in suspense all night. Tell me who it is, man," I insisted.

"Emma Barnett," he said excitedly.

I instantly visualized Emma in my head and really began smiling then. "Man, you lyin'." I chuckled. "You right, I ain't heard from her in at least three years, maybe more. How come I ain't seen her in here tonight?"

"Probably 'cause she sittin' way up top on the other side. I wouldn't o' seen her either if I hadn't went over there to holla at my brotha and my sistah-in-law 'bout a hour after we got here," Will told me.

I was only halfway listening to him, 'cause while he was talking, I was remembering the luscious ass Emma had on her.

"Man, she still the same? How she look?" I asked.

"Man, she look better than a mug," he stated with extra enthusiasm. "And so did her friend she had wit' her."

"Friend?"

"Yeah, it gets better, my brotha." Will lit up even more. "She wanna see you tonight. In fact, her and her friend wanna see both of us tonight. I went ahead and took the liberty of tellin' 'em we'd meet at the GTL right after the program." Will cut his eyes at me. "That's cool wit' you?"

I was already thinking of a good lie to tell Reena. "Is it? Man, please. You and me gon' ride together or what?" I said, confirming our plans for the night.

"Yeah, that'll be fine." Will nodded. "You just come on down to my house, then we'll drive down to the hotel to meet 'em in my black Buick."

"I can hardly wait."

Shit, it had already been three months since the wedding, and things were going just dandy with Reena and me. After our weekend honeymoon was over, we returned home and fell into a nice husband-and-wife routine. We'd work through the day and fuck nearly every night. To be a forty-five-year-old woman, Reena had an extremely high sex drive. At least in my opinion she did. She was the first woman I'd had at that age who wanted to fuck every day, sometimes twice a day. It was an interesting experience at first, but I was getting a little bored with the same ole, same ole. I hadn't had no new pussy since weeks before we got married. A night out with an old flame was just what I needed. Yeah, I was gon' get all up in Emma's stuff. Will and I were getting ready to make our way outside when he nudged me.

"Don't look now, man, but you ain't gon' believe who comin' our way," he said, barely moving his lips while looking over my shoulder. Before I turned around to look, there she stood.

"Good evenin', Charles. Will," she said, gesturing her head.

"Good evenin', Bettie," Will replied.

"How you doin'?" I said very cool.

"May I see you privately for a minute?" Bettie asked politely.

It was a surprise to see her not so uptight and bitter, but it was an even bigger surprise to hear her say she wanted to see me in private.

"Sure," I said without delay. "Let's walk out to the parking lot to your car. That is, if it's all right."

"Yes, that's fine," she said.

"Will, don't go nowhere. I'll be right back," I said, walking away with her.

"A'ight," Will answered.

Bettie and I made our way through the crowd and walked out to the parking lot. She had a somewhat severe look about her. It almost looked as if she was in some kind of trouble and was dreading asking my help to get her out of it. Whatever she had on her mind humbled her unbelievably well, especially considering the way she'd acted when we last ran into each other at the Fairfield Inn parking lot.

"All right, what's going on?" I asked peacefully as we walked.

Bettie's serious look intensified as she started talking. "Listen, Charles, I am by no means tryin' to get in your business, but I heard somethin' very disturbin' from a reliable source. And well, I thought you should know," she said with certainty. Her grim, concerned tone grasped my full attention.

"Okay, what is it?" I asked as we approached her car.

"It's about your wife, Charles," Bettie replied cautiously.

"What about her?" I frowned, staring at Bettie.

"From what I've been told, she has some problems," Bettie stuttered.

I could tell Bettie was reluctant to say whatever it was she'd supposedly found out about Reena.

"Some problems?" I repeated, hoping she'd go on and get to the point. "What kinda problems?"

"Some very, very serious ones," Bettie continued. "You need to watch yourself, Charles. I mean, like I said . . . I'm not tryin' to get in your business, but after hearin' what happened with the last guy she was dating, I guess I felt like it would be wrong not to at least warn you, regardless of what happened between us. After all, I wouldn't wish anything fatal on you or nobody else." Bettie's troubled expression was now worse, and she really disturbed me when she said the word "fatal."

# ReChella

"Wait, wait. Hold on just a minute, now. Fatal?" I held one hand in the air. "When you say some serious problems, can you elaborate a li'l more? And what happened with what guy she used to date? I'm just not gettin' it. I wish you'd just come on out and tell me what you wanna tell me, Bettie." A deep array of concern came over me, and Bettie and I peered at each other intensely.

For a second or two, I think we actually forgot that we ended our marriage not being able to stand each other. Her concern was more than clear, and at that moment, I appreciated it.

"Okay, okay," she said, slowly gesturing one hand in front of her. "Charles, she was seein' this man down in Holly Springs for about two years, and she found out he was cheatin' on her—"

"Well, hello." Another female voice cut off Bettie's words. "I'm not interrupting anything, am I?" Reena asked, easing up without warning.

Bettie and I were so engaged in the conversation, neither of us realized that Reena was headed in our direction. We both looked surprise. I turned my attention to Reena.

"Naw, baby . . . uhh, uhh, you ain't interruptin'. I happened to see Bettie in the lobby, and I was just hollerin' at her to clear up any misundastandin' 'bout the last time we ran into each other in Southaven." I spit out the first thing that came to mind.

I didn't know why, but for some reason, this eerie feeling came over me when Reena walked up. And Bettie sure didn't waste no time getting the hell out of dodge.

"Is that a fact?" Reena asked with a cunning smirk on her face as she parked herself alongside me and locked her arm in mine. "Good evening, Bettie."

"Good evening, Reena," Bettie replied, opening her car door.

"Don't hurry on account of me." Reena shot Bettie a wicked sneer.

"I was about to leave anyway," Bettie snapped, then got

in her car and took off without saying another word.

"Was it something I said?" Reena laughed sarcastically.

"Naw, you didn't say nothin'," I answered, playing it off like Bettie and whatever she was talking about didn't matter. "She's always a smart-ass, anyhow. You know that. Come on, let's head back to the lobby." I hated that Bettie didn't get a chance to finish telling me what she'd started, but I told myself I'd get in touch with her later so she could tell me the rest. I had a serious case of curiosity now.

"Charles, I don't think I like the idea of your ex-wife being up in your face like that," Reena said as we walked back toward the church.

"Baby, she the last person you need to worry 'bout," I said with assurance.

"Oh, really?" Reena stopped in her tracks. "Well, who's the first?" She seemed to have slipped into uptight mode all of a sudden.

"Nobody." I yanked her hand to keep walking. "I was just lettin' you know you don't have to worry 'bout no mess like that."

"I don't? Well, that's good to know, because I don't want to have to." The sternness in Reena's voice was steadily increasing. "You know, in spite of everything that happened with you and Bettie, she's still in love with you, Charles."

*Where the hell did that come from?* I asked myself silently, stopping in my tracks now. "I know you don't believe that," I stated firmly.

Reena began nodding like I had asked her if she wanted to fuck. "Oh yeah, she's got it bad for you, Charles. Why else would she be screwing her way through your gospel group buddies?" Reena asked me the question then answered it for me. "I'll tell you why. Because somewhere in her sick, perverted little mind, she thinks she's staying close to you by being with them." Reena talked as if she knew her theory was fact.

"What?" I demanded, shaking my head.

Reena wasn't making a bit of sense, but she insisted on continuing with her foolish belief.

"It's true," she stated with confidence. "I know it seems hard to believe, but those are the facts. Your singing buddies are close to you, so she figures the closer she is to them, the closer she is to you. It's that logical to her."

What kind of crazy-ass shit was that? And what kind of crazy-ass mind could have thought of that? I had to put her in her place.

"Ain't nothin' logical 'bout what you just said, Reena. Besides, Bettie was wit' one member of my group, Preston. She ain't been wit' none of the other guys. Now, those are the facts," I retorted.

"How do you know that? You think they're going to openly admit it to you? Preston wouldn't have told you if you hadn't caught him red-handed. And furthermore, why are you defending Bettie?" Reena demanded angrily.

We had almost reached yelling level. I knew I needed to calm things on back down.

"Look, baby. I'm not defendin' anybody. Least of all, Bettie. All I'm sayin' is, I think you a li'l off base, and to be honest wit' ya, I don't really care who doin' what, 'cause ain't none of it gon' affect me and the guys' brotherhood," I said calmly and with certainty, which seemed to irk Reena even more.

"All right, Charles, but don't let me have to say I told you so." Reena turned away from me, indicating that the subject was now closed.

Will was waiting at the front of the church as Reena and I walked up.

"How you doin' tonight, Reena?" Will asked courteously.

"I'm fine, Will. How are you?" Reena answered.

"Charles, you gon' trail me on down to the house so we can work on that project, or you got to make a stop first?" Will asked.

"Naw, I'm gon' take my wife by the house first, then I'll be on down. I won't be too far behind ya," I told him.

Reena shot me a *where the fuck you going?* look as William walked away.

"What are you talking about, Charles? You're taking me

home and going where?" she demanded.

"Oh hell, I forgot to tell ya. Me and Will gettin' together at his house to work on some important group business," I answered as she and I headed to the truck.

"What kind of group business can you all be working on this time of night?" Reena's question was filled with doubt, which made me mad as hell, 'cause I hadn't given her a reason not to trust me.

I was tensed now, so my reply was sure enough on the rude side. "Number one, it's only ten-thirty. That's not late. Number two, that's why it's called group business. It ain't for nobody else to know. That includes you."

"But, Charles," Reena contested.

"Excuse me for interruptin', but what's the big deal?" I asked angrily. "I just told you where I'm goin', and that should be good enough for you. What's wit' the third degree? I haven't done anything to deserve it. Are you thinkin' somethin' or worried about somethin' that you need to share with me? 'Cause if you are, it's completely unfair, ya know." I laid it on thick.

She seemed to mellow out after hearing my *I'm angry and wounded* pitch.

"You're right. I'm sorry, honey," she said softly, sliding over in the truck and laying her head on my shoulder. "I guess I just let my imagination run wild when I saw you talking with Bettie. Forgive me? I know you wouldn't do anything to hurt me. " She stayed quiet 'til I dropped her off at home.

Afterward, I drove straight to Will's, and as planned, we met Emma and her girlfriend at the Gulf Travel Lodge in Sardis, better known as the GTL Motel. The little place was only about fifteen minutes south of Senatobia, but it was the most secluded one around. Will and Emma's friend checked in their room, and me and Emma checked in ours.

Emma hadn't changed much at all. She was still hotter than the Georgia asphalt, and soft on me like a bail of freshly picked cotton. She swore the only reason she left Senatobia in the first place was because I up and married

Bettie instead of her after Ruth died. Emma reminded me that after everything she and I had gone through over all those years, she should've been the one walking down the aisle with me.

She and I reminisced and caught up on some of the time we'd missed in the last three years or so, but most importantly, we fucked real good for old times' sake. Emma put on a magical show for me. I didn't make it home 'til about 4:00 that morning. I walked in the house humming a silent, new tune that was cut damn short, damn quick. Reena was waiting for me on the den sofa in the dark. She sat there in her black nightgown, staring straight ahead.

"It's her, isn't it? I was right, wasn't I?" Reena asked gently without turning to look at me as I walked into the den.

"Hey, you still up?" I asked, surprised, ignoring the question she'd asked. I strolled over to the sofa and stood behind her.

"Answer my question," Reena said delicately, as if she was forcing herself to stay calm.

"What question, baby?" I asked, hoping to sound confused.

"Is . . . it . . . her?" Reena spelled the question out that time, so I couldn't ignore it. My next best thing was to play dumb.

"Is what who? What you talkin' 'bout?" I asked, leaning over her.

"Are you fucking Bettie?" Reena asked candidly, turning around to face me now.

"You got to be kiddin' me. We went through this earlier. I ain't fuckin' nobody but you." My fake innocent eyes stared into Reena's.

She didn't say anything for a few minutes, then she allowed a few words to tenderly slide through her lips. "Charles, I only asked you about Bettie to give you a chance to be honest with me."

I sighed and tried to speak as tenderly as she had. "Reena, I don't know why you thinkin' what you thinkin' . .

. but you wrong. That's all I can say."

Reena definitely had the right string, but the wrong yo-yo. She may have suspected that I had done a little dirt that night, but she was way out in left field thinking it was with Bettie.

Reena raised up from the sofa. "I can see the lust in your eyes . . . and I can smell the sex all over you." She began walking toward the bedroom door. "I can take a lot, you know. Much more than most women, because I'm logical and very practical. If you want to come clean and be honest with me, we can try to work something out. I'm all for it," she uttered, peering at me threateningly. "But my advice is to do it now, before everything goes bad."

Watching her turn away from me and go into the bedroom with that glum look, and hearing how words that were supposed to be "upset words" eased out of her mouth, gave me that same eerie feeling I'd gotten when she tipped up on me and Bettie in the parking lot earlier that night.

# Chapter Eighteen

The next several weeks weren't any better. I couldn't stay away from Emma. It was almost like she had drugged me. When I didn't get a chance to see her on the weekend, I met her on weekdays during work hours, mostly in Memphis. Reena knew that things between me and her had taken a turn for the worse. Her silent treatment and nonchalant attitude toward me gave me all the room I needed. Plenty of times I'd be out with Emma, and because I knew Reena wasn't going to say anything when I got home, I stayed on and had my fun with ease. As much as she loved sex, Reena had even cut me off from that, which was fine, because Emma was fucking my brains out. I guess she was trying to make up for lost time.

Nevertheless, I got the surprise of all surprises one Friday night when I made it home a day early from a job-related trip. I unlocked the door and went in the house. All seemed normal. As I walked toward my bedroom to put up my grip-case and suit-bag, I heard music coming from upstairs. Marvin Gaye's "Sexual Healing" caught my attention. *Why on earth did she come up here to listen to music? If it was to avoid me, she knew I wasn't gon' be here 'til tomorrow,* I thought as I reached the top of the stairs. As I stood in the hallway, I could've sworn I heard additional music coming from the bedroom next to my office, and it wasn't the "Sexual Healing" song, either. Maybe I was just tired from the long ride. Yeah, that had to be it, I figured. I made my way to the door of the room where Keshundra stayed when she was there. "Sexual Healing" rang out loud and clear from that room, but you couldn't tell me I didn't hear a man's voice faintly moaning under the music. I leaned my head into the door to listen closer.

"Mmm. Mmm. Mmm. Mmm." Reena's unforgettable, high-pitched squeal emerged from inside the room.

Without hesitation, I turned the knob and stormed into

the room. I didn't want to believe what I was seeing. Reena was stretched out in the bed butt naked, rolling her ass like a wild woman on a Ferris wheel, and I had to do a double-take at the man humping between her legs fiercely.

"What the hell!" I yelled out. "Reena!"

At the sound of my voice, they jumped up, looking like they'd seen a ghost, and began grabbing for the covers to hide their naked asses.

"Charles! What are you doin' here?" Reena exclaimed, snatching the sheet up over her breasts.

"Lawd have mercy! God almighty, help me! Brother Charles, I'm sorry! Please don't overreact," he screamed, crying like a damn punk.

"Deeberry!" I yelled, shaking my head from side to side. "Can't say I'm surprised. I knew you wasn't nothin' but a low-life ape in the woods, but I woulda gave you more credit than to be comin' up in a man's house."

I was more angry about them fucking in my house than I was about them fucking each other.

"Look, brother Charles . . ." he started.

"I ain't yo' damn, brotha, so don't say it no mo', nigga," I cut him off. "Just get yo' shit and get the fuck outta my house befo' I do somethin' to ya," I told him.

Reena didn't even try to get up from the bed. She calmly reached over and turned off the stereo, still holding the covers up over her.

Deeberry was gathering his clothes together as fast as he could.

"Please, let's try to talk about this in the right way," he begged nervously.

"Talk? Look, man, ain't shit to talk about. I don't need no excuses or explanations from neither one of y'all." I glanced from him to Reena. "I just want you and yo' ho to get the fuck outta here right now."

Up 'til I said ho, Reena had kept her cool, even with the dull, lifeless frown she had on her face.

"Ho?" she snapped. "Who are you calling a ho? Is that what you call that bitch you been fucking?" She peered at me with eyes of evil, then slung the covers off her and jumped up naked as a Jay-bird. "Yes, I fucked him. So what? It ain't no more for me to do it than it is for you to do it. You think you have a different set of rules just because you're a man. Well, guess what? Men ain't the only ones with needs. Women like to fuck too. Wake up and smell the new millennium. This ain't 1920, nigga. Wives ain't just laying around at home waiting on sorry-ass husbands like you to come home and fuck 'em, especially if you bringing the dick home tired out and used up by somebody else. Put up or shut up, 'cause I'm gonna get mine. Ain't no ifs, ands, or buts about that." She stopped talking just long enough to reach down and grab an exotic, sheer black robe off the floor and quickly slip it on.

"You been out in the streets doing what you want, with who you want, then coming home all times of the night for weeks," she continued. "And I haven't been running behind you or hounding you about any of it. But you got the nerves to come up in here tripping. You better calm the fuck down. Hell, it ain't nothing but pussy. He can't get it all."

For a brief moment, I looked at her, shocked that she had the nerve to be standing up in my house saying some shit like that.

"Come up in here tripping? In case you done forgot, this is my house, smart-ass bitch," I barked.

"And I'm gettin' out of it, Brotha Charles." Deeberry tossed his nervous words in. He'd quickly jumped in his clothes as best he could while Reena was gabbing her mouth at me. He took a couple of steps to walk past me and go out of the door.

*Claccck!* My fist landed smack-dab in the middle of his jawbone. *Plicckety-plow!* He hit the damn floor.

"Not without one of them first," I stated angrily.

He grabbed the side of his face that I'd punched, while at the same time getting up, groaning. "Ohh . . ."

"Now you can get the hell outta here." I gestured my hand for him to leave.

Reena dashed to his aid. "Charles, that shit wasn't

called for, and you know it," she exclaimed.

"Naw, that's all right. I'm fine," he said, holding his jawbone. "I had it comin'. I didn't have no business in his house," Deeberry admitted pitifully.

"Damn right you didn't. Now get to steppin'," I demanded.

Reena looked like she wanted to rip my heart out. The wickedness in her eyes penetrated right through me, but that was my house, and I was going to say just what I wanted. "And you don't have to worry none, 'cause you goin' right out wit' him." I pulled the door back wide to let them out. Deeberry stepped out into the hall first, then Reena started walking behind him.

"You son of a bitch, this isn't over by a long shot," she declared, gawking at me as she passed by.

"It's as over as it's gon' get, baby," I assured her.

"You black bastard." She swung back around, trying to slap me. I blocked the lick and grabbed her hand.

"You better keep yo' hands to yo'self if you know what's good for ya," I said as we tousled around.

Deeberry jumped in, trying to break us apart. Reena was scuffling, trying her best to hit me.

"I'll kill you! I'm not going anywhere! You started all of this shit anyway. I begged you to be honest with me before it got out of hand, but you just couldn't tell the truth. If you had, it wouldn't have gotten this far, motherfucker," she screamed hysterically. I didn't see one tear fall as she yelled.

"Reena, please stop! Calm down and let's just leave like he told us to," Deeberry pleaded, struggling to restrain her.

"No! Turn me loose! He started this whole thing, and now he think just because I did it, he's gonna put me out with no strings attached. That's a lie!" She continued scrapping and scraping at me. Her robe came undone, showing her whole naked front, but she still didn't cease fire.

I had no intentions of hitting her, but she wouldn't let up. And Deeberry obviously couldn't handle her. As relentless as she was, I hated it, but I knew I was going to have to knock some sense into her.

*Smaccck!* I couldn't hold it back any longer. I slapped the hell out of her. I figured she would've increased her yelling and fighting even more after the lick, but she did just the opposite. She stopped hitting me instantly and dropped her arms down alongside her like a robot. Look like she'd gone into shock or something. Neither Deeberry nor I said anything right away. We just gazed at her. Over a period of a few seconds, her eyes became even more red, and her expression changed to blank. It was like her mind had snapped and checked out of reality. Her body was right there with us, but by the look in her eyes, her mind wasn't even on this damn planet. She'd transformed into this cold, distant being right in front of us. I didn't give a damn what her problem was. I just wanted both of them out of my house. Deeberry panicked even more.

"What's wrong wit' her? What you do to her?" Deeberry asked, sniveling. "Man, you know you don't hit no woman like that."

"Hell, you act like you couldn't get her off me, and she wouldn't stop. I had to do somethin'," I stated in my defense.

Reena began walking slowly toward the opposite end of the hall, still engrossed in her spaced-out look.

Deeberry called to her. "Reena, you all right?"

She didn't respond, just kept going. By now she had made it mid-way down the hall in front of the bathroom.

*Where the fuck she goin'?* I asked myself silently. "You goin' the wrong way to be leavin'," I yelled to her.

She didn't so much as attempt to turn around and answer me. She kept going 'til she reached my office door, then opened it and disappeared on the inside without a word.

"What you doin' in there?" I yelled to her again, then looked at Deeberry. "You need to take this woman on outta here before I end up beatin' her ass and the police get involved, then you gon' be knee deep in mo' trouble than you want with the church and everybody else too."

He let out a deep sigh, like he was regretting it, then started up the hall after her.

"Reena, come on. Let's get out of here before some real trouble start," he exclaimed, walking just as slow as she had.

I walked behind him, so I could find out what in the hell she was doing in my office.

"Y'all betta not be done fucked around and left nothin' in my office, either. That's probably why she done took her crazy ass in there to get some kinky shit y'all done left behind," I said loud.

Deeberry stopped walking just past the bathroom door and turned to me. "Charles, ain't nobody been doin' nothin' in yo' office. And by the look on Reena's face, I hope you ain't got no knives or weap—"

"She got a gun!" I yelled, cutting him off as the office door swung open and I looked straight at Reena, pointing a gun in our direction.

*Bang!* Deeberry and I fell to the floor, covering our heads with our hands.

"Reena! Please stop! Don't do this. It ain't worth it! Put the gun down," Deeberry yelled to her.

"Forget that. She done went off the deep end. She don't hear you," I said, trying to get up in a crouching position to make it back to one of the bedrooms to take cover. Just as I rose slightly, I looked straight into her isolated eyes. They were black as a pit. She again raised the gun and pointed it directly at me without mumbling a single word. Didn't even flinch her eyes. She took slow steps toward me, probably to get a closer shot. I just knew I was a dead man. She was only seconds away from pulling the trigger again.

*Bang!* The shot fired as I made a sprint.

In a matter of seconds, so many thoughts flickered in my mind. Why did it have to end like this? Why didn't I see that Reena was crazy in the beginnin'? That was what Bettie was tryin' to tell me, probably. Where would the bullet hit me? Would I die right away, or would I suffer awhile? How bad would Momma be hurt? What would Deeberry tell everybody? Would I see Gregg again? Would I go straight to Hell, or would God pardon my sins and give me a 'get out of Hell' free card?

"Oooohhhh! I been hit," Deeberry yelled out in pain. "I been hit!"

I quickly turned to see why it was him screaming out and not me. I was once again stunned at the sight before me. I didn't know what was going on, but somebody needed to tell me something in a hurry. I was real glad to not to be the one shot, but didn't nothing make any sense to me as I glanced around in the hall.

"Deeberry? Oh my God," I exclaimed, rushing to his side.

He was lying flat on his back, holding his right shoulder with one hand. Blood ran down between his fingers.

"You a'ight, Deeberry?" I asked, kneeling down beside him.

"I think so," he answered, attempting to rise up. "Yeah, it happened so fast." He seemed to be in agony, but he was still able to sit up on the floor.

Standing over me and Deeberry was a person whom I really needed an explanation of why she was up in my house with them. She and I locked eyes as she handed me a towel.

"Here. Wrap this around his arm and tie it in a firm knot at the end," her soft voice instructed.

I knew she saw the big question mark on my face. After I secured the towel on his upper arm, I helped him to his feet.

"That feel any better?" I asked, gripping his wound-free arm to make sure he was able to stand.

He was frowning something awful. "Yeah, that's a li'l better," he said. "Thank you." Then Deeberry looked past me to the opposite end of the hall, where Reena was lying on the floor out cold. He spoke to the man kneeling over her.

"What's wrong wit' her, man?" Deeberry asked him.

As shocked as I was to see him, I was still glad to here him say what he said. "When I jumped her, I guess I didn't realize how hard I ran into her. We lost our balance and fell down. She hit the back of her head against the wall. She got a pulse, but she out cold. You all right?" he asked Deeberry.

I stood there dumbfounded, looking from one person to the other, but my damn mouth wasn't silent for long.

"Wait! Now, just hold on one damn minute! Somebody better start talkin' and tellin' me just what the hell goin' on up in here," I shouted.

Their eyes traveled back and forth between the three of them, not able to decide who was going to say what. Seconds flew by. Still, nobody said anything. They looked like they just didn't know what to say.

I was very impatient now. "Awww, hell. Ain't no need of bein' shy now. I guarantee y'all, I ain't gon' ask no mo'. Next time it's gon' be the police doin' the askin'. Now, what the fuck all of y'all doin' up in my damn house?"

"Charles, please. Just calm down, man," Preston said softly. "You got us . . . you caught us. This is exactly what it looks like. Ain't nobody gon' try to deny nothin'. We all got together here 'cause you wasn't s'ppose to be back 'til tomorrow night. Reena suggested it." Preston could hardly look me in the eye.

"This ain't no damn hotel. Why my house?" I asked furiously.

"I just told you. Reena asked us to come," Preston repeated.

"What y'all been doin', havin' one big orgy?" I was on edge big-time.

"Don't be ridiculous," Preston stated. "Look, they was in that room doin' their thing, and we was in this one over here doin' ours. Don't nobody in here get down like that, and you know it."

"No, I don't know it. From what I can see, I really don't know shit about any of y'all mofos. And evidently, y'all don't know shit 'bout Reena. That heifer is crazy as hell and will do anything wit' anybody. Y'all might not have had a orgy goin' on at this point, but rest assured, being up in here wit' her freaky ass, y'all was well on ya way to havin' one by dawn, and ya didn't even know it," I declared harshly.

All that was going on right in my house, I was outdone. I had to stop and think about it for a minute. Before I knew it, I'd let out a slight laugh. "Damn, all this time people been 'round here talkin' 'bout how ruthless and immoral I am. But I gotta hand it to ya. Y'all some sneaky-ass bastards. Ain't this a damn trip?" I feasted my eyes on my unsuspecting sister-in-law. "And you? Who woulda thought you'd be caught in the middle of somethin' like this. I wouldn't have suspected you in a million years. But you know what they say. It's always the—"

"Charles, please. We get the picture." Her soft, proficient voice interrupted my speech. "We're all adults, and we're all prepared to accept responsibility for our actions. I know I am. We can point fingers and discuss all of this later. Right now, we have a man wounded, and a woman laying out cold on the floor. We need to be getting some help out here for them. Now, if it's all right with you, I'll go call an ambulance and the authorities," Linda said sadly as she began walking toward my office.

"Now, wait a minute, y'all," Deeberry spoke up. "Everybody in town gon' know 'bout this mess befo' midnight. Ain't it some way for us to try to get the necessary help we need, and at the same time keep this under wraps?"

"Nigga, please," I stated. "You shoulda thought about that befo' you sneaked yo' phony ass up in here. Have you forgotten you up in my damn house wit' my wife? That gunshot got to be done ran yo' temperature up and gave you a high fever, 'cause you hallucinatin'. I ain't coverin' up nothin' for ya." I began walking toward my office behind Linda.

Preston was still standing over Reena's half-naked, motionless body. As I went past him, it really sunk in that one of my best buddies was in on all of that conniving shit behind my back. That twisted my feelings more than I wanted to admit. I didn't even know what to say to him one-on-one, but I damn sure wasn't gon' let him know that he'd gotten to me that time. I parked my eyes upside his head.

"Look up in that linen closet and get a sheet to cover her up. That is, unless you wanna leave her exposed and fuck her right there," I stated, hoping to sound unfeeling.

I saw the gun that she'd used lying on the floor. I reached down and carefully picked it up with only my index finger and thumb.

"Just wanna make sure don't nobody else get no bright ideas." I nodded at Deeberry.

"I don't see no sheets, Charles," Preston said, shuffling through the bottom of the linen closet.

"Look at the top," I told him then closed my office door, leaving him and Deeberry out in the hall with Reena.

Linda was standing behind my desk, holding the cordless phone in one hand and fumbling through the telephone book with the other one.

"Linda, I'll make the call," I said, walking over to her.

She handed me the phone and stood aside. I dialed a number.

"Hello," a woman answered.

"Hello, I need to speak to Will, Francine. This Charles," I said with urgency.

"All right, hold on a minute, Charles," Francine said.

Linda stood quietly and watched me as I waited for Will to come to the phone.

"Hey, Will. What's up, man?" I said.

"Nothin' much. You at home, man? I thought you wasn't coming back 'til tomorrow night," he said.

"Yeah, I wasn't s'ppose to, but I got back early."

"Well, maybe you can catch up on a li'l rest, fella," he said.

"That woulda been a good idea, except I got a mess here at home you ain't gon' believe 'til you see it for ya'self." I briefly filled him in and asked him to get over to my house as soon as possible.

# ReChella

When I hung up, Linda gave me a puzzled look. "Charles, why did you call Will instead of the police?" she asked softly.

"Relax. I'm callin' 'em right now." I dialed the non-emergency phone number to the police department and gave them the necessary information to dispatch a car and send an ambulance to my house.

After I hung up the phone, I dropped down in the chair behind my desk. Linda stood on the side of my desk, evidently lost in thought. Sure, I knew the basic circumstances of the night's events, but I still couldn't wrap my mind around the fact that Linda was mixed up in all of it. I just had to ask her about it now that we were alone.

"Linda, I'm not here to judge you, attack you, or try to make you feel bad," I said gently. "Believe me, I'm the last person in the world qualified to do that." I exhaled. "Honest to goodness, I just have one question. May I ask it?"

"No, because I'm not going to answer." Linda cried, dropping her face in her hands. "Ohhh, my God. I can't deal with this right now. I just can't." She wept softly.

Damn, I didn't expect that. I handed her some Kleenex from my desk. I felt sorrow for what I knew she and my brother were getting ready to go through if he found out. I could only imagine what she felt. Before that night, if somebody had given me a choice to nominate a couple for their commitment and fidelity to each other, Kenny and Linda would've been my first choice. Obviously, I was wrong. I was on the outside looking in, and there was no way of really knowing what was going on behind their closed doors. All I knew was every time I saw them, they wore happy, in-love faces. Guess I wasn't the only one pretending most of the time. The way Linda was crying, yet still refusing to offer any kind of explanation for her actions, was so strange to me.

"Linda, maybe it'll help if you talk about it. Just get some of it out," I suggested carefully.

"Talk about what, Charles? Huh?" she snapped, tears really gushing from her eyes now. "Talk about how Kenny gets to fuck outside of our marriage anytime he feels like it, and I get to secretly clean the different shades of lipsticks off his shirts? Or talk about how I pretend like I don't hear his pager going off in the middle of the night, or how the phone rings and every time I answer she hangs up, but when he answers fifteen minutes later, he's suddenly got to run see a buddy or run a errand that he'd forgotten about? Or maybe we can talk about how he brought her into our home and fucked her in our bed and she left me a calling card just to let me know she'd been there. He didn't even know about what she'd left, because only a woman would think to do what she did."

Damn, she threw me all the way off. I wasn't expecting to hear any of what she said. I sat there with my mouth hanging open, listening. Linda was crying a river, sniffling delicately, though.

"Ohhh, and you're gonna love this one. Let's talk about how for the first time in little old conservative, boring Linda's life, she starts an affair a few months ago and decides to do something outrageously scandalous just to spice things up a little and, and—"

Shit, I couldn't take anymore. "Linda, please." I dove into her pity party and rose to comfort her. "Hey, I'm sorry. I had no idea about all of this. None whatsoever." I embraced her. She really let out a load of quiet, hard tears when I hugged her. "Linda, this may sound crazy, but in a weird way, I kinda understand why you did what you did. What I don't understand is why you did it over here with Reena knowing all about it. And Deeberry too? I mean, how did all of that come about? You've never been one to socialize much." I still talked to her as gently as I could.

"Charles, she came to me and confided in me about you over and over again. I felt sorry for her in the beginning, but I didn't tell her about Kenny. Well, not at first." Linda rested her head on my shoulder, still sniffling and talking at the same time. "Reena told me about how much you were hurting her, and how much she loved you. She and I started going places together, shopping at the malls and out for drinks sometimes. She was my friend, the only friend I've had for a very long time. So, after she told me about Pastor showing an interest in her and she'd decided to go out with him, well, what kind of friend would I have been not to tell her about me and Preston?"

I shook my head in disbelief. "Linda, do you know what kind of man Preston is? You still foolin' wit' him after what you know about him and Bettie?" I asked with concern.

"I didn't care about that, Charles. I don't love Preston. Preston is no more than someone to have sex with. I love Kenny; always have and always will. I still want to be with Kenny for the rest of my life, but I just can't handle him cheating. He's been doing it for years, and the only way for me not to sit up in the house and go crazy, worrying about him doing it, is to do it too," she explained.

"I didn't see nobody else's car in the yard. How'd you get over here?" I asked, changing the subject.

"I rode with Reena. She picked me up at my sister's house earlier today," Linda said pitifully.

Linda was very distressed and fragile as she rested in my arms. I'd seen times when I would've tried to take all the advantage I could of a woman in her vulnerable state. But as I consoled her, surprisingly, all I felt was love and concern for her and my brother. That moment with her was one of the very few times in my life that I'd actually held a woman in my arms who wasn't blood kin, and all I wanted from her was for her to be all right.

"Charles, Reena comin' to," Deeberry exclaimed from the other side of the door.

"A'ight. We on our way out," I yelled back then whispered to Linda. "Come on, Linda. Dry your face up. I'm gettin' you outta here." I motioned for her to follow me out the door.

"What are you talking about?" she asked, wiping her face.

"Listen, just go along wit' me. Whatever I say, agree to it," I told her just before I opened the door and she and I walked back out into the hallway.

# Scandalous

Preston and Deeberry were kneeling down on the floor over Reena. They had placed a wet towel on her forehead in addition to covering her with the sheet. Linda also kneeled down to take a closer look at her.

"She stirrin' a little, but she haven't opened her eyes yet," Deeberry said.

"Well, when she do open 'em, just make sure y'all keep your eyes on her. She got some damn mental issues, and I don't want her wanderin' 'round in my house no mo'.'" I looked down the staircase. "Y'all ain't heard the doorbell yet?"

"Nahh, ain't nobody come yet," Preston said. "I ran downstairs to check, but—"

*Ding dong.* The doorbell rang.

"That's probably Will. I'll be right back," I said, hurrying down the stairs to open the door. "Man, am I glad to see you. Get on in here," I told Will then closed the door behind him.

"I got here as fast as I could," Will said. "Now, you know we gon' have to do somethin' 'bout Preston this time, don't ya?" Will sounded very agitated.

"I agree, but we gon' have to do that later," I quickly stated. "Right now, I need you to get Linda outta here and take her to her sistah's house befo' the police and the ambulance get here. I don't want her in the middle of all this shit. Our family been through enough as it is . . . and well, I wanna spare my brotha on this one."

"I feel ya. And I agree. Where she at, man?" Will asked.

"Come on. She upstairs."

We hurried up the stairs. By then, Reena was propped up against the wall with her eyes partially open, but she still wasn't responding to anybody, just sitting there dazed-out.

"Damn, if this ain't a sight to see." Will gasped, taking a quick look at everybody and boggling his head. "Shit, the wrong one was doin' the shootin'. Charles, you got some patience, my brotha. If this was my house, we'd need a few body bags and the damn coroner too. This bullshit don't make no—"

"Will, please," I interrupted him. "We gon' handle this, man. Just get her on outta here." I turned to Linda. "Linda, go wit' Will. He gon' take you to yo' sistah's house, then you go on home, ya hear?"

"What?" Linda asked, looking baffled. I quickly furrowed my eyebrows and widened my eyes at her to remind her of what I'd told her to do.

"Ohh . . . uhh, okay," she stuttered, remembering my instructions, then started down the hall.

"Wait a minute. Where she goin'?" Deeberry asked, watching Linda. "I thought we was all mixed up in this together."

I shot him a *shut the fuck up* look. "I guess you thought wrong. Linda ain't the one who got shot, and she ain't the one who did the shootin', so therefore, ain't no reason for her to stay here. It's yo' ass and Reena's ass that's gettin' strung up," I snapped. "And well, Preston, you was the one who knocked Reena out, so look like you gon' be hangin' on the same limb wit' them two." I stared at Preston. "You got any objections?"

"Nahh, I ain't got none," Preston said peacefully.

"Wise choice. You already got enough explainin' to do. Ain't no need of addin' a explanation about Linda to the list." I bullied his ass.

"How you gon' stand there and agree wit' that, Preston?" Deeberry asked, sounding upset.

I didn't give Preston a chance to answer. I answered for him. "Preston got a wife and kids at his house. You ain't got nobody at yours. The only person you had to hide from was me, nigga. And seein' that I'm the one who caught ya, well, I'll just let you fill in the rest."

"Y'all know this ain't gon' work. How we gon' explain Reena and . . . and two men?" Deeberry hesitated.

"Simple. She was fuckin' both o' y'all," I stated bluntly. "And don't act like you wouldn't have went for it." I didn't give a damn about what happened to nobody but Linda. My uncaring statement told 'em that.

233

Deeberry finally shut his damn mouth, looking disappointed.

"Will, y'all go head befo' the folks get here," I urged.

Not five minutes after Will and Linda got out of there, the police showed up at my doorstep. The ambulance was only a few minutes behind them. Deeberry, Preston, and I gave a statement. We pretty much stuck to the true happenings of the incident, except nobody mentioned Linda's name. Since Preston had provided the transportation for him and Deeberry to come to the house, he used that as the only reason for him being there. He told the police that he'd fallen asleep in the bedroom next to my office while waiting for Deeberry, so they could go back to where they'd parked the car at the dead-end spot up the road. I could tell the officer had his doubts, but he didn't scrutinize.

The thing I hated most was that Deeberry could use my protecting Linda as a means to get me to give him some slack about the church members finding out what he'd done. I told myself I'd just cross that bridge whenever I got to it.

Reena was the only one not able to give a statement. She had to be carried out on a stretcher. The paramedics couldn't even get a response from her. She looked like she was trapped in a distant world. The paramedics believed that she was in some kind of traumatic shock as a result of everything that happened. They asked me to look through her things for any medicines that she may have been on. A police officer was assigned to accompany her to the hospital and remain there, guarding her 'til she was aware enough to answer for the criminal charges that had been brought against her. The paramedics transported Deeberry along because of his bullet wound.

# Chapter Nineteen

By the time the official inquisition was over, Will had made it back from dropping Linda at her sister's house. Preston, Will, and I sat in the den, talking.

"How was Linda when you dropped her off, Will?" I asked.

"She was still a li'l shaken up and uneasy, but she said she was gon' be a'ight," he answered.

"Did she . . ." I started.

"Excuse me, Charles," Will interrupted me. "I don't mean to cut you off or nothin', but I just can't put this off no mo'." He was clearly upset. "I got a few questions I wanna ask."

"A'ight," I said. "Ask anything you want."

"My questions ain't for you, Charles." Will turned to Preston, who was sitting at the opposite end of the sofa. "They're for you," Will said.

"I figured that," Preston replied, glaring back at him. "What you want me to say, Will? I mean, I was wit' Linda. I wasn't the one wit' Reena." Preston humped up his shoulders.

Will screwed his face into a huge frown. "That's a bunch of bullshit and you know it. That's not all you guilty of. You up in his house. A man you call yo' brotha, and you knew his wife was fuckin' a man he can't stand. You was helpin' the man get away wit' the shit, Pres," Will stated firmly.

"I wasn't helpin' 'em get away wit' nothin'. Reena and Deeberry had that shit planned out from the git-go," Preston exclaimed, defending himself.

"Was you gon' tell Charles about it, man?" Will point blank asked Preston.

Preston hung his head down with no indications of answering. I sat quietly in observance.

"That's just what I thought," Will said after Preston

didn't answer. "Not tellin' your brotha is just like helping his enemy. Our group ain't about that, Preston. You know the rules. You got away wit' that shit one time wit' Bettie, but that was his ex-wife, so he wasn't messed up about it. So, the group looked over it too. But now, you bold enough to come up in this man's house without him knowing. Why? For goodness sakes, why?"

Will briefly paused for an answer, but Preston remained silent. His expression said he wasn't answering no questions, so Will continued. "You sing wit' him, you ride wit' him, you eat wit' him, you drink wit' him, you in a brotherhood wit' him. I mean, we took oaths and made pledges for the good of our group. If we can't trust each other, who can we trust? Frankly, the way you disrespectin' Charles tells me a lot. If he can't trust you, hell, can't none of us trust you."

Will let out a deep breath, looking like he was about two seconds away from whupping Preston's ass, but Preston still didn't say shit. I couldn't believe that he was just gon' sit there and not even try to explain why he was fuckin' over our friendship like that.

"Charles, it's on you, man," Will said angrily.

"I'm through wit' it, Will. Y'all can take it up at the next group meetin'," I said, looking at Preston. "But I do wanna say that I appreciate you savin' my life, Preston. When Reena was pointing that gun at me, I looked right at her and she sho' nuff had a good, clean shot. If you hadn't thrown her off balance, she probably would've killed me. I thank you for that, man." Throughout the evening, I'd thought about Preston jumping in the way he did, but I was too mad to even mention it or thank him. I was glad it finally came out.

Preston was clearly irritated by our interrogation. He finally lashed back. "Tell ya what. I'm gon' save y'all the trouble of goin' befo' the group." He sprung to his feet angrily. "I quit. Who the fuck do y'all think y'all are? Both of ya got some nerve. Gon' sit up here and put me on trial 'bout some shit y'all been doin' forever. Why are the rules of the brotherhood different when it comes to y'all? Huh? 'Cause y'all the so-called founders of the group, that mean y'all got a different set of rules than the rest of us? Now, that's what's bullshit," Preston declared.

"What you talkin' 'bout, Preston?" I asked, frowning.

"I'm talkin' 'bout my wife, you son of a bitch!" Preston yelled, flying off into a fit. "Did you go befo' the mothafuckin' group when you fucked my wife?" he demanded.

"What? Yo' wife?" I asked in astonishment, jumping up from my seat. "I ain't never been wit' yo' wife."

"You a damn lie! I know you did! I heard the talk around town. I just never had any proof," Preston stated in a rage.

"That's 'cause wasn't no proof to have, nigga," I stated.

"Now, hold on a minute, y'all," Will intervened, standing up too. "Preston, you wrong, man. I don't know where you been gettin' yo' information from, but this ain't never happened. I can promise you that."

"Who the fuck you s'ppose to be, the one keepin' up wit' who he fuckin' and who he ain't fuckin'?" Preston demanded sarcastically. "Besides, Will. Yo' word ain't no good wit' me. You gon' take up for him anyhow. We all know that." Preston had somewhat lowered his voice. He motioned toward the door.

"I ain't takin' up for nobody. I'm just tellin' you the facts." Will gritted his teeth and tightened his lips, looking like he was trying his damndest to be patient with Preston. "I'm tellin' ya, man. Charles ain't the one you want. He ain't done nothin' wit' yo' wife. But I got to know, is that why you been doin' all this fucked-up mess 'round here, 'cause you think Charles fooled wit' yo' wife?"

Will and I glared at Preston, waiting for an answer.

"You damn right I did. And I don't have no regrets about it." Preston was fearless. He meant he didn't give a damn about nothing.

That nigga had been out for revenge on me for some shit I didn't even do. I was about to lose it. I had to calm myself quick. I tried speaking to him in a more peaceful manner. "Preston, all I can say is you way off. Way off. I didn't do it, man."

"Yeah, right. Sure you didn't." Preston wasn't the slightest bit moved by my sincerity, but he did cool his yelling a notch.

Will and I seized eye contact, and I knew we were thinking the same thing. I just hated for it to come to that.

"Can I ask you a question, man?" I asked respectfully of Preston.

"I don't care what you ask me. Ain't no way you gon' convince me otherwise." He sneered at me.

"A'ight, that's fair enough," I said. "Did you confront yo' wife about it? I mean, if I supposedly had an affair wit' her, did you ask her about it?"

"Yeah, I asked her about it, and she lied just like you lyin' now," Preston said bitterly.

"Well, why haven't you asked me about it too? At least gave me the chance to have a say in my own defense befo' you tried, convicted, and sentenced me." I kept my eyes on him.

"I just told you I didn't have no ironclad proof."

"Well, you musta had somethin', my brotha, 'cause you found me guilty."

"Yeah, I had somethin'." Preston's words dripped slowly out of his mouth while he peered at me with eyes of hatred. "C. Jennings. I found that name in some of my wife's private belongings, plus all the talk that was goin' on in my family about her cheatin' on me wit' one of my own group members."

"And that was enough for you to find me guilty?" I asked, boggling my head.

"You damn right it was. It may not have been ironclad, but it told me what I needed to know," Preston replied.

I dropped back down in my seat and exhaled, fighting hard to hold back my words—words that I swear I didn't want to say.

Will knew what I was struggling with, so he took over

the conversation. And now, his peaceful side had surfaced. "Preston? Please believe me, man. You falsely accusing Charles. He didn't do what you sayin'."

"Oh, really. Well, how do you know? Huh? How do you know that for sure, Will?" Preston argued.

Will turned to me, and he and I once again seized eye contact briefly. Then he turned back to Preston and slumped his head. I was dreading what he was getting ready to say, but wasn't no way around it.

"I remember when it happened a few years ago," Will said, sounding regretful, and took in a deep breath. "It wasn't Charles . . . it was Gregg."

Preston looked like he went into automatic shock after hearing what Will said.

"Now, what kinda lyin', bullshit is that? Everybody know Charles the biggest ho in the group. Always was, always will be. How can y'all stand in here and lie on a dead man who can't defend himself?" Preston said with disbelief.

"Naw, man, I wish it was a lie. I know you and Gregg was tight. Y'all had a close friendship goin' on," Will continued. "When we found out about him and her, we talked to Gregg and he promised to leave her alone. So you see, he did break it off. And you right, we didn't take it befo' the group, because he went ahead and complied."

Preston looked like somebody had kicked him in the teeth.

"I don't believe a word of this shit," Preston said skeptically. "And furthermore, you can't hear too well. I said C. Jennings, not G. Jennings. What you gon' do next, tell me my wife made a mistake and wrote a C instead of a G?"

"Nahh, she wrote what she meant to write . . . and I did hear you the first time," Will said confidently. "You don't know how bad it makes me feel to have to tell you this. C. Jennings was Gregg's initial too. He just never used it, and very few people, if any, knew about his first name. Maybe only family knew. But the ones that did, knew how bad he hated it. None of us ever used his first name or even made reference to it. Corwin Gregg Jennings was his full name."

Preston stood in the doorway, speechless.

I felt sorry for him. "He tellin' the truth, Pres," I said. "I'm sorry you had to find out this way, but like you said, he dead and he can't tell you nothin' you might need to hear right now. And well . . . I just can't speak for him. But I will say this: He hated he did it after it happened. That's why he ended it as soon as the three of us sat down and talked."

Preston was still silent as a mouse. A look of illness came upon him, then he turned and walked out of the door without saying a word. William and I talked about things a while longer, then he left too.

Later on, I called to check on Momma and to let her know what was going on. After exchanging greetings and small talk, I cut right to the chase.

"Listen, I got somethin' very serious to tell you, but I don't want you to get upset 'cause everythang fine now. All right?" I said then waited for her response.

"What is it?" she asked anxiously.

"Tell me you ain't gon' be gettin' upset first, Momma," I insisted.

"Come on wit' it, now. I'm all right," she stated firmly.

I knew there was no way for me to keep her from getting upset. I just thought I'd at least try.

"Well, it happened when I got back home earlier tonight," I said.

Momma listened tolerantly as I filled her in on all the details. As I expected, she went berserk just at the notion of me being shot at.

"I knew it was somethin' strange 'bout that gal. I just couldn't put my finger on it. I did my best to look past what I felt, 'cause you was so crazy 'bout her. And all this time that heifer was crazy as hell. I just be damn." Momma flew off the handle in her well-known, shrill, angry voice.

"I tell ya what. She done messed wit' the wrong set o' folks. Charles, why didn't you call me and yo' brothas when this shit first happened? I done told you 'bout bein' out there needin' yo' family and won't call. Where you say they took her crazy ass? I betta not ever see her out nowhere. She coulda killed you, boy. Lawd, I swear some of y'all gon' give me a heart attack yet. It don't make no damn—"

"Momma." I raised my voice into the phone, trying to get her attention and calm her down. "It's all right. She gone now, and she ain't comin' back."

"You damn right she ain't comin' back. I hope I do see her ass even step one foot in yo' driveway out there." Momma's keen voice and heavy breathing combined was driving me bonkers, but I knew she was mad as hell.

"Momma, you remember that program we sung on in Memphis at the Pilgrim Zion Baptist Church?" I asked.

She paused momentarily to recall. "Yeah, I remember," she said.

"Well, that night after the program was over, Bettie came to me and was tryin' to tell me somethin' she'd heard on Reena. It was 'bout somethin' bad that happened between her and some man she'd been wit' at one time," I explained as best I could remember.

"What man? He live here in Senatobia?" Momma asked.

"Nahh, Bettie said he lived in Holly Springs, and Reena found somethin' out about him. Ahh, I can't remember what. Anyhow, my take on it was Reena did somethin' to the man. I can't be for certain, 'cause Bettie never finished tellin' me, but I do remember her sayin' Reena had some serious problems and I needed to be careful."

"Aww, you mean Bettie told you that?" Momma asked surprised.

"Yeah, it surprised me too. But she said in spite of what happened between her and me, she didn't wish nothin' fatal on nobody. When she said *fatal*, she really caught my attention, but that's when Reena came up outta nowhere and interrupted us. I thought about it a few weeks later, but I never got back in touch wit' Bettie to let her finish tellin' me the whole story. I wish I had now. It may woulda saved a whole lot o' trouble. The first thing to pop in my head after the incident tonight was that's probably what Bettie was gon' tell me—Reena tried to kill that other man."

241

"Lawd have mercy. What's the matter wit' her? Do her folks know she crazy? I mean, I been knowin' her momma and daddy for years and they ain't like that. 'Course now, I ain't seen 'em in a long time, so they may be done changed," Momma said.

"I'm sure they know somethin' wrong wit' her. The paramedics even said the state she was in indicated that somethin' more than we could see was wrong. They asked me if she was on any kind of medication, and I told 'em none that I knew of. They still wanted me to look through her things just to be sure. Momma, I went through her drawers and found a medicine bottle stuck down in a little bag in the back of one of 'em."

"What was it, Charles?" Momma asked anxiously.

"To be honest, I can't pronounce it or spell it . . . Pxehil . . . somethin'. But the paramedics said it was a medicine prescribed for psychosis."

"Psychosis? Lawd, she crazy as hell, ain't she?" Momma asked.

"Sho' is," I said.

Momma let out a big sigh. "Charles, I told you not to marry that gal so quick. You didn't know enough 'bout her. You can't just go rushin' into stuff like that without askin' God for some kinda insight. You s'ppose to know betta."

"Yeah, I know that, Momma." I knew it was time for me to hang up. Momma was getting ready to go into one of her long, religious speeches. "Look, Momma, it's been a long day and a even longer night. I'ma go get a shower and turn in. I'm real tired." I declare, I didn't feel like listening to no lecture.

"All right, I'ma try to get hold o' Kenny and Wayne, so I can tell 'em 'bout all o' this. Lawd, I still can't hardly believe it. Pastor annnnd Preston mixed up in all this togetha. That crazy-ass woman was actually coatin' both of 'em at the same time up in yo' house." Momma sounded disgusted.

"Momma, I didn't say she was coatin' both of 'em at the same time. I said I walked in on her and Deeberry in the act. Preston was stashed back in the bedroom next to my office," I repeated for the sake of clarity, but if I knew Momma, she was gon' hear what she wanted to hear anyway.

"Yeah. Waitin' on his turn if he hadn't already had her. Ain't no need o' tryin' to sugar coat it. When you get through talkin', it's all still the same thang. She was coatin' both of 'em at the same time. Now, I don't know what you and the group gon' do 'bout Preston, but the church gon' definitely have to do somethin' 'bout Pastor. Shit, I don't even know why I'm still callin' him that. I mean Deeberry." Momma corrected herself, and it tickled the hell out of me to hear her take over my disrespectful word for Deeberry.

"After I get Wayne and Kenny, I'ma start callin' 'round, lettin' some of the other deacons and members know too. You sho' you don't want one of yo' brothas to come down and keep you company tonight?" Momma asked.

"Nahh, I'm goin' straight to bed after I shower. But if y'all can come down in the mornin' and help me pack up Reena's stuff, that'll be good," I told her.

"All right. I'll tell 'em, and we'll be down 'bout nine or ten in the mornin'."

"Okay, Momma. Goodnight."

# Chapter Twenty

That following Saturday was just as grueling as that Friday had been. Momma, Richard and Bo came over to my house to help me clear out Reena's things. There was no doubt, our relationship was history. What sane man would reconcile with a woman whose mind had snapped to the point that she'd tried to kill me?

After the four of us bagged all of Reena's stuff, we delivered them to her folks' house. Her father and mother wasn't happy about things, nor were they happy to see me, but it was their daughter who had the sanity problem, and my guess was they already knew about it. Word of the incident spread over town like wildfire, and once again the Jennings name was the town cover story, with the exception of Deeberry's bullet to the shoulder being the headliner.

The church and deacon board called an urgent business meeting for that Sunday morning at 11 o'clock. Regularly scheduled Sunday school was held at its normal 10:00 A.M. hour, but 11:00 worship service was cancelled, so we could have the business meeting. All of the members of Mt. Pleasant piled in to hear the details of the Friday night happenings and vote on what to do about Deeberry. The old jack-leg bastard was still able to be there in spite of his shoulder injury. Somebody told me that the doctors had removed the bullet, bandaged him up, and already released him. His arm was in a sling, but he was good as new.

At the business meeting, once the facts were presented and everybody found out exactly what their beloved pastor had done, the votes were not in his favor. He was ordered to turn over his church keys and have his desk and pastor's study cleaned out before we locked the church for the day.

He refused to leave the grounds, claiming he wasn't the only one in the church guilty of wrongdoings. Though the members had the last word, as pastor, he was well within his rights to have a final speech.

I was against it. I knew he was going to use any dirt he could dig up to plead his case, including Linda. I disputed the notion of him making a final speech as long as I could. All of the brothering on the deacon board agreed that his last words wouldn't change the decision that had already been made, but he still couldn't be denied his final speech. We had to stay within the guidelines of his initial installation. Mr. Dixon, Kenny, Wayne, the other four deacons and I sat around the narrow, walnut-oak table in the front of the church, maintaining our unanimous decision as the meeting came to a close.

Deeberry was not allowed to take his usual place in the pulpit, therefore he stood behind the floor podium to speak. Everybody listened closely as he cleared his throat, peering over the church at the members.

"As I look out across the sanctuary today, I see the church is full. I see a lot of faces that I haven't seen in months, even years." Deeberry's rickety voice was already getting on my nerves, and he hadn't said but a few words. "Most Sundays, the crowd be so thin in here we can almost hear echoes. It's always the same faithful few. But look at us now. We got wall-to-wall show-up. So, I guess that old sayin' is true about how people won't get up and come to church to praise and worship God, but they sho' will pile in for a meetin' to talk about some mess . . . or to desecrate another saint." He kept dabbing the corners of his eyes with a white hanky, seeming to wipe away tears. Let me tell it, he wasn't doing nothing but putting on another one of his faked-out, dramatic performances. Like me, some of the members were impatient as hell.

"Don't nobody wanna hear all that mumbo-jumbo! Why don't you just do what you was told and leave?" one angry male member yelled out from amongst the crowd.

Deeberry quickly glanced across the audience to see who'd made the statement.

"My brother, this is my time to speak. Everybody else had theirs, and I would appreciate it if you'd allow me the opportunity to speak my peace," Deeberry uttered peacefully.

"This ain't nothin' but a waste of time. Ain't nothin' you say gon' change our decision, so just spare us all your lies and leave," another angry male member yelled out.

This time, Deeberry was a little more firm. "I ain't goin' nowhere. God put me in this place, and this where I'ma stay," he exclaimed.

"You gettin' outta here, or else you gon' get carried out! We ain't puttin' up wit' no fornicating, adulterous preacher," another outraged male member from the audience shouted.

The meeting had run rather smooth and in order up 'til that point. But now, things seemed to be taking a wrong turn.

"Brother? You ever heard of forgiveness? We have all sinned and fell short of the glory of God," Deeberry stated, looking like he was trying his best to keep his cool. "I'll be the first to admit I made a dreadful mistake . . . and I'm sorry. God knows I am."

"Don't be puttin' God's name in this! You knew better! What kind of example have you set for the young folks at this church? Sleepin' 'round in another man's house wit' his wife while he outta town. That's why you got shot. That was part of ya punishment," one of the mothers on the mother-board yelled out sternly.

"That's right! You nearly 'bout got my son killed," Momma shouted.

"Yo' son ain't no saint, Sister Mildred," Deeberry stated. "In fact, he a looong way from it. Did any of y'all carry on like this when Bettie walked in on him foolin' wit' her own sistah? Or what about Sister Katie? Everybody know the real reason she left the church. Her and Charles had a long-time affair goin' on. He lusted after . . . and bedded his own brotha's wife. Everybody in town know 'bout it." Deeberry was anything-goes now.

I knew it was only a matter of time before he started pulling out all the punches. I swear, I was a half second off his ass for bringing my name up. "You better keep me outta yo' mess! I ain't on trial! This meetin' 'bout you," I barked at him, pointing all the while. Oh, how I wanted to shut him up before he did some real damage. He'd angered more than a few people. And when Momma was mad, she was a couple of folks all by herself.

"Stop lyin' on my boy! All o' that mess a bunch of lies anyhow! Just go on, leave." Momma's shrill shout defended me.

"Have you ever asked him about all of it? Or when you heard about it, did you just automatically assume it was lies? Why won't you ask him 'bout it?" Deeberry insisted, glaring at Momma. "I'll tell ya why. 'Cause all of y'all know he ain't nothin' but a—"

"Now, hold on. Hold on one minute." Wayne jumped up and cut Deeberry off before he could finish his sentence. "Evidently, y'all done forgot where we at. Simmer down, so we can carry on like civilized folks. We may not be in service, but we still in church." Wayne gave Deeberry a look of warning as he addressed him peacefully but firmly. "And Pastor, please . . . please, don't raise yo' voice at my momma no mo'."

If only Deeberry had taken Wayne's advice and shut his mouth before it was too late. But that was too much like right.

"Brotha, don't stand up here and issue no orders out to me," Deeberry replied angrily. "Ain't none of y'all got no room to talk. If yo' brother so faultless, why didn't he tell everybody the whole truth 'bout Friday night? That's right, the whole truth."

That was my cue to shut him up by any means necessary. I just couldn't let him sabotage Linda like that, 'cause I knew where he was headed.

"Deeberry! We tired of listenin' to this mess. This meetin' is over," I quickly stated, jumping up from the table in an attempt to deter him.

Wayne now engrossed a deep frown as he stood looking confused, peering at Deeberry. I knew everybody else was probably just as confused by the statement as Wayne was. Everybody except Linda, that is. Before I could silence him, Deeberry quickly turned to Kenny, who was still seated at the table, and shot off.

"That's right, Brotha Kenny. Yo' wife, Linda, was held up in that same house wit' the rest of us. She was there wit' Preston. And Charles slipped her outta there befo' the police even made it to the house. Call himself tryin' to protect his family, but look like to me he made things worse." Deeberry sounded boastful as he peered into Kenny's eyes. "He coulda told you in private, but instead, you done found out at a business meetin' in front o' yo' whole family and all yo' church members."

*Blooopp!* Wayne whooshed over and dropped Deeberry like a bad habit. Kenny didn't even get a chance to get up from the table and get to Deeberry to shut his mouth. Wayne did it for him. The look in Wayne's eyes while Deeberry was running his mouth tipped me off that he wasn't far from a well whupped ass. I just hate Wayne didn't get to him before he did the damage. Wayne didn't fuck with nobody, but when it came to his family, he would snap a nigga in half real quick.

"Wayne! Stop, Wayne! Get him off of him, y'all," Momma shouted, fearing that Wayne was gon' really hurt Deeberry by him already being shot.

Wayne knocked Deeberry to the floor, pinned him down, and was bashing his face in repeatedly with his huge fists, punch after punch after punch. I was loving every damn minute of it. It took me, Kenny, Richard, AJ, and two of the other deacons to get Wayne off of him.

"Come on, Wayne! Let him go," Richard shouted.

"Get off of him! Wayne, I ain't worried 'bout what he said," Kenny yelled to Wayne. "He ain't worth you goin' to jail, man! He ain't worth none of us goin' to jail!" Kenny was trying his best to calm Wayne down.

We had to peel Wayne off of Deeberry. Wayne's fist splatted against Deeberry's jaw and sank into the skin, imprinting all four of his knuckles. It sounded like somebody slapping two whole sides of fresh cut beef together.

"Somebody get that nigga outta here," AJ yelled, talking about Deeberry after we'd gotten Wayne off of him.

We held onto Wayne tight to keep him from getting back at Deeberry. The other deacons and a couple of male members got Deeberry up on his feet and were helping him back to the pastor's study. He was fucked up, too. His face and nose were bleeding, and his shirt was ripped halfway off of him. They all but had to carry him out of there. The members of the audience were in a big uproar. The church was so noisy, we could barely hear what each other was saying. It was plain to see that nearly everybody was stunned over what had just been revealed. Wayne was panting and still mad as hell.

"Wayne, get ya'self together. We in the house of God," Richard said, trying to calm him down.

Kenny took Wayne by the arm. "Come on, man. Let's get outta here," Kenny insisted. "I'm all right. I ain't worried 'bout Deeberry."

If Kenny was in any way upset about what Deeberry had revealed to him, he did a good job of covering up his emotions in front of everybody. Whether it was true or not, the accusation alone had to be a hard pill to swallow, especially in front of all those people.

I guess Linda couldn't take it anymore. I saw her zoom out of the church in tears. Momma made sure we had Wayne under control, then she hurried out of the church behind Linda. Sharon followed them.

Somebody needed to bring some order back to that out of control crowd. I took it upon myself to do that.

"Look, y'all, go on outside wit' Momma 'nem. I'm fixin' to close this meetin' down and tell everybody to go on home," I stated firmly. I walked to the podium and picked up the microphone.

"Charles," brother Dixon said, grabbing my hand just as I raised the microphone to my mouth. "Go on home wit' yo' family. They need you. Me and the other deacons a take care this." Brother Dixon took the mic from my hand and nodded for me to leave.

I saw his sincerity and concern. I was moved that he was trying to be helpful instead of judgmental.

"Thank you, brother Dixon," I said, taking his advice and leaving on out of the church.

The second I stepped on the outside of the church, Bo walked up to me. "Charles, Momma want everybody to come up to the house right now."

"A'ight," I answered.

I knew that it was going to be a long evening. By the time we all made it to Momma's house, things seemed to have calmed down, but that was only because nobody was talking. I bet everybody's thoughts were about to jump out of their skulls.

The time was about 1:00 P.M. We all sat quietly in the living room. Some sat on the sofa, some on the love seat, some in chairs. The way we were staring at the walls and floor reminded me of when me and my brothers were younger and Momma used to gather us up to get on us about some misbehaving that we'd all taken part in. Even though I was way older than the rest of the boys, she'd scoop me up too.

Just like back then, Momma didn't waste no time. She quickly put her purse and things in her bedroom, walked straight back in the living room, and stood in the center of the floor. Hurt, anger, confusion, disbelief, and many more emotions engrossed deep in Momma's face. She peered all around as she stood before us.

"Will somebody please tell me what in the hell is happening to our family?" she demanded slowly. "Every time I turn around it seems like some big chunk of shit and mess is sweepin' through this damn town and some of our family members is caught right dead in the middle of it. And to tell you the truth, I'm tired of hearing the Jennings name being dragged through the streets like this. Every one of y'all grown, and I've always tried my best to be here for my family. I know I may overstep my boundaries sometimes, but I try hard not to get in y'all's private lives. We are a family . . . and family s'ppose to stick togetha. I know I raised y'all boys without a daddy, but I raised ya in the church, and I did the best I knew how." Momma expressed herself with great sorrow.

I wished I could just snap my fingers and make things okay as I listened to her go on.

"Now, I know all of y'all know right from wrong. That's why I refuse to believe that any of you would take part in this garbage folks keep gossipin' 'bout. And I know none of y'all don't believe it either. Six brothas, and for the ones of ya who blessed enough to have wives, well, yo' wives are sistahs to yo' brothas. Real siblings don't act the way folks talkin' 'bout y'all been actin'. No relationship is perfect. That's why you got to keep God in yo' lives first . . . and other people who don't mean you no good out of yo' lives."

"Momma," Kenny called out. "I don't mean no disrespect, but I'm leavin'." Kenny's sudden announcement surprised Momma and the rest of us.

"Leavin'?" Momma asked, raising her eyebrows, a sure sign that she wasn't pleased.

"Yes, ma'am. Leavin'," Kenny repeated.

He stood his ground. The firm tone in his voice reminded me of how he used to insist on things being his way when he was a kid, and most of the time he pretty much got it after he'd thrown enough fits.

"Why you leavin', Kenny? This is Sunday evenin'. The Sundays that I cook, the family always have dinner togetha." Momma sounded suspicious as to Kenny's reason for wanting to leave.

"I know that, Momma, but today ain't just a regular day," Kenny stated.

"Why? Because of what happened today?" Momma demanded. "We all heard what that lyin', desperate-ass, so-called preacher said. The whole church heard him. That's all the more reason for us to be here and try to work through this thing like civilized adults. The last thing I want is for this family to be torn apart, and accusations like he made can do just that, Kenny."

"Well, Momma, I'm not really concerned wit' that right now," Kenny said, rising from the sofa.

"You should be. What's more impor—"

"What's more important is the truth about all of this," Kenny blurted out, raising his voice at Momma.

AJ jumped up instantly. "You need to lower yo' voice, man. Don't be hollin' at Momma like that."

It was evident that the circumstances were bringing out the worst in everybody.

"Sit down, AJ," Momma snapped, turning toward AJ. "I got this." Then she turned back to Kenny. "Well, who do you want the truth from, Kenny? Yo' wife sittin' over there, and yeah, you and her can talk about this in the privacy of yo' own home, which is the way it oughta be. But we got one mo' li'l problem. Yo' brotha been accused too, so that's where I come in . I ain't gon' stand by and watch y'all fall out over somebody else's lies." Momma was fluttering her eyelids like crazy.

"How do we know they lies?" Kenny exclaimed, turning away from Momma and facing Linda. "Was you there, Linda? Huh? Was you wit' Preston like the man said?" Kenny's upset emotional state had finally surfaced. He sounded very unsure and very angry.

Linda sat quietly on the loveseat across the room, tears seeping from her eyes as she stared up at Kenny. "Don't you stand there and yell at me like you're some kind of saint," Linda snarled at Kenny, rising from her seat too. "What if I was there?"

I was one shocked nigga, and so was everybody else. Linda actually raised her voice at Kenny.

"If you was, then you ain't nothin' but a damn slut," Kenny barked.

*Smacck!* Momma slapped the hell out of Kenny before he even knew what had hit him. He stood staring down at the floor, speechless.

"Have you lost yo' cotton-pickin' mind, boy?" Momma uttered angrily. "Where is your respect? You don't talk to no woman like that."

Degrading words to a woman in front of Momma was something she wasn't about to stand for. Kenny knew better. I guess he just lost it for a minute. I was regretting it, but I knew I had to go on and say something sooner or later. I told myself I may as well go on and get it over with.

"Look, Kenny," I said, rising rose from my seat on the sofa behind Kenny. "Why don't y'all just calm down and talk about—"

"Ain't nothin' to talk about," Kenny snapped, cutting me off. "She just answered my question. So, since she did answer it, I guess we now know Deeberry was tellin' the truth about you sneakin' her outta there." Kenny peered at me in ultimate anger. "You wasn't gon' even tell me 'bout it, was you? Was you?" he demanded.

I gazed at him with no response, but it didn't prevent him from continuing.

"That's like approvin' of what she did, and if you would do that to one brotha, if you would do that to me, then you would've done what they say you did to Gregg wit' Katie."

I didn't want to believe what was happening. The last thing I wanted was a confrontation with Kenny, but he made me snap before I knew it. "That's a lie! What I did, I did to protect you! To spare yo' feelin's, and save you from bein' hurt," I shouted back in anger. Kenny didn't budge, though.

"That's a bunch of crap, and you know it! What you did was hide you a ace in the hole, so you could bring it back up later and use it to get what you want from her!" he shouted, pointing at Linda but still peering at me. "Well, there she is! You can have her, 'cause I'm through wit' her just like I'm through wit' you. As far as I'm concerned, I got four brothas livin', and two dead!" Kenny stormed to the front door and flung it open.

He then turned back around and re-parked his rage-filled eyes back on mine, but now he wasn't yelling anymore. "Betrayal. Charles, you ain't nobody but Judas all back over again," Kenny uttered effortlessly. "I'm nothing even close to being Jesus but at least now, I know what he experienced when he felt Judas' lips of betrayal on his jaw." After that, Kenny walked out the door.

Nobody said anything else, not even Momma. I walked out behind him and left for home. The first time in my life I'd done something selfless and without motive, and it came right back to bite me in the ass. That old saying about what goes around comes back around accompanied me in my thoughts all the way home.

My telephone was ringing as I unlocked my door. I rushed in and picked it up.

"Hello," I answered.

"Hi, Daddy." My daughter Tina's soft, tenor voice carried through the phone receiver.

It probably wasn't the best time to talk to her, but it had been so long since the last time we'd talked. I instantly tried to take my mind off everything that happened at Momma's house, so I could have a decent conversation with her.

"Well, well. You finally decided to call ya old man. To what do I owe this pleasure?" I asked.

"Daddy, why can't you just say hi, how are you doing, how's school? Things like that," Tina asked politely.

"Seein' that I haven't talked to you in about three months or so, it's just a pleasure to hear from you. So, I figured I owed somethin' for some reason," I answered. "Tell you what . . . how 'bout I take a wild guess at the reason you called? Momma called you and told you about what happened Friday night wit' me almost gettin' shot, and to keep from feelin' guilty, you struggled wit' yo' conscience to at least call and check on dear old Dad, right?"

I heard her take a deep breath before she responded. I knew I was in for it.

"Daddy, I didn't bring this subject up, but since you did . . . you didn't know anything about that woman when you up and married her in the first place. I don't know why you did that," Tina said critically.

"Oops, well, there it goes. I knew we weren't far from it,"

I continued with the sarcasm. "Look, Tina, everybody make mistakes. And one day you, Amy, and Karen gon' have to realize that yo' old man just ain't perfect."

"Daddy, we know you're not perfect, but everybody's supposed to learn from their mistakes. That's what Momma taught us. Thing is, you never learn from yours, because you keep making the same ones."

I now took a deep breath. "I know neither one of y'all will ever forgive me for marryin' Bettie after yo' momma died, but I done come to accept that, and I just can't worry 'bout it no mo'."

"Excuse me, Daddy?" Tina's voice rose with intensity. "You didn't marry Bettie after Momma died . . . you married Bettie *immediately* after Momma died. And believe me; Amy, Karen, and I know you're not perfect, because we were the ones at home comforting Momma when you were out doing your thing. Momma didn't deserve the bad things you did to her all those years. From the time I was little, I can't remember one single day that she didn't shed tears over you. And still, after everything you did, she loved you more than anything," Tina uttered sadly.

"Yeah, well, I can't do nothin' 'bout that, now." I tried to sound cool and composed, but hearing shit like that from either of my girls always got to me. "I'm not gon' start this same old conversation wit' you, Tina. You and yo' sistahs gon' have to grow up and let that stuff go at some time another. It's in the past, but every time we talk, the conversation always manages to end on this subject." I wanted to hurry up and get off the subject before I ended up hurting my baby girl's feelings.

She was still very sensitive about her mother; therefore, she demanded to be heard, no matter what.

"Let it go? Let it go?" Tina's agitation grew. "I can't believe you, Daddy. You're the one who can't let stuff go. You can't even let it go long enough to get your life in order. You were married to Momma for nearly thirty years and she stayed at home, took care of us, and allowed you to do whatever you wanted with whomever you wanted, and she still remained faithful to you because of her one weakness—she truly loved you."

I could hear the hurt in her voice as she continued talking. "Then, when Momma died, you married your next best candidate to take her place. Bettie didn't work out because you found out she wasn't going to take the same things that Momma took. So, Bettie divorced you. And then right after Bettie, you married your next best candidate to take her place. Reena didn't work out because you found out she wasn't going to take even a portion of what Bettie and Momma had taken. And to top it off, Reena tried to shoot you in your own house. Who's next, Daddy? When is it going to be enough? After one of these women that you don't really know anything about has finally put you six feet under ground?" Tina refused to stop talking until she got her message across, loud and clear.

I thought it was best not to interrupt her. I would have only made it worse and prolonged it even more. "Momma was a true and gentle woman, a unique woman. No other woman's going to do what she did. She put up with your infidelity, yet still remained faithful to you. She loved you unconditionally; therefore, she let you do what you want, when you want, and still came home without any consequences. You were supposed to have been a role model for us, but since you were unsuccessful at that, why don't you try to be one for Amy and Karen's kids? They are your grandchildren, you know." Tina didn't take no pity on me while speaking her mind.

As bad as I hated it, I knew she was right about everything. It was just something about constantly hearing it from my own children, even though they were all grown up. Oh, how I wished me and my three girls would have had a better understanding. All in all, I just couldn't let Tina know she'd gotten to me. I continued to play it cool.

"Baby girl, are you done?" I asked nonchalantly.

I heard her let out a deep sigh.

"Yes, Daddy," she said glumly. Like always, she probably felt that her lecture had no affect on me. If only she'd known.

"Well, thank you for callin' to check on me, and as you can see, I'm fine. You've done your good deed. So, now, you can call up yo' sistahs and let 'em know you talked to the old man, and he's the same." I don't know why I always did smart-ass shit like that. It just automatically came out.

"Bye, Daddy. I love you," she said unhappily.

"Bye, baby girl. I love you too," I replied.

I loved my children very much, but I'd always known I would never be the father they wanted me to be. When they first grew into teens, I wanted to have a better relationship with them, but since it wasn't so, I just did what I'd always done, providing a comfortable, worry-free financial life for them until they were able to take care of themselves. Tina never admitted it to me, but I felt the reason she chose to get her own apartment while attending college was to ensure that she wouldn't have to come home as often. I made sure her check was deposited into her account on time each month. I had to admit, their level-headedness was instilled in them by their mother.

# Chapter Twenty-One

"Charles!" A man's voice called out to me as Emma and I were about to get in the truck. "Hold up, man," he called again.

I looked in the direction of the voice to see who it was.

"Preston?" I hollered back.

I hadn't seen Preston or heard anything from him since the night he quit the group and stormed out of my house. Emma and I stood on either side of the truck, watching him walk toward us.

"This should be interestin'," Emma said teasingly.

"That it should," I said, smiling at her.

"How y'all doin' this evenin'?" Preston asked, approaching us.

"We doin' a'ight. How you doin'?" I said, semi-smiling and remembering to be cautious from the last time we'd been in each other's company.

"Aw, I'm good." He glanced from me to Emma. "Listen, can I holla at you a minute, man?" He looked genuine.

"Yeah." I nodded then looked over at Emma. "Give me a few minutes."

She was already opening the truck door. "Nice seein' you, Preston," Emma said, getting in the truck.

"You too, Emma," he replied, waving one time at her.

"So, what's up? How happen you came out, man?" I asked as he and I walked to the back of the truck and stopped.

"To be honest, man, I didn't come to hear the singin'." He nodded from side to side. "I came on out 'cause I wanted to get a chance to holla at you. "Hell, I'm 'bout ten cars down." He pointed to the other end where he was parked. "When I first got here, I rode through the parkin' lot tryin' to spot yo' truck. And ten cars down is the closest I could park to ya. Ain't that a trip?" He laughed. "It's got to be a full house in there, ain't it?"

I laughed with him. "Yeah, man. It's wall to wall, you already know. You wasn't gon' come in at all?"

"Yeah, I was gon' run in for a few minutes, just to let you know I wanted to see you befo' you left, and maybe holla at the fellas briefly. Why you leavin' so early, anyhow? If I hadn't o' still been out here, I mighta missed ya. "

"Aw, I told Momma me and Emma was gon' leave when I came off stage so we could make it to her house in time enough to eat wit' everybody else."

Preston gave me a surprised look. "Aw, you mean yo' Momma cookin' on a Saturday? It must be a special occasion or somethin'."

"Believe me, when she told me she was cookin', I said the same thang. And so did everybody else. She didn't say so, but she probably got somethin' up," I told him.

Everybody new how Momma loved to cook, but everybody also knew her day for big cookin' was on Sunday. Unless it was a special occasion, she rarely cooked on Saturday, because she did it for Richard, AJ, and Bo, Monday through Friday.

Preston drew a frown. "In fact, the mo' I think about it, her and Ms. Hattie 'nem ain't at the program this evenin'?" He really sounded surprised now.

I chuckled. "Weird, ain't it?"

He gave me a quick grin then became more serious. "Look, man. This ain't the easiest thang in the world for me, but I just wanted to apologize for my part in what happened at your house that night. I know it's been 'bout two months, now, and my apology may be a li'l late, but I guess better late than never," he said, peering right at me with sincerity.

I was quite surprised to hear him say what he said. Yeah, it had been two months since all of that shit went down, but like the incident that happened with Bettie even before the one with Preston 'nem, things were finally starting to take shape again. As I stood there listening to Preston, I saw the genuineness in his eyes and I realized how glad I was to see him.

I was now just as serious as he was. "Look, Pres—"

# Scandalous

"Hold up, Charles," he said, holding his hand in front of me. "Let me finish sayin' this, man."

"A'ight," I said peacefully.

"I talked to my wife several times 'bout what went down, and well, she finally came clean. She told me it was Gregg, not you." Preston sighed sorrowfully. "I know I can't take back nothin' I did, but I wanted to at least apologize to you. I care for y'all like my own brothas. Hell, we are brothas. None o' this shit shoulda ever happened.

How could I not accept my brotha's apology after that? I accepted it graciously. "Apology accepted, man," I said, reaching out to shake his hand. "Like I told you that night, I wish I could say somethin' on Gregg's behalf, but the fact is, I just can't speak for him." My sadness about it all was hard to hold back. Preston and I shook hands.

It may sound crazy, but I was actually glad to know that everything he'd done behind my back, he'd done as an act of revenge. In my logic, doing it for revenge was better than just doing it for no reason at all. That said to me that he probably wouldn't have done it in the first place had he not thought I'd already done it to him. Believe it or not, I found consolation in knowing that. Maybe because I knew that I'd done it to my own blood brother for years, and for no reason at all. Preston and I buried the hatchet right there on the spot.

"So, you comin' back to the group, Pres?" I asked him.

"I don't know. Even if I do, it won't be right now. I'm tryin' to take some time out and work on some o' me and my wife's shitty problems. You know what I'm sayin'?" he replied honestly.

"I feel ya," I said, looking around to the sound of my truck door opening.

Emma leaned out. "Look, I hate to interrupt y'all, but Charles, Momma gon' throw a fit. You know she told us to come straight on over there."

I looked at my watch. "Damn," I whispered. "Look, man, she right. You know how Momma can be. Is it a'ight if I holla at you a li'l later?" I asked hastily.

"Yeah, that's cool." He nodded. "I said what I came to say. But call me later on tonight if you ain't busy." He was motioning to walk away now. "I'ma probably run in and holla at the fellas for a minute or two anyhow."

"A'ight," I said, backing away. "I holla at ya, man."

I hopped in the truck and Emma and I took off.

"So, what he want? Don't be holdin' out on me," Emma asked smoothly, gazing at me from the passenger side.

I smiled, glancing at her. "I hope you wearin' ya seatbelt, 'cause you ain't gon' believe me when I tell ya, and you might fall out o' the truck," I said jokingly.

Though I couldn't give her all the details, I'd told Emma about Preston's apology by the time we pulled into Momma's driveway, and Emma was just as surprised about it as I had been, but she was ecstatic that he and I were talking again. She even encouraged me to remain optimistic that it probably wasn't gon' be too much longer before Kenny and I reconciled. I wasn't too sure about that one, but I was happy that she was always so positive and encouraging.

We got out of the truck to go in the house. Being encouraging was one of Emma's good qualities. Of course, the way her sizeable hip portions contoured and curved inside that two-piece red suit she wore was one of her better qualities. I smiled naughtily as I slacked a step or two behind, watching her saunter up on Momma's porch. That ass of hers was wearing that red skirt out.

Emma certainly didn't have to be introduced to my family, because Momma had known her since she was a child. Our families grew up not too far from each other's neighborhood. Aside from the last three years that Emma had been staying up north, she'd been on the scene in my life, pretty much all my life. Just as many as Ruth had. Therefore, Momma and the rest of my family didn't have to worry about Emma being another strange and crazy Reena. I felt very comfortable with Emma, and she was definitely helping me to bury some of the crazy shit that the previous months had carried. She didn't mind spending a few nights at my house, then going back to her own place until we decided to do it all over again. Our renewed relationship was off the chain.

When she and I walked in, everybody was just sitting down at the dining room table getting ready to eat.

Momma shot me the "in trouble" eye. "It took long enough. Y'all must didn't go on as early as you thought?" she asked, gazing at me as I pulled a chair out at the table for Emma, then slipped into the one next to her.

"Yeah, we went on at the right time," I answered. "That ain't why we late getting here."

I went ahead and told everybody about Preston and his apology. They didn't seem to care one way or the other. Momma, on the other hand, was somewhat doubtful, but she didn't complain too much. We all went ahead and ate 'til we got full, laughing and talking the whole time.

Momma grinned, watching Emma eat.

"Emma, you still eat like you did when you was li'l, just like a bird," Momma said teasingly.

Emma laughed. "I know. I was the only one of all my sistahs and brothas who ate small portions. Whewww, the rest of 'em ate more than Bo and Wayne put together."

"I done told y'all 'bout puttin' my name in stuff I ain't in," Wayne teased, finally finishing up his second plate and exhaling a long wind from his full belly.

"My baby watchin' her figure," I said boastingly, smiling at Emma as she blushed from my remark.

"Well, if that's the case, she been watchin' it since she was 'bout four years old," Momma joked. We all laughed.

"Momma, you still ain't told us why you cooked today," I said, looking at her.

"Yeah, why did you cook today?" Wayne asked. "I been tryin' to figure that out all evenin'."

Sharon looked at Wayne rather abruptly. "Stop lyin', Wayne. You been too busy feedin' yo' face to try to figure anything out," she stated humorously, which extracted our laughter again.

A somewhat serious and sad expression came over

Momma's face as she looked around at us.

"I thought maybe if I change things around a li'l, I could get everybody here togetha at one time, so you and Kenny could talk," Momma uttered softly, nodding once at me. "It just ain't right for y'all brothas not to be speakin' to each other, Charles."

Well, that certainly changed the mood at the table. Now everybody looked somewhat glum.

"Momma, I know that. But it wasn't my decision for it to be like this," I said regretfully. "You know how stubborn Kenny is. I can't help he won't listen to reason."

"Charles, you got to make him listen." Momma gave me a pleading look. "You got to find a way to make it right, son. Make it right. You got to."

*Make it right. Make it right,* I repeated to myself. Those words sure enough rang a bell in my head. It came to me that those were the last words the angry man's voice had said to me during his last visit, or dream, or whatever it was. Now, Momma was saying it too. She was imploring me to "make it right," just like he had. What did it mean? What was going on? I asked myself silently, feeling a sensation of weirdness all over.

"You hear me, Charles?" a soft voice interrupted my thoughts.

I took a brisk head shake. "Ahh, huh? You say somethin', Momma?" I asked, trying to collect myself. I obviously didn't hear whatever she'd said to me.

"You daydreamin' or somethin'? I asked you have you seen him," Momma said.

"Who?" I was a little confused now. That "make it right" thing had thrown me off. "Have I seen who?" I peered at momma.

"Who?" Momma demanded. "Yo' brotha, that's who."

"Oh, I'm sorry, Momma." I apologized. "I just got distracted."

"We can see that," Bo said smart-alecky. "You wanna come on back to earth and join us now?"

"Naw, I ain't seen him," I said, ignoring Bo's comment.

"Any of y'all talked to him?"

"Nahh, I ain't seen him this week," Bo said.

"Me neither." AJ shook his head.

"That's what tonight was s'ppose to be for." Momma slumped her head down.

"I saw Linda in town last week," Sharon said.

"Did you talk to her?" Wayne asked, turning to look at Sharon.

"Briefly," Sharon replied.

"Is she still stayin' wit' her sistah?" Momma asked, raising her head.

"Yeah, she there for now, but she told me she was fixin' to get her an apartment."

"Apartment?" Momma frowned. "What she need wit' a apartment?"

I could tell that Momma didn't like the sound of what Linda getting an apartment may have meant—a permanent separation, maybe.

"She been stayin' wit' her sistah since her and Kenny separated. Maybe she tired o' that and need her own space," Richard said. "You know how y'all women is 'bout ya space."

Momma boggled her head with this long look of grief on her face. "All I know is the family reunion comin' up in a few weeks and it's sad enough Gregg ain't gon' be there. I can't stand not havin' the rest o' my boys there togetha." She paused a second. "All these bad thangs been happenin' in our family. I'm tellin' y'all they ain't nothin' but warnin's from God. The Bible teach us that warnin' comes befo' destruction. Well, I think we need to pay mo' attention, 'cause the Lawd tryin' to warn the Jennings family that Satan workin' hard to destroy us. That mean we got to stick togetha."

Momma's words went through me like a hot iron stick. It was almost as if someone was speaking through her and talking directly to me. Then she'd already mentioned those "make it right" words. As bad as I wanted to talk more about it, I just couldn't deal with it at that time. No, I didn't want to deal with it. I pushed my feelings aside and concentrated on making Momma feel better.

"For what it's worth, Momma, I been tryin' to call Kenny. I even left him several messages. He won't take my calls or answer the messages," I said. "Now, you know if he won't forgive Linda and talk to her, I ain't got a chance."

"I don't wanna hear that kinda talk, Charles," Momma insisted. "Kenny still a li'l upset right now. He'll come to his senses after a while, and put a end to all o' this nonsense. I want both o' y'all at that family reunion, like always. You just keep tryin' to let him know you sorry 'bout the misundastandin', all right?"

"All right," I agreed unexcitedly. "I'll do—"

*Ring. Ring.* My cell phone interrupted. I unclamp it from my belt.

"Hello," I answered.

"Hello. Long time, no see," a slightly familiar female voice whispered soft and seductively into my ear as I held the phone. "I been dreamin' 'bout you, wet dreams. In fact, when I wake up from the dreams, my panties be soakin' wet. It's about time I quenched my thirst. I know you remember how hot and wet I used to be for you. I'm caressing myself right now. Ahhhhh . . . mmmm. I'm gettin' it ready for you. Come meet me and get some pussy, Charles," the soft voice begged.

I was so absorbed in the mesmerizing phone chat, I almost forgot that everybody sitting around the table was able to see my reactions to the person on the other end of the phone. I quickly snapped out of it, and played it off.

"Hello, hello," I repeated into the receiver, pretending like no one was answering me. "Hello? I ain't gon' hold on forever. Whoever this is, you don't call somebody's cell phone and conversate wit' a person who already there wit' you."

Now she spoke to me again after hearing my "not alone" hint. "Oh, you can't talk right now, huh? Well, can you meet me tonight about 9:30 out on Gravel Bush Road? I promise, it'll be worth yo' while," she said enticingly.

By the time she finished her sentence, I'd figured out who the tantalizing voice belonged to, and I couldn't have been more astonished, but I played it off rather well.

*Keshundra. Now, what do she really want,* I asked myself suspiciously.

"Hey, man. Who you talkin' to? I thought you had the wrong number for a minute," I said aloud as if I was talking to a man. I hoped that Keshundra was at least smart enough to play out the charade with me,

"What you want me to say?" Keshundra asked mischievously. "You want me to talk dirty to ya? Or maybe moan into the phone a li'l bit?"

"Naw, naw, man. You ain't got to do that. I can meet wit' you 'round 9:30. We gon' go over that project again, or you done already worked somethin' out?" I said rather cool.

"Naw, I ain't worked nothin' out yet, but I plan to when I see you. I'ma fuck yo' brains out." She sniggered deviously. "So, I guess we on for tonight?"

"Yeah, man. I'll holla at you later," I said with relief, ending the call and rejoining the conversation with my family.

Emma and I hung around Momma's house with everybody for at least thirty more minutes. The whole time, I couldn't stop wondering what Keshundra wanted after all that time. I knew what she'd said on the phone, but after the way she sold me out, her word didn't carry too much weight with me. Still, I had to admit, she'd gotten me all stirred up in just those few minutes. I hadn't seen her since that fucked-up night Bettie caught us together, but I kept picturing her well rounded tits and ass. Shit, I found myself fantasized about Keshundra all the way home. So much so that the second Emma and I stepped into my house, I began touching her and feeling on her, trying to satisfy the thirst that Keshundra had left me with. It was Emma's body that I was getting ready to fuck, but it was definitely Keshundra's face I was visualizing.

Emma's and my pit stop in the kitchen was a bit awkward, but I couldn't keep my hands off her, and she didn't seem to mind. I groped her, kissed her, fumbled over her. She responded by returning my aggressive touches. She grabbed a handful of my crotch and rubbed firmly. I began to grow through my pants. Emma and I ravished each other's mouths. It seemed that our tongues couldn't get deep enough into each other's throats.

"Ahhh, ahhh," I panted.

Our breathing was our only means of verbal communication. Our eyes said much of what we didn't say aloud.

"Ahhh, ohhh." I buried my head in her bosom atop her V-neck jacket.

I kissed at random, while she continued gripping my crotch. We rolled around against the kitchen sink. We began kissing and tonguing again as we rolled. She suddenly stopped our kiss and backed a short distance away from me, then began undressing herself. I stood still against the sink and watched tentatively. She unbuttoned her red jacket, took it off, and dropped it on the floor. She unzipped her skirt and slid it off, then dropped it on the floor. She then quickly eased out of her panty hose. All that remained was her navy blue bikini panties and lace bra. I looked into her eyes and took my time searching over her mocha body. Her hips stood out like big ham hocks as she sauntered back over to me and removed my already unbuttoned jacket, then unbuttoned my shirt and took it off along with my tie.

Slowly gliding her tongue over my chest, she then reached her hands down and unfastened my belt and pants and pulled at them until they fell to the floor. I used my feet to maneuver out of them. I stood before her in my underwear and socks. My erection had gone full stretch and was hard as an iron pipe. She continued kissing over my chest, then finally began moving downward. As she headed south, I rubbed through her soft hair and firmly clutched the back of her head with one hand. She soon fell to her knees in front of me and began softly biting at my hard-on through my shorts until they were slightly wet with my penis saps and her saliva. She pulled one end of my underwear up and slid my stiffness through the side. She rested my underwear on the side of my hard cock and balls, then slowly began licking away.

The feel of her warm tongue increased my heartbeat and caused more secretions to seep from the small opening of my dick into her mouth. She licked, she sucked, she jawed, she tongued the tip of it. Sap and saliva dripped down it and down the corners of her mouth. Our panting and breathing had turned into moaning. As she carried on eating me up, she spread open her legs in her kneeling position and began rolling her ass. Her thick, chunky hips and thighs stood wide open, swaying in the air as I watched. My mouth watered to taste her. I knew that her pussy was just as drenched and wet as my dick. I felt my own spit began to drip down the sides of my mouth. I also felt my peak coming on. I grabbed hold of my dick with one hand as she fed on it, and grasped the back of her head tight with the other one and shoved it in her mouth even more. She took it in the back of the throat like all those many times before. I thrust and thrust, rolling my ass vigorously as I continued feeding it to her. The way she sloshed on it reminded me of a pig slopping his wet dinner. Emma wasn't Keshundra, but she could hold her own exceptionally well. She quickly pulled her titties over her bra and let them hang free.

"Ummmm, ummmm," I moaned.

The louder my moans grew, the harder she sucked. I was ready to blow. She suddenly replaced her mouth with one of her hands and vigorously applied friction up and down on my dick.

"It's comin', it's comin'," I whimpered.

My moaning changed to complete words at that point. The second she heard my warning words, she boosted her big, fluffy tits up under my dick and squeezed them together with my dick lying in between both of them. She made a tittie-breast sandwich that sheltered and cuddled my balls and cock. She slid her tits back and forth, and forth and back until she got me off. My cum shot between her breasts and underneath her chin and neck.

"Ohhhhh, ohhhh," I huffed in and out.

She quickly reached across the sink, tore off a wad of paper towels and wiped her chest clean, while still locked in silence.

Needless to say, I had to speak up. "Baby, I got two words for you," I said lively.

She looked at me and smiled. "What are they?"

"Monica Lewinsky," I laughed large. "Monica ain't got nothin' on you, baby," I boasted.

Emma smiled back at me. I always said something encouraging to her after each time she went down on me. I already knew she wasn't going to let me drop my cum-load down her throat, or even in her mouth. Emma was old-school like me, only three years difference in our ages. And although over the years she'd learned to enjoy the art of oral sex, she would only do it up to the point that her man was about to blow out the cream, then she'd use her hand or some other means the rest of the way. I, on the other hand, had learned to like the taste of my woman's sweet cum on my tongue. Emma's method wasn't bad at all. The way I looked at it was simple. At least she was good at the part she did choose to do.

Emma didn't make any comment after my Lewinsky tease. She only smiled at me in silence and began backing toward the kitchen table. I followed her like a dog on a leash, still visualizing her face as Keshundra's. I embraced her, and we began to kiss yet again. I dangled my tongue in her mouth, she dangled hers back in mine. I slithered my tongue down under her neck as her head leaned back. I made my way to her tits, unclamped her bra, and slung the bra on the floor with the rest of her things.

Her nipples were still stoutly budded. I licked and suckled them, leaving traces of wetness all around them. I danced my fingers down to her cunt, ripped off her bikini panties, and rambled all through her hot, wet pussy. Her clit was as hard as her nipple buds. I caressed and massaged her clit between my fingers. She groaned and spread her legs wide. She reached down and rubbed my hand through her wet pussy. I tickled around the entrance of her cunt with my middle finger. It pleased her. She abruptly rammed my finger up in her pussy-hole. I began slowly finger-fucking her, sliding my finger in and out, and wiggling it inside. She rolled her pussy over my hand as I fingered her.

"Fuck me. Ohhh, fuck me, baby," she whispered into my ear as she probed in and around it with her tongue. "I want you to fuck me now," she demanded.

We leaned over the sturdy, walnut wood kitchen table and carried along with our foreplay. I eased my finger out of her and moved my hands around to rub and squeeze two palms of her ass cheeks, then motioned to lift her onto the table. She assisted in the lift. Lying flat on her back, she stretched her legs wide and used both of her hands to open her pussy lips for me. I stroked the insides of her upper thighs as I gazed into her eyes.

"Fuck me," she uttered. I wasted no time in sliding my throbbing cock inside of her and began slowly thrusting.

"Ohhh, ohhhh, ummm," she muttered as I gradually increased my thrusting.

"Harder . . . come on, harder," she begged.

I gripped the sides of her hips, yanked her closer to me, and forcefully rammed in and out of her juicy pussy without missing a stroke. She met my forceful strokes with her own firm pussy stroking. She started to shriek her climaxing sound. I then rolled harder and moved one hand to her bare, exposed clit and finger-massaged it. That intensified her good feeling. She began rolling her widened cunt back at me harder. She grabbed and squeezed her tits while I thrust inside her and worked her clit. I soon felt another orgasm approaching. We stroked and rolled continuously until we delivered our package. She creamed my dick, and I splattered her pussy. Cum dripped on our lower bodies as I pulled my dick out of her. We took a minute to get our breath, then we each headed for the showers.

Emma already knew about my supposed 9:30 meeting with Will. She didn't want to stay at my house alone, so she decided to stay at her place that night. As soon as Emma left, I collapsed across my bed to take a nap and re-coup, so I'd be fully prepared to bust Keshundra's back out—right before I interrogated her ass and figured out the real reason she wanted to see me.

# Chapter Twenty-Two

The back road where Keshundra had asked me to meet her was well hidden and secluded. Nobody ever traveled that road or used it since it was a straight dead end. Trees, bushes, and weeds were all that was visible. The road itself was very narrow, and a person would have to be familiar with it to even know it was there.

I arrived there before Keshundra and parked on the side of the road. I turned my headlights off and sat listening to my radio while waiting for her to show. A few minutes vanished, and her white Altima pulled in behind me and the headlights promptly turned off. I hopped out of my truck and strolled around to the back. Luckily, the moonlight was full and bright, and although we were well hidden from any person's view, the moonlight gave us a well lit spot to occupy.

She got out of her car wearing a short, skin-tight black skirt and an equally tight, cut-off black top with no sleeves. Her bare stomach and exposed thighs jumped right out at me. The rocks crunched underneath her black, slip-in sandals as she approached me.

"Well, well, good evenin'. Long time, no see," she said, running her fingers through her free-flowing hair as she searched me from head to toe with a sneaky smirk.

I tried to come off as nonchalant and a little pissed too. "You already said that on the phone. Did you forget?" I snapped.

She grinned, resting her hands on her hips. "You can drop the nonchalant act. If you wasn't interested in seein' me, you woulda hung the phone up the second you realized it was me. And you sho' wouldn't have agreed to meet me out here."

"So, what's all this about?" I eyed her from head to toe like she'd done me. "You ain't made up wit' yo' sistah yet? 'Cause if you have, I know she wouldn't approve of you comin' to meet me."

She shot me a instant frown. "I don't give a shit about BJ or what she would approve of."

"Really? Well, it certainly didn't seem that way the night all the shit unraveled. You started cryin' and singin' like a yellow-bellied canary. I could hardly believe you fell apart like that. You'd always put on this front like you had it all together." I didn't take no pity on her turn-coat ass.

Her screwed up face told me she didn't like what I'd said, but I didn't give a damn. Like I figured, she declared there was a good excuse for all of it.

"That night when BJ rolled in on us, my only concern was keepin' her from tellin' my parents. That's the reason I put on the big, I'm-so-sorry, cry-baby show for her. And you damn right, I would've told her anything she asked, because she had put it all together anyway. Lyin' to her woulda pissed her off even more, and that woulda made her go straight to Momma and Daddy."

"Did you have to shift all the blame on me?" I demanded. "You told Bettie shit that you didn't even have to bring up, like about Katie, for example." I could feel myself getting a little hot-tempered the more we talked about it.

Keshundra raised her hands in surrendering position. "I ain't gon' even try to front. You right, I did all o' that on purpose to try to gain some leadway wit' BJ. I volunteered info to her so she wouldn't be as mad at me, but it still didn't work. She ended up tellin' Momma and Daddy 'bout it last week . . . and it almost killed 'em." Keshundra looked a little sad now, so I came on back down a few notches.

"Why she wait all this time? It's been damn near a year," I asked gentler.

"Evil, lowdown, cold, vindictive, and not to mention she gettin' ready to marry some preacher she been fuckin'," Keshundra exclaimed.

"Preacher?" I frowned. "What preacher?"

"He pastors a church over in Holly Springs. His name is Jerry somethin'. Anyway, her and the coordinator been makin' arrangements for the wedding, so Momma and Daddy asked her why wasn't her only sistah gon' be in it. They already know me and her ain't been havin' nothin' to do wit' each other for a while now. All this time, me and her been makin' up our own li'l excuses for 'em. So finally, they got us togetha and asked us about the rumors they'd heard on why you and her split up. That's when BJ went ahead and spilled the beans. I told Momma and Daddy that I'd all but jumped in front of a truck tryin' to beg her forgiveness, but she was the one who wouldn't talk to me." Keshundra sighed deeply. "Anyway, BJ told me maybe that would do it."

"What would do it?" I asked, puzzled.

"Jump in front of a truck. Preferably your truck. That way, I would be ran over dead, and you would be in prison for killin' me. That was the last thing she said to me a week ago. I thought about it and I decided to take her advice and come get in front o' yo' truck . . . but not to get ran over, just to fuck. It would kill her to know I was still fuckin' you." Keshundra gave me her mischievous smirk again.

Yes, I was very much in love with the "fuckin' me" idea, but I was too suspicious to give in just yet. "So, you plannin' on tellin' her?"

"I ain't tellin' her shit," Keshundra snapped. "It'll do me good enough just to know I can fuck you when I want. And she didn't stop nothin'. Besides, BJ can't judge nobody. She done did mo' shit than me and you put together. I'll never forget what she told me on my eighteenth birthday. That was even befo' I lost my virginity." Keshundra laughed.

"What she tell you?"

"She told me if I learned how to fuck a man the right way, I wouldn't ever want for anything as long as I lived." Keshundra stopped smiling at me. "So, tell me. Did it work on you?" She strolled over and stood in front of me, leaning into my chest, and began gently rubbing my shoulders. I was already beginning to stick straight out in my slacks. Her soft thighs pressed against my stoutness. The moon's incredible brightness revealed to me how deep she was staring into my eyes. Maybe it was just me, but her same sensual perfume, her sexy clothes, and the way her hair accented the sides of her face as it blended together with the magically lit moon, mesmerized me. The air around her was intoxicating. It had me too still to even move my hands and feel her in return as she felt over me. She soon fixed that by firmly gripping the back of my neck with one hand and pulling my head down to meet hers. As our mouths almost touched, she gently licked over my lips with her damp tongue.

My tongue automatically jumped out to play with hers. She used her free hand to grasp one of my hands, and at the same time she stopped the tongue-enticing around my lips. She stepped away from me just a smidgen and gave me another full view of her sensually perfect body. As she held on to my hand, she gradually parted her legs, leaving only a peep of a gap between her thighs. She never broke eye contact with me as she slowly steered my hand toward her stomach, then moved it on down until it reached the top of one of her thighs, which was exactly where her very short skirt stopped. She placed my hand underneath her skirt, then wiped my fingers through her sizzling, moist pussy. I felt the sleek secretions from her on each one of my fingers.

"You ain't wearin' no panties?" I asked excitedly.

"Why would I do that?" Her seductive voice whispered as she slid my fingers through her pussy again. "Easy access, baby."

She didn't have to slide my fingers through a third time. I instantly took charge by grabbing the sides of her hips and forcing her up closer to me. I slipped my hands around to her ass cheeks, gripped the bottom of her skirt, and fiercely yanked it up as high as it would reach to her waist. Her ass and pussy were completely exposed. I then picked her up, clasping to the bottom of her cheeks, and she wrapped her legs around my waist and her arms around my neck. I hurriedly carried her over to her car and sat her bare cheeks down on the hood with her knees elevated, and pulled her thighs wide apart.

Evidently, the car had cooled enough for her to sit on it. She didn't complain. She leaned back and rested on her elbows while her pussy gapped open for me. I carried my mouth straight into it. It was just as I remembered—tight and hot, yet succulent and juicy. I swiped my tongue over it from wall to wall, not missing a spot. I then flicked my tongue in and out of her slippery pussy hole. She wanted more.

She grabbed hold of the back of my head, rubbed her hands over my hair, and hastily pressed my face deep into her pussy while grinding and rolling it around in my face at the same time. I stiffened my tongue and tongue-fucked her as hard as I could. She squealed out for more. Her pussy was filled with wet pre-juices. I scoured my face around in her cunt, still flicking my tongue in and out of her hole every other second. When my mouth, jaws, chin, and even nose were layered with her slippery-slick out-pourings, I shifted my tongue onto her clit and sucked just the way I knew she liked it.

"Ohhhhh, ohhhh," she moaned as I sucked on it. It grew larger and stiffer as I continued.

"Ummm, ummm," I sounded out in enjoyment.

Keshundra worked her pussy faster and with harder strokes, indicating that she was accelerating toward her ultimate finish. And an ending it was. She pressed my mouth into her pussy all the way through her orgasm, then immediately slid down from the car, unzipped my pants, fumbled until she pulled my hard dick through my fly, and leaned over the car with her ass cheeks facing me. I bent down and kissed on top of her big, caramel ass.

"Come on, give it to me. Stick it in," she begged as she spread her legs and re-opened her pussy from the back.

Her skirt still rested around her waist. I finished unfastening my pants and pulled my underwear just below my balls, then hurriedly crammed myself inside of her sweltering cunt. I gripped her hips and ass cheeks tight as I thrust in and out of her. She returned my thrusts with her own rolls and strokes. We gyrated and twisted our asses for quite some time. Then I leaned over her back and pulled her cut-off top up over her big, plump titties. When they sprang out, I squeezed and caressed them in both my hands as I continued thrusting in her.

"Ohhh, I'm cummin'. I'm cummin' again," she mumbled as she pressed her ass harder into my crotch, while rolling her saturated pussy over my dick. She let off yet another keen orgasm, and I, in turn, filled her pussy up with a nice load of thick cum.

I leaned and rested over her back for only a minute after we'd finished. Then she turned around to face me and leaned back on the car, smiling devilishly. I tossed her a brief smile back, then bent over and inserted my tongue in her mouth and we shared a hot-ass kiss.

"Too bad I wasn't disappointed. Maybe I wouldn't wanna see you no mo'," she said as I moved back and fixed my clothes on me.

"That is too bad, ain't it? 'Cause I don't need to be involved wit' somebody who gon' sell me up the river at the first sign o' trouble," I said jokingly, but really meant it.

She must have caught on to the "really meant it" part. "Look, I'm not gon' keep explainin' somethin' I've already explained. Besides, you ain't married to nobody . . . and don't nobody tie me down. I do what I want when I want," she whined defensively, fixing her clothes on her.

"Naw, I ain't married to nobody, but I'm seein' somebody," I said voluntarily.

"Yeah, that must be the ole girl you couldn't talk in front of when I called. Well, good for you." She was sarcastic now.

"Her name is Emma. I been knowin' her a long time, and yes, now we're seein' each other. She means a lot to me, so you make damn sho' you stay outta her way," I said sternly.

"I could care less about the bitch. She ain't got nothin' I want. Hell, I just got what I wanted," Keshundra snapped then eyed me once-over. "So, I guess you think I'ma take the old side-mistress spot, huh?"

"I didn't say that. You did."

"You know you want me to," she said with pride. "Look, my number should be on yo' cell's caller ID. Hit me up when you get a chance. I s'ppose to be meetin' Derrick in a few." She held out her arm, trying to see her watch in the moonlight.

I gave her a disagreeable look. "So, you gon' run out here and fuck me real quick, then meet up wit' Derrick and fuck him too?"

"Derrick ain't gettin' no pussy tonight. Believe me, he ain't no competition behind that." She shot me a wink as she backed toward the front of her car.

"Yeah, whatever." I turned around and headed to my truck.

# Chapter Twenty-Three

The minute I walked out of my attorney's office that Monday morning about 11:15, I wanted to do a jig right there on the sidewalk. Instead, I dialed Will up on my cell to let him know the papers were finally signed and sealed. That's right, after two months, my short marriage to Retarded Reena was officially over. After my attorney's preliminary investigation, he informed me that we would simply file to get the marriage annulled on the grounds of Reena's incontestable mental illness, and her failure to inform me of her past criminal record, which was a direct result of her mental competency. And also, she had a dependency on that damn medicine prescribed for psychosis to help maintain her mental stability. As if all that wasn't enough, he found out a short time later that she'd been taken from Senatobia hospital and hospitalized in a psychiatric care facility in Whitfield, near Jackson, Mississippi. Her parents wound up having to admit her there for an extended stay. I was once again a single man, and might I add, one who'd decided to take it slow for a change with the rushing into marriage shit. Will congratulated me on the good news.

"Yeah, I'm glad it's all finally over wit', man," Will said happily. "I know one thing. You one o' the luckiest bastards I know. Livin' wit' a fool like that . . . she could've missed a dose o' that medicine, snapped, and killed you any minute." He sighed deeply.

"Damn, man. Thanks a lot for the encouragin' info," I stated sarcastically.

He laughed. "Aww, you know what I mean, fella. But seriously, though, Charles. I can't figure out how she and her folks kept all o' that information hid so well. I mean, I realize it happened in Holly Springs, but hell, Holly Springs ain't but forty-five, fifty miles from Senatobia."

"I hear you on that. But for one thing, as soon as it

happened, they sent her to mental place up north somewhere for treatment, so she was gone outta Miss'sippi for a pretty good spell. It mighta died down 'cause she wasn't around no mo'."

"Damn, might have," Will grumbled. "Look, the man she was wit', was he originally from Holly Spring?"

"I ain't sho' 'bout that. But from what my attorney's investigator said, Reena had been livin' wit' him for 'bout two years. And everythang was fine 'til she found out he was messin' wit' another woman. Then things went real bad, real quick. Evidently, she done had the mental problems for years. That's why she take the medication." I sighed.

"Well, like I said, I'm glad the shit over wit'," he stated with relief, then changed the subject. "So, has the li'l hot tamale called you since Saturday?"

He was referring to Keshundra. When I made it back home that Saturday night after Keshundra and I fucked, I gave Will a call and told him what happened. He and I tripped about it, plus he told me that Preston apologized to him at the program too.

Later that evening at first dark, I had picked up a few items for the house at Wal-mart, and was putting the shopping bags in my truck on the passenger side. The parking lot wasn't too full. The cars parked were scattered about. I guess that's why the soft woman's voice that called to me seemed to come out of nowhere.

"Hi, Charles," she spoke gently.

I turned around and saw that the pleasant female voice was coming from just who it sounded like. Lora Powers, one of my more sophisticated past flames.

"Hey," I spoke back, looking at her. "How you makin' it along these days?" I probed her from head to toe.

She smiled, holding a couple of shopping bags. "I'm doing good. And you?"

I tried not to sound too enthusiastic on purpose. "I've been managin' . . . but I ain't been the same since you told me you couldn't see me no mo'. I been missin' you, Lora."

# ReChella

She gave me a look of disbelief. "Really? Well, seem like to me you been spreading yourself around pretty good." You been divorced from the second wife, then remarried, then divorced from the third wife, and now you all but shacking up with who may very well be wife number four. Off hand, I'd say you haven't had time to miss me."

Her response wasn't quite what I wanted to hear, but I wasn't going to give up that easily. My more sad face was ready for round two.

"That's no further from the truth than I ever heard. I've missed you a lot. Some people just can't get outta yo' system as easily as others. You one of 'em. But I know you probably ain't gave me a second thought."

I laid it on real thick, but her cool expression didn't seem to be changing much, so I took it to a more serious approach. "And please, I know everybody in town know all about that other shit that happened. I ain't fixin' to stand here and discuss it, or make myself relive it again. Now, if you came over here to speak, then you've done it. And if that's all, I got to get this stuff home. Emma gon' help me 'round the house a little bit befo' she go back to her place."

Voila, and there emerged the "change of heart" expression on Lora's smooth, bright face.

She somewhat hesitated before she said anything. "So . . . she got her own place? I mean . . . Emma. She doesn't live with you?"

I nodded carelessly. "Yeah, she got her own place, but she stay wit' me some time. Why?" I asked.

Lora tossed me a sudden insulted glare. "Oh, so, after fifteen years or so of sleeping with me, I all of a sudden can't ask you a question?" She curled her lips. I was beginning to get to her.

"You can ask me anything. You always could. What you and me had all them years was good. We did what we did, we had fun, and our spouses never knew. You the one who broke it off. That night when you told me you couldn't see me no mo', I honestly didn't believe you. But then you stopped answering any of my calls, so I moved on," I said disappointedly.

I hastily closed the passenger door and eased by Lora to go to the driver's side and get in. I did that to make it seem like what she was saying wasn't important. Of all the things about her, I knew she couldn't stand to be ignored. Sure enough, she followed me around to the driver's side and stood between me and the door as I sat in the truck. She gave me an apologetic look.

"Maybe I made a mistake," she stated humbly.

I pretended to be puzzled. "About what? Comin' over to speak to me, or droppin' me like a bad habit back then?"

"Look, I didn't drop you like a bad habit, Charles. I simply told you that the critical condition my husband was in was too much for me to handle. I felt so guilty with him laying up in the room down the hall helpless . . . and you and me in another room not far from him, doing our thing."

"I understood that. But other arrangements could have been made, baby. I didn't wanna lose you," I said grievously. "So, it's been what, three years since we been togetha? I know you been wit' somebody else in all that time. Who?"

She shot me a suspicious look before she answered. "I've had a couple of fly-by's, but that's in the past like you told me," she admitted carefully. "I don't care to talk about it. Truth is, I've missed you. I can admit that."

The inviting look in Lora's eyes and the gentle hand-stroke she reached over and rubbed down my upper thigh said it all. Then she asked me to meet her at her house in about twenty minutes. I dropped those sacks off at home and drove straight to her place.

The second I stepped in her door, she began pulling my clothes off, and I did the same for her. Memorable moans and groans from yester-year sang in the air in her bedroom.

"Oooh, oooh. Don't stop. Keep it right there," she whispered softly as I thrust in and out of her. "Yes, yes, Charles. Oooh, fuck me, baby. Charles, it's so good, baby. You can't ever leave me again. Nobody can do it to me like you." We fucked long and hard.

# ReChella

Her bedroom had the same clean, crisp atmosphere just like I remembered. As Lora and I became re-acquainted while making love, I took careful inventory of everything I used to love about her: her long, black, even hair that I mowed my fingers through; her smooth, brown skin that I licked from inch to inch; her brown eyes that I gazed into from time to time as we fucked; her medium-sized frame, jiggly-cheeks and plump breasts that I pacified myself on while me and her stroked our way to an intense orgasm. When we finished, we lay side by side in her big, king-sized bed. She propped her head up in one hand and lay on her stomach as we shared conversation.

"Damn, multiple orgasms? You made me have multiple orgasms?" she said, inhaling deeply. "You've always been able to rock my world, but damn. I see you've learned some new tricks."

"What tricks you talkin' 'bout?" I asked, pretending not to know what she was talking about.

"Don't be silly. You know exactly what I'm talking about. I remember back in the day, you wouldn't even consider going downtown. Please, tell me who changed your mind. I'm dying to know." She leaned over and lavished a big kiss on my lips.

"Let's just say I had a big change of mind about it," I said after she moved from my lips. "What? I didn't do a good enough job for you?" I asked playfully.

She widened her grin. "A good enough job? Are you kidding me? I can hardly keep my legs together just thinking about it."

"Good." I pulled her head to me and we kissed again.

"So, tell me, how's your husband?" I asked, retracting from the kiss.

She let out a lengthy sigh. "He's pretty much the same, if not worse. His initial prognosis changed to a final diagnosis several months ago."

"What was the diagnosis?" I asked, crinkling my forehead.

"He'll be quadriplegic for the rest of his life. The

chances of him ever moving any part of his body from his neck down are one in ten million. After the accident, there was too much damage to his spine." Lora looked regretful.

"But the last time I spoke to you, you told me there was at least one optimistic doctor out of all the ones who had seen him."

"Yeah, at the time, that particular doctor was working on some kind of new experimental technique."

"So, what happened wit' that?"

"After nearly two years of testing and having no profound results on him, the doctor finally agreed that the degree of the accident was too severe to be reversed."

I shook my head sympathetically. "I'm real sorry to hear that. Victor was a pretty good guy when he was up and about, and I'm sure he's still the same, even though he in this kinda shape."

"Well, I've gotten used to the idea now, but in the beginning, it was very difficult for me to deal with. That's why I stopped seeing you. Every time you and I would get together and make love in this room, after you were gone, I'd go into Victor's room to check on him, and the look in his face drove me crazy. It seemed like his eyes would be saying he knew somebody had been in here with me," she uttered in remorse.

"That was just your imagination. Ain't no way he could have known. Not only was he confined to his bed, but he could barely get two words outta his mouth. And didn't you say his hearin' was damaged too?" I asked.

"Yeah, partially. He wasn't completely deaf, though. And it wasn't my imagination. Like I told you, it was my guilty conscience," she insisted.

"Lora, it ain't like we started the affair after his accident. It was already goin' on. You and me had been seein' each other for years. Shit, Victor used to be pretty tough wit' the women himself. Who was that girl you caught him wit' that time?"

"Some heifer that lived in Coldwater. I tried to beat the hell out of her too." Lora laughed.

"Yeah, all of that classy sophistication went leapin' out the window when you rolled in on Victor and her," I said in good humor.

Lora and I burst into laughter, then I rose and sat straight up in the bed.

"Is Victor still in the same room?" I asked curiously.

"Yeah, the room down the hall on the left. He's still in that one," she answered, sitting up too.

I was tempted to walk down the hall and peep in on him, but I didn't.

"How yo' son like college?" I asked. "I heard he had started a while back."

"Vic, Junior, like college fine. And don't be trying to change the subject." She narrowed her eyes at me.

"Listen, baby, I just didn't want you to start that guilty conscience thing all back over again. That's why I was remindin' you Vic wasn't no angel. He did some pretty fucked-up shit in his early days like the rest of us. And you know for yo'self, the only reason me and you started gettin' togetha here at yo' house was 'cause you couldn't leave him by himself at night," I reminded her.

"Yeah, I know. And I'm afraid the situation still the same on that. He has a nurse here with him all day while I'm at work, but I have to be here with him at night."

I glanced at her nightstand clock, knowing it was time for me to get on out of there. "Speakin' of night, I better be getting' ready to go. I dropped them sacks off at home and told Emma I'd be right back," I said, scooting out of the bed.

"You know, you never answered my question." She placed a pillow at her back and rested against it at the head of the bed.

"What question was that?" I asked, putting my clothes on.

"Is Emma going to be the next Mrs. Charles Jennings?" Lora's question sounded as refined as she claimed to be.

"I don't remember you askin' that, but maybe she is, one day." I buttoned my shirt. "But it won't be no time soon. I ain't rushin' into marriage no mo'.

Lora slightly crinkled her forehead. "Is Emma okay with that? 'Cause I know you been knowin' her for a long time."

"Emma's fine wit' it. And if for some reason she decides she ain't fine wit' it no mo', then that's gon' be her problem," I stated firmly. "Why you askin'?"

"No reason." She looked unsure.

"Sure there's a reason. Come on out wit' it."

She hesitated before answering. "Well, if you think about it, me and you have just as much history as you and her. Why marry her? Why not marry me?"

*What the fuck?* I said in my head. I tried to cover up my surprised look before I answered her. "That would be a li'l hard to do, since you already married. You forget yo' husband down the hall?"

Her face drew a blank. "Charles, the doctors don't think Victor got too long to live."

"Oh, I didn't know. I'm sorry to hear that." I leaned over and stroked her leg caringly.

"So see, you and me can be together and make it right at the same time," she said expectantly.

I looked at her like I'd seen a ghost. "What?"

"I said we can be together, Charles, and make it right," she repeated.

*Make it right. Make it right,* I thought, feeling that same weirdness I'd felt at Momma's just two days ago, when she'd said those very words to me. I quickly snapped out of my thoughts. Not only had Lora freaked me out a little by saying those words, I hated to burst her bubble too. So, I replied as carefully as I could.

"Tell you what. Let's give it some time and see what happens, okay?"

"Okay." She slowly smiled, nodding yes.

I then hurried the hell out of there and headed home. Lora was right about our history together, and I adored her. No doubt, she would have made a fine wife, but like I said, marriage was the furthest thing from my mind.

When I arrived home, Emma's car was gone, but a note was waiting for me on the kitchen table. It read: *Charles,*

# ReChella

*my sister called me and asked me to take her to Hernando to pick up an important package from a friend of hers. I got finished with all the cleaning, and I fixed you a large chicken salad and left it in the refrigerator. I don't know how long she's gonna be, so I'll probably just see you tomorrow. Have a good night. I love you, Emma.*

I finished the salad, showered, and went to bed, only to find out I couldn't fall right off to sleep. My mind kept recalling everything Momma had said on Saturday at the evening dinner. I tossed and turned for quite some time, which was odd because I didn't have any problems sleeping that Saturday night, nor that Sunday night. So, why was I unable to go to sleep a whole two days later after what she'd said? I pictured how sad her face was when she talked about the family reunion, and how she wanted all of us to be there. I realized that things really were going to be different this year, because so much had changed since the last reunion. But what could I do to make things right? The family reunion was in two weeks. That was not a lot of time, I thought, still tossing back and forth. That was the last thing I remember thinking before I shut my eyes.

# Chapter Twenty-Four

*Damn, them two weeks went by fast. Here we are at the family reunion already,* I said to myself as I gazed across the backyard at everybody. Some were eating, some were drinking, and everybody was having fun. I'd already had more than my share of food, and after a rather tiresome game of volleyball that my team lost, I had to run in the house and change the dirty T-shirt I fell on the ground in.

"Emma, I got to go change this T-shirt. I'll be right back," I called to her, panting for air.

"Okay," she replied. "Bring me a towel back with you?"

"A'ight."

I stopped at the fridge for a cold glass of water, then went to my bedroom to change. Just as I plopped down on the foot of my bed and pulled off my shirt, there was a knock at the door. I got up and opened the door. I was very surprised to see the person who was standing there—so surprised, I didn't say anything right away. I just stood there staring at her, so she spoke up.

"Hi, Charles." She gazed back into my eyes. "I hope I'm not disturbing you, but I just wanted to talk to you for a few minutes if I may. Don't worry, nobody's seen me yet," she said softly.

I slowly backed away from the door and opened it to let her in, then closed it again. She had such a peaceful appearance about her.

"Are you going to say anything?" she asked, looking at me. She had on a brown skirt and tan blouse with brown pumps. I snapped out of my surprised state.

"Ohh . . . ahh, yeah," I stuttered. So many questions darted through my mind. "I'm . . . I guess I'm just surprised to see you in here, I mean here . . . at the reunion, Linda." I finally got my words out.

She seemed to force a smile. "Yeah, well, I knew this was the day of the famous Jennings reunion and I didn't want to miss it. I talked to Sharon last week, and she told me the cookout was going to be at your house this year. She also told me Kenny said he wasn't coming because it was going to be at your house." Linda sighed. "Anyway, I just decided to come on by and see everybody."

"Well, it's nice to see you. I didn't mean to be rude. It's just been a while since I've seen you. You kinda caught me off guard." I was finally getting a hold of myself. "Everybody's out back. How'd you get in the house without anybody seein' you?"

She gestured her hand. "I parked behind the other cars and walked into the garage to ring the doorbell. After I rang for a while and nobody answered, I tried the knob. Voila, it came right open. I didn't wanna just go straight out in the crowd. I was hoping to talk with somebody who's still in the family first, to make sure it's okay for me to be here."

"You and Kenny divorced yet?" I asked playfully.

"No," she answered.

"Then don't be silly. Of course it's okay for you to be here. You're still family regardless of what's going on wit' you and him." I was more relaxed now. "Besides, this is my house, and you can come anytime you want to."

"Can I do it right now?" she asked, giving me a funny look.

I started for the door to let her out. "Sure, you can go on out now. I just ran in to change my T-shirt. Tell Emma I'll be out in a minute."

"I don't mean go out there. I mean what you just said. Come anytime I want. If you meant it, then I'd like to do it right now, with you," she uttered softly, walking toward me, then gave me slow, wet kiss on my jaw.

Thank goodness I hadn't opened the door yet. I was too shocked.

"Linda, come on now. You don't wanna do this," I said, pulling my face away from her.

"Yes, I do wanna cum . . . and I want you to make me do it. So, stop pulling away from me, and let's cum quick before somebody decides to interrupt us," she whispered, embracing me and kissing my jaw again.

"Why are you doin' this?" I asked gently, not pulling away this time. "You know once we cross the line, we can't ever take it back."

I tried so hard to keep from giving in. Just the thought of having her in my bed made my dick hard. I never thought I'd see the day when Linda would pursue me. She ignored my resistance and caressed all over me, kissing me, rubbing my bare chest, my back, my shoulders, and the back of my head and neck. I couldn't fight it any longer. I began kissing and caressing her too. Then I reached back and turned the lock on the bedroom door.

The second I squeezed her soft breasts through her blouse, she came out of the blouse, skirt, and shoes in almost an instant. I wasn't too long behind her in taking off my tennis shoes, jogging pants, and underwear. We embraced each other again, kissing and caressing, while scuffling our way to the bed. I quickly pulled the covers back, and we eased underneath them.

"I don't know why, but when Kenny turned me away, it did something to me. The only thing I've had to console me and keep me warm inside is the way you held me that night in your office. The more I tried not to think about it, the more it kept popping in my mind," Linda whispered as we continually kissed and licked over each other's bodies.

"Yeah, I remember that night, Linda. But I wasn't tryin' to make a pass at you. I was just tryin' to make sure you were safe, and the incident didn't hurt you and Kenny." I slowed up on the kissing. For some reason, I felt I needed to be honest with her about my innocent motives that night.

"I know you weren't suggesting anything, Charles." She stopped and looked at me. "Maybe that's why I've wanted you so bad since that night, because you sincerely tried to help me and didn't want anything in return." She kissed under my neck gently. "Let's stop talking and start fucking." She grasped my dick and guided it into her heated pussy as I rolled on top of her.

We lay in the middle of the bed at the head with me

thrusting in her fiercely. She was so warm and wet. My dick glided against the tenderness of her pussy. "Ohhh, yes," she moaned in whispers while squeezing my ass cheeks. I humped all the more. Then I leaned my head down and we engaged in a deep, intense kiss while still rolling our asses.

"Oooh, Linda, you got some good pussy, baby. It's so—"

*Baaamm!* A loud, busting-open-the-door sound interrupted us. I instantly rolled off Linda. We both grabbed for the covers to hide ourselves. We could hardly believe our eyes as we looked at the person standing before us.

"Kenny! Oh my God," Linda yelled out. And without another word, her eyes cocked upward and she fell back on the bed. She fainted cold. That left me all alone to face Kenny.

My heart was racing. "Kenny, this ain't what it seems. I swear. It wasn't like this in the beginnin'. This just happened, man. You got to—"

"Shhhhhhh!" Kenny held his index finger to his lips, shushing me. He glued his eyes on me as he stood in the middle of the doorway. The door was still wide open after he'd kicked the lock off and broke it. Him catching us couldn't have happened on a better cue if it had been planned out. He wore dark blue Levi jeans, a black T-shirt, and a pair of white tennis shoes.

"You know, it's a funny thing, big brother. I didn't have a clue that anything was goin' on between you and Linda," Kenny said calmly, strolling into the room and standing at the foot of the bed, looking down at me. "When I accused you of wanting to get her into bed that day at Momma's house, I was more upset than anything. I honestly didn't believe it. Later on, I told myself you really were trying to protect me and her. Sorry to say I was wrong."

Kenny smiled at me fearlessly. He never broke a sweat. He spoke boldly and very calmly, as if he already knew what to expect when he made it to my house. His relaxed attitude shook me up all the more.

"Kenny, I don't know what to say except I'm sorry." I quickly glanced over at Linda. "But I think we need to make sure Linda all right."

I thought if I got him to focus his attention on Linda, maybe I could get up and get my clothes on without having a brawl and drawing in any more of the family.

"Aww, Linda's all right. You don't need to be worryin' 'bout her. She the least of yo' problems right now," he said with assurance.

"Kenny, she out cold. She might need a doctor or somethin'."

"Trust me, big brother, Linda a lot better off than you are. She don't need to see any of what's fixing to happen." His tone of voice changed from calm to bitter in a hot flash.

"Any of what?" I asked cowardly, feeling a few chills pass over me. "Look, I'm fixin' to get up and put my clothes on before somebody else come in the house. Then we can talk about all of this." I still held on tight to the covers, but I made a motion to get up and get my clothes. Kenny quickly reached around to the back of his waist and grabbed a gun. He pointed it straight at me.

I broadened my eyes instantly. "Kenny, what you doin'?"

"What am I doin'? What am I doin'?" he asked real cool, narrowing his eyes. "I'll tell you what I'm doin'. I'm ridding our family of the worst mistake Momma ever made. You a bad seed, Charles, and I'm sendin' you back to hell wit' yo' real daddy. Ain't no human daddy made nobody like you." Kenny extended his arm and pointed the gun even closer at me.

"Please, Kenny. Please don't do this. We can work this out," I begged him for my life. I even felt tears began to roll down my cheeks. "Please, I'm yo' brotha, Kenny. How can you do this?"

His eyes were as cold as a block of ice.

"That's my question exactly." Kenny nodded his head at me. "How could you do it? You're my brotha, my blood. We came out of the same womb. How could you do it?"

Kenny spoke as if he'd been programmed on what to say. The more he talked, the more I realized I'd heard those words, or very similar words before. He continued.

"I swear, you ain't nothin' but a back-stabbin' son of a bitch. Linda's my wife, not yours. Today, I'ma let Momma and the rest of the family know what kind of sick bastard you really are. Today you gon' pay for everything you've ever done. And the beauty of it is the entire family will get to see who you are firsthand. You layin' up here butt naked and dead, wit' yo' black, rusty dick stickin' in yo' mouth, right beside myyy wife. That's right, after I shoot you, I'm gon' cut yo' dick off and put it in yo' mouth."

I couldn't believe what I was hearing. I knew I'd heard those same words before. It was Gregg's final promise to me at the gravesite after the funeral. I was shocked beyond belief. How could Kenny know what Gregg had said to me? I'd never told nobody but Will, and I knew he couldn't have told nobody. There was only one other way that Kenny could have known. I almost fainted just at that notion.

Kenny continued talking. "Big brotha, before I kill you, I just want you to know who gets the credit for tippin' me off 'bout you and Linda's li'l rendezvous here today." Kenny's eyes were unbearable to look at. "My brotha. The same brotha you betrayed in the same way you've betrayed me. That's right, Gregg. I was at home on the sofa asleep, and all of a sudden he just appeared befo' me and told me what was goin' down. He also told me what you did to him for all those years wit' Katie."

"Please, Kenny. Have mercy," I cried.

Linda couldn't offer any help in my pleading. She was still out cold.

"Don't ask me for mercy. Ask God. And you better ask Him befo' you take yo' last breath." Kenny let out this evil laugh. "Oh yeah, Gregg wanted me to give you a li'l message. He swore that he was gon' be watchin' everything you did and every move you made. He said he wouldn't rest 'til he'd ruined you. Well, I'm taking care of all that for him. You won't get a chance to do this to none of our other brothas."

"No!" I screamed, thrusting my hands up, trying to get

out the way of his shot.

*Bang!* It was too late. I felt the bullet hit me straight in my chest. *Bang!* Kenny fired again, and the second one hit me in the chest not far from the first one. I fell back on the bed with my arms hanging alongside me. I couldn't move.

*Bang!* He fired again, and the third bullet entered straight into my chest, not far from the first two. The pain from the three bullets was horrendous. My chest frame felt like it was caving in. Everything around me became a big blur. After a few seconds, I felt myself moving around inside my own body. The life was seeping right out of me. Everybody and everything I'd ever known, seen, lived, done and even thought, flickered briefly back to mind. I also felt emotions from each of the incidents, like I was reliving them. Just before I closed my eyes, I saw a big, shadowy figure appear over me.

"Hello, Charlie boy. Long time, no see. You miss me?" The deep, revengeful voice spoke to me.

I couldn't respond. I was stiff and aching. The only thing I could do was listen as the last bit of breath ran out of me. He gazed down at me with eyes of hatred.

"Bet you thought you'd seen the last of me. Naww, it wasn't gon' be that easy, son. My promise to you had to be fulfilled. And now that it has, I guess I'll see you on this side, huh? Tell you what. I'ma have a little pity on you and speed on your sufferin'." He wrapped both of his big, cold hands around my neck, choking me.

I still couldn't move my body, but I felt a struggle from within, an inner me, who was conscious and able to move around, but just not in physical form. I guess it was my spirit-man. Gregg continued choking the last breath of life out of me.

"Die, you bastard, die!" he yelled. "I warned you to make it right, but you kept ignoring the warnings. All you had to do was ask the ones you've hurt for forgiveness, then repent and make it right. I knew you wasn't gon' make it right. You got a warning through Momma. You got a warning through Lora. When Katie told you 'bout her visit, a visit similar to yours, that was even a warning! And what about all that tragedy you lived through? Those were warnings. Boy, you signed yo'self up for Hell!"

The harder Gregg squeezed, the harder my inner-self fought to get him off, even though my physical body was stiff as a board and locked in silence. I also heard faint cries from my inner-self. Finally, after all this time, it all made sense to me. Like Gregg said, I'd had all the warnings that I needed to make it right, especially all the tragedy that I'd managed to live through, but I willfully ignored it. At that moment, I realized that it didn't matter if those strange incidents were labeled as dreams, visions, guilty conscience, or unexplainable miracles from God. They were tailor-made warnings for me to get my life in order. Now, it was too late. Everything was about to be over for me. No more dishonesty, no more cheating. I was about to meet my maker, and even I had sense enough to know that I was not prepared to stand before the throne and face God.

Suddenly, something different happened. I felt two soft hands tugging on my shoulders and arms. The hands were warm against my skin and to my surprise, didn't hurt when they tugged over the bullet wounds in my chest. The touch of the hands also rendered feeling back into my physical body. I instantly went straight for my neck and began clawing at the big, choking hands that were crushing the last few drops of wind out of me. Everything was black and blurry. I was desperately trying to focus and free myself in the scuffle. A few seconds later, I heard what sounded like help for me. It was her gentle hands that rescued me.

"Charles! Charles! What's wrong?" a woman's voice called to me as I scuffled and clawed to get Gregg's huge hands from around my neck. Then suddenly, I was able to yell out too.

"Stop! Stop! Get off. Get off," I yelled as I slowly began to focus in on my surroundings. I was soon able to see all around me. That's when I realized it was Emma's sweet voice that I'd heard and the soft touch of her hands that rescued me. She stood right there in front of my bed as I glanced from place to place over the room. There was no Linda, no Kenny, no Gregg, no gun, and when I flung my hand to my chest to touch my wounds, there were apparently no bullet holes.

I hopped out of bed and stood in front of Emma, staring into her concerned eyes. The morning light was shining bright in the room, the time on the clock was 8:12 A.M. There was no aroma or sign of any food that had been cooked for the family reunion, and as unstirred as things were, it didn't even look like the family reunion was going on.

"Charles, what's wrong, baby?" she asked, putting her arms around me to hug me. "I think you were havin' a bad dream. When I came in the room, you were mumblin' real crazy and tryin' to move, but you seemed to be tied down or somethin'. And I've been callin' you since 6:30 this mornin'. I called the house and the cell all the way up to 'bout 7:45, and when you didn't answer, I got worried, so I jumped in the car and drove down here as fast as I could. I didn't know you were goin' to be off work today."

I still didn't say anything. I only hugged her tightly. Just like the times before, the incident seemed so real. But one thing was different this time. I didn't care whether it was a dream, a vision, or what. I got the message loud and clear. I felt myself trembling in her arms.

"It's okay, baby," she said softly, trying to console me. "That musta been some dream. You're tremblin'."

I pulled back and looked in her eyes. "It wasn't a dream," I said gently but very confident. "It was a warning."

Emma's forehead wrinkled. "A warning?" she repeated. "Why are you so pale? Are you sick? Is that why you didn't go to work?" She asked me question after question. I honestly didn't feel like answering any of them, but I wanted to ease her mind.

The night before, I remembered eating the salad she'd left for me, then showering and going straight to bed. I also remembered that I wasn't able to fall asleep for quite some time, thinking about how sad Momma was from everything that had happened. I must've tossed and turned a mighty long time, because I couldn't remember exactly what time I finally fell off to sleep. Whatever time, it must have been when the dream started, and obviously, it lasted 'til Emma came in and woke me up. Wow. I'd slept clean through my 5:45 A.M. alarm clock, my telephone and cell phone calls from Emma, plus I was now over an hour behind for work.

What a dream. It didn't take me long to explain all of that to her, then she understood. And as for me, things couldn't have been more clear. I felt so different, so thankful for one more chance, a chance that I didn't intend on ignoring this time. I knew what I had to do, and I knew I had only two weeks in which to do it. Considering the circumstances of all my ill behavior, it really seemed like an impossible task to get any of the people's lives that I'd affected to listen to anything I had to say. But one thing for sure, I was going to do everything in my power to "make it right."

# Chapter Twenty-Five

The day finally arrived, and it wasn't a dream either. The Jennings family's three-year reunion was underway. Our out-of-town family members rarely visited over the years. They hardly even made it to funerals, weddings, or any kind of occasions of that sort. But one thing for sure, none of them ever missed the tri-year reunion. Yeah, that was one time everybody gathered in full. Maybe because we all knew it would be another three years before the entire bloodline would get a chance to see each other again.

It was customary for us to have the Saturday cook-out at the Sardis Dam, but in the dream I'd had two weeks prior, the cook-out was held at my house. I felt like that was some sort of sign, so I told Momma I really wanted to have the cook-out in my backyard this year. And so it was.

Emma, Sharon, Wayne, and I were responsible for barbequing all of the ribs, steaks, chicken, and hamburger patties. We also fried fish in the deep fryer. Before Momma left her house, she cooked all of the extras and brought them over that morning before the rest of the family arrived. She brought spaghetti, baked beans, greens, potato salad, dressing, coleslaw, and plenty of desserts.

Family from all over was at the reunion: nieces and nephews, close cousins from Memphis, and distant cousins from Missouri. Momma's two brothers and two sisters from Chicago made it to my house about 12:00 that Saturday afternoon.

Tina drove up from Cleveland, and made it to the house just before Amy and her family, and Karen and her family arrived. Amy's and Karen's husbands rented a van big enough for both families to drive down from New Jersey. In spite of my daughters' and my differences, the reunion time always seemed to bring out our best behavior. Plus, I'd called all three of them on conference the week before, and we'd all aired some of *my* dirty laundry. I was finally able to say some of the things they'd wanted to hear for so long. And what made it so great was I actually meant what I said. They expressed how glad they were to see me at the reunion, and I had a ball with the grandchildren.

Ms. Hattie and Mrs. Sadie Mae sat at one of the picnic tables with Momma and her siblings, as usual. They laughed and talked about everything under the sun.

I took a few moments to stand in the yard and gaze around at everybody. I was amazed at how everything so closely resembled the way it was in my dream. I thought about how that particular day would still be a memorable time, recorded in history, just like the many other reunions had been when the long-gone family members were once with us. The sun hovered high in the sky and beamed so pretty, as if it were specially shining down on us. The wind stirred just enough to help the large shade tree keep everybody cool. The sound of laughter and children playing enchanted the atmosphere. Family and good friends were scattered all about, mingling, reminiscing, and catching up on the last three years' events. Food was plentiful, and fun was widespread.

A couple of the cousins from Memphis brought along a huge, inflatable water-slide and pumped it with helium for the kids to play on. That was all-day amusement for them. The only quiet place on my property was inside the house, and it remained quiet unless somebody needed to take a quick bathroom break. The tall, ten-foot tent that we assembled in the yard to set the tables of food in suited the occasion well. It was sturdy enough to stand tall and house any ten or twelve persons fixing plates, and at the same time protect the food from any unwanted insects.

The two weeks leading up to the family reunion were two of the busiest I'd had in a long time. But I was at ease, because I'd kept my word for a change and tried my best to make things right so the family could move forward.

My first, and by far hardest task was when I sat down in front of Momma the day after my dream to make her understand that her Charles wasn't the always-lied-on, perfect man she thought she'd raised. I poured my heart out to her, maybe not every gory detail, but enough for her to know that I had a lot of problems—a lot of problems I'd created myself from the time I was a young man. It pained me to see her cry, but it was better than continuing to live a lie. In the end, it worked out, because she realized I was finally beginning to see the light, even after all those years. We talked for hours. Her last words to me before I left her house were, "God got to be savin' you for somethin', boy. And now that you on the right path, you betta stay there."

Then there was Katie. I couldn't blame Katie for not answering any of my ten or fifteen phone calls. After everything I'd said to her the last time we were in each other's company, I didn't blame her for not wanting to talk to me. And even after I wound up knocking at her front door, I had to tell her I'd had a visit from Gregg before she let me in. My talk with her wasn't for hours and hours, but I still had a lot to get out. By the time I was done telling her the truth about the gravesite incident at the funeral and all the warnings I'd gotten from Gregg, she was down on her knees in the middle of the floor, crying and shouting. When she finally got up and composed herself, she thanked me for being honest and confirming even more for her, her visit from Gregg. She told me she could continue on with her life the way she'd been doing for the past several months, even more positive now, because she felt there was more closure added.

I don't think they were her last words, but somewhere toward the end of our conversation, she peered straight into my eyes and said, "At this very moment, I can honestly say I know what it feels like to care for you as a *real brother*, because I never thought I'd like you again, even as a person."

I made my way to Bettie's job one evening right before she got off, and asked her for a few minutes of her time. She seemed to be more curious about what I wanted than anything. We sat down in front of a couple of sodas at Blazing Steer's. First and foremost, I thanked her for the *almost* warning, and told her it was my fault for not getting back in touch with her to hear the whole story. I could tell she was a little anxious at first, but after I made my apologies for all the hurt I'd caused her, she listened patiently, then told me that for some reason, she believed I was sincere. She didn't go into detail, but she even admitted that she'd chosen to be with Preston for all the wrong reasons, and I was among those reasons. She told me about her upcoming wedding, and I congratulated her and wished her all the happiness that I didn't give her. Her eyes told me she cared a lot for her fiancé, and she was happy.

The words I remember most from her were when we'd gotten up to leave and she laughed a little and said, "If I'd known all it was gon' take to bring you to your senses was to shoot at you, I would've done that before Reena did." We laughed on the way out of the restaurant.

Undoubtedly, the most difficult person I had to talk to was Keshundra. She'd called me up one evening, whining about how bad she needed to borrow twenty-five hundred dollars. Evidently, she was behind on a few bills in her apartment, but she said Derrick was moving in with her and he was going to be paying all the bills from now on. She told me once they were caught up on everything, she'd pay me back. I was too happy to give her the money—not loan, *give,* but on one condition: that she not call me or contact me anymore. I told her things had changed for me, and I couldn't see her anymore. The first thing she did was hang up the phone in my face. The second thing she did was call me right back. I didn't bother to go into detail, but I told her I was going to be faithful to Emma. No more sleeping around.

Right after Keshundra laughed in my face, she said to me, "Make it a even three thousand and I'll forget I ever knew you."

It wasn't the most ethical thing to do, but when I met her to give her the money, I told her if she ever broke her promise, she would have to pay it back. I knew she understood that kind of language more than anything else.

I'd already mentioned to Will a little bit about my change of heart, leaving out all the dramatics, though. I knew the dream scenario would bring up every excuse he and I relied on to make justification for stuff we didn't want to accept. The minute he heard the words "I ain't messing around no more," he asked me about Keshundra. I assured him I had nothing more to do with her. Right after he told me I was just going through a phase, he was too tickled to know he could now holler at the hot tamale, as he called her.

Lora expressed how sorry she was for becoming re-acquainted with me only to lose me all back over again, only this time through no fault of her own. I apologized to her for leading her on in any way, and told her I'd always be a friend.

It was nothing short of a miracle when Kenny finally agreed to talk to me. I must've pleaded and begged on his answering service for days before he softened up enough to call me back and tell me I could come over to his house. I poured my heart out, lock, stock, and barrel, about the real reason I'd done what I'd done on that tragic night at my house.

Kenny to got up after sitting there quietly listening to me all that time and said, "If you finished, you know where the door is." Then he walked straight back to his bedroom and closed the door even before I left. It hurt like hell, but what could I do?

I didn't quite know what to expect when I pulled up in Reena's parents' driveway, but I sure as hell didn't expect for them to turn Cujo loose on me when I stepped up on the porch. That big St. Bernard came out from around their house, barking and foaming at the mouth just like on the movie *Cujo*. I didn't know I could run so fast. I jumped in my truck and spun out of their dirt driveway, leaving a big cloud of dust.

It was obvious I was going to have to make other arrangements to try to find out about Reena. I told my attorney I wanted to help her and her folks with any financial burdens they weren't able to handle, and also try to make it easier on her if they found her capable enough to answer for the criminal charges. He told me he'd contact them and get right on it. So, I all I had to do was wait to hear from him.

Like I said, it was a very busy two weeks for me, but I didn't regret any of it. Well, maybe a few things didn't go as I'd hoped, but I didn't plan on quitting just because they didn't come to pass in that time frame. I'd work on it as long as it took. But for now, I was just going to seize the moment and enjoy the beautiful day of events. I swear, those children couldn't have had more fun if they had been on the waterslide at Disney World.

I was turning the meat over on the grill when Emma ran up to me with this excited look on her face.

"Got a surprise for ya," she said, grinning real wide.

I smiled back at her. "Grinnin' and all excited like you are, let me guess. You won the lottery."

She shoved me with her elbow. "Even betta. Come on." She grabbed my arm, pulling me toward the house. She was literally sparkling with joy. That really made me curious.

"What's the surprise?" I asked, trying to keep up with her as she yanked on my arm. "Come on, what's the surprise?"

"Just hold your horses, baby. You 'bout to find out," she answered, still smiling.

We made our way in the house and she motioned for me to go into the den.

"Now, look woman," I said jokingly. "I don't know what you got sta—" I cut my words short when I walked in the den.

I was overjoyed at the sight before me, so overjoyed I couldn't say anything. No other people could have made the day more complete.

"Kenny? Linda?" I said, looking back and forth from one of them to the other as they stood side by side.

Kenny gave me a slight smile. "Now, somebody need to be video-tapin' this. Charles Jennings, speechless?" Kenny joked. "You do remember inviting us, don't you?" He began coming toward me.

I was smiling even more now. "Do I? Yeah, I do!" I stated excitedly, moving toward him. We hugged then shook hands. Thanks for comin', man." I nodded slowly.

He peered at me genuinely. "Naw . . . thank you for what you tried to do for us," he said with care. "I've hurt her too. It may take a minute, but I think we gon' be a'ight."

That was music to my ears. I walked over and hugged Linda too.

"Well, folks started gettin' here 'round twelve. It's just now 2:30, so I think we got plenty mo' food left," I said playfully, knowing we had enough food to feed an army.

The three of us laughed.

"If Wayne and Bo done got at the food, it may not be enough left," Momma said, coming out of my bedroom, a big smile spread over her face too.

"Momma, what you doin' in there?" I asked hastily.

"Chile, I wouldn't o' missed this for the world." She stopped near Linda and threw her arm around her. "Now, let's go see how much damage ya brothas done did to the food."

Momma was hiding in my bedroom, listening all the time. I crumpled my forehead, pondering.

"Hold on a minute," I said. "Momma, when you find out about this? I mean, when you find out Kenny and Linda was comin' to the cook-out?"

"Last week," she said. "Believe me, I wanted to tell ya, but they asked me not to. Said they wanted to surprise ya. I really didn't wanna keep you in all that wonderin' 'bout ya talk wit' Kenny. And the only thing that kept my mouth togetha was when Emma told me you said you'd been prayin' for him to come around. Hadn't been for that, they'd jus' had to been mad at me." Momma let out a jolly laugh, then we all headed outside.

I guess I was so excited about seeing Kenny and Linda,

# ReChella

I didn't pay much attention to anything else. Now that we'd been on the outside for a modest amount of time, I was gazing out across the yard yet again, and I noticed Kenny and Linda chatting with Wayne and Sharon. I swear, I had to do a triple-take when I realized Linda was wearing a brown skirt, tan blouse, and brown pumps. And Kenny was wearing dark blue Levi jeans, a black T-shirt, and white tennis shoes. I could hardly believe my eyes. They had on the exact same clothes they'd had on in my dream. How amazing was that?

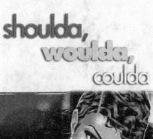

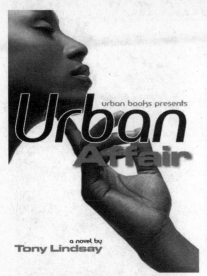

DECEMBER 2005
1-893196-27-5

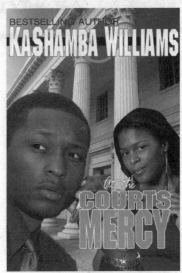

JANUARY 2006
1893196-29-1

FEBRUARY 2006
1-893196-41-0

FEBRUARY 2006
1-893196-37-2

MARCH 2006
1-893196-32-1

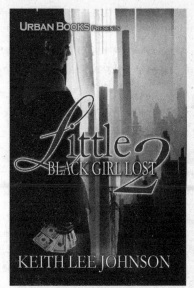

MARCH 2006
1-893196-39-9

MARCH 2006
1-893196-33-X

APRIL 2006
1-893196-34-8

# OTHER URBAN BOOKS TITLES

| Title | Author | Quantity | Cost |
|---|---|---|---|
| Drama Queen | LaJill Hunt | | $14.95 |
| No More Drama | LaJill Hunt | | $14.95 |
| Shoulda Woulda Coulda | LaJill Hunt | | $14.95 |
| Is It A Crime | Roy Glenn | | $14.95 |
| MOB | Roy Glenn | | $14.95 |
| Drug Related | Roy Glenn | | $14.95 |
| Lovin' You Is Wrong | Alisha Yvonne | | $14.95 |
| Bulletproof Soul | Michelle Buckley | | $14.95 |
| You Wrong For That | Toschia | | $14.95 |
| A Gangster's girl | Chunichi | | $14.95 |
| Married To The Game | Chunichi | | $14.95 |
| Sex In The Hood | White Chocalate | | $14.95 |
| Little Black Girl Lost | Keith Lee Johnson | | $14.95 |
| Sister Girls | Angel M. Hunter | | $14.95 |
| Driven | KaShamba Williams | | $14.95 |
| Street Life | Jihad | | $14.95 |
| Baby Girl | Jihad | | $14.95 |
| A Thug's Life | Thomas Long | | $14.95 |
| Cash Rules | Thomas Long | | $14.95 |
| The Womanizers | Dwayne S. Joseph | | $14.95 |
| Never Say Never | Dwayne S. Joseph | | $14.95 |
| She's Got Issues | Stephanie Johnson | | $14.95 |
| Rockin' Robin | Stephanie Johnson | | $14.95 |
| Sins Of The Father | Felicia Madlock | | $14.95 |
| Back On The Block | Felicia Madlock | | $14.95 |
| Chasin' It | Tony Lindsey | | $14.95 |
| Street Possession | Tony Lindsey | | $14.95 |
| Around The Way Girls | LaJill Hunt | | $14.95 |
| Around The Way Girls 2 | LaJill Hunt | | $14.95 |
| Girls From Da Hood | Nikki Turner | | $14.95 |